Pre...
Proposals

A convenient marriage…for baby's sake!

Three passionate novels!

In November 2007 Mills & Boon bring
back two of their classic collections,
each featuring three favourite
romances by our bestselling authors…

PREGNANT PROPOSALS

His Pregnancy Ultimatum
by Helen Bianchin
Finn's Pregnant Bride
by Sharon Kendrick
Pregnancy of Convenience
by Sandra Field

MISTRESS BY CONSENT

Mistress by Agreement by Helen Brooks
The Unexpected Mistress by Sara Wood
Innocent Mistress by Margaret Way

Pregnant Proposals

HIS PREGNANCY ULTIMATUM
by
Helen Bianchin

FINN'S PREGNANT BRIDE
by
Sharon Kendrick

PREGNANCY OF CONVENIENCE
by
Sandra Field

MILLS & BOON®
Pure reading pleasure

Harlequin Mills & Boon Limited,
Eton House, 18-24 Paradise Road, Richmond, Surrey TW9 1SR

PREGNANT PROPOSALS
© by Harlequin Enterprises II B.V./S.à.r.l 2007

His Pregnancy Ultimatum, Finn's Pregnant Bride and
Pregnancy of Convenience were first published in Great Britain by
Harlequin Mills & Boon Limited in separate, single volumes.

His Pregnancy Ultimatum © Helen Bianchin 2004
Finn's Pregnant Bride © Sharon Kendrick 2002
Pregnancy of Convenience © Sandra Field 2002

ISBN: 978 0 263 85527 2

05-1107

Printed and bound in Spain
by Litografia Rosés S.A., Barcelona

HIS PREGNANCY ULTIMATUM

by

Helen Bianchin

Helen Bianchin was born in New Zealand and travelled to Australia before marrying her Italian-born husband. After three years they moved, returned to New Zealand with their daughter, had two sons, then resettled in Australia. Encouraged by friends to recount anecdotes of her years as a tobacco sharefarmer's wife living in an Italian community, Helen began setting words on paper and her first novel was published in 1975. An animal lover, she says her terrier and Persian cat regard her study as as much theirs as hers.

CHAPTER ONE

'MIA!'

A slender form almost identical to her own burst forward the instant Mia emerged into Sydney's airport arrival lounge, and within seconds she was engulfed in an enthusiastic hug.

'Hey,' she protested with a musing laugh. 'It's only been five months.'

A sisterhood of two, no parents since their untimely death a decade before, the girls had been the best of friends for as long as they could remember. Sibling rivalry didn't exist, never had, and each was sure it never would.

Petite in height, sable-brown hair, dark brown eyes, their likeness was such they had on occasion been mistaken for twins.

Yet Alice was the elder by two years, divorced with a nine-year-old son.

Mia caught hold of her sister's arm. 'Let's get out of here.'

It took a while to collect her bag from the carousel, clear the busy terminal and join the flow of traffic heading towards the city.

It was great to be home, although *home* was something of a misnomer, for she no longer had a home as such. During the past few years she'd lived on university campus studying for a pharmacy degree.

Mia rolled her shoulders in a bid to ease the lingering tension from too many sleep-deprived nights leading up to end-of-year exams, the lack of caffeine, and a weariness that had little to do with either one of them.

'So, tell me,' Alice begged. 'What's new?'

Hell. Where did she start? Not at all might be best, she decided, while her sister was negotiating busy inner city traffic. It would take a while to reach the northern suburb of Manly, and the kind of news she had to impart was better told seated at Alice's dining-room table while sharing a pot of tea.

'The exams went okay,' Mia reiterated cautiously, aware she'd said as much via email.

'*And?*'

'It's good to be back.'

Alice gave her a searching look as the car drew to a halt at a controlled intersection. 'You look pale. Tired,' she elaborated.

Mia offered a faint smile. 'Thanks,' she managed ruefully. 'Just what I needed to hear.'

'Nothing some home-cooked food and a good night's sleep won't cure.' The brisk tone was accompanied by a competent smile.

Alice was the ultimate earth mother, taking pride in producing wholesome hearty meals, home-baked cookies and bread, charity bakes. She sewed, stitched, crocheted, knitted, and took pottery classes. It didn't stop there, for she also took art, sculpted, and set oils on canvas. She served on her son's school committee, ran as president of the parent-teacher association, and excelled in organisation of all things.

Ask Alice was an invisible bandana her sister wore with pride, for *helping* had become a mission in life. It made up for the five years of Alice's marriage during which her husband conditioned her to believe she served little purpose and possessed no self-worth.

Mia took in the familiar sight beyond the windscreen. Old buildings merged with new, dull, well-worn red brick jumbled together with renovated terrace houses, newly lacquered ornamental iron railings vying with broken wood palings. An endearingly eclectic mix that marked inner-city suburbia.

Traffic, as usual, maintained a hectic pace in a never-ending river of vehicles jostling for position in a bid to catch the next set of lights and minimise road time.

City smells, combining aged buildings, fuel fumes, summer heat. Trees with spreading branches bordering a green-grassed park, and, above, a cloudless blue sky.

Mia turned her attention to her sister.

'How's my favourite nephew?'

'Great. Matt is doing well in school, enjoyed a terrific soccer season, and is heavily into tennis for summer,' Alice enthused. 'He's studying piano, guitar, and is a whiz at chess. He began martial arts classes this year.'

Maternal love was unconditional, and Alice believed in the 'busy mind, active body' theory...totally. Fortunately her son was an enthusiastic advocate who viewed each new venture as a conquerable challenge.

'I can't wait to spend time with him.' They shared a mutual affection that dispensed with the generation gap, a love of sports, action movies, books. Pals, she accorded fondly, and hoped the *friendship* part of their relationship would never change.

'He has plans,' Alice warned, and Mia offered a wry smile.

'Uh-huh. I take it para-gliding, bungee-jumping and all other dangerous activities are a definite no-no?'

Alice made a sound that was part sigh, part groan.

'Don't,' she warned. 'Even in jest.'

Traffic was heavy as they crossed the harbour bridge, and only began to ease as they cleared the inner northern suburbs.

There were coves with moored craft, a marina, and heavy greenery hugging the elevated rock-face where luxurious homes perched high sharing magnificent views of the inner harbour and city.

Sun-dappled water, stunning architecture…a place where she'd been born and spent her formative years. Excelled and survived, loved and been betrayed, only to emerge as a strong, determined young woman whose focus became unwavering in pursuit of her goal.

Except for one little blip that had the power to change her life for ever.

Alice's home was situated in a wide tree-lined street, a solid double-brick structure with medium-size rooms her sister redecorated with considerable flair at regular intervals.

Externally it was similar to many houses in the established suburb, but indoors it held an air of homeliness that was both inviting and relaxing.

'Coffee, tea, or something cold?' Alice queried as she preceded Mia down the hallway.

'Tea would be great.' There was only one guest room, which she occupied during university vacations, and she deposited her bag, released her knapsack, then she quickly freshened up before joining her sister in the kitchen.

Aromatic tea steamed from two cups, and there was a selection of home-made cookies set out on a plate.

'We have an hour before I need to go collect Matt from school,' Alice declared, indicating a chair opposite. 'So...out with it.'

She could prevaricate, brush off her sister's intuitive questioning, or at least delay giving an answer until...*when*? Tonight, when Matt was asleep? Tomorrow? There was never going to be a *good* time.

'I'm pregnant.' No lead up, just the basic fact. Yet the very starkness of her announcement caused acute anxiety as to Alice's reaction, for Mia's stance on pre-marital sex was a shared, well-known fact.

Together, they'd laughed about it, exchanged views, pursued the 'fors' and 'againsts', whether saving oneself for the *right* man and marriage didn't belong way back in the previous century! 'What if the sex turns out to be...well, *less* than anticipated?

How will you *know* if you have nothing to compare it with?' Alice had teased.

Now, there was a tremendous sense of vulnerability along with the anxiety. Everything she'd believed in, all that she'd held dear in her emotional heart, was laid bare, and open to criticism.

It was bad enough she'd resorted to self-castigation every day…every waking *hour*, since that fateful night.

'Just…*I'm pregnant*? That's it?' Alice demanded, aghast.

Mia closed her eyes, then opened them again. Dear heaven, what was the matter with her? 'I need to fill you in,' she managed ruefully, and caught her sister's intent expression.

'In spades. No detail spared. And it would help to know whether I'm to congratulate, commiserate, console, or rejoice with you.'

Her stomach executed a somersault, then went into free fall. 'Commiserate,' she admitted, and didn't know whether to laugh or cry.

'You weren't—?' Shock and anger meshed with a fighting spirit second to none. 'It wasn't—?'

'*No,*' she reassured at once, her own shock a visible entity. 'Nothing like that.'

Alice leaned forward and covered her sister's hand with her own. 'So—what happened?'

The genuine concern evident in her sister's expression almost moved her to tears, and she shook her head in self-chastisement of the emotional roller coaster she'd been riding for the past few weeks. One minute she'd be fine, the next a teary mess.

Where did she start? *'Who,'* she corrected wryly. Oh, yes, it was definitely *who*.

'I assume he's to die for,' Alice opined with a faintly wicked smile. 'Considering he managed to persuade you to discard every one of your preconceived convictions about sex before marriage?'

His image came sharply into focus, haunting, taunting her with what they'd shared together. The excitement, the ecstasy…and her wantonness to experience it again, and again. A willing pupil beneath a skilled lover's touch, she reflected.

'Incredible,' she said simply, aware of the warmth flooding her cheeks as she held her sister's gaze.

'Off the planet, huh?' Alice's grin was replaced with curiosity and a degree of mild reproof. 'You didn't tell me you were with anyone.'

Alice's surprise was understandable, given they spoke on the phone each week and resorted to email almost every day.

'I'm not.'

Her sister's eyes narrowed fractionally. 'If you don't give me the rundown…the *total* rundown,' she endorsed, 'I'll be forced to take dire action!'

Mia managed a faint smile. 'The short version won't wash?'

'Don't even think about it!'

There was nothing else for it but to start at the beginning…something she should have done at the onset, instead of dropping a verbal bombshell in her sister's lap.

'I was supposed to meet a friend at an evening function.' A night out had seemed a good idea at the time, following weeks of intense study. It had also provided the opportunity to dress up...a marked change from wearing the usual university garb of jeans and tee shirt. 'She didn't show,' Mia went on to explain. 'When I checked my cellphone there was a text message to say she'd become suddenly ill.' She effected a faint shrug. 'I didn't know anyone there, and I was about to leave when I noticed a fellow guest standing alone on the other side of the room.'

A man whose magnetic presence had made the room and everyone in it fade into insignificance.

Even from a distance he'd had an alarming effect on her equilibrium. Disturbing, disruptive, *lethal*. In that instant she'd instinctively known her emotional life was about to go into a tail-spin.

Yet not even she, in her naïvety, could have possibly imagined how the evening would end, or its far-reaching implications.

Nor would she have believed she could fall so quickly, so easily beneath a man's spell.

Not one day passed when she didn't query her sanity in mindlessly giving in to temptation...yet that was a misnomer, for she'd been fully aware of her actions, and honesty demanded acceptance she'd been a willing, eager participant.

'You dated him?'

Oh, hell, this was where it became...difficult. 'Not exactly.'

Alice's expression sharpened. 'What do you mean...*not exactly?*' There was fleeting comprehension, followed by full-blown shock. 'You slept with him that same night?'

There hadn't been much sleep, only sheer physical and emotional exhaustion in the early pre-dawn hours.

'Dear God, Mia.' Her sister's voice reduced to a stunned whisper. 'What were you thinking?'

She closed her eyes against the anguish of her foolishness. 'That's just it. I didn't *think*.'

Her sister's eyes narrowed. 'I take it the sex was consensual?'

'Oh, hell, *yes*.' The man, the night, the sex filled her mind in vivid detail. His powerful image, his touch, everything about him was indelibly imprinted in her mind.

Alice discarded her tea and sank back in her chair. 'You had a wild night with someone you'd never met before?' She shook her head in silent disbelief. 'My sensible sister who's so selective with her body she steadfastly refused to sleep with the man who wanted to put a ring on her finger?'

How could she explain all it had taken was one look, and she'd felt her bones melt? Recognition on some intense instinctive level that went beyond anything she'd ever known before.

'Someone must have spiked your drink.' It was the only logical explanation Alice could summon, and Mia shook her head.

'I wasn't drinking.' There was nothing, no one to blame but herself.

'Have you told him you're pregnant?'

How could she, when she didn't even know his name, let alone where he lived, worked?

Her silence was sufficient answer, and Alice's features softened with distress. 'He's married?'

The thought almost destroyed her. If only for the reason it pegged him as a cheater, and made a bad situation worse. 'I have no idea.'

'Yet you had unprotected sex?' Her sister's face paled at the implications. 'Are you insane?'

'One of the condoms broke.'

Alice's gaze widened. 'One?' She waited a beat. 'Oh, my.'

Oh, my didn't come close. The sex had been mind-blowing, passion at its zenith…for her. Had it been the same for him? He hadn't said, but then neither had she. In truth, she hadn't been capable of uttering a word.

'You don't have his name? Anything?'

It sounded crazy to admit an exchange of names hadn't seemed important at the time. Worse, it hadn't even entered the equation.

'I left while he was still sleeping,' Mia revealed after an agonising silence, not adding her sense of sick shame, or the furtiveness with which she'd donned her clothes and crept from the room, the hotel, and summoned a cab.

Oh, Lord…how could she have discarded every moral she'd held dear all her life for one night with a man she'd never met before? Worse, would undoubtedly never see again?

It didn't make sense any more *now* than it had

then. And she couldn't even claim her decision to go with him had been clouded by alcohol.

'Are you considering a termination?'

Pain clenched deep inside, a tangible entity that momentarily clouded her eyes. She wanted this child. So much so, she couldn't bear the thought of extinguishing its foetal life. It was a part of her, *him*. A vivid reminder of what they'd shared. 'Do you think I haven't agonised over that decision every hour of every day?'

'And?'

'I recognise the wisdom associated with termination, given the circumstances,' she offered slowly as she met and held her sister's gaze. 'But I don't think I can do it.' She lifted a hand and smoothed a stray tendril of hair behind her ear, then attempted a faint smile that somehow didn't quite come off.

As close as they were, she couldn't bring herself to admit that what she'd initially damned as unbridled lust was something much deeper, more meaningful than just the slaking of physical need. It touched her heart, her soul, and captivated both on a level she hadn't dreamed possible.

The child she carried represented part of that.

'No verbal warning about bringing a child into the world and raising it as a single mother?'

'I look at Matt and *know* my life would be as nothing without him,' Alice assured quietly. 'He's my light, my laughter, my joy.' She paused in reflective silence as she chose her words. 'There are a number of working mothers in today's world. I guess I have to say emotionally it would be easier to share things with a supportive partner,' she added. 'Someone who could cut me some slack every now and then. Share the responsibility. However, if you want reassurance single parenthood can work...I have no regrets, not one.'

'I know it.'

Alice's hands reached out and covered her own. 'I'm sure whatever decision you make will be the right one.'

For me? Or the child?

It was something that had kept her awake nights, diminished her ability to study, and with morning sickness beginning to kick in she was forcibly reminded of the need to make a choice...soon.

'If seeing the pregnancy through is an option, you could transfer to a university here and move in with me.'

Tears sprang, clouding her vision, and she blinked to dispense them.

Unconditional love. It was beyond price, and infinitely precious. 'Thanks.'

'But...?'

Alice knew her well. Too well. 'If I take that option, the responsibility is my own.'

'I kind of figured you'd say that.' An absent-minded sip from her cup brought a murmur of disgust. 'I'll make fresh tea.'

Mia checked her watch. 'You don't want to be late collecting Matt.'

Her sister groaned. 'I need to take him on to the tennis club for coaching.'

'We can pick up something to go, and drink it while we watch him.'

They did, and Matt's enthusiastic welcome lightened Mia's heart a little as she applauded his good shots with as much fervour as his mother.

Was this where she'd be in ten years? Cheering her son or daughter on from the sideline? Ensuring there was a host of extra-curricular activities to strengthen the mind and body, thus avoiding the pitfalls of vulnerable youth?

The conception of this tiny foetus growing inside her womb was a mistake. Yet its presence existed. If she carried it to term, it would never know its father. And what empathy could she hope to achieve as a mother with her child if she went with honesty and revealed the child's existence was the result of a one-night stand with a stranger?

'Did you see that backhand?'

She had, in an abstracted way. 'Poetry in motion,' she conceded, punching the air for Matt's benefit.

At that moment her cellphone buzzed with an incoming SMS message, and she frowned as she read the text.

'Problem?' Alice queried, and Mia offered a rueful smile.

'Nothing I can't handle.'

Alice's gaze held hers. 'But not one you particularly want to?'

Mia rolled her eyes in an expressive gesture. 'It's—awkward.'

'Explain *awkward*.'

'It's from Cris.'

'One of the students you share lectures with?'

'Yes. His family are Sydney based.'

'That's a problem, *how*?'

'He's nineteen, and he hasn't told his family he's gay.'

Alice's expression didn't change. 'Okay, so why do I get the impression there's more to it than what you're telling me?'

Mia took her time in answering. 'He's a nice guy.'

'And you feel protective of him?'

She summoned a mental image of the tall, lean young man who made her laugh, shared his sharp brain and the benefit of a photographic memory. 'I value his friendship. We share two of the same lectures, and tend to hang out together.'

'There's a preconceived image on campus he's your toy boy?'

'No.' She'd formed friendships with several fellow students and enjoyed their company. Yet she wasn't a *girlie* girl who lived to follow the latest fashion trends, and she veered away from the thinly veiled sexual overtones prevalent in many of the male students.

Cris didn't cause her to put up barriers on any level.

'I've been invited to dinner on Thursday evening.'

'I think you should go,' Alice opined as Matt finished up with his coach and came off the court. 'How difficult can it be?'

Maybe Alice was right. And besides, if she declined on some fabricated excuse the invitation would inevitably be extended to another evening.

SMS made for easy, quick communication, and within minutes it was set, with Cris alerting he'd collect her at six.

'It'll be fun,' Alice assured as they walked to the car.

Mia wasn't so sure. Twice the next day she considered cancelling. Wednesday she made the call, only to cut the connection.

Thursday was way too late, for only an emergency would do…and her patron saint refused to oblige her with one.

Consequently Mia dressed with sophistication in mind. Stiletto heels, the classic black dress, minimum jewellery with the exception of stunning drop ear studs. In the need to complete the image, she swept her hair into a smooth knot and secured it, then teased a few tendrils free to curl below each temple.

'*Don't go,*' a tiny voice warned as she collected her evening purse and exited the guest room. *Fool*, she admonished. No one would eat her. Besides, she was capable of taking care of herself.

'Looking good.'

Mia offered her nine-year-old nephew an affectionate smile. 'You think?'

'*Wow*, definitely,' Matt declared with a male appreciation beyond his years.

'Your ride has just pulled into the driveway,' Alice forewarned a few seconds ahead of the sound of a car door closing.

Mia rolled her eyes expressively. 'I wish this didn't seem like such a big deal.'

Somehow 'the family would like to meet you' had

seemed a light-hearted invitation at the time, but, now it was imminent, she wasn't so sure.

'Cris is a fellow student, a friend. I'm sure his family are very nice.'

The name *Karedes* numbered high among the city's social echelon, and *nice* was debatable, given Cris' version of his family.

Elder brother, Nikolos, who ruled the Karedes Corporation with a fist of steel; their widowed mother Sofia, whose influence was superseded only by Angelena the family matriarch, Nikolos and Cris' widowed paternal grandmother.

The doorbell pealed, and Mia drew in a deep breath as she crossed into the hallway.

'Hi.' Her greeting held genuine warmth for the young man standing in the aperture.

He was attractive, with dark soul-searching eyes, a warm smile and generous heart; his tall frame and lean features held promise of the man he would become.

Introductions were made with ease, and minutes later Mia slid into the passenger seat of a Porsche.

'Yours?' she teased as he sent the car purring down the street.

'It belongs to my brother.'

'And he lets you borrow it?'

'When I'm home.' Cris effected a negligible shrug. 'He has others.'

'As in *plural?*'

'Uh-huh.'

A shiver slid down her spine, for which she had

no logical explanation. 'Perhaps you should fill me in on the evening's game plan.'

The Porsche growled to a halt at a traffic intersection, and he spared her a penetrating look. 'You're a friend I happen to regard with affection.'

'Platonic friend,' she conceded, and earned his swift smile.

'That's the description I've offered.'

'Good.'

'They'll adore you. What's not to like?'

Mia offered a slightly rueful smile. There was a part of her that wanted to tell him to turn the car round and take her home.

Get a grip. It was only one evening. A few hours. She'd exchange social pleasantries, decline the obligatory glass of wine and eat fine food.

Rose Bay held an eclectic mix of well-established homes, many with panoramic views of the harbour, and *stately* came to mind as Cris eased the Porsche to a halt outside a magnificent set of ornate wrought-iron gates guarding entrance to a sweeping driveway that led to a double-level plantation-style home in cream-plastered brick.

Wide bi-fold doors, timbered shutters, pillars and an elegant *porte-cochère*, set in beautiful landscaped grounds, the home...*mansion*, Mia amended...gave hint to serious family wealth. *Very* serious wealth.

Something Cris had neglected to mention.

As if to compound it, a Maybach sat parked beneath the *porte-cochère*. Its opulent lines were easily identifiable as the ultimate in the Mercedes group.

'You're impressed.'

It was a statement, uttered without emotion, and she allowed her gaze to settle on his features. 'Am I meant to be?'

His expression became unreadable as he drew the Porsche to a halt in a designated parking bay. 'It's only stuff,' he said quietly. 'Material possessions gathered and passed from one generation to another as a visual attestation to entrepreneurial success.'

'Which you hate?'

'No. I merely prefer not to hang onto the familial coat-tails.' He reached for his seat belt as Mia undid her own. 'Okay, let's go do this.'

'Face the fray?' she teased lightly, and was rewarded with a teasing smile.

'You got it in one.'

Seconds later they gained the spacious bi-level marble-tiled external entrance, and two large panelled doors swung open to reveal an impeccably attired butler.

'Good evening.'

A *butler*? Why should she be surprised?

Cris executed an introduction. 'Costas has been with the family for years.'

'The family are assembled in the lounge.'

When it came to strict formality, she'd take warm spontaneity any time. Didn't families of Greek origin fall into the latter category?

Perhaps not.

Mia crossed the wide expanse of marble-tiled floor at Cris' side, a few steps behind the butler, who paused on reaching what she presumed to be the lounge.

'Ma'am, your son and his guest are here.'

It was a large, exquisitely furnished room in which two women were seated and a man stood in side profile beside a wall of French doors.

A man whose height and stance struck a familiar chord. One Mia instantly dismissed, despite the swift curl of apprehension twisting her stomach.

The younger of the two women rose to her feet and moved forward.

'Mia. How nice to meet you at last.'

'My mother, Sofia Karedes,' Cris alluded with a smile. 'Mia Fredrickson.'

'Allow me to introduce my mother-in-law.' Sofia indicated the older woman remaining seated. 'Angelena Karedes.'

The matriarch, Mia concluded, meeting Angelena Karedes' intense unwavering gaze. Nothing, she deduced, would pass unnoticed beneath those sharp dark eyes.

'Mia.' It was a polite acknowledgement, nothing more.

'My elder son, Nikolos.'

He turned, and she felt as if her heart suddenly ceased beating.

No. The silent cry rose up from the depths of her soul. It couldn't possibly be…

There had to be a mistake. How could Cris' brother and the man with whom she'd spent a wild night of unbridled sex be one and the same?

Yet his identity was beyond doubt. His height and breadth of shoulder were achingly familiar. So too were his broad-sculpted facial features, the strong jaw, dark eyes, and a mouth that was to die for.

All it took was one look, and her bones began to melt.

Dear heaven…just thinking about what they'd shared almost brought her undone.

He knew. It was there in the depths of his eyes, the sensual curve of his mouth…an instant recognition that appeared fleetingly as he moved forward to greet her.

She wanted to obey an instinct to turn and run, and it was only courage that forced her to remain.

'Mia.'

Her name on his lips sent the blood surging through her veins, heating her body to fever pitch, and it was all she could do to utter a brief acknowledgement.

Did he recognise her discomfort? Worse, did anyone else in the room sense it?

She wanted to rage against fate for being so unkind. It was bad enough accepting she'd discarded every moral she'd held dear for all of her adult years. Difficult to condone it had happened with a stranger. Discovering she was pregnant went right off the Richter scale.

Yet *this*…this was her worst nightmare.

CHAPTER TWO

MIA tried for calm politeness, and held the instinctive feeling she failed miserably.

'Nikolos.' His name on her lips sounded strange, even to her own ears, and she dismissed the inclination to close her eyes, then open them again in the hope she was locked into some nightmarish dream.

In the name of heaven, *get a grip*. In the list of awkward situations, this took top place in her book. But doubtless not in his.

In his late thirties, Nikolos Karedes bore the air of a seasoned sophisticate, well-versed in every social nicety.

Yet she'd caught a glimpse of the man beneath that façade…someone who'd destroyed her previously held defences with galling ease. Worse, she'd allowed him to.

As if she'd had a choice, she reflected wryly, aware of the intervention of a divine power over which she'd had no control.

Had it been the same for him? That instinctive knowledge they were twin halves of a soul? Or was it merely fanciful thinking on her part?

The latter, she perceived with rueful acceptance. Without a doubt.

So her name was *Mia*…Nikolos perceived. The petite sable-haired young woman who'd managed to get beneath his skin in a way no other woman had. The thought, *taste* of her had driven him mad with longing since that unforgettable night they'd spent together twelve weeks ago. She was an itch he couldn't scratch…heat and light and passion, and so much more.

Did she have any idea how he'd felt when he'd woken and found her gone?

Or the steps he'd taken in subsequent days and weeks to try to discover who she was? Each avenue he'd explored had brought no result. It was as if she'd appeared out of nowhere, only to disappear.

He'd wanted to wring her neck…dammit, his own, for not anchoring her close to him in sleep so that her slightest move would have brought him awake.

There were occasions when he wondered if he'd dreamed the entire night, *her*…yet he retained a vivid memory of her scent, the clean, fresh smell of her hair, the silky smoothness of her skin beneath his hands, his mouth.

As to her response…the tentative surprise, the burgeoning sensuality beneath his touch, her generosity in giving herself up to him so completely… It had proven a powerful aphrodisiac that had changed *want* to *need* through the night, and seeded an emotion he hadn't cared to define.

Mia glimpsed the momentary darkness evident in his dark, almost black eyes. The faint edge of mockery, and something else she was unable to determine. Anger? Why *anger,* for heaven's sake?

'Please take a seat.' Sofia indicated a chair close by, and Mia sank into it with a feeling of relief.

'What can we offer you to drink?'

Something strong to settle the wild tango in which her nerves were indulging would be great…except alcohol in any form was a no-no. 'Thank you. A soda,' she indicated. 'Or mineral water.'

Mia was acutely aware of Cris' interested gaze, and that of his grandmother. Sofia seemed intent on acting the gracious hostess. As to Nikolos…his part in this wretched tableau was something at which she could only hazard a guess.

What had held the portent of being a difficult evening had taken a shift for the worse.

How long before she could leave? Two hours, three?

Mia accepted a frosted glass from the proffered tray.

'Cris has spoken very highly of you.'

She could do polite conversation. 'We share a few classes at university.'

'How old are you?' Angelena Karedes demanded, and earned Sofia's chiding protest.

'Please. Mia is a guest.'

Oh, hell, could the evening get any worse? 'Twenty-seven.' She waited a beat. 'Would you like to check my driver's licence?'

The old lady's eyes gleamed. 'Sassy. I like that.' The gaze didn't shift. 'What do you see in my nineteen-year-old grandson?'

Mia's chin tilted slightly. 'A friend.'

'Hmm.'

One word, that wasn't really a word at all, yet it conveyed a wealth of meaning.

'*Yiayia*,' Nikolos chided gently. 'Enough. You embarrass our guest.'

The matriarch's sharp gaze speared her own. 'Are you embarrassed, child?'

'Do you mean me to be?'

'Dinner is served.'

Costas' announcement was timely, and brought an inward sigh of relief that was short-lived as she found herself seated opposite Nikolos.

Accident or design?

Design, Mia decided. As the eldest male and presumably head of the family, there could be little doubt the reason for his presence was to check out his younger brother's *friend* and deduce an ulterior motive for the friendship.

Familial protectiveness or necessary caution? Undoubtedly both, and, while she could see the sense of it, she abhorred the not-so-subtle interrogation.

Would she have felt differently if Nikolos weren't present, and part of it? Innate honesty compelled an affirmative answer.

He disturbed her...mentally and emotionally. It was almost as if every nerve cell recognised him on a base level, and she had to fight to retain her composure.

Difficult when he was *there*, almost within touching distance on the opposite side of the dining table.

The thought of eating anything made her feel ill, yet good manners ensured she sampled a few morsels from each course...of which there seemed far too many. Or was that merely her imagination, due to her acute sensitivity of the man seated close by?

'Are you a perpetual student,' Angelena queried, 'intent on gaining academic successes without putting theory to practice?'

'If I'd known you would be so intensely interested in my background, I could have brought my CV for your perusal.'

Strike one for Mia, she accorded silently, and heard Cris' appreciative chuckle.

'Are you going to give it up, *Yiayia*?'

His grandmother lifted one eyebrow. 'Have you known me to retreat from anything?' She turned her attention back to Mia. 'What field were you in before choosing to pursue a pharmacy degree?'

For one second she considered going for shock tactics, then opted for fact. 'I was a cosmetics consultant.'

Those shrewd eyes sharpened. 'In a department store?'

'On referral from cosmetic surgeons to teach patients how the skilful use of cosmetics can minimise facial disfigurement.' Exacting work, with often pleasurable results.

'I imagine it was gratifying,' Sofia indicated with interest. 'Did you work with children, or mainly adults?'

'Both.'

Between them they were gradually building up her profile, and she mentally chastised herself for her own cynicism in wondering if it wasn't some preconceived test.

Mia sipped water from her glass, and when it came

to dessert she passed on the baklava and settled for fresh fruit.

Another hour, she perceived, then she could plead a need to leave.

'Are you intent on seducing my grandson?'

Now there was a question!

Nikolos fingered the stem of his wine goblet as he waited to see how Mia would handle the elderly lady's irascible manner, intrigued by the slight tilt of her chin, the faint edge of defiance deepening her dark brown eyes.

'No.'

'You are a refreshing change from the simpering socialites who trip over themselves to attract my grandson's attention.'

Costas' appearance was a welcome intrusion. 'Coffee is served in the lounge, ma'am.'

Thank heaven the evening was almost at an end. For the past few hours she'd felt like a specimen beneath a microscope…dissected, analysed, and categorised.

Mia requested tea, and when she finished she stood up, thanked Sofia, Angelena, then she turned towards Cris.

'Would you mind calling me a cab?'

'Don't be ridiculous.' His protest was immediate.

'I'll drive Mia home,' Nikolos inclined smoothly.

A silent scream rose and died in her throat. Oh, dear Lord, no. She didn't want to be alone with him. Hell, she didn't want to have anything to do with him!

Except somehow she couldn't dismiss an instinctive feeling he intended to allow her no choice.

'A cab is fine,' she managed evenly, tempering her firm tone with a polite smile.

'No.'

If she thought he'd let her escape so easily, she was badly mistaken. Nikolos leant down and brushed his lips to Angelena's temple, then accorded Sofia a similar gesture of affection.

'Goodnight. I'll be in touch.'

Mia cast Cris a desperate glance, and received a faintly raised eyebrow indicating a silent *What's the fuss?*

If he only knew!

'This isn't necessary,' Mia said quietly minutes later as Nikolos opened the passenger door and stood waiting for her to slip into the front seat.

'You want to cause my mother distress by beginning an argument on her doorstep?'

She flung him a dark glance as she slid into the car, and the door closed with a refined click before he crossed to the driver's side.

The instinct to get out and run was uppermost, and she banked it down.

'I'll accept a ride to the nearest cab-stand,' she indicated stiffly as Nikolos eased the vehicle towards the gated entrance.

'Afraid, Mia?' he posed as the Mercedes gained the leafy avenue and gathered speed.

Sheer bravado was responsible for her answer. 'No.'

'You should be.'

'I don't see why.'

He spared her a brief glance. 'No?' She looked so delightfully petite seated against the opulent leather. 'You'd have me believe what we shared was of little consequence? A one-night stand between two consenting adults?'

Her heart thudded in her chest, then kicked to a faster beat. 'Something like that.'

'The *hell* it was.'

She wanted to hit him, and would have if he hadn't been in control of a car. 'There's a cab-stand at Double Bay. You can drop me there.'

Nikolos' hands tightened on the steering wheel as a knot tightened in his gut. Something primeval stirred deep within in the knowledge he'd been her first and only lover. He tamped down the need that rose so swiftly, and stifled a husky oath in self-castigation.

He was far beyond the ready lust of a teenager. Yet this woman had the power to test his control, and it irritated him. Worse…thoughts of her kept him awake nights, and ruined him for any other woman he could easily have bedded. Heaven knew there were a number from whom he could choose.

Except it was Mia's features he wanted to see, the warmth of her smile…and he gently extricated willing fingers, made a seemingly reasonable but regretful excuse and went home alone.

'When we've talked,' Nikolos declared. 'I'll take you home.'

'We have nothing to discuss.'

He brought the vehicle to a halt at a set of traffic

lights and turned towards her briefly. 'Yes,' he reiterated hardily. 'We do.'

'Do you insist on a post-mortem with every
woman with whom you've had sex?'

The lights changed, and he moved the vehicle forward with the flow of traffic. Minutes later he entered
Double Bay and after finding no convenient parking
space he swung the car into the entrance of the Ritz-
Carlton hotel, requested valet parking, then led her
into the hotel lounge.

Refined elegance, she perceived as a waiter hurried
forward to usher them to a table, took an order for
tea, then unobtrusively retreated.

Mia schooled her features as she deliberately met
Nikolos' dark gaze. 'Can we get this over with?'

Was that her voice? She sounded so calm, when
inside her nerves were shredding into a tangled mess.

'Why did you leave?'

Her eyes widened slightly, then became shadowed.
Twelve weeks had passed since that fateful night, yet
every detail was etched in her mind. The magic of
his touch, the unleashing of emotions she hadn't
known she possessed...

Dear God, how could she have stayed and faced
him in the morning? Calmly risen from the bed,
showered, dressed, shared breakfast, then walked
away as if the night had meant nothing more than
the sharing of good sex?

Instead of an earth-shattering experience that had
changed her perspective, her life?

'There was no reason to stay.'

'No name, no contact number,' Nikolos pursued

silkily. 'No means by which I could get in touch with you. Why?'

'I was unaware there was any protocol involved. What would you have had me write on a note? "You were great?"' She was on a roll. '"Call me some time and we'll do it again?" Would that have fed your ego? Salved your conscience?'

He didn't move, but she had the sensation his body coiled like a tightly wound spring.

'You gifted me your virginity. That had to mean something.'

His words were silky smooth and dangerous, and Mia barely repressed a shiver as sensation unfurled deep within at the memory…his disbelief, the husky curse, and his gentleness as he'd led her through the threshold of pain to pleasure beyond her wildest imagination.

And afterwards…dear heaven, *afterwards* he'd held her all night long as she'd become a willing wanton eager for his touch. Again and again.

'It wasn't such a big deal.' And knew she lied…big time.

'No?' His gaze didn't shift.

'The prophylactic broke, remember?'

One of them.

The waiter arrived and laid out their tea, then took his leave.

'If you weren't taking precautions prior to intimacy,' Nikolos continued, 'I imagine you covered any possibility of pregnancy with a prescription for the morning-after pill?'

'I considered it unnecessary.' Foolishly, she ac-

corded in silent self-castigation. What on earth had
she been thinking of? Yet when she *had* thought,
she'd rationalised her cycle hadn't been in the fertile
zone.

So much for the *norm*, the majority!

She became aware of Nikolos' intent gaze, and
held it with difficulty.

'And was it unnecessary?' he pursued quietly.

Oh, dear Lord, how did she answer that?

His eyes darkened and assumed a ruthless intensity
as her silence stretched too long. 'Mia?'

'My body, my responsibility,' she managed quietly, aware she was just barely holding it together.

'Dammit, you weren't alone in that bed.'

'What do you want me to say? ''Was it as good
for you as it was for me?'' Or are you afraid I'll slap
you with a paternity suit, demand a large financial
settlement, or run to the media and besmirch the
Karedes name?' She was like a runaway train that
couldn't stop. 'Or maybe all three?'

'The truth will do for a start.'

She held his gaze fearlessly. The *truth*? 'I took a
pregnancy test three weeks ago, and had the positive
result confirmed by a doctor the following day.'

He waited a beat as he attempted some measure
of control. 'Tell me, was I never to know?'

Her hand shook a little as she took time out to add
milk to her cup. 'Reality check, Nikolos. Just as you
didn't know my name, you hadn't given me yours.'

The breath hissed from his mouth. 'Have you
had—?'

'An abortion? No.' The foetus inside her was a

living entity. The thought of having it forcibly removed from her body made her feel ill. 'This child is my responsibility.'

'Mine, also. I'll ensure you have specialist obstetrical care, and take care of all medical expenses.'

'I don't want anything from you.'

'If you think I'll walk away from this, you're mistaken.'

'You have no rights—'

'Yes, I do.'

The thought of sharing the child hadn't entered her head. Now that it did, it began to assume gigantic proportion.

'I intend bringing up the child alone.'

'No.'

'What do you mean…*no*? The decision isn't yours to make.'

'The child will bear the Karedes name.'

Mia replaced the cup carefully down onto its saucer, then sank back in her chair. 'Fredrickson,' she corrected.

'*Karedes,*' Nikolos declared with chilling softness.

'As I don't intend changing my surname, *Fredrickson* will appear on the birth certificate.' She rose to her feet and caught up her bag. 'It's been some evening. Your grandmother suspects I've snatched Cris for a toy boy and showed no mercy in her interrogation.' She glared at him, and barely restrained herself from picking up the ashtray and throwing it at him. 'As if that's not enough, you shanghai me and take up where they left off.'

'Sit down.'

'Go to hell.'

'Sit down—please.'

The *please* almost did it, except she refused to give in. 'I'll have the concierge summon a cab.' She fixed him with an angry glare. 'If you try to stop me, I'll—'

'Do what?' Nikolos drawled.

'Call Security and file a harassment charge.'

'You might care to rethink that.'

'Why?' It was a cry from the heart. 'You're bent on detaining me against my will.'

'This conversation would have been better served in private.'

'We've said all there is to say.'

'No,' Nikolos drawled imperturbably. 'We haven't.'

She was tired, she had a headache, and she'd had *enough*. 'It's simple. I'm going to keep the baby. I don't want your help…financial or otherwise. And I'd rather not see you again.'

His appraisal remained steady, and unnerved her…as he meant it to. 'Tough. Because not seeing me again isn't an option. Nor is refusing my help.'

Mia didn't like his imperturbability, or the hint of elemental ruthlessness beneath his deceptively mild exterior.

Nikolos Karedes possessed an animalistic sense of power that was vaguely frightening. He had no hold over her, no means to force her into any situation she didn't want or covet.

So why did she have the feeling he was intent on taking control? With or without her consent.

It was crazy.

Without a further word she turned and walked to the concierge's desk, requested the attendant summon a cab, then when it swept into the entrance she made her escape.

As the cab eased forward she saw Nikolos emerge from the entrance and lift his hand in silent acknowledgement as he slid behind the wheel of his car.

Any satisfaction she experienced at initiating independence diminished with the knowledge Nikolos Karedes knew who she was, where Alice lived, and her anonymity no longer existed.

CHAPTER THREE

'THE guy you slept with and Cris' *brother* are one and the same? You're kidding me...aren't you?' Alice challenged with a stunned expression as they shared lunch together at a café overlooking the harbour.

It was by way of being a celebration, given Mia had successfully confirmed a three-week placement in a local pharmacy. There was also an indication she'd be offered part-time work during the long summer holidays.

Alice expelled a long drawn-out breath, concern clouding her features. 'Unbelievable.'

A slight understatement, if ever there was one, Mia acknowledged silently. 'It made for an uncomfortable evening.'

'Added to the subtle grilling re your friendship with Cris?'

'*Subtle* didn't enter the equation.' Mia rolled her eyes expressively. 'Cris' grandmother breathed fire and brimstone.'

'A dragon, huh?'

'Oh, yeah. And then some.'

'And?'

She met her sister's gaze, interpreted the silent query, and fielded it. 'You're not going to let up, are you?'

'Got it in one.'

'Nikolos insisted on driving me home, we stopped off for coffee, and we…talked.'

'As in?'

'He asked, I told him, he offered help, I refused,' Mia declared. She paused to sip chilled water from her glass. 'Then I walked out and caught a cab.'

'Not the best move.'

'It seemed a good idea at the time.'

'So what happens now?'

'Nothing, hopefully.'

'You think he's going to dismiss the fact you're carrying a Karedes *heir*?' Alice's voice held a slightly incredulous note.

She'd known for three weeks, and in that time she'd considered the baby *hers*. Her responsibility, therefore her decisions were the only ones that would count.

Now she was forced to accept the father of her child intended to take an active role in its life. Which meant Nikolos Karedes would intrude in *her* life. Something she needed like a hole in the head.

There was a part of her that wanted to cut and run. *Sure,* a tiny imp silently derided. That's *really* going to work!

'You do realise just *who* Nikolos Karedes is, and the power he has in this city?' Alice queried.

A chill shiver slithered the length of Mia's spine. Why did she get the feeling she was losing a battle that had yet to be fought? It was crazy.

If only she hadn't decided to spend the long summer break in Sydney…except she had, and it wasn't possible to go back and change a set of circumstances that had brought her into contact with the man with whom she'd conceived a child.

So…she'd deal with it. All she had to do was remain resolute. Nikolos Karedes might imagine he possessed a few rights. But they had to be limited, surely?

'I'm self-supporting, and entitled to make my own decisions,' Mia reminded gently.

A half-share in their parents' estate had allowed her to purchase her own apartment and have an investment portfolio. An apartment she'd leased out when she'd entered university. Her furniture had been placed in storage, and most of her clothes were stored at Alice's home.

'With regard to yourself,' Alice agreed, frowning with concern. 'However, when it comes to the child, Nikolos Karedes can insist on a DNA test, and with proven paternity he has legal rights with regard to custody, education.'

Mia felt the blood drain from her face. 'You're positive about this?' A ridiculous query, given Alice worked as a para-legal, and possessed an extensive knowledge of the law. 'What if he doesn't choose—'

'To stake a claim?' Her sister paused for a few seconds, then offered gently, 'Hasn't he already stated he intends to be part of the child's life?'

That put a different perspective on going solo. 'So what do you suggest?'

'Establish a convivial friendship with the man.'

'Are you mad?'

Alice shook her head. 'It wouldn't be wise to make an enemy of him.'

The mere thought of him in that role sent a chill shiver feathering the length of her spine, and she placed a protective hand to her waist.

A silent groan of despair rose and died in her throat. How could she have been so foolish as to think she was in control, and able to call the shots?

As to Nikolos Karedes backing down…forget it.

Friends. How could they be friends?

She didn't want to think about it. In fact, she refused to consider anything about the man for the rest of the afternoon.

Mia checked her watch. 'We should go do some shopping before we collect Matt from school.'

'A bid to divert the subject of conversation?'

'Got it in one.'

Alice lifted both hands in a gesture of defeat. 'Okay, time to butt out.'

'No,' Mia contradicted gently. 'I love you dearly, and value your opinion, your advice.'

'But…?'

'I'd prefer not to spend time second-guessing Nikolos Karedes' next move.'

'So let's go enjoy the rest of the day, huh?'

Mia's cellphone pealed within minutes of leaving the café, and she took the call.

'Mia? It's Cris.' His voice held amusement. 'Last night. You and Nikolos. What *was* that?'

If only you knew! 'You could have rescued me.'

'Darling, you were doing just fine on your own.'

'You think?'

'Sweetie, if I was hetero I could almost be jealous of how fast he moved in for the kill. So he drove you home, *and*…?'

'There was no *and*…'

'Of course not. But—'

'I left and took a cab.'

His soft chuckle almost undid her. 'No woman walks out on Nikolos Karedes.'

'This one did.'

'Wish I'd been there.'

'Any fallout from last night?'

'Oh, you could say that.' His humour was infectious. '*Yiayia* lectured me on the age difference, my studies, the family honour. Sofia added her concerns, and brother Nikolos subjected me to one of his discerning looks over breakfast. Incidentally,' he added following a fractional pause. 'Nikolos has your phone number.'

'You gave it to him?' she demanded incredulously.

'You mind?'

Yes, she did. Very much.

'Oh, hell.' Cris swore quietly. 'Want me to go into damage control?'

There was little point. 'No.' She drew in a deep breath, then released it slowly. 'I'm out shopping with Alice.'

'Enjoy. We'll talk soon.'

'Cris?' Alice queried as Mia cut the call.

'Uh-huh.'

'I think,' Alice offered cheerfully, 'we need to do some serious retail therapy.'

'It's that or chocolate,' Mia hinted darkly, and led the way into the next trendy boutique.

It was after four when they arrived home, and it took little prompting for Matt to tend to his homework before dinner.

Mia deposited an assortment of bright carrier bags in her room, then changed into cargo pants and a tee shirt before joining Alice in the kitchen.

They were about to begin preparations for a steak salad when the doorbell rang.

Alice dried her hands, and smoothed a hand over her hair. 'I'll get it.'

A few minutes later she returned carrying a large bouquet of pale roses in cream, peach and apricot. 'For you.'

Mia felt the nerves in her stomach tighten. Who would send her flowers? It couldn't be… She plucked the card, and read the slashing signature.

Nikolos.

No message, just his name.

'Should I guess?' Alice prompted, and Mia shook her head as she extended the card.

'Kind of makes a statement, don't you think?'

'I'll get a vase.'

Mia drew a deep breath and released it slowly. 'How do you feel about discarding dinner and we'll take Matt and go grab a burger? My treat.'

'Yes.' Matt's victory gesture clinched it, although his mother added the rider, 'Finish your homework first.'

It was a futile act of defiance, but it felt good as

Mia switched off her cellphone *en route* to the nearest burger outlet.

'You think that's going to work?' Alice queried mildly as they collected their order and made for one of the outdoor tables.

'It's something I can control.'

Matt's enthusiasm for a departure in routine was catching, and his natural flair for humour brought laughter during the ride home.

Until Alice turned the car into their street and Mia caught sight of Nikolos' Mercedes parked at the kerb.

'Wow,' Matt breathed with boyish reverence. 'That's right outside our house.'

Mia cursed beneath her breath, and endeavoured to still the nerves turning somersaults inside her stomach. Nikolos emerged from behind the wheel as Alice entered the driveway.

'Let me out before you take the car into the garage,' Mia instructed quietly. 'I'll get rid of him.'

'Don't like your chances.'

It took only seconds to slip out from the car, and she turned to face Nikolos Karedes as the automatic garage door slid closed.

He was too tall, his shoulders too broad…and he was altogether too much. Strong masculine features projected a forceful image that meshed elemental sensuality with leashed strength.

Designer jeans and a chambray shirt replaced the elegant suit and tie of the previous evening, and the casual look in no way diminished his animalistic aura of power.

Mia took in the faint grooves slashing his cheeks, the tiny lines fanning out from his eyes, the curve of his mouth, and conducted a mental count to five as she attempted to slow her heartbeat.

Attack was the best form of defence…wasn't it? 'What are you doing here?'

'You left me little choice,' Nikolos drawled. 'Your sister's answering machine wasn't activated, and your cellphone is switched off.'

'We were out.' With the obvious intention of being incommunicado. She should have known he wouldn't let it rest for long. 'We said all there was to say last night.'

'No,' Nikolos drawled. 'We didn't. You chose to leave before we were done.'

Her fingers curled into a tight fist. 'I have nothing more to say to you.'

He glanced towards the neat fences, the surrounding houses. 'I suggest we have this conversation elsewhere.'

'Why?' Mia demanded, sorely tried.

No one had worked their way beneath her skin as this man did. She was incredibly aware of his sensual alchemy and the effect it had on her. Potent, devastating and infinitely dangerous. She could recall in vivid detail how it felt to have his mouth possess her own, the touch of his hands on her body…how he could make her *feel*.

She didn't want to go there. Didn't want to remember. Not in the daylight hours. It was bad enough he haunted her dreams, invaded her subconscious, and lingered there all through each night.

'We're going to share a child together.'

Her eyes flared, widening into deep dark pools as she regarded him. '*I'm* the one who's pregnant. Whose body will nurture and expel the child into the world, feed and care for it.'

His expression didn't change. 'All the more reason for us to take time to get to know each other better.'

She waited a beat. 'I think we've already taken care of that, don't you?'

One eyebrow slanted. 'One night of intimacy doesn't constitute a relationship.'

'There isn't going to be a *relationship*!'

'Friends,' he amended. 'It would be a start, don't you think?'

'A start to *what*?' She was on a roll. 'Civility? Sharing the occasional meal, observing the social niceties? I don't think so!'

'What are you afraid of?'

Oh, man, you can't begin to comprehend! 'I don't see it would serve any purpose.'

'You didn't answer the question.'

Mia heard a slight sound and turned to see Alice framed in the open doorway, a polite smile creasing her attractive features.

'Hi, I'm Alice. You must be Nikolos.' The smile curved a little wider. 'Perhaps you'd like to take this indoors and continue your conversation over coffee.'

Coffee? Indoors? *Are you mad?* Mia demanded silently, and met Alice's bland expression as Nikolos inclined his head.

'Thank you.'

Matt's boyish enthusiasm acted as a merciful distraction, and within minutes Mia followed Alice into the kitchen.

'Traitor,' she accused quietly as she took down cups and set them on matching saucers.

'You could hardly stand out on the lawn indefinitely.'

'Want to bet?'

It didn't take long for the coffee to percolate, and Matt leapt to his feet the instant Alice appeared in the lounge.

'Nikolos has a cruiser.' His eyes gleamed with excitement. 'Guess what? He said we can all go out on it. With him. Sunday.' He was trying hard to act cool. 'If it's okay.'

'That's nice of him.'

Nice? Mia sent Nikolos a dark glance that intimated she knew exactly what game he was playing. The mere thought of spending a day in his company set the nerves inside her stomach turning somersaults. It wasn't a comfortable feeling!

'We can go, can't we?'

Mia could see Alice wavering towards acceptance. Understandably, given Matt's enthusiasm. He was such a great kid, and he didn't deserve to be denied a wonderful day's outing.

'Mia?'

Sibling loyalty at its best, for it gave her the opportunity to decline. One Nikolos Karedes expected her to take, she perceived, from the faint challenge evident in his dark gaze.

The very reason she summoned a smile. 'How

could I be the one to disappoint my favourite nephew?'

Matt's response was a joyful whoop.

A day spent in Nikolos' company. How hard could it be, given her sister and nephew would be there as a buffer?

Nikolos finished his coffee, then rose to his feet and took his leave.

'I'll collect you on the way to the marina on Sunday morning. Shall we say nine?'

Mission accomplished, Mia accorded silently as Alice accompanied him to the front entrance. With determined effort she stacked cups and saucers together and took them through to the kitchen.

Alice joined her there minutes later, and they regarded each other in silence for a few seconds.

'Don't hold back,' Mia offered quietly, and Alice rolled her eyes.

'For what it's worth, I don't think you have a snowflake's chance in hell of dismissing him from your life.'

'You base that opinion after having spent ten minutes in his company?'

'Intuition?' Alice ventured, and took time to check her watch. 'I'll organise Matt off to bed. Give me ten minutes.'

'More coffee? Or tea?'

'Tea.'

Mia took care of the dishes, and was in the process of pouring tea into two large mugs when Alice entered the kitchen.

'Shall we take this into the lounge? Maybe slot in a DVD and view a movie? Or do you want to talk?'

Mia shot her sister a faintly rueful smile. 'A movie.'

'You're on.'

They sat together in companionable silence as the movie played, and when it was over they closed everything down and went to their separate rooms.

CHAPTER FOUR

SUNDAY held the promise of being a beautiful day, the sun ascending in a cloudless blue sky. A gentle breeze moved the air, dappling the water's surface as Nikolos eased the powerful cruiser out into the harbour.

Wow had been Matt's appreciative description when Nikolos had led them to the large boat at its marina mooring.

Fitting, Mia agreed, for a seaworthy vehicle of sufficient size to hold several passengers and throw a small party.

Splendid accoutrements with fine attention to detail, it was an expensive craft only the wealthy could afford.

'You could live here,' Matt declared, attaching himself to Nikolos' side. 'And go anywhere.'

'I don't get to use it very often. Mostly it gets chartered out for private entertaining.'

Doubtless at an exorbitant fee.

'Matt appears to have nominated Nikolos as his new idol.'

Mia encountered Alice's regretful glance. 'He doesn't get to be around men very often.'

'Today he has two,' she offered lightly, watching as Cris took over the wheel and left Nikolos free to point out places of interest.

She had to admit he appeared to have a natural empathy with her nephew, providing information with casual grace for a young brain eager to soak up knowledge about the cruiser, its measurements, capacity, engine.

Yet, despite its size, Mia was very aware of being trapped in a relatively small space out on the water with no escape until Nikolos brought the cruiser in to berth late that afternoon...seven, eight hours from now.

Alice, Matt and Cris provided a welcome distraction, although she had to wonder if her emotional tension was evident. She hoped not!

Nikolos was *there*, the focus of her existence, and she was incredibly aware of his every move, each glance, the depth of his dark gaze whenever it came to rest on her.

Thank heaven for sunglasses, for they served a dual purpose in shading her expressive eyes. Although it worked both ways...she couldn't determine his expression, either!

Yet being in such close proximity brought alive the sexual chemistry they shared, until it almost became a palpable entity.

Every nerve-cell in her body tautened to screaming point, and she was conscious of every breath she took.

It was maddening to be so aware of him, to retain such a vivid memory of what it felt like to be held in his arms...his scent, the feel and taste of his skin beneath her lips. And to know she wanted his touch. Craved it, in a manner she found vaguely shocking.

Did he guess? Dear heaven, she hoped not!

Sydney was her home town, the city where she'd grown up, and she thought she knew its origins, the history behind the harbour bridge, the dramas associated with the design and building of the famed Opera House.

Yet she became fascinated as Nikolos had Cris take the wheel while he gave Matt a verbal recount, and pointed out places of interest.

'Mia, come look at this!'

Matt's excited voice brooked little resistance as Mia followed Alice to where Matt stood.

'See that house? Nikolos said a former prime minister lived there.'

She was barely conscious of a subtle shift in position, only that Nikolos had somehow moved to stand beside her, his solid frame close to her own.

Too close, Mia decided as his arm brushed hers when he pointed out the home belonging to a famous Australian actress.

Was his touch deliberate, or was she merely being fanciful?

Seconds later there was little doubt as he slid an arm around her waist, lingered there, then smoothed a path up her back to capture her shoulder.

It was fleeting, outwardly casual to any onlooker. Except she felt all her skin-cells leap into tingling life, and she suppressed a shivery sensation threatening to wreak visible havoc.

What was *wrong* with her? It wasn't possible for one person to have such a devastating effect on another...was it?

Mia wanted to move away. Yet conversely, she needed to stay. If nothing else, to prove she could.

Nikolos Karedes knew precisely what he was doing, and she refused to give him an atom of satisfaction.

Yet, despite her calm exterior, inside she was a mass of nerves. Breathing was an automatic act, yet she became conscious of every breath she took, each exhalation.

Once, she could have sworn his breath teased her hair when he moved to stand behind her, and her whole body stiffened as he leant forward and grasped the rail, effectively caging her in.

The temptation to dig an elbow into his ribs was impossible to resist, and she'd barely congratulated herself on the small victory when she felt the imprint of his body against her own.

It lasted only seconds, but it was enough to lock the breath in her throat.

She could *kill* him…and would, she determined, at the first opportunity.

Almost as if he *knew*, he moved away and placed a hand on Matt's shoulder. 'How about we relieve Cris at the wheel?'

Matt's response was immediate. 'We? As in you and me?'

'Sure. Are you up for it?'

As if Matt needed to be asked! His face was a study in pride, pleasure and euphoria as Nikolos allowed him to feel the powerful engine beneath his hands as he stood in front of Nikolos at the wheel.

'He sure knows how to capture a young boy's

heart,' Mia voiced lightly as Cris joined her, and incurred his musing look.

'Afraid he might use similar tactics to capture yours?'

'My interest doesn't rest with cruiser specifications.'

Cris' expression sobered. 'Nikolos has a reputation as a skilled negotiator, and he can be ruthlessly tenacious when it comes to getting what he wants.'

'You're telling me this, because...?'

'He wants you,' he stated simply.

The engine stilled, and Cris checked his watch. 'We've stopped for lunch.'

Alice had insisted on preparing a picnic hamper filled with a variety of salads, bread, and home-baked fruit pies. Nikolos withdrew cooked chicken and cold cuts from the cabin fridge, and retrieved chilled drinks.

A retractable table and collapsible wooden chairs on the main deck made for a relaxed atmosphere, and it was much more informal than eating in the main cabin lounge/dining area.

Matt was in his element, his natural curiosity endearing as he plied Nikolos and Cris with numerous questions. Cars, boats, countries they'd visited.

'And you, Mia?' Nikolos queried with apparent idleness. 'Any places of interest you particularly enjoyed?'

'New York, Hawaii.' She cast Alice an affectionate glance. 'Paris.'

'It's a beautiful city,' Cris relayed. 'Friendly people, great food, fantastic ambience. Especially in the south.'

'Mia can speak French. She does martial arts, too,' Matt declared in a bid to impart information about his favourite and only aunt. 'Mum and I went to watch her in competition. She's awesome.'

Mia bore Nikolos' interested gaze with equanimity.

'Any other hidden talents?' he drawled. When she refrained from answering he transferred his attention to Alice, who merely grinned as she offered, 'You expect me to risk my life?'

His sensually moulded mouth curved to form a musing smile as he countered, 'Family loyalty?'

'Self-preservation,' Mia answered on her sister's behalf.

In retrospect it was a carefree day spent in convivial company, and for Mia it was wonderful to see Alice relax and enjoy herself, while Matt's pleasure was a matter of pure delight.

It more than made up for spending several hours in Nikolos' presence, for she was acutely aware of him in a way that tied her nerves in countless knots.

Did he know? Dear heaven, she hoped not.

She'd never experienced this depth of emotion before, or felt so mentally and emotionally attuned to anyone to quite this degree.

It wasn't a feeling she coveted. It was almost sickening. Then she held back the laugh threatening to burst from her throat. Was there such a thing as lust-sick?

Honesty compelled her to admit she wanted his

touch. To be able to experience again the depth of emotion, the heat...Why not call it how it was—the *ecstasy* she experienced in his arms.

How could she be so intensely vulnerable? So weak? It was ridiculous.

Consequently it was something of a relief when Nikolos eased the cruiser into its berth at the marina.

'Do you need to clean out the bilges?' Matt queried as they disembarked, his eagerness to help clearly apparent.

Nikolos ruffled the boy's hair. 'The marina staff take care of it. You can come with me to the office when I hand over the keys if you like, while Cris goes ahead with your mother and Mia to the car.'

'I think *idol* just moved up to *god,*' Mia murmured as they reached the car park.

'He's a great kid,' Cris complimented as he unlocked the boot and stowed their gear. 'We'll take him out again.'

'That's so kind. He's had such a wonderful time. We all have.' Alice's enthusiasm had Mia silencing a protesting groan.

What hope did she have of minimising her contact with Nikolos, when he already had Alice and Matt on side?

Minutes later she turned and saw Nikolos and Matt walking towards them. Her stomach lurched at the sight of man and boy together, and her mind took a quantum leap into the future. To the years ahead when Nikolos would spend time with their son or daughter.

She saw all too clearly how Nikolos would swing

their child high onto his shoulders, the laughter, the fun they'd share together. The affection, the love.

Yet a child spending equal time with each parent, emotionally torn between both. Probably with step-parents and step-siblings to cope with, and perhaps resentment at not belonging to one family or the other.

It wasn't an ideal picture, and for a brief moment she felt stricken at the implications of what the future might hold.

Matt's excited voice intruded, and Mia summoned an affectionate smile as he drew close. It would be wonderful to return to the simplicity of being a child, she mused. To have the unconditional love of a parent, few complications in life, to seize the day and squeeze the most enjoyment possible from it.

She caught Nikolos' intent gaze, met and held it for a few timeless seconds, grateful for the dark lenses shading her eyes so their expression remained indiscernible.

It was almost six when Nikolos turned into Alice's driveway. Summer daylight saving meant it would be light for two, perhaps three more hours.

Mia determined to engage Matt in a few games of chess. It would help focus her mind on something other than the tall, powerful man who seemed intent on turning her life upside down.

'Thanks for a wonderful day.' Alice's and Matt's voices echoed in tandem, and Nikolos smiled as Mia added her own.

'I have tickets to a private gallery showing on Tuesday evening. A percentage of the ticket price and sold items will be donated to one of the charities the Karedes family are known to sponsor. I'd like to invite you both as my guests.'

'Alice?' Please say you can't get someone to sit with Matt at such short notice, she begged silently.

'That would be lovely. Matt is due to have a sleep-over with a friend.' Alice's features creased with friendly warmth. 'Can I check and have Mia confirm with you?'

'Of course.'

Mia crossed to the rear of the car to retrieve the picnic basket, aware Nikolos fell into step beside her.

'You're not playing fair,' she accused quietly.

'No?' He undid the boot and they both reached for the basket simultaneously.

Nikolos' fingers brushed her own, and her skin cells felt as if they burned from the contact.

'I'll be in touch,' he drawled as she turned away and began walking up the path.

She didn't look back as the car engine purred to life, and she declined to join Alice and Matt as they waved a friendly farewell.

'Wasn't it a cool day?' Matt queried seconds later. 'That cruiser is something else. Nikolos is a great guy. I like him.'

'Go wash up,' Alice bade. 'While Mia and I organise something to eat.'

'On my way.'

'You look as if you want to bite my head off,' Alice said as soon as Matt was out of earshot.

Oh, hell. She made an attempt at humour. 'Is it that obvious?'

'I'm your sister, remember?'

And far too perceptive for Mia's peace of mind. 'I'd prefer to keep any contact with Nikolos Karedes to a minimum.'

Alice's eyes were startlingly direct. 'Can't you see he's not going to give up?'

'I have no intention of accepting every invitation he extends, just because—' She paused, and Alice completed the sentence.

'You're carrying his child?'

'Yes, dammit!'

'You'd like it better if I renege Tuesday evening, and you show as his partner?'

'You know the answer to that one.'

Alice arched an eyebrow. 'So?'

Matt's appearance in the kitchen saved Mia from elaborating further.

Their evening meal comprised cold cuts and a salad followed by fresh fruit, and afterwards Mia suggested chess.

'Loser gets to take out the trash for the next week.'

Matt rose to the challenge with a grin. 'Guess that's going to be you.'

'Want to bet?'

Alice called a halt at eight-thirty. 'Time for bed, Matt.'

'I'm about to sweep Mia off the board,' he protested, and gained a five-minute reprieve.

'Yay!' He raised a fist in the air in triumph.

Mia spread her hands. 'Tomorrow night I get to win.'

He gave her an infectious grin. 'In your dreams.'

She reached forward and mussed his hair. 'Make sure yours are good ones.'

'You, too.' He picked up the chessmen and packed them away. 'Goodnight.'

Mia cleared away the teacups and stifled a yawn as she stacked the dishwasher, glancing up as Alice re-entered the kitchen.

'If you don't mind, I'll grab a shower, then have an early night.'

'All that fresh sea air,' her sister declared sagely.

'Uh-huh.' Not to mention a day fraught with tension.

Nikolos Karedes had a lot to answer for, Mia determined as she slid into bed. His powerful image filled her conscious mind, and even in sleep he invaded her dreams…haunting evocative sequences that left her wanting.

The privately owned gallery catered to the social élite whose main purpose in life was undoubtedly to be seen at events such as this, Mia perceived as she glanced in idle speculation around the large, elegantly furnished room.

Works of art graced the walls, occupied strategically placed stands, displayed with deliberate precision.

Invitation only, the evening's exhibition featured works by three of the city's well-known artists.

'Alice, how nice to see you here.'

Mia glanced at the immaculately attired man who greeted her sister, and offered a smile as Alice introduced him.

'Craig Mitchell. A legal partner and my boss.'

Mia noted the faintly heightened colour tingeing Alice's cheeks, and lifted an eyebrow in silent speculation when he moved away.

'Don't even go there,' Alice warned quietly, and Mia's mouth curved a little.

'Hidden interest?'

'No.'

And cows jumped over the moon, she accorded silently as she cast her sister a speculative glance. 'Uh-huh.'

'It's quite a gathering, isn't it?'

Mia had to agree. 'A collection of the beautiful people dressed in their finest.' She sipped chilled water from her glass, and could almost have wished for something stronger.

'Speaking of which,' Alice voiced quietly, 'one of the most stunning women in this room is moving this way.'

Stunning didn't quite cover it, she decided as she followed her sister's line of vision. A model? Actress? Certainly no ordinary mortal. Tall, long flowing dark hair, classically moulded features, and beautifully attired in a black figure-hugging gown.

Exquisite make-up, Mia added as she drew close, aware just how long it took to create such perfection.

'Nikolos.'

Oh, my. Sultry tones with the hint of an accent she couldn't begin to place. And a proprietorial manner that irked as much as it irritated.

Mia watched as Nikolos turned towards the sable-haired beauty, and saw his features crease into a polite smile.

'Anouska.'

He was good. Skilled, she amended, in the art of social behaviour. So adept, she had little idea whether the exquisite female was friend, acquaintance, or lover. The next question had to be past or present?

Anouska inclined her head towards Cris.

'Home for the holidays?'

'Yes.'

Anouska returned her attention to Nikolos. 'Friends from out of town, darling?' The faintly languid drawl held a teasing quality as she arched an enquiring eyebrow.

'Mia,' Nikolos indicated by way of introduction. 'And her sister Alice.'

Anouska's smile was a mere shadow as she subjected Mia to an encompassing appraisal. 'Should I know you?'

Cris offered, 'Mia is—'

'The mother of my unborn child,' Nikolos concluded quietly.

Mia felt as if everything faded from the periphery of her vision. There was only their small tableau, five people momentarily frozen in time.

The illusion lasted mere seconds, and was broken as Nikolos caught Mia's hand in his and lifted it to his lips.

What was he doing?

She promised herself she'd do him physical harm at the first opportunity.

The room and its occupants came back into focus, together with the background chatter. She glimpsed Cris mime a silent whistle, and Alice appeared to be holding her breath.

'Really, darling,' Anouska protested lightly. 'Your sense of humour is questionable.'

Nikolos' expression didn't change. 'Humour wasn't my intention.'

Mia attempted to tug her hand free, only to have Nikolos tighten his hold.

A malevolent gleam appeared so fleetingly in Anouska's dark eyes, Mia had to wonder if she imagined it.

'You've kept her well hidden, darling. There hasn't been so much as a whisper of any one of several women who might have any—' Anouska paused with a delicate lift of one eyebrow '—shall we say *meaning* in your life.'

Ouch! Sour grapes were never attractive.

'Understandable,' Nikolos drawled. 'Given I prefer to keep my private life—' his pause was deliberate '—private.'

Anouska didn't bat an eyelid. 'Can we assume there will be a shotgun wedding in the near future?'

Forget sour grapes, Mia dismissed silently. The woman might take the cake in the stunning stakes, but her tongue was pure acid.

'No doubt word will circulate when I've been able to persuade Mia to make an honest man of me.'

He was ice, to an almost frightening degree. Lethal, whom only a fool would choose to have as an adversary.

'Something I'm disinclined to do,' Mia offered in an attempt to set the record straight.

'How…amazingly unperceptive of you.'

'Yes,' Mia said sweetly. 'But then, my values verge towards the unusual.' She visualised a mental high-five. Score one for Mia! It was easy to summon a winsome smile. 'If you'll excuse me? I should go examine the exhibits.'

Nikolos made no move to relinquish her hand as he chose to walk at her side, and she waited only seconds before bursting into restrained speech.

'Just what did you think you were doing back there?'

Amusement tugged the edges of his mouth. 'Shall we say…setting the record straight?'

'Really?' Cool, she could do *cool*. 'And that's necessary…because?'

'I have no reason to hide the fact we've made a child together.'

'I'll have returned to Brisbane before my pregnancy is visible.'

His gaze was startlingly direct. 'No, you won't.'

'Excuse me?' It was amazing she managed to keep her voice calm.

'You heard.'

Her eyes glittered with indignation. 'I have a commitment—'

'To complete your registration examinations at the end of next year,' Nikolos completed. 'Something which can be arranged here. As can your assigned pharmacy placements.'

'You've made enquiries?'

One eyebrow lifted, and his mouth assumed a mocking curve. 'Did you think I wouldn't?'

She shot him a glare that would have felled a lesser man. 'You have no right—'

'Yes, I do,' he said quietly.

Alice's cautious reminder of legal fact backed up by DNA returned to haunt her. 'After the birth,' she qualified tightly, wondering how on earth she would cope with seeing Nikolos on a regular basis, much less relinquishing her child to him for regular custody visits.

His fingers threaded through her own, and tightened when she attempted to pull free.

'Must you?'

'Is it such a hardship to present a united front?'

Mia contrived for superficial serenity, and achieved it…just. 'I don't like playing games.'

'Who said it was a game?'

She swallowed the lump that rose in her throat, aware the conversation had taken a subtle shift, and she became intensely conscious of his close proximity.

The scent of him, a combination of male muskiness and expensive cologne mixing with the clean smell of freshly laundered clothes.

It was all too easy to visualise the hard body beneath the trappings of his fine tailored apparel. Broad-shouldered, lean-hipped, the chiselled perfection of well-honed muscles, how they flexed with each move he made, the washboard stomach and tight butt.

'Would you deny me the pleasure of seeing our child grow inside you?'

Oh, dear heaven. Heat suffused her veins at the mere thought of its conception. How she lay awake night after night reliving in vivid detail the touch of Nikolos' hands, his mouth, each caress...the electrifying passion they'd shared several times through the dark hours, until the first light of dawn when she'd quietly dressed and slipped silently from his room.

It was too much. *He* was too much.

'By making a public statement, you've irretrievably connected the two of us together. Something you could easily have avoided.' She met his gaze and held it. 'So why didn't you?'

He slanted her a musing glance. 'To ensure there's no doubt to whom you belong.' He paused fractionally, then added quietly, 'Or to whom I owe my loyalty.'

She got it in one. 'Anouska.'

His eyes speared hers, dark and unfathomable. 'You doubt I can handle Anouska?'

'No.' He could handle anyone he chose, undoubtedly with chilling efficiency. She just didn't want to be one of them.

Where had that come from?

She wasn't *falling* for him...was she? A hollow laugh rose and died in her throat. Who was she fooling?

Could he guess at the state of her emotions? The utter turmoil he'd caused? Or were her hormones adding to the mix?

'What do you think?'

Mia registered Nikolos' voice and dragged her attention back to the exotic landscape displayed in splendid isolation.

Bold colours apparently splashed at random on canvas, but somehow meshing to depict a scene that captured and held the imagination.

'It would need a room all of its own,' she ventured, and listened as he discussed the artist with knowledgeable expertise of his work.

They moved from one exhibit to another, pausing every now and then to devote more than a passing examination of anything that took their interest.

'I have tickets for the Thursday evening performance of *The Merry Widow*,' Nikolos intimated as they reached the last exhibit.

Mia turned towards him. 'Are you asking me out?'

'Yes.'

'On a date?'

'Is that so strange?'

Just the two of them, alone, with neither Cris nor Alice as a buffer.

'You need to think about it?'

She met his teasing gaze, and summoned a brilliant smile. 'No.'

'Is that a no you don't need to think about it, or no you refuse?'

'I'd enjoy a night at the theatre.'

A flashlight exploded close by, one of a series of flashes as a photographer captured shots for the social pages.

Nikolos Karedes was newsworthy, so it was a

given his photo would feature among those of the city's social echelon.

Doubtless the appearance of an unknown woman at his side would cause conjecture. Mia wondered just how long it would take for the rumour mill to begin its speculative journey, and how much fact would be among the fiction.

Worse, what would Sofia's reaction be when she checked the social pages, and news of Nikolos' revelation reached her ears? As it would.

'Sofia, Angelena and Cris are aware of the situation.'

Oh, heavens, he'd *told* them? 'You read minds?'

'You possess expressive features.'

Oh, *great*. Just what she wanted to hear. 'Thanks.'

He'd set the cat among the pigeons. She could almost hear the flutter and flapping of wings as the Karedes matriarchs absorbed the news.

'Naturally they expect to resume their acquaintance with you.'

'I don't think I'm ready for another interrogation just yet.'

His husky laughter came as a surprise. 'I promise not to leave you alone with them.'

'That's what worries me.'

'My mother will adore you. You're providing her with a longed-for grandchild. And Angelena is a pussycat at heart.'

'You could have fooled me.'

She watched idly as Anouska posed with professional ease and exchanged a few words with the photographer.

Ensuring the man noted the designer label she wore? Or that her feet were shod in Manolo Blahnik's?

Doubtless such detail bore importance, Mia accorded with unaccustomed cynicism.

It took a while to circulate the room, for many of the guests were associates and business acquaintances who used such social occasions to touch base.

Mia smiled and indulged in polite conversation with each introduction, fielding the subtle and not so subtle queries thinly disguised as an exchange of social pleasantries.

It was a relief when the evening drew to a close following an announcement that record funds had been raised to benefit the nominated charity.

The guests began to disperse, and Mia slid into the passenger seat, silent as Nikolos sent the car whispering through the city streets.

Alice, ever the polite hostess, offered coffee when the car drew to a halt in her driveway, and Mia held her breath hoping, praying Nikolos would decline.

'It's kind of you, but I have to catch an early morning flight to Melbourne. Another time?'

Minutes later she followed Alice indoors, pausing in the lounge to step out of her stilettos.

Alice copied her actions, then offered a level glance. 'Want to talk?'

She felt all talked out, and tiredness seemed to close around her like a shroud. 'Can I take a rain check?'

'Of course.' Alice's features held concern. 'You look beat. Try to get a good night's sleep.'

As if that were likely to happen. She'd probably lie awake replaying the evening over and over in her mind.

CHAPTER FIVE

MUCH to Mia's surprise she slept well, and woke feeling relatively refreshed. She could smell fresh coffee, and longed for it, except caffeine was a no-no.

Today she and Alice were just going to potter around the house completing chores, talk, and simply relax.

It made for a leisurely day, and one they enjoyed. Alice's week off from work would soon end, and, with Mia's holiday employment about to begin, it was pleasant to fill the cookie tins, freeze muffins for Matt's school lunches, and simply catch up.

Nikolos Karedes didn't get a mention, and that suited Mia just fine.

There were a few friends she needed to touch base with, and she made the requisite phone calls, checked with the leasing agent who handled her apartment, and took in a movie with Alice next day.

It felt strange to be embarking on a date with Nikolos. There was a part of her that wanted to opt out. The unwise part urged her to throw caution to the wind and go with it.

How difficult could it be? They'd attend a lauded theatre production, he'd drive her home, she'd offer polite thanks...and the evening would be done.

Who do you think you're kidding? Mia queried

silently as she selected deep red silk evening trousers with matching camisole and jacket, slipped her feet into stiletto-heeled sandals, and added minimum jewellery.

Already her nerves were every which way but loose, and she was conscious of every breath she took as she slid into the passenger seat of his luxurious car.

Emotional havoc reigned as raw passion swirled deep within, spinning its sensual web. It was madness, utter insanity to be so affected by him and the intense sexual chemistry he was able to generate.

Fate and circumstance had thrown them together once, and now they were bent on showing their hand again. This time she wouldn't be able to cut and run, for her connection with Nikolos was forged by virtue of the child she carried.

'When did you return from Melbourne?' It seemed a logical query, and she met his musing glance as he paused at an intersection.

'The late-afternoon flight.'

'I imagine it was a successful trip?'

'Yes.' Intense negotiations, a particularly stubborn adversary who knew he had nowhere to go, but determined to play hardball just for the hell of it.

'I imagine you travel frequently?'

'It's an integral part of my position as head of the Karedes empire.'

Did he have a woman waiting for him in a number of cities around the world?

'No.'

His quiet drawl startled her. 'I beg your pardon?'

'I don't bed women indiscriminately.'

'You expect me to believe I was an exception?'

'It was an exceptional night.' He waited a beat. 'For both of us.'

And then some. She retained every second of it... The faint prickling sensation at the base of her neck; how she'd glanced away from the group she'd been with and met his gaze, literally across the crowded room, and felt as if she'd been struck by an electrical force so strong she'd become powerless to move.

He'd threaded his way through the mingling guests and engaged her in conversation...and never left her side for what remained of the evening.

Afterwards she'd accepted his invitation to share coffee in the lounge of his hotel. Even then she'd known how she wanted the evening to end. The excitement, apprehension...and the passion. To explore the previously unexplored with this man.

It had been...unbelievable. He was unbelievable. She'd forgotten who or where she was, or why. There had been only *him*, the night, and the most wonderful experience of her life.

Mia focused her attention beyond the windscreen, and chose silence until they reached the theatre foyer, where patrons merged and mingled while waiters circulated offering champagne and orange juice.

She recognised a few of the well-known glitterati, aware of Nikolos Karedes' position among the élite social set.

To be seen at his side, socially, undoubtedly caused speculative interest among his contemporaries. Introductions and polite conversation became the order of the hour, and she began to wish she could sip something stronger than orange juice as Anouska swanned into view looking as if she'd stepped straight from the cover of *Vogue* magazine.

Her gown was one of those barely there creations in tangerine silk...strapless, backless, and moulded her slender curves to perfection.

'There you are, darling.' The husky tones were exactly as Mia remembered. So too was the smile, the seemingly liquid dark eyes expressing blatant sensuality...and the body language that of a woman on the make.

Oh, my, this was going to be some evening!

'Anouska.' Mia was so polite, it was almost a travesty.

'Mya...or is it Mary?'

This could only get worse. 'Mia.' The correction held a faint emphasis that caused the woman's eyes to narrow slightly before she redirected her attention.

'Nikolos. Such a shame I couldn't join you in Melbourne. The boutique. Scheduled invitation-only fashion showing. You know how it is?' She lifted an elegant shoulder. 'Maybe next time?'

So it was war, huh? One-sided, but war nonetheless.

'I don't recall issuing an invitation.' Nikolos' voice held a degree of wry cynicism Anouska chose to ignore.

'Darling—' the protest was prettily voiced and accompanied by an alluring smile '—since when did I need one?'

Saved by the bell…or, more pertinent, the electronic buzzer, Mia breathed with relief.

Short-lived, she determined as Anouska accompanied them into the auditorium and took the same row.

Nikolos indicated their seats, and Mia deliberately took the one farthest of the two, aware the fashionista slid into the seat immediately adjacent his.

Oh, this was going to be just peachy! The mistress on one side, with the mother of his unborn child on the other.

'Maybe I should leave?' she queried in an undertone as the orchestra set up.

Nikolos leaned in close. 'Don't even think about it.'

He was close, too close. If she turned her head, his lips would almost brush hers.

'She has prior claim.'

'No, she doesn't.'

'Like I care?'

He caught hold of her hand, and held it fast within his own. When she endeavoured to break free, he traced the delicate veins at her wrist in a gesture meant to soothe.

Mia's response was to dig her nails in *hard*. Not that it had the slightest effect, for Nikolos merely enclosed her hand within both of his.

The curtain rose, and it became all too easy to lose herself in the magical production, the actors, the singing.

Scene changes were slick, and intermission came far too quickly, breaking the spell.

Anouska rose to her feet. 'Coming out for a drink, darling?'

'Not for me,' Mia negated politely, and offered Nikolos a stunning smile. 'But don't let that stop you.'

'Nikolos?' The tone held an edge of impatience Nikolos chose to ignore.

'Don't wait for us.'

Anouska gave an imperceptible shrug and eased her way into the aisle.

'Playing games comes with a price.'

'Really?' Mia didn't miss a beat. 'Anouska has a neon sign with *mine* pasted to her forehead whenever she's near you. Or hadn't you noticed?'

'She owns an exclusive fashion boutique in Double Bay,' he informed silkily. 'We're social acquaintances, nothing more.'

'Really?'

His eyes narrowed. 'You disbelieve me?'

'I didn't say that.'

'If I owed loyalty to another woman, I would not have—'

'Seduced me?' Mia intercepted. 'Let's tell it like it was.'

'My memory recall has it as being entirely mutual.'

That night would haunt her for the rest of her life. She swallowed the slight lump that had risen in her throat. 'Okay, so it was mutual.'

A faint smile curved the edges of his mouth. 'Such honesty.'

Mia rose to her feet. 'I think I need some fresh air. On my own,' she added as he joined her.

'Forget it.'

'I don't need anyone to hold my hand.'

'Tough.'

Her eyes flared with withheld anger. 'You really are the—'

His mouth closed over hers in a kiss that tore the words from her throat as his tongue swept briefly over hers, tasted, lingered, then withdrew, leaving her speechless.

'You've walked out on me twice,' Nikolos said quietly. 'I don't aim to let you do it again.'

Mia didn't offer so much as a word, for there wasn't one coherent thought in her head at that precise moment.

She was too aware of the taste and feel of him. And worse, much worse, was the urge to pull his head down to hers and repossess his mouth.

There were people in the auditorium…witness to the electric tension fizzing between Nikolos Karedes and his unknown companion.

She told herself she didn't care, but she did, and hated the soft colour suffusing her cheeks as she preceded him into the crowded foyer.

Locating the powder room was easy, and waiting in line provided sufficient time for her to regain a sense of relative calm.

Nikolos was there when she re-emerged into the foyer, and she walked silently at his side as they returned to their seats.

Anouska sent her a killing glance as the curtain

lifted, and, although Mia did her best to dismiss the woman's expressed venom, it stayed with her through much of the final half of the production.

There were occasions when she'd been the victim of envy, even jealousy. But nothing she'd experienced came close to the momentary hatred visible in Anouska's eyes.

The message was plain...*Watch your back*.

It was a relief when the curtain came down after a resounding ovation, and they made a move to leave.

Anouska placed a hand on Nikolos' arm. 'Coffee at the usual place?'

Are you kidding?

Nikolos removed her hand. 'I think not.'

The fashionista offered a conciliatory moue. 'Can't be much fun, darling, having a pregnant mistress.' She leant towards Mia with apparent concern. 'Morning sickness, tiredness...how are you coping?'

'Well, thank you,' Mia responded sweetly. She cast Nikolos a winsome smile. 'I can easily get a cab home if you want to share coffee with your friends.'

'No.'

Anouska's eyes widened with playful coquetry. 'If Mia's happy...' she let her voice trail deliberately '...to allow you an open relationship?' She lifted her shoulders and formed a seductive smile. 'Darling, you know where I am.'

Talk about eating a man alive!

'What do you think you're doing?' Nikolos demanded with deceptive mildness the instant Anouska was out of earshot.

Mia spared him a telling look that had no effect whatsoever. 'Returning the favour.'

'For?'

'Setting the cat among the pigeons.'

They cleared the foyer and reached the street. Nikolos' car was in secure parking, and they walked at a leisurely pace.

'Would you like to go somewhere for a drink?' Nikolos queried as he eased the powerful vehicle into the flow of traffic.

'Why not?' she managed lightly. It had begun as a date...they might as well finish the evening as one.

'You aren't going to add the proviso as long as it's not one of Anouska's favoured haunts?'

'I was hoping you'd figure that out for yourself.'

His husky laughter caused sensation to feather its way down her spine.

Nikolos chose a trendy café on the city outskirts, and placed an order for tea and coffee as soon as they were seated.

'So,' he began idly, holding her gaze. 'Why don't you tell me something about yourself?'

'Such as?'

His mouth curved to form a musing smile. 'Why not start at the beginning?'

'You mean you haven't had me investigated?' she queried with unaccustomed cynicism.

He wasn't about to tell her that no one managed to gain access to the Karedes inner family circle without security measures being observed.

The waiter delivered their order, his service faultless as he set down condiments.

Nikolos reached forward and poured her tea, added milk and sugar. It was a surprisingly unexpected gesture.

'I know you chose to study pharmacy after several years in the workforce.'

Was he legit? Mia had no way of knowing.

'Sydney born, bred and educated. Alice is my only sibling. Our parents died in a plane crash when I was in my teens. I gained training in specialist cosmetology, dated, became engaged to a doctor.' The next part was painful. 'I wanted the sex to wait until our wedding night.' She effected a seemingly faint shrug. 'He agreed, but took his pleasure elsewhere. I found out, we split, and I enrolled in a Brisbane university.' Her life, encapsulated in a three-minute time-frame. 'You?'

The coffee was how he liked it, strong, black and sweet.

He searched Mia's features, glimpsed the faint edge of emotional damage and tamped down anger at the man who'd caused it.

'Born in Perth of Greek heritage, educated in Sydney, spent two years in New York, two in Athens. Returned to Sydney when my father and grandfather were killed in a car accident.'

'You left out the women,' she said solemnly.

His dark eyes held faint humour. 'You expect me to say there were many, when they number far fewer than you imagine.'

She met and held his steady gaze. 'I guess it depends on the individual interpretation of *few*.'

Mia finished her tea, and sought to end the evening. 'It's getting late.'

Nikolos extracted a note and slid it beneath his cup to cover the bill, then he stood up and led the way to his car.

'How do you feel about dinner Saturday night?'

'Another date? So soon?'

He deactivated the locking mechanism, opened the passenger door and waited until she was seated before crossing round to slip behind the wheel.

'Call it a briefing in preparation for Sunday lunch with Angelena and Sofia.'

Oh, hell, for a moment she'd forgotten the official family conference. 'Will Cris be there?'

The car eased into the flow of traffic, gained speed, only to pause at a set of lights.

'You want Cris to return the favour of ally?'

Mia was suddenly alert to his tone, and she momentarily froze. Nikolos couldn't know...

'Did you think I was unaware of my brother's sexual proclivity?'

She felt as if she were skating on thin ice. What did she say? Hell, what *could* she say? 'Cris is a friend.'

'Your loyalty to him is commendable.'

Mia searched his features, and caught very little of his expression in the dim interior of the car. 'He's a nice guy.'

'Yes, he is, and I'll do everything in my power to protect him.'

Relief eased the tension, and she offered quietly, 'Perhaps you should tell him that.'

'I already have.'

But what of the Karedes women? 'Your mother and grandmother?' Mia queried cautiously.

'It's Cris' choice to confide in Sofia when he's ready.'

It came as a surprise when Nikolos drew the Mercedes to a halt at the kerb outside Alice's home.

'I've acquainted them with the truth of my involvement with you.'

Oh, *nice* one! '*Thanks*. So now I'm a slut for having sex within hours of meeting you.'

'No.'

'What do you mean...*no*?'

Did she have any idea how magnificent she was when battling anger? Her eyes glowed with it, and her body tensed as tight as a finely tuned bow.

She brought out the most incredible instincts in him. Instincts he hadn't known he possessed.

'They trust my judgement.' His slightly accented drawl held a tinge of humour, which served to incense her.

'Really?' She lifted a hand and clicked her fingers. She was on a roll, and couldn't stop. 'Just like that?'

'They have no reason to disbelieve me.'

Mia didn't attempt to hide her scepticism. 'You think not?'

Mia summoned a mental image of Angelena Karedes, and gritted her teeth. Enduring Sunday lunch was going to be as tricky as attempting to walk through a minefield!

'You'll be treated with dignity and respect.'

On the surface. But what of the hidden undercurrents?

Mia released her seat belt and reached for the door-clasp.

'You forgot something.'

She turned towards him in puzzlement.

'This.' Nikolos captured her head in both hands and lowered his mouth to hers in a kiss that tore her composure to shreds.

It would be so easy to invite more, to touch him as she wanted him to touch her. Attempt in some way to ease the ache deep inside.

Except it wouldn't be enough, for either of them.

His lips trailed to her temple, then explored a delicate cheekbone before settling at the edge of her mouth.

'I—please,' she said in a desperate voice. She couldn't stay. Daredn't.

Nikolos stifled a husky groan as he traced the soft curve of her mouth with his lips, felt their faint quiver as she sought control, and sank in for an evocative tasting.

'Go,' he bade gently as he relinquished her. 'I'll call you when I've confirmed a booking for Saturday evening.'

Mia unlatched the door and slid from the passenger seat without so much as a backward glance.

It took mere seconds to reach Alice's front door, insert the key, then close it behind. With a defeated movement she leant back against it and closed her eyes.

Dear heaven.

She was filled with the taste and feel of him, every sensory nerve-end *alive* with deep, aching need.

For twelve weeks she'd schooled herself to accept a certain rationale, employing logic and reason to her inexplicable behaviour on that fateful night.

There were the vivid dreams as her subconscious forced her to relive the cataclysmic assault he'd had on her senses. And her willing participation.

Now that she'd seen him again it was worse, so much worse than she could have ever imagined. For she was caught in a trap, legally bound to allow him access to their child once it was born, and committed to maintaining contact, sharing decisions, *seeing* him on a regular basis.

Any thought she'd entertained of moving on, creating a new life for herself and rearing a child on her own no longer existed.

Nikolos Karedes would find her, wherever she went, whatever she did. He was that sort of man. Possessed of omnipotent power, with sufficient wealth and resources to hunt her down. Worse, he could inevitably use that power to pursue his own ends.

It wasn't fair, Mia railed silently as she moved through the house to the bedroom she occupied.

But then, when was life ever fair?

CHAPTER SIX

SEVERAL hours of intense retail therapy had done much to bring Mia's wardrobe up to date…something that hadn't ranked high on her list of priorities over the past three years, given university apparel mainly comprised jeans, cargo pants, tee shirts, with an added jacket during winter.

The need to discuss how they should handle lunch with Sofia and Angelena seemed reasonable, and Mia wasn't averse to Nikolos' suggestion they talk over dinner.

'Another date with Nikolos?' Matt teased as Mia entered the lounge minutes ahead of the time Nikolos specified he'd be there.

'It's not a date,' Mia explained, and incurred a boyish grin.

'Looks like a date to me.'

She rolled her eyes in mild exasperation. 'You want me to take you horse-riding in the morning?'

'Okay, so it's not a date.'

'Thank you.'

'Stop it, you two,' Alice admonished with a laugh, and gave Mia her full attention. 'You look gorgeous.'

There was something about a basic black dress, faultless make-up, and minimum jewellery. Black stiletto heeled pumps, a stylish evening purse…

'Seriously gorgeous,' Matt endorsed, wriggling his eyebrows in mock admiration.

'You're a menace,' Mia accorded with affectionate indulgence. 'Fast forward ten years, and heaven help the female population.'

'*Ten?* I was thinking maybe five.'

'Try seven, minimum, or you're jail-bait.'

'Threats, promises, and blackmail?'

It was difficult to contain her laughter. 'All three, and more,' she declared. 'And what your loving mother doesn't finish, I will.'

'Two women ruling my life,' Matt declared, throwing his hands up in mock despair. 'What guy has *two*?'

Mia tilted his chin and planted a kiss on his forehead. 'You do, and don't you forget it!'

'Car just pulled up.'

Levity fled in a second, and was replaced by nervous tension. Did nerve-ends fray? Or stretch to breaking point? Hers felt as if they did both, simultaneously.

How was it possible to experience such a conflicting mixture of emotions? It didn't make sense.

But then, nothing had made sense from the first moment she'd set eyes on Nikolos Karedes.

All she had to do was look at him as he preceded Alice into the room, and everything else faded from her vision, her mind.

His tall, broad frame bore superb tailoring. Armani? Fine blue cotton shirt, silk tie several shades darker, hand-stitched shoes.

'Hi.' Even to her own ears, her greeting sounded incredibly banal.

Nikolos inclined his head. 'Hello.' He turned towards Matt. 'Hi there.' His mouth curved to form a wide smile as he quizzed, 'Is that warpaint?'

Recognition was instantaneous as he used a hand to scrub the lipstick from his forehead, explaining, 'Mia kissed me.'

'Lucky fellow.'

Nikolos' voice held a teasing drawl that did strange things to her composure. Did he realise the effect he had on her? Probably. In fact, she was sure of it!

'Shall we leave?' she managed coolly in a determined bid to exert some measure of control.

'Have fun,' Matt offered innocuously minutes later as Mia followed Nikolos to the car.

The restaurant he'd chosen was situated in one of the inner city suburbs, and intimately small. The sort of place where bookings were made weeks in advance.

'The chef is a personal friend,' Nikolos relayed on being greeted with affection and ushered to what had to be the best table in the house.

'Fine food, wine and exemplary service,' Mia accorded lightly.

He wanted to reach out a hand and trail his fingers down her cheek, cup her chin and outline the curve of her mouth with his thumb.

Except she'd probably bite him if he did.

The thought amused him, and for a moment he was seriously tempted just for the hell of it. Except it might lead to her walking away from the table, out of the restaurant, and hailing the first cab that passed.

She really was something else, he mused as he pretended interest in the wine list. There was no coquetry, no false smiles or attempt at seduction. What was more, she didn't appear to give a *jot* for his wealth or social position.

She possessed beauty that came from within. It was evident in her smile, the teasing gleam apparent in those liquid brown eyes whenever she was with her sister and nephew.

For the time-span of one night…a total of too few hours, she'd plumbed the emotional depths and gifted him everything she was, all she could be, and more.

He wanted back what they'd shared. Dammit, most of all he needed *her*. Beneath him, over him. Innocently generous, eager to please, and passionately genuine in her ecstatic reaction to every pleasure he chose to bestow.

Since when had *want* become *need*?

Mia chose a non-alcoholic spritzer, ordered a starter and a main course, then settled back in her chair. An hour and a half, two hours at the most, and they should have reached comparable tactics.

She picked up her goblet and sipped the cool drink, then set it back down. 'I imagine you've given tomorrow's game plan some thought?'

'Angelena and Sofia are aware of the facts, and that any decisions made will be our own.'

'But?' Mia queried bluntly.

'They offered a few suggestions.'

'I hardly dare ask.'

The waiter delivered their starter, checked Nikolos' wine goblet, then quietly retreated.

'Relatively, they mirror my own.'

Mia forked a delicate morsel from her plate and savoured it. 'So we have an impasse.'

'Not entirely.' His voice was deceptively mild, and she carefully replaced her fork.

'Go on.'

'You could marry me.'

'Excuse me?'

'Marriage,' Nikolos reiterated with hateful ease. 'Consider the benefits as opposed to sharing the child between two parents in different residences.'

'You're insane.'

'Am I?'

'You base what is meant to be a whole-of-life decision on one night of good sex?' *Good* didn't come close.

'Our sexual compatibility is a bonus.'

'No,' she said steadily.

'You don't agree it's a bonus?'

'No, I won't marry you.' He could give her everything she could ever want or need. A lifestyle almost without equal.

'Would you care to give me a reason why not?'

'I'd always know it was a choice you felt impelled to make.'

'You're so sure of that?'

How could it be anything else? 'Yes,' she said simply.

'What if you're wrong?'

'I had the textbook engagement,' she reiterated

quietly. 'Friends for two years, engaged for one. As it turned out, I hardly knew him at all.'

'So come live with me.'

Her eyes widened. 'I beg your pardon?'

'Move in with me, share my life, and determine whether marriage to me would be so abhorrent.'

'I don't think that's a good idea.'

'Afraid, Mia?'

'Of course not.' And knew she lied. If she went with him she'd never want to leave. And that was a luxury she couldn't afford.

While some women might eagerly settle for material possessions and social prestige in exchange for sexual favours, she wasn't one of them. Nor could she accept or condone a string of affairs in an open marriage.

'So what do you have to lose?'

You can't begin to know! she thought. To exist in a relationship where she knew she didn't have his heart and soul would only be half a life, and one she'd rather not have at all.

'I'm Alice's guest for the summer vacation.'

'That isn't a problem.'

Mia raised one eyebrow. 'Really?' She waited until the waiter cleared their plates before continuing, 'So I get to visit Alice and Matt whenever I'm not at work, socialising, or sleeping with you. Is that how you envisage such an arrangement?'

Nikolos' eyes narrowed. 'It isn't my intention to impose any restrictions on when and where you spend time with your sister.'

'Except you'd expect to take priority.' She examined the contents of her goblet, then speared his gaze with her own. 'Tell me, do you always get your own way?'

'Mostly.' He leaned back in his chair and regarded her carefully. She was something else…vibrant, sassy, and far too independent for his peace of mind.

'Perhaps you should make me aware of Angelena and Sofia's *suggestions*?'

'In order to be prepared?'

'I imagine your mother will be politely circumspect in comparison to Angelena.'

Nikolos' husky laughter sent sensation slithering down her spine. Worse, she appeared to have a host of butterflies in her stomach fluttering their wings madly in an attempt to escape. Neither was a comfortable feeling.

'*Yiayia* is adamant a Karedes heir should be born within the legitimate bounds of marriage,' he drawled, and Mia rolled her eyes in expressive dismissal.

'No exception acceptable.'

'None,' he agreed. 'Sofia suggests the announcement of an immediate engagement, followed by marriage in the foreseeable future.'

'Before the child's birth.'

'Preferably.'

She looked at him carefully. 'You're prepared to go along with that?'

'Would I suggest it if not?'

Doubtful. He wasn't a man to be coerced into anything, much less marriage. 'So tomorrow I stand alone against the three of you?'

Nikolos regarded her thoughtfully. 'Are you going to renege on lunch?'

And appear a wimp? 'No.'

The edges of his mouth twitched with musing humour as the waiter presented their main meal. 'I'm pleased to hear it.'

Tomorrow's confrontation held all the connotations of being a familial battle. One any sane person would go to any lengths to avoid.

Mia looked at the food displayed on her plate with artistic flair, and wondered if she'd be able to do it justice, for her appetite seemed to have fled.

Worse, her stomach appeared to be on the verge of a revolt. Morning sickness? In the evening? *Now?* The powder room was *where*?

There was barely time to utter 'excuse me' as she leapt from her chair and made a dignified dash to the designated powder room.

Minutes later she took a deep breath and placed a hand to her stomach. Everything seemed fine, but maybe she should give it another minute or two before venturing back to the table.

Mia glanced up as the door swung open, and she gave an involuntary gasp as she saw Nikolos in the aperture. 'You can't come in here.'

'Watch me.' His eyes narrowed as he raked her slender frame. Her features were pale, and her eyes seemed too large for her face. 'Are you okay?'

'I'm fine.' She smoothed a hand over her hair. 'Let's get back to the table.' She managed a faint smile. 'A cup of tea would go down well.'

He arranged it with considerable speed, and she

sipped the brew appreciatively, feeling better with each passing minute.

'Nikolos.' The voice was feminine and familiar. 'Who would have thought to find you here?'

Mia didn't need to turn in her chair to determine just who was standing close by.

'Anouska.'

Coincidence? Maybe. Or perhaps Anouska, aware of Nikolos' favoured eating places, could have phoned to check if he had a booking here tonight.

Mia moved slightly and murmured a polite greeting, noting the silk evening trouser suit, the jewellery, and superbly applied make-up. The fashionista looked a million dollars, and was very aware of the fact.

Mia was reminded of a preening peacock, aware she had the gender wrong. A peahen was utterly plain.

Anouska's male companion was too smooth, his smile too practised. Artificial superficiality was alive and well.

'We have a reservation, but perhaps we could join you?'

Great. Just what she needed. Another round with Anouska vying for one-upwomanship.

'We were just leaving.'

They were? He'd barely finished his main meal, and, even if he intended passing on dessert, he had yet to order coffee.

Was he doing this for her benefit? Or because he chose not to handle Anouska's company?

Whatever the reason, Mia felt a certain gratitude

as Nikolos beckoned the waiter and requested their bill.

'If you'll excuse us?'

Anouska's pout was pure Hollywood. 'Shame, darling. We could have had some fun.'

It depended on one's definition of *fun*, Mia determined as she rose to her feet and offered a polite 'goodnight'.

In the car, she sat in silence observing the passing night scenery, the bright neon advertising signs, the traffic.

'Nothing to say?'

Nikolos' drawling voice held a tinge of humour, and she turned towards him, aware of his profile in the semi darkness of the car's interior. A profile that assumed angles and planes beneath the illumination of oncoming headlights.

'What would you have me say?' Mia countered lightly.

'Anouska doesn't want to give you up? Thanks for a lovely meal? How about, Please take me home?'

His soft laughter sounded impossibly husky in the close confines of the car.

'Thanks,' Mia added quietly, and incurred his sharp glance. 'For making a quick exit.'

'How are you feeling?'

Don't sound as if you care. The thought that he might almost brought her undone. 'Fine,' she managed evenly. Physically, she accorded silently. Emotionally was something else.

Alice's house was in darkness with only the outside light burning when Nikolos brought the car to a smooth halt at the kerb.

'I'll see you tomorrow,' Mia indicated as she reached for the door-clasp.

He leaned towards her and trailed light fingers across her cheek. 'Midday. I'll collect you.' He traced her lower lip with his thumb-pad, felt its slight tremble beneath his touch, then sank back in his seat. 'Sleep well.'

Mia slid out from the passenger seat and crossed the path to her sister's home. Seconds later Nikolos' car purred to life as she closed the door quietly behind her.

Mia rose early and drove Matt to his horse-riding lesson, commended his skills, and returned in time for a late breakfast, after which Alice left with Matt for a day at the beach, offering a humorous last-minute instruction.

'Don't let the dragon ladies win.'

'Slay 'em,' was Matt's throwaway directive, accompanied by a figuratively graphic sword thrust-and-parry movement.

'Your talent should be displayed on the stage,' Mia responded in a droll voice, and laughed when he wriggled his eyebrows expressively.

'You think?'

'Go,' she begged. 'I need peace and quiet in which to plan my modus operandi.'

'You'd have more fun with us at the beach,' Matt declared. 'You could bring Nikolos.'

Now there was a thought…'Maybe another time,'

she said lightly. 'Today I have to do the grown-up thing.'

'Serious stuff, huh?'

You can't begin to believe how serious! 'You could say that.'

'Good luck.'

Her smile was heartfelt. 'Thanks.'

It was relatively early, and she put a load of washing into the machine, tidied the kitchen and did some household chores.

Tomorrow she was due to begin work at the pharmacy, and she checked her student identification tag, organised her uniform, then hit the shower.

What did one wear when going into battle? Mia mused as she checked through her clothes.

Lunch with the Karedes matriarchs loomed like a spectre before her, and she chose a sleeveless silk dress in jade green with a wide scooped neckline, and a bias-cut skirt.

It was stylish in design, feminine, and provided a sophisticated image.

Make-up was cleverly understated with emphasis on her eyes, and she wore her hair in a smooth French twist, added minimum jewellery, then slid her feet into stilettos.

She checked her watch, then caught up her clutch purse and walked through to the lounge in time to see Nikolos' car pull into the driveway.

Mia drew in a deep breath and released it, then opened the door.

Party time.

Well, almost, she amended as she locked up and

turned to meet Nikolos, whose height and breadth of shoulder seemed vaguely intimidating this close. Or maybe she was just acutely aware of him at a base level, knowing how it felt to be enfolded against that hard-muscled chest…and in need of being offered such a sanctuary again, for comfort and reassurance.

Oh, for heaven's sake, get a grip!

'Hi.' She caught his smile and offered one of her own.

'How are you?'

'Fine,' Mia admitted honestly. 'Apart from feeling as if I'm about to enter the lions' den.'

His mouth curved with humour. 'I won't let them eat you.'

'Ah, you'll parry verbal swords for me?'

'Count on it.'

She effected a slight mock curtsy. 'My knight in shining armour.'

Nikolos' eyes gleamed as he caught hold of her hand and brought it to his lips. 'My pleasure.'

The gesture quickened her pulse and sent warmth flooding her veins. A fact she managed to disguise by pinning a smile in place and holding it there.

He led the way to the car and saw her seated before crossing round to slip in behind the wheel.

It took a while to reach Vaucluse, and enter the lovely tree-lined avenue where Angelena's stately home was situated.

A gold Lexus stood parked beneath the portico, and Nikolos parked beside it.

'Ready?'

Her eyes met and held his. 'Let's go do this, shall we?'

They were greeted at the front door by a manservant and ushered indoors. Mia was aware of a large foyer, panelled walls, oil paintings and antique furniture as Nikolos led her into a formal lounge where Angelena and Sofia were seated in separate chairs.

'Nikolos,' Angelena acknowledged, and inclined her head towards Mia. 'Mia.'

'*Yiayia.* Mother.'

Formality was obviously the order of the day, with a certain disapproving stiffness that hardly augured well.

Sofia offered a conciliatory smile that was perhaps meant to soften Angelena's stance. Although Mia wasn't prepared to bank on it.

'Please,' Angelena began. 'Take a seat and be comfortable.'

Comfort wasn't exactly a word Mia cared to associate with the matriarch. She could conjure up a few that seemed more suitable as she selected a chair, aware Nikolos chose to remain standing.

How long would it be before the purpose of this visit was mentioned? Social drinks first, then straight into the fray? Or did Angelena intend to feed them first?

Drinks, Mia determined minutes later as she accepted a soda.

'Lunch will be served shortly,' Angelena informed. 'After which, we will address the current situation.'

Polite civility at all costs, Mia mused. So she was

to be offered food before being metaphorically fed to
the lions? On the grounds she might be more mellow
and less prepared? In order to fall in with whatever the
matriarch deemed an acceptable resolution?

It was a relief when lunch was announced. A meal
where the food was superbly presented and, without
doubt, delicious. Although Mia's tastebuds appeared to
have gone on strike.

She was supremely conscious of Nikolos seated at
her side, aware just how his close proximity was adding
to her nervous tension.

'You've hardly eaten a thing,' Sofia noted with apparent concern. 'Would you prefer something else?
Some salad, perhaps?'

'I'm fine,' she reassured, knowing it was an exten-
sion of the truth. The thought of her stomach going
into revolt *here* was the last thing she needed.

'I developed the most unlikely cravings when I was
pregnant with Nikolos,' Sofia offered with a faint smile.
'Food I'd never liked suddenly became all I wanted to
eat. In weird combinations.'

Mia passed on dessert and chose a selection of fresh
fruit.

'We'll have coffee in the lounge,' Angelena declared
when her manservant appeared and began clearing the
table.

Okay, Mia accorded silently. This is when the fun
begins!

Sure enough, the matriarch waited only as long as it
took for them to relocate to the lounge and be served
coffee and tea before she launched directly into the
specific purpose of today's invitation.

'We need to discuss plans.'

Plans? 'There are no plans that I'm aware of,' Mia began, only to incur a long, piercing look meant to diminish her into subservient silence.

'You will, of course, marry.'

The matriarch's tone carried unequivocal conviction, and Mia unconsciously held her breath for a few seconds before she ventured with polite civility, 'I don't see marriage as a prerequisite to having or raising a child.'

'Yiayia,' Nikolos admonished gently. 'It is for Mia and I to make a decision.'

The temperature in the room seemed to drop a few degrees as Angelena took pains to compose herself.

'I find it totally unacceptable for a Karedes heir to be born out of wedlock.'

Mia felt as if she'd been suddenly flung back into the previous century. 'I have no intention of denying my child its place within the Karedes family,' she said calmly, 'but I won't be coerced into a marriage I don't want.'

The matriarch's faint indrawn hiss of disapproval was more visible than audible.

'You *do* realise the importance of the Karedes name?'

Mia's chin tilted fractionally. 'More important than the future happiness of a child born into a marriage based on convenience in which both parents find themselves trapped?'

If it were possible for Angelena to draw herself more tightly together, the effort was made. 'My grandson is a wealthy man in his own right, and possesses a generous disposition. You'll lead a fulfilling life, and doubtless bear more children.'

'To further the Karedes dynasty?'

'Of course.' Angelena fixed Nikolos with a dark beady stare. 'You have proposed marriage, I assume?'

'Naturally,' Nikolos drawled with hateful ease. 'Did you imagine I would not?'

'And?' the matriarch demanded imperiously.

Mia didn't wait for him to answer. 'I turned him down.'

The elderly woman's eyes dilated. 'I beg your pardon?'

This was rapidly digressing into a full-scale argument, albeit refined…just.

'You expect me to commit to a man who doesn't love me? Live with him, sleep with him, raise children with him?' She waited a few seconds. 'Look the other way when he takes on a lover or two, or more? Accept and condone his behaviour?'

Haughty didn't begin to describe Angelena's expression.

'You dare accuse Nikolos of such indiscretions?'

Oh, my. 'I don't know Nikolos well enough to judge him.'

'You didn't think of that when you leapt into bed with him.'

'The desire for sex was entirely mutual,' Mia corrected as she held the elderly lady's gaze. 'Last time I heard, consensual sex isn't a crime.'

'*Yiayia,*' Nikolos chastised. 'Enough.'

'I agree,' Sofia declared. 'Let's not make demands.

Instead, we should welcome Mia into the family, endorse our support for whatever decision she chooses to make, and resolve to get to know her.'

An ally? The day suddenly became marginally brighter.

'An excellent suggestion,' Nikolos concurred as he placed his cup and saucer onto a nearby table. 'Now, if you'll excuse us? Mia and I have arrangements for the remainder of the day.'

They did?

'You realise I will not let this rest?'

'Yiayia,' he warned with dangerous silkiness. 'In this instance, you have no choice.' His voice gentled. 'Try not to concern yourself overmuch, hmm?'

Mia was surprised to see the faint shimmer of tears in the elderly lady's eyes before she blinked them away.

'How can I not?'

It was almost three when they left, and Mia sat in silence as Nikolos eased the powerful car through the gates and turned into the tree-lined avenue.

A number of conflicting thoughts fought for supremacy, some of which she didn't want to face. At least not here, not now.

Was she being a fool to stubbornly refuse contemplating a life with Nikolos? She would be inextricably bound up with him via legal custody rights. Marriage would provide stability in more ways than one, together with the bonus of sharing his bed.

It was impossible to ignore the surge of warmth flooding her veins at the thought of having him reach for her through the night, their shared intimacy and the hundred and one sensual delights their lovemaking would provide.

Sure, a tiny imp taunted. You'd contemplate using good sex as a basis for a lifetime commitment? *Are you mad?*

An elderly woman's tears have led you to give Nikolos' proposal a moment's consideration, when common sense dismisses it out of hand?

What had seemed so clear-cut less than twenty-four hours ago now provided an element of doubt. Minuscule, but there nonetheless.

'I thought we might drive up to the northern beaches.'

Mia turned towards him, aware of his forceful image, the well-defined facial structure that combined with a dramatic mesh of intense sensuality and power.

'We could have dinner, maybe take in a movie,' he continued.

'Dinner,' she agreed. 'I'll take a rain check on the movie. I start work tomorrow.'

'I'll endeavour to return you to Alice's home at a respectable hour.'

Mia detected a degree of musing humour in his voice. 'You're not going to argue with me?'

He offered her a quick glance before returning his attention to the road. 'Would it do any good?'

'No.'

Nikolos activated a CD and soft background music flowed through the sound system. It was relaxing, almost therapeutic, and she wondered if he used it as a de-stressing device.

Entrepreneurial power-broking had to involve deci-
sion-making at a high level, maintaining constant touch
with directorial and managerial staff, keeping track of
every movement within the company.

His physique denoted he took time to work out. Did
he follow any sport? Was he a team player or did he
prefer a solo activity?

'Ask,' Nikolos drawled as he eased to a halt at a
traffic intersection.

'And you'll answer?'

'You have twenty questions in mind?'

'Very funny.'

'Changed your mind?'

'Do you travel often?'

'Frequently. Interstate, overseas.'

'For long periods of time?'

'Most business can be wrapped up in a day or two
within Australia.' He effected a faint shrug. 'Overseas,
taking flights into the equation…four or five days.
Maybe a week. For a few years I rotated almost equally
between New York, Athens, Tokyo and Sydney.'

'With no one place to call home?'

'I have apartments in each city.'

She should have guessed. 'Must be easier than living
out of a suitcase.'

'Indeed.' But lonely, he could have added. Long
flights, an empty apartment at the end of it, a solitary
bed…with only the occasional selective exception.
Business had become his focus in a bid to prove he
was a worthy successor to his late father.

Until recently. One night was all it had taken to make him question his priorities.

One woman.

Who, because of fate and a broken prophylactic, would bear their child.

Would she believe he wanted her in his life? Dammit, *needed* her, as he'd never needed any other woman?

Patience, he instilled silently. He manipulated multimillion-dollar deals on a weekly basis. Dealt and went head-to-head with some of the biggest power-brokers in the world. He could handle a petite, sable-haired slip of a woman…couldn't he?

'All those long flights and intense business meetings,' Mia ventured. 'What do you do to keep fit?'

'Martial arts. It combines body and mind, and promotes self-discipline.'

It figured.

They spent a relaxing few hours exploring the northern beaches, and enjoyed delicious seafood in a waterfront restaurant before taking the highway south.

It was almost ten when Nikolos eased the car to a halt outside Alice's home, and Mia offered a polite 'goodnight' as she reached for the door-clasp.

Only to feel his hands close over her shoulders as he turned her towards him, then his mouth covered hers in a kiss that literally robbed the breath from her throat.

There was hunger, and so much more…passion that threatened the fragile tenure of her control. She *ached* with it, and became lost in the sensual thrall until there was only him…and deep, throbbing need.

It was Nikolos who broke the contact, easing back gently as she brokenly voiced her regret.

'Go *now*,' he bade huskily. 'Or I take you to my apartment. Choose.'

Oh, God. As if there was a choice! Yet there was only one she could make. 'I can't,' Mia whispered, and knew she lied. It would be so easy to go with him. So very easy.

'Then go, Mia.'

She did, quickly slipping from the passenger seat in a bid to put distance between them. Otherwise she'd give in to temptation and throw self-caution to the wind.

She didn't look back as she walked swiftly to the door, and inside she made straight to her bedroom where she leaned back against the closed door for an age, until her rapid breathing steadied, and the heightened tension began to lessen.

Then she slowly removed her clothes, cleansed off her make-up, and slid between the sheets to lie staring at the darkened ceiling until sleep took her captive.

CHAPTER SEVEN

THERE was something intensely satisfying about being in the workforce and employing theory with day-to-day practice. It was an ongoing learning experience that Mia enjoyed, especially the interaction with customers requiring information about prescription and over-the-counter medications.

The head pharmacist proved courteous, and helpful with each of her enquiries, his manager likewise, and the staff were friendly.

The customers were a mixed group of people of varying ages and nationalities, some extremely colourful, others quiet, even diffident.

Careful shoppers, some elderly and visibly frail for whom Mia felt oddly protective. Brash young teenagers who swaggered in, wearing fashionably tattered jeans, designer tee shirts, shades and sporting various body piercings.

There were also the less favourable customers on methadone programmes, and the addicts who came in for their sealed packs of needles.

The young girls who wanted to fill in time by sampling perfumes, cosmetics, trying out lipsticks, requiring advice on blushers and mascara, and the dreaded acne.

It made for an interesting and varied day, and she

emerged from the pharmacy at quitting time to find Nikolos standing indolently at ease on the pavement.

'What are you doing here?' The words slipped out before she gave them much thought.

'Whatever happened to *hello*?'

His musing drawl brought a tinge of soft colour to her cheeks. 'I didn't expect to see you,' she managed evenly.

'I thought you might appreciate a ride home.'

'Taking care of the Karedes heir?'

His eyes narrowed. 'I'll let that pass.'

'Kind of you.'

He indicated the Mercedes parked at the kerb. 'You want to argue?'

'I feel I should, just for the hell of it.'

'Maybe you could compromise?'

'As long as you don't intend making a habit of playing chauffeur.'

'Get in, Mia.'

It was easier to comply, and seated inside the luxury vehicle she had to question her sanity. Hormones, she decided as Nikolos slid in behind the wheel and drove her the short distance to Alice's home.

'I could have walked.'

'Is that a token objection, or an attempt to argue?'

She cast him a steady look. 'Oh, why don't I go for broke, and admit to both?'

'Let me get you home, then you can change and I'll feed you.'

'Excuse me?'

'We'll go have dinner somewhere.'

'You can go have dinner. I want a shower, food, and an early night.'

'You can have that. I'll even throw in a foot massage.'

She closed her eyes at the thought of such bliss, then opened them again in time to see him pull in to the kerb outside Alice's home.

Behind a four-wheel drive. A very shiny, new-looking Mercedes four-wheel drive.

Alice had a visitor?

'Yours,' Nikolos elaborated, indicating the vehicle.

'No,' Mia said firmly.

'I insist.'

'I don't need transport.'

He handed over a set of keys. 'Consider it a gift. Indulge me.'

'*Why?*'

'Because I'll sleep easier.'

'That's a valid reason?'

'It is to me.' He dropped the keys into her lap. 'Now let's go inside, shall we?'

'Alice will have already organised dinner.'

'I don't imagine she'll mind if you give it a miss.'

Alice didn't mind at all. So much for sibling loyalty! Although that wasn't strictly fair, Mia decided as she hit the shower. Alice wanted whatever was best for her.

Designer jeans, a jacket over a vest top, low-heeled sandals, just a touch of make-up, and she was ready.

Nikolos chose a small Italian restaurant only a few

kilometres distant, where the redolent aroma of pasta sauce set the digestive juices flowing. Bruschetta, a small plate of delicious tortellini was *perfetto*, combined with light background music…it teased the senses, calmed and lifted them.

The service was warm and friendly, the atmosphere, with its small tables dressed in red and white checked gingham, empty Chianti bottles with their candles…

It was charming.

'Thank you.' Mia forked the last mouthful, then pressed the napkin to her lips.

'For?'

'Bringing me here,' she said simply, and watched his mouth curve into a musing smile.

'My pleasure.' He leaned back in his chair. 'How was your first day?'

'Interesting.'

One eyebrow lifted. 'That's it? The entire day encapsulated into one word?'

'The elderly like to chat. Mothers with young children want quick service, and teenage girls spend time trying out the make-up testers.'

The waiter cleared away their plates, and asked if they'd like to see the dessert menu.

'Not for me.'

Nikolos ordered tea, and coffee for himself.

'I imagine you spent the day wheeling and dealing, meetings, phone calls.'

He reflected on one particular problem and the fact it required his personal attention. 'I fly out to New York on the late-evening flight.'

She looked at him more closely, and glimpsed the fine edge of tension. Fine lines fanned out from the corner of his eyes, and there was a brooding quality apparent she couldn't define. 'I take it this wasn't factored into your schedule?'

'No.'

'How long will it take?'

'Four, five days.'

Their tea and coffee arrived, and he took his black with sugar. 'We have an invitation to attend a pre-Christmas party on Saturday evening.'

'*We* do?'

The corner of his mouth lifted at her emphasis. 'Yes. Are you going to object?'

'Will it make any difference?'

'I intend to make an appearance. I'd prefer to have you join me.'

Mia offered him a solemn smile. 'In that case, I accept.'

He drained the rest of his coffee as she sipped the remainder of her tea. 'Shall we leave?' He signalled for the bill, paid when it came, then he led her out to the car.

'Thanks,' she offered quietly when he drew in to the kerb outside Alice's home. 'I hope everything goes well in New York.' She reached for the door-clasp, only for his hand to close over hers.

'Not so fast.'

'Nikolos—' Whatever else she might have said remained locked in her throat as his mouth possessed hers in a kiss that tore her composure to shreds.

Hard, passionate, it swept her towards a place she

badly wanted to be, and her hands crept up to link together behind his head as he deepened the kiss.

It wasn't enough, and she was hardly aware of the faint despairing groan that sounded low in her throat as he began to withdraw. Slowly, and with infinite care, until his lips, his tongue, soothed instead of ignited her senses.

Then she was free as he lifted his head, and her eyes were wide luminous pools as she looked at him.

Nikolos brushed gentle fingers down her cheek, then bent and trailed his mouth gently over her own.

'I'll call you.'

Mia wasn't capable of uttering a word, and she simply nodded, then she opened the door, slid out, and stood watching as he cleared the driveway and accelerated down the street.

'What do you think about having a barbecue on Sunday?' Alice queried next morning as she checked the time, then drained the last of her coffee. 'Just a few close friends. Ask Nikolos when he phones.'

Casual outdoor eating held a definite appeal. 'Sounds great.'

'Five minutes, Matt,' Alice reminded as she headed towards the hall to fix her make-up.

'Maybe you could drop me to school,' Matt suggested wistfully. 'Just a small detour on your way to work?'

Mia tilted her head as she regarded him across the breakfast table. 'Tonight after dinner we'll take the four-wheel drive for a test spin. Okay?'

He punched a fist high in the air. *'Yes.'*

Mia left the house a short while later. It was a lovely summer's day, the sky clear with scarcely a drift of cloud, and she cast the four-wheel drive a glance, admired its solid lines, the shiny paintwork, and walked right on past.

Walking was good, she assured silently. Stubborn single-mindedness had nothing to do with her decision…and knew she fooled no one.

The morning passed quickly, and she took an early lunch break, choosing to eat a healthy chicken salad sandwich in a nearby park. Bottled water, a magazine, a comfortable bench beneath a shady wide-branched tree…what more could anyone ask?

The gardens were lovely, with splendid stands of strelitzia providing colour, adding to an array of native plants, and in the distance a jacaranda in full bloom casting a carpet of pale lilac petals beneath its branches.

There were birds perching high, undisturbed by the sounds of traffic and human habitation, and their calls held a pleasant melodic quality.

'Enjoying your lunch?'

Mia glanced up from the magazine and her eyes widened at the sight of Anouska standing a few feet distant.

Chance was a fine thing, but having the fashionista appear here, now, was stretching coincidence too far.

Which meant Anouska had elicited information from a source…the question was *who*? Alice was a definite no. Nikolos? Doubtful.

'Anouska.' Cool, calm and collected. She could do all three. 'Just passing through?' As if.

How difficult would it be to determine the suburb where Alice lived and phone a few pharmacies in the area? Would a temporary staff member's name be confirmed?

Depending on the basis for such a query, it was possible.

'I doubt you're that naive.'

'Nikolos.' As if there was any doubt.

Anouska examined her flawlessly polished nails. 'I like a girl who gets to the point.'

Mia made a study of checking her watch. 'Can you wrap it up in five?'

'Darling, I can do it in less.' She flashed a brilliant artificial smile, then honed in for the kill. 'I shall suggest Nikolos insists on DNA. I've no objection if he supports your child. It's just that I intend to have his ring on my finger.'

Mia held the fashionista's pseudo gaze. 'By fair means...or foul?'

'I see we understand each other.'

Mia stood up. 'If you're done, I really have to get back to work.'

'Watch your step.'

'Ditto, Anouska. In spades,' she added as she turned and took the path to the roadside. Within minutes she entered the pharmacy, took time to freshen up, then she resumed work. Rattled, but not shaken, she assured with an attempt at silent humour.

Anouska's threat was almost a joke, except she had the feeling the fashionista was deadly serious.

Why Nikolos? Surely there were other men among the social élite who were rich, attractive and eligible?

Or was Anouska delusional? Fixated on an emotional tie that no longer existed. If it ever had.

The park scene replayed itself over several times during the course of the afternoon, and it was a relief when closing time came.

The walk home cleared her mind, and Matt's welcoming grin, his enthusiasm for a ride in the four-wheel drive swept aside Mia's lingering concern as they discussed their respective days over dinner, then, dishes cleared, she retrieved the set of keys and led the way out to the vehicle.

It was a dream to drive, so smooth and comfortable.

'Wow,' Matt accorded as she headed towards French's Forest, then she headed down to the Spit, found a parking space close to an ice-cream parlour and bought them each a luscious sundae.

They didn't linger long, as Matt had a homework assignment to complete before bedtime.

'I want one of these when I'm old enough to drive,' Matt said with fervour as Mia brought the vehicle to a halt some time later.

'Dream big, study hard, and maybe,' Alice said affectionately as they went indoors.

'Yeah, I know,' he said with boyish enthusiasm. 'One day.'

Mia contemplated sharing Anouska's surprise appearance with Alice as they sipped hot tea while viewing a favourite comedy on one of the television channels.

Then the moment was gone, and it wasn't until

she lay in bed that it returned to haunt her. Tomorrow, she decided on the edge of sleep.

Except there was a power cut through the night, and the alarm didn't go off. Consequently they woke later than usual and everything became a mad rush to get out of the house on time.

The day didn't get any better. One of the pharmacy staff called in sick, a truculent child ran amok and emptied an entire shelf of its contents, and an indignant customer insisted Mia had sold him the wrong over-the-counter cough medicine, when she knew she hadn't served him at all.

Mistaken identity? However, retail policy favoured the customer, and he was sufficiently appeased with her apology together with a bottle of the 'correct' medicine.

Mid-afternoon a florist-emblazoned box was delivered with her name on it. Inside were two dozen roses in delicate peach, cream and apricot, and a card bearing *Nikolos*. She sent him a text message, thanking him.

His image rose to the fore, strong, powerful, and a force all on his own. It was easy to recall how it felt to have his mouth possess hers, the touch of his hands on her body…the deep, all-consuming passion he aroused in her without any effort at all.

She could understand Anouska wanting him. What woman wouldn't? Except the emotional aspect of a relationship needed to be equal, and obsessive behaviour shouldn't enter the equation.

Which led her to wonder how far the fashionista would go.

Mia didn't have long to find out. Next morning when Alice left for work she noticed the four-wheel drive had two flat tyres.

'It was fine last night.' A perplexed frown creased her forehead as Matt crouched down for a close inspection.

'One could be a puncture,' Alice offered, and shook her head doubtfully. 'But *two*, both kerbside?'

'I'll have to call a tyre shop and organise for replacements.' She checked the time. 'Go, or you'll be late. I'll ring you during my lunch break.'

'Check my business card file by the phone. You'll find a contact number there.'

She did, and made the call, then she set a brisk walking pace to the pharmacy.

It was late morning when she managed to check with the tyre firm, and it didn't help to learn both tyres had been punctured with a sharp object.

'Intentionally?'

'Yeah, without doubt. You need new ones.'

She wrangled a little on price, gained a discount, and arranged for two new tyres to be fitted.

Lunch was an egg and salad sandwich eaten at a nearby café, where she made the call to Alice from her cellphone.

'Craig Mitchell,' a deep masculine voice answered.

'Mia Fredrickson, Alice's sister.'

'I remember. We met at the gallery exhibition last week,' he acknowledged warmly. 'Alice has just stepped out to retrieve a file for me. Shall I have her call you?'

'Please, my cellphone number.' She made a spur of the moment decision. 'Are you free around midday on Sunday? Alice and I are planning a barbecue lunch for a few friends. It's very informal. We'd like to have you join us.'

'Thank you. Can I contribute anything?'

Mia effected a silent *yes* following his acceptance. 'Just yourself. You have the address?'

'It's on file.'

'We'll look forward to seeing you.'

She cut the call, and sipped her cool drink, assuring herself it wasn't matchmaking as such…merely giving fate a helping hand.

Not that Alice would consider it that, she mused as she flipped through a magazine and waited for her sister to return the call.

When it came she steeled herself for exasperation, maybe irritation…and found herself on the receiving end of both.

'Just what do you think you're doing?'

Here we go…'Craig? The barbecue?'

'Yes!'

'You object?'

'You could have run it by me first.'

'And given you the opportunity to find any number of reasons why Craig shouldn't be invited?'

'I prefer to keep my professional and private lives separate.'

'It's only a barbecue, with a few friends.'

'And Matt,' Alice said heavily. 'Had you thought how it might affect him, having a strange man turn up at the house?'

'Craig is your boss, for heaven's sake.'

'He's also someone Matt has never met. You know I haven't dated since David walked out.'

Instead, her sister had thrown herself into being both parents rolled into one.

'Maybe it's time you did,' Mia offered gently. 'And I'm sorry you think it's such a big deal.'

She recalled only too well how Matt had reacted with Nikolos on the cruiser. The tinge of colour in her sister's cheeks when Craig Mitchell had made an appearance at the gallery…and the warmth apparent in the man's eyes when they had rested on Alice.

'You don't understand.'

'You can handle what you feel for Craig while it remains a professional relationship,' Mia relayed, 'but you're not at all sure how you'll deal with him if it becomes personal?'

'Something like that. Did you organise new tyres?'

'Yes.' Her mouth curved at the edges with the sudden change in their conversation, and took another direction, suggesting, 'Do you feel like taking Matt out for fish and chips tonight? My treat.'

'I should cook—'

'Why? You cook most nights.' Every night. 'Let's pick up fast food and go eat it down by the waterfront. Out of packets,' she added for good measure.

'I know why Matt relishes you holidaying with us,' Alice said with mock severity, and Mia laughed.

'Fast finger food, no plates, no cutlery. Shock, horror.'

'Okay, we'll do it. I'll see you at home.'

The sun still retained much of its warmth as Mia left the pharmacy at the close of the business day.

Her mind strayed to Alice, and she thought how nice it would be for her sister to have a man in her life again. She deserved someone who would protect and care for her, and welcome Matt as his own.

Alice's husband had been a manipulative chameleon whose worst side had appeared soon after the ink had dried on the marriage certificate. Becoming a father hadn't been on his agenda, and Alice had come home from work one day to find the house had been completely emptied. A messy divorce had followed.

A faint sound caught her attention, she saw a blur of movement, then hard hands grabbed her shoulders and attempted to push her to the ground.

Mia went with the momentum, carrying her attacker's body in an arc that put him flat on his back. He lashed out with his foot and connected with her ribs, an action which gained him an essential few seconds to scramble out of reach and get to his feet.

He was young, lean, and identification was impossible...he was wearing a ski-mask.

He motioned for her shoulder-bag, and when she didn't comply he made a grab for it.

Anyone with any sense would have simply handed it over, but she was angry...*really* angry. She clenched both hands together and aimed a hard upward thrust to his jaw, heard his howl of pain, and watched him turn and run.

Martial arts training had finally paid off. And she

still had her bag, with most of her dignity intact. Except for a bruised rib or two, she was fine.

'You okay, miss?'

A young kid on a bike wheeled up to her and braked hard, swinging the rear wheel round with a flourish. 'I saw that guy. Want me to chase him?'

Hell, no. 'Don't,' she cautioned. 'He's long gone.'

'I'll walk you home in case he comes back. You're staying at Matt's house, aren't you?'

She hated to squash the youngster's sense of chivalry. 'Yes, I am. And thanks, it's kind of you.'

'No problem.'

Five minutes later he walked her up to Alice's front door, rang the bell, despite Mia assuring him she had a key, and when Alice opened the door he relayed the story with all the importance of a young police cadet.

Matt raced out, and a kind of organised pandemonium followed with Alice insistent on a hospital check-up.

Minutes later Mia found herself bundled into Alice's car with Matt in the rear seat, and each and every one of her protests ignored.

It took a while, between an examination, an ultrasound, before she was given a medical all-clear. The foetus was fine, and she had two bruised ribs.

She turned towards Matt as she slid into the passenger seat. 'I'm hungry, champ. How about you?'

He offered an infectious grin. 'Starving.'

'Okay, so we get to take fish and chips home.'

'I don't think—' Alice began, only to have Mia interrupt.

'We need to eat. Why not make it easy and fun?'

'Fun and easy is cool,' her nephew endorsed.

'Matt—'

Half an hour later they arrived home with individual steaming packets, which they ate as finger food at the dining-room table.

'I think I'll go take a shower,' Mia indicated. Her ribs were giving her hell, and she refused to take anything to relieve the pain. 'Shan't be long.'

She was back in ten minutes, clad in a comfortable cotton nightshirt and a light cotton robe, her face free of make-up and her hair tied back in a pony-tail.

Mia took one look at Alice's stern expression and Matt's crestfallen features. 'What's up?'

'Nikolos rang. I told him about your accident, and hospital,' Matt relayed. 'Mum said I shouldn't have.'

Alice lifted a hand and let it fall again, concern clouding her eyes. 'I took the phone from him, but it was too late.'

'I'm sorry,' Matt said with a seriousness beyond his years. 'I forgot Nikolos was away, and he might worry about you.'

'I told him you were fine,' Alice added quickly. 'He's ringing back.' At that moment the phone rang. 'I guess you'd better answer it.' She turned towards her son. 'Go take a shower, Matt.'

Mia crossed the room and picked up. 'Hi.'

'Nikolos.' His voice sounded deep, and, unless she was mistaken, barely controlled. 'Alice assures me you're okay. Are you?'

'The baby's fine.' The all-important Karedes heir.

'Reassuring, but it wasn't my question.'

Oh, my, time for a deep breath. 'I have two bruised ribs.'

A few seconds' silence followed the revelation. 'Perhaps you'd care to give me your version of what happened.'

She did, in brief, and heard his husky oath in response.

'Obviously you chose not to drive.'

'Two flat tyres sort of precluded that.'

There was an electric silence. 'Would you care to run that by me again?'

'I've had it taken care of.'

'Why do I get the feeling there's a lot you're not telling me?'

And then some, Mia reiterated silently and rolled her eyes in exasperation.

'I assume you've reported both events to the police?'

'Not as yet.'

'I'll have Cris instigate enquiries, and I'll take the next flight out.'

'You're kidding me?'

He wasn't. 'I'll call you tomorrow.'

She'd suddenly had enough. 'There's no need.' She cut the call before he had a chance to respond.

The phone rang ten minutes later, and she exchanged glances with Alice. 'If it's Nikolos, I don't want to talk to him again tonight.'

Within seconds Alice held out the receiver. 'It's Cris.'

'News travels fast,' Mia said without preamble, and heard his faint chuckle.

'How are you?' There was concern apparent, and she dismissed her irritation. This was Cris...not Nikolos.

'I'm fine. Really,' she added.

'I'm glad. Meantime, we need to file a police report. I'll come over in the morning and bring someone with me.'

She took a deep breath, winced, and let it out carefully. Breathing deeply was not a good idea. 'I leave for work at eight.'

'Maybe you should consider taking the day off.'

This had gone far enough. 'Nikolos is indulging in a severe case of overkill.'

'And don't mess with me?' Cris queried with musing humour.

'Got it in one. I'm going to hang up now and go to bed. Goodnight, and—' she waited a beat '—thanks for the call.'

'Do you think that's wise?' Alice prompted as Mia made them each a cup of tea.

'Which particular part?'

'Why not go for broke?'

'I'd rather not discuss anything involving the name Karedes,' she declared darkly, and glimpsed her sister's faint smile.

'Like that, huh?'

Matt poked his head into the room. 'Goodnight.'

'Sleep tight,' Mia bade lightly, and failed to raise a smile.

'You really are okay, aren't you?'

'Absolutely.' She lifted a hand and placed it over her heart. 'Promise.'

His sigh of relief was heartfelt. 'That's all right, then.' He even managed a smile before disappearing from sight.

'Cute kid,' Mia complimented when she was sure he was out of earshot. 'You're doing a great job with him.'

'He'd hate to hear you call him *cute*.'

It was Mia's turn to grin. 'I know. He's adorable.'

Alice stifled a smile. 'That, too.'

They sipped their tea in silence, then Mia turned towards her sister. 'Are you mad I asked Craig to visit on Sunday?'

'Nervous would be a better description.'

'You'll be with family and friends. It's not as if you're alone on a date with him.'

Alice became pale. 'I don't think I want to go there.'

'Take it one day at a time,' Mia offered gently, and stood up. 'I'll go key a fact-list into my laptop, and give Cris a disk.'

'You're really sure about work tomorrow?'

'Do you need to ask?'

'No, I guess not,' Alice said with resignation.

'Thanks for the hospital thing, and staying with me.' A warm smile curved her generous mouth. 'You were great.'

CHAPTER EIGHT

MIA woke next morning after a restless night's sleep, dressed, ate breakfast, and, following a close inspection of the Mercedes four-wheel drive, she took Alice's advice and drove to work.

Once there, she sent Cris a courtesy text message confirming she was at the pharmacy, then she donned her uniform and got on with the day.

One that became increasingly busy as morning shifted to afternoon, broken only by the appearance of Cris and a plainclothes policeman intent on filing a report of yesterday's assault.

It was late when she took her afternoon tea break, and she emerged from the staff-room ten minutes later to find the pharmacy manager deep in conversation with a dark-suited man whose stance and rear profile were all too familiar.

Nikolos.

Almost as if he sensed her presence, he turned towards her, and she could only stand there, momentarily incapable of moving as he closed the distance between them.

His expression was unfathomable, his eyes so dark they were almost black, and his mouth was set in lines that would instil fear into any adversary.

'Mia.' He lifted a hand and brushed gentle knuckles over her cheek. 'Go get your bag. You've finished for the day.'

'I—'

'Just do it, hmm?'

She wanted to protest, and almost did, except instinct warned against it. Instead she moved a fraction, caught the pharmacist's nod of approval, then she retrieved her bag from the staff-room and accompanied Nikolos out of the shop.

'How come you're back so soon?'

He cast her an all-encompassing look. 'I was in LA when I spoke to you last night.'

Had she any idea what he'd gone through in the last twenty-two hours? Imagining, fearing the worst, unable to see her, touch her? Totally reliant on verbal reassurances he knew could mask the true reality?

He'd made a few phone calls, pulled a few strings, and taken the next Sydney-bound flight out of LAX, arriving early afternoon. He'd caught a cab to his apartment, showered, dressed, and driven to the pharmacy where, Cris had text-messaged him, she'd ignored his directive and chosen to work.

He reached for her, closing his hands over her shoulders, then he slid each palm and cupped her face.

'*Theos,*' he uttered huskily as he smoothed a thumb-pad across each cheek. 'When I think what could have happened to you.'

His head lowered and his lips brushed hers, gently and with such care his touch was as light as a butterfly's wing.

It brought a faint sheen of unshed tears to her eyes, and she blinked rapidly to disperse them.

'I'm fine,' she managed shakily, knowing the words were a travesty. Right now she felt as if her bones were in the process of serious meltdown.

Nikolos traced the curve of her lower lip, felt it tremble, and he groaned as he trailed a path to the sweet hollow at the edge of her neck, savoured it, then he buried his mouth against the sensitive cord, nipped gently, and felt her body shake.

He wanted desperately what he knew he shouldn't take...and he told himself it was enough just to hold her, kiss her. For now.

Except he knew it would never be enough. For as long as he lived, he'd want, *need* her. In his life, his heart...dammit, in his bed.

He shifted slightly, and covered her mouth with his in a gentle exploratory kiss that teased with the evocative promise of passion...leashed and in control.

For her sake. He'd called in a favour and had a medic friend request a faxed copy of Mia's hospital medical record. Cris' faxed copy of the police report had been waiting for him when he'd first walked into his apartment a few hours ago. Together they detailed an account that chilled him to the bone, and added to a growing suspicion he entertained.

If he was correct...

Only a fool would act before there was sufficient proof, and no one could accord him a fool, he determined grimly.

It shouldn't take long. Days…possibly a week. Then he'd deal with it.

Meantime, he'd ensured there would be someone watching over her. For her own safety. Dammit, for his peace of mind.

The sound of voices, a car-horn blast brought their surroundings into sharp focus, and Nikolos effected a musing grimace. 'Let's get out of here.'

'The four-wheel drive is in the rear parking lot,' Mia indicated, only to have Nikolos catch hold of her hand and thread his fingers through hers as he turned her in the opposite direction.

'You're coming with me.'

'Unless you're intent on taking a circuitous route,' she ventured minutes later as his car gathered speed. 'You're going the wrong way.'

'We're going home. My home,' Nikolos corrected, and absorbed her sudden silence.

'I don't even know where that is.'

He spared her a quick glance. 'Seaforth. I have an apartment there.'

'I see.'

'That's it?'

'What would you have me say?' Mia queried, aware her pulse had quickened its pace. Every nerve-end seemed to quiver, heightening her senses to an almost uncomfortable pitch.

Was it inevitable, this crazy, wild feeling he was able to generate within her? To be affected to this extent was a madness she couldn't afford.

Mia focused her attention on the passing scene beyond the windscreen, noting the escalation in home style and value as they drew close to Seaforth.

Nikolos' apartment building was perched high overlooking Middle Harbour with splendid views of Port Jackson, and Mia didn't offer so much as a word as the Mercedes swept down into an underground car park.

If she had an ounce of sense, she'd insist he retrace the journey and take her to Alice's home. Except it was a bit late for that.

Maybe she could stop the lift at the main lobby, alight, and call a cab?

'Don't even think about it,' Nikolos warned as he summoned the lift.

'I'm not sure this is a good idea.' Too late, a tiny imp taunted. Much too late.

The lift doors opened, they stepped inside, and he depressed the uppermost button. The penthouse.

Electronic speed ensured they reached the top floor within seconds, and Mia preceded him into a spacious lobby, from which they entered a large, beautifully furnished lounge that at first glance combined a pleasing mix of beige, camel and cream.

She caught splashes of colour in paintings adorning the walls, and a wide expanse of tinted glass offering a panoramic view.

Had he employed a professional interior decorator? Or chosen the furnishings and colour scheme himself?

'It's beautiful,' she complimented, turning to face him, and felt her eyes widen as he shrugged off his jacket.

She watched as he tossed it over a nearby chair, and she was prepared to swear she stopped breathing when he took her bag and placed it onto the long buffet.

'Come here,' he bade gently as he caught hold of her hand and led her towards a large, comfortable sofa.

In one fluid movement he sank onto it and carefully pulled her onto his lap.

'Comfortable?'

There was something evocative about his warm strength, the feel of hard muscle and sinew caging her loosely within his grasp.

Mia breathed in the clean smell of him…freshly laundered cotton mingling with soap and the muskiness of his expensive cologne.

The temptation to curl into him and just *be* was almost too much to resist, and she held her breath as he tucked a fall of her hair back behind one ear.

She felt *safe*, in a way she never had before. As if nothing and no one could touch her while she was with him.

His lips brushed the top of her head, and he ran the palm of one hand down her thigh, lingered at her ankle, then eased one shoe off, then the other.

A sound that was part surprise, part resistance, passed her lips when he took her foot in one hand and used his thumb to massage the sole, gently working a kind of subtle magic over every bone in one foot before moving to render a similar treatment to the other.

Dear heaven, she could get used to this.

'Okay?'

Very much so. 'Are you trying to seduce me?'

'Is it working?'

She could almost hear the smile in his voice. 'I don't think I should answer that.'

'Care to fill me in on the past few days?'

She discovered a fascination for the fine stitching on the pocket of his shirt, and she traced the signature initial. 'Not particularly.'

Mia lifted her head and met his dark gaze. There were fine lines fanning out from the corner of his eyes, and the vertical groove on each cheek seemed deeper than she remembered. 'When did you last sleep?'

'Concern for my welfare, Mia?'

She ignored the query. 'Are you hungry?'

The edges of his mouth lifted. 'Now there's a question.'

'I'm talking *food*.'

'You want to go eat?'

'Depending what you have in your fridge and pantry, I could fix something.'

One eyebrow slanted as his eyes assumed a musing gleam. 'You really want to do this?'

If she remained held in his arms for much longer, it might not be a good thing. Already her resistance was in tatters, and staying with him wasn't an option. 'Yes.'

She wasn't prepared for the way his mouth closed over hers, or the slow, exploratory sweep of his tongue as he took evocative liberty with the moist cavern of her mouth in a kiss that made her ache for more.

Mia sensed rather than heard his faint groan, then he stood and placed her carefully on her feet. Bare feet, which diminished her height and made her incredibly aware of his height and breadth of shoulder.

'I guess it's the kitchen, huh?'

'Unless you want to change my mind?'

'I think something domestic is a wise choice,' she offered gravely.

Nikolos traced the edge of her jaw, lingered at the corner of her mouth, then let his hand drop. 'Wisdom, hmm?'

'I'll text message Alice and let her know I won't be home for dinner.'

The kitchen was a dream, with expensive appliances, a well-stocked fridge and pantry, and Mia set to work creating a meal from scratch. Pasta with a delicious sauce, garlic bread, and a steak salad to follow.

It was kind of nice to share the meal and clear up together afterwards. He made conversation easy…so easy she was scarcely aware of the passage of time until she happened to glance at her watch.

'I'll ring for a cab.'

'No, you won't.' He caught up his keys while she collected her bag.

Darkness had fallen, the sky a deep indigo with a sprinkling of stars. The view of the city night-scape was magical, and she paused to admire it as they walked through the lounge.

The basement car park was brightly lit, and their

footsteps echoed in the concrete cavern. Minutes later Nikolos cleared security and took the Mercedes to street level.

It didn't take long to traverse the distance between Seaforth and Manly, and he parked close to the four-wheel drive.

'I'll collect you at six-thirty tomorrow evening.' He leaned in close and took her mouth in a brief, hard kiss. 'The pre-Christmas party, remember?'

He waited until she slid behind the wheel and ignited the engine, then he followed her to Alice's home and didn't drive off until she was safely indoors.

The evening had to be accorded an incredible success, Mia determined as she stood beside Nikolos in the large entertainment lounge of a beautiful home in suburban Woollahra.

It was clearly evident no expense had been spared with interior furbishing, with marble-tiled floors, magnificent marble pillars, exquisite French antique furniture, and works of art adorning the walls.

Fellow guests sipped champagne from crystal flutes and nibbled bite-size canapés as they touched base with friends and mingled.

The women were beautifully gowned, wonderfully bejewelled, and hair styled by whoever happened to be currently in vogue.

Skilfully applied make-up was an art form, and there were instances where Mia would have loved to take a woman aside, advise against a chosen toning and make suggestions to her benefit. A different, more subtle shade, a softer rouge application, and the eyes...the right touch and colour could work magic.

One matron came close to assuming clown-like features, for the colours and emphasis were a cosmetic disaster. While another had used such a heavy hand with the kohl and mascara wand, it was a travesty.

Use the magic, she wanted to offer, don't abuse it.

Was this how it was for each creator in a specific field? Did a seamstress cast a critical eye over the gowns, unconsciously noting flaws and making mental adjustments for improvement? Would a jewellery designer check cut, setting, and gem quality?

Going a step further, would a cosmetic surgeon subconsciously check for work done? An eyebrow lift, nose job, cheek implant?

'Having fun?'

Mia lifted her head a little, met Nikolos' musing gaze, and offered a warm smile. 'How could you imagine otherwise?'

His soft laugh stirred her senses and sent warmth singing through her veins. He had the craziest effect on her, everything about him as familiar to her as if they'd known each other in another lifetime.

Was that possible? Could it be she was fighting the inevitable?

Nikolos caught hold of her hand and lifted it to his lips. 'Don't ever change, *pedhi mou.*'

'A compliment?' She pressed a hand to her heart. 'I'm suitably charmed.'

His teeth nipped gently at her knuckles, then he soothed the faint mark with his tongue. 'Will you be quite so brave when I take you home?' He buried his lips in the palm of her hand. 'Mine,' he added as he lifted his head.

Mia felt her eyes widen as sensation arrowed through her body, activating all her fine nerve-ends until she became a quivering mess.

For several long seconds she was incapable of uttering a word, for there was instant vivid recall of the night they'd spent together, of how it had been between them…and the promise of how it would be again.

'Will you deny me? Yourself?'

Oh, dear God. 'You're giving me a choice?' Her voice was so quiet, it was little more than a whisper.

'You have doubts?'

She closed her eyes, then opened them again. The temptation to be with him, enjoy once again the intimacy they'd shared…dammit, she was pregnant with his child, for heaven's sake!

Could he even begin to comprehend just how much she wanted to be with him?

'Yes,' she said with simple honesty, 'because it would never be just one night.'

'And that would be so bad?'

She didn't answer. Couldn't.

'Nikolos.'

The feminine purr was all too familiar, and Mia felt her heart sink as she turned to find Anouska standing within touching distance.

The fashionista had outdone herself this evening in figure-hugging black. A strapless satin bustier showed her impressive breasts to maximum advan-

tage while displaying a tiny waist, and a long black
skirt was split almost to the hip-bone. Stiletto heels
added to her majestic height, and her make-up was
flawless.

'Darling, wonderful to see you. How was New
York?'

Nikolos retained Mia's hand as he lowered his
own. 'Anouska.'

Mia offered the polite smile, and barely refrained
from gritting her teeth when Anouska traced the
seam of Nikolos' jacket with the tip of a scarlet-
lacquered nail.

'You haven't called me.'

Nikolos removed Anouska's hand.

The pout was pure Hollywood, and her eyes per-
fected a sultry pose. Practice makes perfect? Mia
queried silently.

'I adore this time of year. So many functions. You
are attending the awards presentation dinner next
week?' She cast Mia a critical glance. 'You must find
it difficult to find clothes, being so petite. I doubt
even I could find anything suitable for you in my
boutique.'

Cat's claws drawn and ready, Mia perceived, and
faced the challenge with admirable panache.

'I mostly shop in the teen section, and leave my
evening wear to a dressmaker.'

One eyebrow lifted with distinct disdain. 'You
sew?'

'No,' she responded carefully. 'I have a friend who
does.'

'Really?'

A friend who happened to be a well-known designer, whose clothes were sold in exclusive boutiques such as the one owned by Anouska.

In fact, unless she was mistaken, the gown Anouska wore was one of Lisa's designs.

A silent bubble of laughter rose in her throat at the irony of the situation.

Mia's gown bore classic lines in floral silk georgette with a fitted bodice and spaghetti straps, and a skirt whose hemline swirled with every move she made. The colours complemented the creamy texture of her skin, and she wore her hair in a simple knot atop her head, with diamond drop earrings and a diamond pendant that had belonged to her mother.

'The Parkinson-Stiles are throwing a tennis party on Wednesday evening. You'll be there, of course?'

'I'm afraid not.' Nikolos placed an arm around Mia's waist. 'If you'll excuse us?'

If looks could kill, Mia would have been struck dead on the spot. A shivery sensation slithered across the surface of her skin as she digested the venom evident momentarily before it was masked beneath a brilliant smile.

'Of course. Enjoy yourselves. I'll catch up with you later.'

Not if Mia could help it!

However, Anouska wasn't one to let opportunity slip through her fingers, and the fashionista managed to intrude more than once on one pretext or another.

'You're looking a little tired, poor darling. Is the social scene proving too much for you?'

Anouska's voiced concern was so artificial, Mia found it difficult to remain silent.

'I'm sure our hostess will accommodate you in one of her guest suites if you need to rest for an hour or two?'

'How considerate,' Mia managed sweetly, wondering if the other woman realised just how much of a challenge it was for her to be polite.

Nikolos brushed light fingers down her cheek and gave her a smile to die for. 'Home, hmm?' Nikolos declared gently. 'We'll locate our hosts and bid them goodnight.'

It took a while, and Mia waited until Nikolos eased the car out onto the street before venturing, 'Anouska has the hots for you.' And who could blame her?

'We're social acquaintances. Nothing more.'

Mia felt her stomach twist a little. 'She doesn't think so.'

'I've never given her any reason to believe otherwise.'

Perhaps not, she allowed dubiously. Yet it was obvious Anouska believed there was more to it than mere acquaintanceship. Much more. So much so, her overactive imagination had created something that didn't exist.

Mia tossed up whether she should relay Anouska's mid-week confrontation in the park, only to dismiss it. She'd dealt with the situation, and, besides, she could take care of herself. Hadn't she been doing so for years?

Yet there was a persistent niggle of disquiet, one she attempted to ignore as a sudden shower of rain splattered the windscreen, rendering the asphalt slick beneath the city street-lighting.

Nikolos traversed the Spit Bridge, then took the left fork to Seaforth and drove to his apartment building.

Mia cast him a studied look as he took the vehicle down into the underground car park. 'You don't play fair.'

He pulled into his allotted space and cut the engine. 'By making a decision?'

'One you've taken for granted is mutual.'

His eyes speared hers. 'You want to tell me it's not?'

She swallowed the sudden lump that had risen in her throat. *What are you waiting for?* an imp taunted. *You went with your instincts three months ago…why not now?*

Besides, her body was alive with a hunger only he could assuage. Need consumed her…need for his touch, his heat. *Him.*

'No.' She reached for the door-clasp and slid out from the passenger seat, then she walked at his side to the lift and rode with him to the uppermost floor.

Mia preceded him into the apartment, aware of subdued lighting, the almost silent electronic swish of drapes closing.

Now that she was here, the nerves in her stomach began an erratic dance, and she turned towards him, tentatively hesitant as he closed the distance between them.

Without a word he cupped her face and lay his

mouth over hers, gently at first, savouring the taste and feel of her, without any pretence at haste.

Dear heaven, this was good. It was like coming home. Here was where she belonged, Mia decided hazily as she opened her mouth to him, glorying in the sensations he was able to evoke.

She closed her eyes and gave herself up to him, returning each kiss with a fervour that built the heat between them until there was need for more, much more than oral contact.

Clothes, she decided dimly. He was wearing too many clothes. With urgent fingers she pushed aside his jacket, and murmured her appreciation when he shucked it off and tossed it onto a nearby sofa.

His tie followed, and she busied herself releasing his shirt buttons, sighing a little when she slid the edges apart and she found warm satiny skin and hard muscle.

Mia pressed her mouth to one male nipple, suckled, then nipped with the edge of her teeth...and heard his husky groan.

Her hands went to his belt and slid the clip free, then she moved to his trousers and eased the zip fastening down over his straining arousal, exulting in the size and strength of it.

His trousers slipped to the carpet, and she traced the slender black silk band at his waist, the hem of his briefs, before feathering a light pattern over the thickened penis, feeling it engorge even further beneath her touch.

'This is a little one-sided, don't you think?' Nikolos murmured huskily as he settled his mouth in the delicate curve of her neck, ravished the throbbing pulse there, and felt her body buck in spontaneous reaction.

With swift movements he toed off his shoes, socks and stepped out of his trousers. His shirt landed on top of his jacket.

Gentle hands moved to the zip fastening of her gown and slid it free with practised ease, then he slipped the spaghetti straps over each shoulder and let the silky fabric slither down to the carpet.

All she wore beneath the gown was a silk and lace thong, and Nikolos traced its line to her waist and followed the lacy edge to her groin.

His touch was electric, and she shuddered as his fingers slid beneath the silk to touch her and explore the sensitive clitoris. A touch as light as a butterfly's wing, back and forth, in tight circles, until she went up and over in a series of orgasmic spasms that shook her very being, so that she held onto him in fear of falling.

With one fluid movement he swung her into his arms and carried her through to the master suite, holding her as he switched on the lights and crossed to the bed where he tossed back the bedcovers before lowering her gently down onto the silken sheets.

With careful fingers he traced the bruising on her ribcage, and uttered something indistinguishable beneath his breath.

Mia lifted a hand and touched a finger over his lips, and her eyes widened as the muscle bunched at the edge of his jaw.

Without a word he lowered his head and pressed

fleeting kisses over the multicoloured mass, then he buried his head between her breasts before trailing a path to one peak.

The tightened bud engorged at his touch, and she cried out as he suckled, only to gasp when his fingers trailed low, stroking, caressing with increasing pressure until she went crazy with need, and began to plead with him. It was then he brushed his mouth down to the sensitive V and gifted her the most intimate kiss of all, savouring as he delighted in her pleasure.

Mia reached for him, and slowly, with infinite care, he entered her, restraining the need to surge in to the hilt.

Silken tissues stretched and expanded to accommodate him, and she dug her nails in deep as she urged him to a quicker pace.

He buried his mouth in the curve of her neck, nipped gently, and felt her response as he began to move, gently at first, then with controlled thrusts that took her to the heights of ecstasy and beyond.

It was a while before Nikolos disengaged from her, and she lifted a languid hand as she threaded fingers through his hair.

'Thank you.'

'For pleasuring you?'

Did she have any idea how beautiful she was? Or how wonderful she looked lying on his bed? He wanted to gather her up and keep her close for the rest of his life.

He lowered his head and brushed his lips to her

breast, lingered there, then moved up to tease her mouth.

'That was all about me,' Mia said quietly, and she felt rather than saw his smile.

'We have the night, *agape*.'

'Uh-huh,' she murmured. 'Now I get to pleasure you.'

With one swift movement she rose and sat astride him, loving the way his eyes dilated and went dark as sin.

She adored the taste of him, the satiny texture of his skin, the flex of muscle and sinew as she explored every inch of him, taking her time and enjoying each hitch of his breath, and the faint groan that growled from his throat.

All the while he stroked her back, tracing the bones that made up her spine, circling the small indentations and gliding over smooth skin before tangling in her hair as he pulled her mouth down to his.

Did it get any better than this? Mia queried silently a long time later. What they shared wasn't just sex. It was something more, much more. *Wasn't it?*

Together they slept, then turned to each other again and again through the night.

In the dark hours of early morning they shared a leisurely shower, where after-play became foreplay, and there was something intensely pagan about making love beneath the beating flow of water.

Deliciously fun with the soft scent of soap, the lingering touch of skilful fingers, a long kiss that became something intensely intimate.

Afterwards, towelled dry, Mia fastened a towel,

sarong-fashion, round her slender curves and began collecting her clothes.

'What do you think you're doing?'

She turned at the sound of Nikolos' husky voice, and gently shook her head. 'Dressing and going home.' Her mouth curved into a warm smile. 'I'll ring for a cab.'

He crossed to where she stood and curved his hands over her shoulders. 'Stay,' he said simply.

'I can't. Alice—'

'Will know you're with me.' His lips brushed hers, teased a little, then went in deep.

He bewitched her, totally, and she clung to him, uncaring when he loosened the towel and carried her back to bed.

Dawn fingered the earth with soft opalescent light, changing grey to colour, bringing the world alive for another day, and Mia stirred, felt Nikolos' arms tighten, and buried her head into the curve of his shoulder.

Soon she'd slip from the bed and text-message Alice, then she'd shower, dress and make breakfast.

Except she slept, and woke to find the bed empty, the teasing aroma of fresh coffee…and was that bacon?

She stretched, and felt the pull of muscles, the acute sensation deep within, and she closed her eyes against the vivid recollection of their lovemaking.

Lovemaking, she reiterated silently. Not just sex, or the shared indulgence of intimacy.

Where did they go from here?

Oh, hell. What was the time? She twisted her head

and checked the digital clock, groaned out loud, then she slipped out of bed, hit the shower, then, dry, she wound a towel round her slender form and made her way out to the kitchen.

Nikolos was dressed in chinos and a polo shirt, looking disgustingly healthy and relaxed, given the amount of sleep he'd had.

He turned as she entered the room. 'Hi.' He crossed to her side and covered her mouth with his own.

Hmm, she could get used to this!

'Bacon and eggs, toast, tea.' He swept an arm to the table set for two.

And coffee. What she wouldn't give for a brimming cup of strong black sweet coffee. Instead she slid into a chair and settled for tea.

'I rang Alice.'

Mia wondered at her sister's reaction, and decided Alice would approve. 'She's planning a barbecue. I really need to be there soon to help out.' The tea was great. Not as great as coffee, but it would do. She picked up cutlery and began doing justice to the contents on her plate.

'We'll leave after we've eaten.' He waited a beat. 'It'll give you time to pack.'

Pack? 'Nikolos—'

'I want you in my life, Mia,' he said gently. 'I need to be in yours.' He held her gaze. 'For all the right reasons.'

Move in with him? The thought of making the apartment her home, returning here after work each night, *sleeping* with him… Should she take that step? *Dared* she?

'After last night, you want us to live apart?'

Occupy a lonely bed, wishing she were with him? Living in denial? Why? As a matter of principle?

Innate honesty came to the fore. 'No.'

His smile almost undid her. 'Marry me.'

Mia's lips parted, and her eyes widened into deep dark pools.

He trailed light fingers down her cheek. 'The ball is in your court, *agape mou*.'

She wasn't capable of saying a word. Instead, she caught hold of his hand and pressed her lips to his palm.

CHAPTER NINE

MATT raced out front as soon as Nikolos pulled into the kerb. 'Hi.'

Mia slid out from the passenger seat and gave her nephew a hug. 'When are your friends due?'

'In about an hour. Mum bought me a new game for my PlayStation.' He smiled as Nikolos crossed to Mia's side. 'It's great to see you.'

'Likewise. Which games do you have?'

Male bonding between man and boy, Mia mused, hoping Craig Mitchell would be as successful at it. 'I'll leave you two to chat while I go help Alice.'

Mia went into the house and made her way through to the kitchen where her sister was putting the finishing touches to a superb-looking dessert.

'I'm sorry I wasn't here to help,' Mia said quietly.

Alice shot her a genuinely surprised look. 'Why? Getting it together with Nikolos is the best thing that could happen to you.'

'You think so?'

'Mia—*yes*. How could you doubt it?'

'You can't agree this is a normal relationship,' she ventured, watching as her sister checked a list.

'You had normal,' Alice reminded. 'We both did. Neither worked out.'

'He's asked me to move in with him.'

Alice didn't miss a beat. 'I hope you said yes.'

A tiny smile lifted the edges of her mouth. 'Trying to get rid of me, huh?'

'Wanting the best for you,' Alice assured gently.

Mia looked at the salads, the bread rolls ready to pop into the oven when needed. 'What can I do?'

'It's all done. Except the outdoor table. You can put out plates and flatware, and the unbreakable glasses.' She indicated a high cupboard. 'They're up there. And the paper napkins,' she added.

It was only a small get-together, with four of Matt's friends and their parents, Matt's tennis coach and his fiancée, and Craig Mitchell.

A pleasant number to mix and mingle and get acquainted, Mia acknowledged, admiring the apparent ease with which Alice organised the food and ensured everyone had plenty to drink, as well as overseeing the boys.

Her sister was an excellent home-maker, and a born mother who should have a brood of children to love, supervise and care for.

Why did some of the good people make bad choices in life?

Nikolos and Craig hit it off very well, and Mia was taken by the lawyer's casual attempt to empathise with Matt. He had just the right approach, and didn't try too hard…there, interested, but not intrusive.

'Playing matchmaker?' Nikolos queried quietly as they carried bowls of leftover salad into the kitchen.

Concern clouded her features. 'Is it obvious?'

He removed the bowls from her hands and drew

her in close. 'No.' He dropped a kiss on the tip of her nose. 'He seems a nice guy.'

'I'd love to see Alice happy.' The temptation to lean into him was difficult to resist. 'We'd better get back out there.'

Nikolos let her go, and followed her outdoors. The boys were kicking a soccer ball around the yard, and Nikolos joined Craig and the tennis coach in passing the ball.

'They're having a good time,' Alice commented, and Mia squeezed her sister's shoulder.

'It's great. Fantastic food, as always, and plenty of it.' She paused, then added quietly, 'Craig is enjoying himself.'

'He seems to be.'

'If he asks you out, I'll come sit with Matt.'

'I don't think—'

'Promise me you won't say no.'

'Maybe,' Alice compromised, and frowned slightly at Mia's light laugh. 'What's so funny?'

'We're giving each other advice on relationships.'

It was after four when everyone began to leave, and five when Craig drove away.

'Wasn't that cool?' Matt asked as they went indoors.

'Really cool,' Mia agreed.

'There's steak and marinated chicken in the fridge we didn't need to use.' Alice tied on an apron and began stacking the dishwasher. 'Why don't you both stay for dinner? Unless you have plans?'

'No plans,' Nikolos assured.

'Want to come see my new PlayStation game?'

Matt suggested with boyish eagerness, and Nikolos offered an easy grin.

'Thought you were never going to ask.'

Together Mia and Alice cleaned up, working with familiar co-ordinated ease until the kitchen and outdoor area resembled its usual ordered appearance.

Laughter and hoots of victory echoed from Matt's room, and Alice rolled her eyes expressively.

They ate at a reasonable hour, given Matt was due in school the next day.

Nikolos appeared relaxed and totally at ease, and Mia was supremely conscious of him, the warmth of his smile, the gleaming amusement in his dark gaze whenever their eyes met.

Was his mind straying towards what they'd shared through the night...and would inevitably share again a few hours from now?

Even the mere thought caused sensual heat to radiate through her body, and whenever her gaze slid to his mouth she had instant recall of the wicked pleasures he could bestow.

One look was all it took, and she became incandescent with primitive desire, so intense she had to wonder if it was recognisable...and inwardly died a hundred deaths at the possibility.

Matt went off to bed at eight, and not long afterwards Mia collected some of her clothes, make-up and toiletries, and left a few things residing in the wardrobe and dressing-table.

Then it wasn't a complete move, she told herself as she filled two large holdalls. Leaving stuff behind meant she still had a place to go to, a bolt-hole should she need it.

Yet the act of moving in with Nikolos made a statement. Just take things day by day, Mia bade silently. Living with him wasn't the final commitment of marriage. She would be free to leave, just as he would be free to tell her to go.

And that was a sobering thought. What if she didn't want to leave? Ever?

Oh, for heaven's sake! Now she was attempting to reach into the future and predict the unpredictable.

'Need some help?'

Mia turned at the sound of Alice's voice and offered a bright smile. 'All done. I've left a few things.'

'It'll always be your room,' Alice reminded quietly, and Mia gave her a hug.

'You're the best.'

'Ditto.'

'I'll ring tomorrow evening.' Mia's smile was wickedly mischievous. 'You can update me on Craig.'

'Oh, sure. Like all of a sudden he's going to change from boss to new best friend?'

'Don't underestimate him.'

They emerged from the bedroom, each with a holdall in one hand, which Nikolos captured as they entered the lounge.

It had been a lovely day, and Mia said so as Alice accompanied them to the front door.

Minutes later Nikolos slung the holdalls into the back of his car, and indicated the four-wheel drive. 'I'll follow you.'

It didn't take long to reach Seaforth, and he swung in front of her when they reached his apartment building, allowing her to follow him down into the basement car park and park immediately adjacent his allotted space.

This was it, Mia contemplated silently as they rode the lift. One step forward to the temporary commitment. The Karedes matriarchs would be pleased.

Had Nikolos apprised them of the move?

'Not yet,' Nikolos drawled as they exited the lift and entered his apartment.

'A man of many talents,' Mia accorded lightly. 'You read minds.'

'Yours has a certain transparency.' He closed the door and placed both holdalls onto the floor. 'Come here.'

He moved in close and lowered his head to hers, taking possession of her mouth in a kiss that took hold of any doubts and dismissed them.

Mia felt as if she were drowning in a pool of emotional sensation, and she clung to him, wanting more, so much more.

She needed to feel his skin without the restriction of clothing, to kiss and caress each pulse-point, until he lost control. She wanted his mouth on her, driving her wild as they both went up in flames.

There was only Nikolos, the moment, and a wealth of sensual pleasure as he swept her into his arms and carried her down to the bedroom.

Living with Nikolos was so much more than Mia had expected. There was no doubt good sex...

lovemaking, she amended with a secret smile, acted as a powerful aphrodisiac.

To be woken early each morning with a lover's touch made for a wonderful start to the day. Days when serving difficult customers and soothing fractious ones didn't faze her at all.

As to the nights…Mia fixed dinner if they stayed in, and when they dined out they chose a small intimate restaurant away from the glitzy social scene. Evenings that became an anticipatory tease to the lovemaking they would share on arriving home.

Socialising as such didn't exist during that initial week, although their absence from the social scene couldn't last overlong.

The Karedes empire supported a few well-known charities, there were certain social obligations, especially with Christmas only a matter of weeks away. Then there were family.

News of Nikolos' and Mia's cohabitation had reached the Karedes matriarchs, which resulted in pressure to confirm a suitable evening to visit.

Craig Mitchell's invitation to have Alice join him for dinner proved a highlight.

'Told you so.' Mia's soft laugh held delight Monday evening. 'When, where? What are you going to wear? Do you want me to come sit Matt, or—?' Inspiration struck. 'He could have a sleepover, and I'll drive him home next day.'

'Whoa,' Alice cautioned. 'One, it's a week night, which means school the next morning. And two, I haven't said I'll go.'

'Alice!' The reprimand held a note of despair.

'*Go.*' She was only just getting started. 'Nikolos won't mind, and I'll drop him to school on my way to work.'

'But what—'

'No *but*,' Mia insisted. 'I'll personally come over there and *shake* you if you refuse.'

Nikolos wandered into the room and stood regarding her with amusement. She was a pocket dynamo. Earthy, loyal, honest, loving… Sexy, sensual. *His.*

He could imagine her going toe-to-toe with anyone who dared question the integrity of anyone she loved. As a mother, she'd beat a lioness hands down.

Attired in jeans, a cotton knit top, her hair tied back in a pony-tail, face free of make-up, she looked about sixteen.

She was an easy read, with expressive features, a generous mouth and eyes a man could drown in. He adored the sound of her voice, her laugh, the way she tilted her chin when she was about to argue. And he loved the way she loved.

To reach out in the night and know she was there, to curl her in close against him and rest his cheek on her head. To hold her, and delight in her response.

'What was that all about?' Nikolos drawled as he crossed to her side when she cut the call.

'Craig has asked Alice out.'

He curved an arm round her shoulders and pulled her in. 'Why should that upset you?'

'She has cold feet.'

'Which you intend to rectify by…doing what?'

His hands were effecting a soothing magic across

her back, and she felt her bones begin to melt. 'You're trying to distract me.'

'Is it working?'

Oh, yes. It would be all too easy to lean in against him, link her hands at his nape and pull his head down to hers. 'Is it okay if Matt has a sleep-over here?'

Nikolos hid a smile at her resistance, knowing what it cost her. 'Of course. When?'

'This week. If I can persuade Alice to accept.'

He nuzzled his lips against the curve of her neck, and felt her go limp. Better. 'And if she doesn't?'

'I'll work on her.' She groaned as his hands slipped beneath her top and sought the clip fastening on her bra.

'I don't suppose you're interested in coffee?'

'My sole interest right now is *you*.' His fingers freed the top button of her jeans.

'You're insatiable.' The breath hitched in her throat as he lay a hand against her stomach.

His mouth touched hers fleetingly, hovered, then settled for a few minutes. 'You want me to stop?'

'Don't even think about it.'

He swung her into his arms and made his way towards the bedroom. 'That's what I thought.'

Mia's hands were as quick and deft as his own in discarding clothes, and she followed him down onto the bed, pinned his arms above his head with one hand, then freed the band from her hair with the other.

She watched his eyes darken as she slowly lowered her head and brushed her hair back and forth across his chest, teasing its length against his male nipples before releasing his hands and sweeping her hair lower, down his ribcage to his waist, the thick length of his engorged penis, to the nest of male hair couching his scrotum.

Seconds later she dipped her head low and used her mouth in an inventive evocative tasting that tested his control and broke it.

Her pleasure was short-lived as he rolled her onto her side and entered her in one slow thrust, only to ease back as he initiated a teasing foreplay that drove her wild.

It was a while before he took her over the edge, joined her there, and held her as she fell.

Afterwards as she lay supine he brushed his lips over every inch of her, slowly and with infinite care, before settling just above her navel.

Mia felt his lips move and sensed rather than heard the sound of his voice. She lifted a languid hand and threaded her fingers through his hair, lightly exploring the slight hollows in his head.

'Did you say something?'

He trailed a path of soft kisses to her waistline, then lifted his head to look at her. 'Just assuring our son or daughter of a loving welcome into the world.' And how he intended to take good care of their child's mother.

It undid her, and she was powerless to prevent the faint shimmering tears, or the single one spilling to run across her temple.

Nikolos saw it, and he swore softly as he gathered her in and pulled up the covers. She surprised and amazed him with her strength and her fragility. A single tear, and he was affected more than by anything she could have said.

She slept, so still and quiet, her body curled into his, and when she stirred in the early morning hours he carried her through to the *en suite* and shared her shower.

Breakfast was a leisurely meal eaten out on the terrace overlooking the inner harbour. The sun shone, its warmth holding the promise of a wonderful summer's day.

'I need to confirm dinner with Sofia,' Nikolos indicated as he drained his coffee. 'Towards the end of the week okay with you?'

She could do this. 'I guess so.' Sofia wasn't nearly as fearsome as Angelena, in whose eyes Mia must surely have taken a step in the right direction from 'one night stand' to 'live-in lover'. Without doubt there would be hope for the transition to 'wife'.

Nikolos stood up, caught up his jacket and shrugged it on, then he crossed to her side and bestowed a brief hard kiss. 'Have a good day, hmm?'

'You, too.'

It didn't take long to clear the table and load the dishwasher, then she put the finishing touches to her make-up, caught up her shoulder-bag, and took the lift down to the car park.

Mia checked her cellphone for text messages during her lunch break. There were two...the first from Nikolos indicating he'd be caught up in a late-afternoon meeting and wouldn't be home until seven.

The second came from Alice, requesting Matt sleep over Wednesday evening.

She'd done it! Knowing Alice as she did, it had taken considerable courage to accept Craig's invitation. She just hoped Alice's boss had the patience to take things slow.

The day had suddenly become brighter, and Mia spent the afternoon in the dispensary assisting with prescriptions at a preliminary level. It was interesting work, matching various drugs to the doctor's diagnosis and checking contra-indications, discussing with the pharmacist how the drug would work, examining the correct dosage, the patient's medication history logged into the computer. What over-the-counter medications conflicted with prescribed medication.

It was a constant learning curve, a challenge that held her intense interest.

Her dream was to own a pharmacy and design the shop fittings to maximum advantage. For the pharmacist, the assistants, the customers.

Security cameras, video surveillance, panic buttons were par for the course with crime and theft at a high level in today's society.

Mia was beginning to recognise the regular customers, mostly residents living close by. There were the usual drive-bys, people who needed aspirin or plasters, cough medicine.

It was close to five when a familiar figure entered the shop, and Mia's heart sank as she recognised Anouska.

This couldn't be good. What could the fashionista

possibly want in this particular shop, if not to cause mischief and mayhem? It was merely a matter of what and when.

At first Anouska appeared to be examining products in the personal hygiene section, then she moved to a stand stacked with packets of prophylactics, selected a variety, then crossed to the counter.

One of the assistants had left early, and the one remaining was busy serving a customer. Which left Mia to step down from the dispensary and tend to Anouska's purchase.

Smile politely, pop the packets in the appropriately sized bag, take the money, and extend the usual pleasantries.

Three, four minutes, and Anouska would be out the door.

Except that wasn't part of Anouska's plan.

'You can guarantee these, I assume?'

Here we go, Mia concluded silently. 'The packet carries instructions for correct usage.'

'They are...resilient and good quality?'

'We only carry quality brands.'

Anouska's mouth thinned. 'Pity you didn't choose wisely when you purchased your own.' Her voice rose when Mia declined to comment. 'But then I imagine falling pregnant was your aim.'

'Your remarks are insulting and uncalled for,' Mia said quietly.

'Really? It's you who is insulting.' She beckoned the pharmacist in the dispensary. 'I want to lodge a complaint.'

To give the pharmacist his due, he listened carefully, explained Mia had not acted in an untoward manner, and suggested Anouska complete her purchases or reject them.

Without a word the fashionista turned and walked out of the shop.

Mission achieved...sort of.

'I'm sorry,' Mia offered, and met the pharmacist's raised eyebrows.

'Whatever for? You weren't at fault.'

Yes, she was. Merely for being in the way of Anouska's objective...Nikolos. What bothered her was the purpose behind the fashionista's visit.

She didn't have long to find out. Half an hour later when she crossed to the car park there was a police car lined up close to the four-wheel drive, with two uniformed officers in attendance. One was taking down details from a man dressed in jeans and tee shirt, while the other was standing guard over a loud-mouthed female vilifying both officers and the witness with deplorable language.

Recognition was immediate. *Anouska?*

At that moment the fashionista turned, saw her, and began screaming a stream of invective. Whereupon the officer cuffed her and pushed her into the rear of the police car.

Mia crossed to the four-wheel drive and was sickened by the words scoured in the metalwork.

'Mia Fredrickson? This woman was caught causing damage to the four-wheel drive registered in your name.' The officer indicated the man who'd just given his statement. 'Your bodyguard has provided us with details, photographic and video evidence.'

Bodyguard?

'Nikolos Karedes hired me.'

At that moment Nikolos' Mercedes pulled into an adjacent space, and Mia watched as he crossed to the group.

'Officers. Jake.'

He caught hold of Mia's hand and lifted it to his lips. 'Mia.'

'Miss Fredrickson has only recently arrived on the scene.'

'Perhaps,' she said in measured tones, 'you might care to explain why this man—' she indicated Jake '—is acting as a bodyguard. Specifically, *my* bodyguard.'

Nikolos' eyes darkened for an instant, then he moved his gaze to the police officers. 'There's no need for either of us to stay?'

'We'll require a statement from you, sir, regarding background facts. Tomorrow? Meantime, you're free to go.'

'Jake, you'll take care of the car?'

'Already organised.'

'Thanks.' Nikolos led her towards the Mercedes, saw her seated inside, then he took the wheel and vacated the car park.

'You'd better give me some answers.'

'I'm sure you're sufficiently astute to have arrived at a few of them,' he indicated as he headed towards Seaforth. 'There was suspicion Anouska damaged the tyres, and paid that young thug to attack you. I hired Jake to run surveillance for your protection.' He eased to a halt at a set of traffic lights. 'Anouska's vehicle was parked several metres down the street from Alice's home on more than one occasion. At night. Last Sunday. She has also been keeping watch on my apartment building at night and in the early hours of the morning.' The lights changed and the car sprang forward. 'This afternoon she visited the pharmacy, then she crossed to the car park and used a metal object to scour marks on the bodywork.'

'You needed to catch her in the act,' Mia said dully.

'Yes.'

'You could have told me.'

'It was considered best not to unduly alarm you.'

'Best by *whom*?' she demanded.

'Everyone involved.'

She shot him a sharp glance. 'Alice knew?'

'No. The police psychiatrist pinned you as the target.'

'Great.'

'You were never in danger at any time.'

He'd made sure of it, and she fell quiet for several minutes.

The sequence of recounted scenes sped through her mind, and she felt the sudden rise of nausea. 'I think I'm going to be sick.'

Please, God, please don't let it happen, not here, not *now*.

She undid her seat belt as Nikolos pulled into the kerb, and she made it out of the car…just.

Seconds later Nikolos was there, and she motioned him aside. Not that he took any notice, and when she was done she directed huskily, 'My bag. There's tissues, wet wipes. Bottled water.'

He fetched them, and minutes later she felt measurably better. 'Let's get out of here.'

As soon as she entered the apartment she made straight for the shower, brushed her teeth, used a mouthwash for good measure, then she stepped into comfortable jeans and a tee shirt.

At least her stomach appeared to have settled, which had to be a good thing, she decided as she emerged into the bedroom.

Nikolos was there, prowling, his expression faintly grim as she met his gaze. 'Maybe I should call the obstetrician.'

'Pregnant women throw up on occasion. It's called morning sickness. Except that tends to be a misnomer, as it's known to happen at any time of the day or night.' She took a calming breath. 'I'll go fix something for dinner.'

'Forget it. We'll order in.'

'Continue treating me like a fragile flower, and I'll hit you.'

'That could prove interesting.'

'Count on it.' With that Mia walked out to the kitchen ahead of him.

It didn't take long to grill a couple of steaks, assemble a salad, and heat bread rolls.

'I thought you were supposed to be at a meeting?'

'I walked out of it when Jake called.'

She handed him a plate. 'Go sit down.' She took her own plate and carried the salad bowl to the table.

Cable television provided visual entertainment for

a while, and although Mia was prepared to swear she only closed her eyes for a few seconds she barely stirred as Nikolos took her to bed.

'Hey,' she protested as he began removing her clothes. 'I can do that.'

'Sure you can,' he said gently and continued divesting each garment. Then he slid her beneath the covers, undressed, and joined her.

He was wonderful, warm, and solid, and she nestled close, and slept.

CHAPTER TEN

MATT'S sleep-over proved a huge success. He loved the apartment, whistled at Nikolos' electronic equipment, ate well, and together they took it in turns to challenge each other's skills with chess. He didn't even protest when Mia called 'bedtime', and later when she checked on him he lay still and contented in sleep.

'No problems?' Nikolos queried when she sank onto the sofa at his side.

'None.'

He curved an arm around her shoulders and brushed his lips to her temple. 'He adores you.'

'It's mutual,' Mia responded simply as she leaned in against him. His warmth held a sensual potency that succeeded in quickening her pulse and heightened all her nerve-ends.

It was magical, witching, primitive and raw. A combination that excited and frightened, soothed and enticed.

The night she'd discovered Nikolos was Cris' brother had been one of the worst nights of her life. Now, she didn't want to imagine a night without him. An admission she chose not to examine too closely just yet. Although putting it off wouldn't achieve a thing.

'Sofia has invited us to join her for dinner tomorrow evening.'

Now there was something to think about! 'A verbal sparring session with the Karedes matriarchs, huh?' Her voice was light, almost teasing as her eyes met his, and she smiled at his musing chuckle.

'It'll be a breeze.'

Much to Mia's surprise, he was right. Cris' friendship was a given, and Sofia exuded friendly warmth over pre-dinner drinks. Even Angelena appeared suitably restrained during the excellent three course meal.

The 'marriage' subject didn't arise, nor was 'wedding' mentioned.

Nikolos had, without doubt, issued specific instructions, which even the irascible Angelena chose to observe.

It had been a pleasant evening, and Mia said so as Nikolos traversed the Harbour Bridge *en route* to the northern suburbs. The night was clear with a sprinkling of stars, the precursor to another fine summer's day.

The following two days involved split shifts to accommodate one of the pharmacy assistants, which meant working Friday morning and Saturday afternoon, and she'd made arrangements to catch up with Alice early on Saturday. Phone calls were fine, but they didn't compensate for meeting in person.

Which they did, sharing morning tea in the tennis clubhouse while Matt had his coaching lesson.

'Craig,' Mia began with a mischievous smile. 'The nitty-gritty,' she teased. 'Not the condensed version.'

'He's…nice,' Alice allowed. 'Kind. Thoughtful.'

'You're describing your boss. I want Craig, the man.'

'He was a gentleman.'

'Didn't kiss you, huh?'

She saw the faint tinge of pink colour her sister's cheeks.

'He's asked Matt and I to a picnic on Sunday.'

Way to go, Craig! This was looking good. 'Naturally you said yes.'

'It should be a pleasant day,' Alice admitted, and rolled her eyes expressively as Mia gave an outrageous grin. 'Your turn.'

'Okay.'

'That's it? *Okay?* How come I get to spill and you don't?'

There was never going to be a better opportunity. 'I guess I'm having a hard time coming to terms with a relationship that doesn't conform with the norm,' she said slowly.

'What's normal? We both had that first time round. The getting-to-know-you, the courtship, engagement. I did the marriage thing.' Alice leaned forward. 'Didn't work for either of us.'

'I imagined falling in love as a gradual thing, something that begins with friendship and develops over time.'

'Not meeting someone and *knowing* in the depths of your soul they're *the one*?'

'Can it be that simple?' Mia queried. A recognition of sexual chemistry…yes. But *love*?

'Sometimes I think it can,' Alice said gently.

'It seems too—' She paused, hesitating over the choice of words.

'Too much, too soon? Too easy?' Her sister leaned forward, her gaze intent. 'Could you live without Nikolos?'

She didn't have to think. 'No.'

'Would you want to?'

Anguish welled up inside and threatened to tear her apart.

'So,' Alice demanded gently. 'What are you waiting for?'

Nothing, absolutely nothing. 'I need to make a phone call.'

It took only seconds to key in the necessary digits, another few to connect.

'Karedes.'

'Is this a good time?' Oh, hell, don't weaken now. 'It's Mia.'

How could she believe he required identification, when the sound of her voice was as familiar to him as his own? Each cadence, the light in her laughter, the warmth when she uttered his name…and the mesmeric hunger when he held her in the throes of passion.

She had the power to turn his world upside down, then send it spinning out of control. It wasn't a feeling he was comfortable with, but one he'd no doubt become accustomed to…eventually, he determined. Maybe by the time he dangled their grandchild on his knee.

Humour at that thought curved his mouth into a musing smile. 'It depends what you have in mind.'

How could she say *I love you* over the phone? 'Would it cause a problem if we cancel tonight?'

Given the nature of the fund-raiser, he could easily send in a cheque. 'Do I get to ask why?'

'I'll explain later. Bye.'

The afternoon became a blur as she summoned Alice's assistance, made phone calls, and begged an hour's grace on her usual finishing time.

Alice, bless her, was waiting in the lobby when Mia arrived there, and together they rode the elevator to Nikolos' penthouse apartment.

'Go shower and change,' Alice instructed. 'I'll take care of the table, and transfer everything into serving dishes.'

Half an hour later Mia emerged into the kitchen wearing minimum make-up, lip-gloss and a touch of eyeshadow. She'd wound her hair into a knot atop her head, and slipped into black evening trousers and a silk camisole.

'Seriously *wow*,' Alice complimented. 'Okay, I'm out of here.'

'Thanks.' Mia's gratitude was heartfelt. 'I couldn't have done it without you.'

She had five minutes, maybe ten, before Nikolos would walk through the door. Time enough to pen the words she wanted to write on a card.

A quick glance at the table revealed Alice had thought of everything, right down to the candles, a delicate centrepiece, gleaming cutlery and crystal.

Nerves were a curse, and hers were waging a war second to none.

What if…? *Don't,* she cautioned silently. There are no *what ifs.*

The sound of a key sliding into the lock heralded Nikolos' arrival, and she summoned a winsome smile as he crossed to her side.

'Hmm,' he managed appreciatively as he reached for her. His lips brushed hers, settled, then went in deep, in an evocative exploration that made her almost forget her plans for the evening.

'I can't persuade you to share my shower?' His hands slid to her waist and held her there.

'Been there, done that,' Mia responded lightly, sinking in against him, loving the way his hands trailed a light pattern over her back. 'And you have ten minutes.' She pressed a kiss to the edge of his jaw. 'Go.'

Bread rolls into the oven, open the wine and let it breathe, check on the dessert…

Mia lit the candles, then transferred serving dishes onto the table as Nikolos entered the kitchen.

The tailored business suit had been replaced with chinos and a chambray shirt, and he'd shaved, his hair still damp from his shower.

Just one look at him, and her bones began to melt.

'Need some help?'

'All done.'

He moved in close and trailed light fingers down her cheek. 'You're nervous. Why?'

It would be so easy to link her hands at his nape and pull his head down to hers.

Except then they wouldn't eat, the food would spoil…and, besides, she wanted to follow the plan.

'I haven't done this before.' Honesty was easy.

Nikolos' mouth curved into a musing smile as he traced her lower lip. 'What, precisely?'

The familiar quickened beat of her heart was visible in the hollow beneath her throat, and she swallowed compulsively in an effort to control it.

Did he know? Could he guess? 'Bear with me,' she managed after a few timeless seconds, silently begging him to understand.

'Would you have me sip through a glass of wine while we indulge in a recap of each other's day?' he queried lightly as he moved to the table and poured a measure of clear amber liquid into one of the crystal goblets. 'Or shall we hold a discussion over the meal?'

There was bottled water reposing next to the wine, and Nikolos filled a glass and handed it to her, then touched its rim with his own.

'*Salute.*' His gaze speared hers, and narrowed slightly as he glimpsed the faint tinge of pink colouring her cheeks. 'A busy day?'

'Some,' she agreed. 'I enjoy working in a smaller suburban pharmacy. The customers are mostly local residents.' As conversation, it seemed incredibly banal, and she indicated the serving dishes.

'Let's eat.' Otherwise she'd never last the distance.

The food had to be wonderful, given Alice's flair for fine cuisine, but Mia barely tasted a thing as she sampled the starter and forked a few mouthfuls from the main course before pushing her plate to one side.

'I'll get dessert.'

'Dessert can wait,' Nikolos declared with deceptive mildness. 'Suppose you tell me why you've been treading eggshells for the past half-hour.'

Oh, hell. The moment of truth! With care she slid the envelope from beneath her side plate. 'I wanted to give you this.' She held it out to him, and watched as he leant forward to take it.

Mia searched his features, watching for the slightest change in expression, and glimpsed none as he slid open the flap and extracted the card.

Choosing it had been a mission, as she'd searched numerous racks, discarding humour for conventional, then changing her mind countless times before selecting a blank card featuring a Monet print.

The words she'd written were engraved in her mind.

I love you with all my heart. Will you marry me and share the rest of my life?

Each second seemed to take for ever as he opened the card, and her heart leapt to her throat.

At last he lifted his head, and his dark eyes met and held her own. 'Thank you.'

She was going to die if he didn't add something…*anything*.

'You doubt my answer?'

Mia made a helpless gesture, unable to trust her voice.

'You think I could make love to another woman the way I make love to *you*? *Theos.*' The husky epithet held a silken savagery as he rose to his feet. 'Or the child you carry is more important to me than its mother?'

His eyes blazed with unrestrained passion…and

something else, much deeper and more profound. 'You're the other half of my soul. My heart.' He crossed to her side and drew her to her feet. 'My life.'

Mia was aware of warmth coursing through her veins, heating her body as it reached every nerve-end. Mesmeric, intensely sensual…passion at its zenith on every level. Of the mind, the heart.

'I love you,' Nikolos said gently. 'I always will. Believe it.'

His mouth took possession of hers with a hunger that was witching, shameless, and she became lost in the rapture of his touch.

His, for a lifetime.

'You sweet fool,' Nikolos chastised in a voice husky with emotion. 'How could you not have known how I feel about you?'

She wound her arms round his neck, lifted her body against his, wrapped her legs around his waist, and hung on as he made his way to the bedroom.

'Mmm.' This was good, better than *good*. It was like reaching for the stars and catching hold of the sun, the moon…the entire universe. She nuzzled his earlobe, nipped, then soothed it with her tongue. 'I wasn't sure you needed *me*.'

Seconds later he gently disentangled her arms, her legs, then slid her down to her feet.

'I'll show you.'

He did. Very thoroughly. And they never got to eat dessert.

It was in the early pre-dawn hours when Mia drifted into semi-wakefulness and became aware of her surroundings, the bed, and the muscular arm that enfolded her close, even in sleep, against a warm, strong, intensely male body.

Love, she determined wistfully, was a wondrous entity. Tenuous, and so infinitely precious. An emotion that should never be taken for granted.

Nikolos was her life, her reason for being. Friend, lover, soul-mate. Always.

Reflective thought drifted slowly through her mind as she recaptured the night they first met, and the force of her cataclysmic reaction.

It was almost as if destiny had played a part, putting them both in the same place at the same time, with fate lending a hand to ensure they met again.

A musing smile played across her generous mouth as she recalled her reluctance to have anything to do with Nikolos Karedes.

Yet he had persisted, dispensing with her resistance as if it was nothing of consequence.

When had she fallen in love with him? More importantly, when had she known it was *love*?

'What are you thinking, *agape mou*?'

The sound of his drawled voice held a musing indulgent quality as he switched on the bedside lamp.

'You heard me *thinking*?' she couldn't help teasing.

The soft light illuminated the room, and she watched as he rolled onto his side and brushed gentle fingers down her cheek. Her mouth quivered as he traced its outline and lingered at one edge.

'I was already awake.' He'd felt a change in the depth of her breathing, registered its quickened pace.

'I love you.' There, she'd said it. Three little words, yet they proved the hardest ones for her to vocalise.

His eyes darkened and became almost black with emotion.

'I tried so hard not to,' she managed with innate honesty.

He leant down and brushed his mouth against hers, soothing the soft contours before taking a slow, sweeping exploration. Teasing, tantalising in an evocative dance that came close to destroying her resolve.

The temptation to deepen the kiss was almost impossible to resist, but she managed it…just, and broke the contact. Only because he allowed her to.

'I want you to know I'm where I'm meant to be,' Mia said simply. 'With you.' She lifted a hand and placed gentle fingers over his mouth. 'Please. I need to say the words.'

She felt his lips caress her fingers, then still.

'You're my world. Everything.' Was that her voice? It sounded impossibly husky and drowning in emotion.

'I gift you my heart, unconditionally. My love.' There was nothing she could do about the well of moisture shimmering in her eyes.

'Thank you,' Nikolos said gently. 'It's a gift I'll treasure for the rest of my life.'

'There's just one more thing.' She moved quickly, taking him by surprise as she reversed their positions and straddled him. 'I get to have my turn.'

Mia lowered her head and brushed his mouth with her own. 'If you want to complain, do it now.'

He didn't utter a word.

CHAPTER ELEVEN

Two weeks later the Karedes family gathered together in the manicured gardens of Sofia Karedes' home.

It was a beautiful day for a wedding, the sun's late afternoon warmth reduced by a soft breeze whispering in from the harbour.

Mia wore an exquisitely crafted gown of ivory silk and lace with a lace-edged veil attached to an elegant headpiece. She carried a bouquet of pale peach-coloured roses, and wore an exquisite diamond pendant and earrings, a gift from the groom…who looked magnificent in Armani.

Alice stood in as the bride's attendant, with Cris acting as Nikolos' best man. Sofia and Angelena took pride of place as mother and grandmother of the groom. Matt was entrusted with the rings.

Costas stood on the sideline, a witness, observer, and Mia suspected, a bodyguard. He also acted as photographer, thus ensuring no unsolicited shots could be released to the media.

There was a sense of unreality as the celebrant intoned the words, and Mia's hand trembled a little as Nikolos slid the wide diamond-studded wedding ring onto her finger.

She was powerless to prevent the shimmer of moisture glistening in her eyes, and her lips parted in surprise as he leant forward and took possession of her mouth in a slow, evocative kiss that brought a soft tinge of pink to her cheeks.

'I don't think you were supposed to do that yet,' Mia murmured as he lifted his head.

'No?'

His voice held a latent sensuality that sent warmth flooding her body.

Then it was her turn to slip a gold band onto his finger, the celebrant concluded the ceremony, and Nikolos kissed the bride.

Affectionate hugs were exchanged and congratulations offered.

'I think I'm going to cry,' Alice warned quietly as the sisters embraced.

'Don't you dare.' Mia's voice shook a little. 'Think *happy*.'

'I *am* happy. You look absolutely stunning.'

'Somebody separate them,' Matt warned. 'We're talking *tears*.'

'Champagne and hors d'oeuvres are set up in the lounge,' Sofia announced, and placed a placating hand on Matt's shoulder. 'Happy tears are okay.'

Mia gently extricated herself and tucked her arm beneath Alice's elbow. 'Let's get you some champagne.'

Nikolos crossed to Matt's side as the party made their way into the house, and paused as the young boy slowed his steps to a halt.

'You'll take care of her, won't you?'

The young boy's earnestness was clearly visible, and Nikolos hunkered down so he was at eye level.

'Mia's special,' Matt continued doggedly.

'Very special,' Nikolos agreed gently, adding, 'I love her very much.'

Matt inclined his head. 'That's okay, then.'

Nikolos rose to his feet in one fluid movement and placed a casual arm round the young boy's shoulders. 'Let's go join the others, shall we?'

Mia saw man and boy enter the lounge, and watched as Nikolos crossed to her side. 'Man talk, huh?' she teased, and felt the breath hitch in her throat as he brushed gentle fingers across her cheek.

He had the ability to make her feel as if she were the only woman in his world. Love was something to be treasured, cherished…a gift beyond price.

'Have I told you how beautiful you are?'

She lifted her head and offered him a captivating smile. 'It's the dress,' she teased. 'All this finery gets to come off.'

His husky chuckle sent her pulse racing to a quickened beat as he leaned in close. 'Removing it will be my pleasure.'

Mia laid the palm of one hand against his cheek and offered him a wicked smile. 'Just be warned I get to return the favour.'

Dinner was served in the formal dining-room. A sumptuous meal with Costas in attendance.

'You'll do very well, child,' Angelena accorded as they sampled the dessert. 'It is a joy to see Nikolos so content.'

For all her blunt manner, the elderly matriarch possessed a soft heart, and Mia took hold of the arthritic hand and gave it a gentle squeeze. 'Thank you.'

There was a wedding cake, its intricate icing a work of art, and a small stack of miniature replicas for each guest, together with toasts to the bride and groom, more champagne, followed by coffee.

After which Nikolos caught hold of Mia's hand and indicated their intention to leave.

Not that they had far to go, for they'd elected to return to the Seaforth apartment. Christmas was only a week distant, and they wanted to spend it with family. Mid-January they'd fly to Athens and take a cruise round the Greek Islands.

'Happy, *agape mou*?' Nikolos queried as they entered the apartment.

'More than mere words can convey,' Mia said gently, and turned into his arms.

'I love you. More than life itself.'

The depth of emotion evident in his voice almost made her cry. 'You're everything to me,' she managed shakily as he gently freed the veil from her hair.

She stepped out of her shoes, and reached for the zip fastening of her gown.

There was a teasing quality evident as they began discarding each layer of clothes, pausing often for a lingering kiss as they slowly made their way towards the bedroom.

The gentle slide of a hand, the brush of his mouth, hers, in a tantalising exploration that fuelled the anticipation, the promise…heightening the sensuality and heating the passion until there was only shimmering, pulsating need.

As it would always be between them.

Love everlasting. Now and for ever.

EPILOGUE

TYLER YANNIS KAREDES made his entry into the world a week early, charming his adoring parents and gaining the adulation of his paternal grandmother and great-grandmother who unashamedly used every opportunity to visit, any excuse to watch over him.

His christening at three months of age was an intimate family event, with Alice, Cris and Matt chosen as godparents. Craig Mitchell was present as an invited guest.

Afterwards, Angelena, Sofia and Alice jostled affectionately for a turn to hold him, noting and commenting on each smile, every gurgle.

'He's enjoying every bit of it,' Mia said quietly as she surveyed the scene being played out in the spacious lounge of her home.

'Captivating his female audience,' Nikolos agreed as he drew her in against him.

'What he needs,' she declared, 'is a sibling to balance the scales of attention a little.'

'Mia—'

'After I sit my registration exams,' she mused thoughtfully, 'would be a good time, don't you think?'

Her delicate perfume teased his senses, and his arms tightened around her slender frame. She was so infinitely precious, so much a part of him. His life, his very soul.

'Not too soon?'

'You object?'

How could he? He'd adored every phase of her pregnancy…the wonder of their child growing in her womb. But nothing had prepared him for the joy of holding their newborn in his arms for the first time.

'My concern is for you.'

Mia's eyes began to mist. 'Maybe it'll be a girl this time.'

At the end of the year she'd gain her degree, and he had his eye on a new shopping complex where a pharmacy would be perfectly located. He already had a team of shop fitters awaiting her instructions, a dossier of CVs for a prospective manager and staff. It would allow her to run her own business, part-time, with the help of a part-time nanny. He intended the package to be his gift to her on their wedding anniversary.

'How soon before our guests leave, do you think?'

His husky voice sent a familiar flood of heat through her body, sensitising each nerve-end, every skin-cell until she ached for him and the sensual delight they shared.

'Another hour?' She sent him a teasing glance. 'Maybe two?'

'How do you feel about an early night?'

Her light laugh tugged at his heartstrings, and she took time to brush her lips against his in a fleeting kiss that didn't come close to easing the desire he felt for her.

It would take a lifetime, and then some. Love, true love, didn't die. It lived for ever, and beyond.

FINN'S PREGNANT BRIDE

by

Sharon Kendrick

Sharon Kendrick started story-telling at the age of eleven and has never really stopped. She likes to write fast-paced, feel-good romances with heroes who are so sexy they'll make your toes curl!

Born in west London, she now lives in the beautiful city of Winchester – where she can see the cathedral from her window (but only if she stands on tip-toe). She has two children, Celia and Patrick, and her passions include music, books, cooking and eating – and drifting off into wonderful daydreams while she works out new plots!

Don't miss Sharon Kendrick's exciting new novel, *Accidentally Pregnant, Conveniently Wed*, out in January 2008 from Mills & Boon® Modern™.

The character of Aunt Finola was based on two
remarkable Irishwomen – the intrepid
Peggy Crone, and my aunt, the gypsy-hearted
Josephine MacCormack.

Also, thanks must go to Willie Burke for his help
on the beautiful city of Dublin and to my darling
(GV) Schubert for his continuing inspiration.

CHAPTER ONE

AT FIRST, Catherine didn't notice the shadowy figure sitting there. She was too busy smiling at the waiter with her practised I-am-having-a-wonderful-holiday smile, instead of letting her face fall into the crestfallen lines which might have given away the fact that her boyfriend had fallen in love with another woman.

The sultry night air warmed her skin like thick Greek honey.

'*Kalispera*, Nico.'

'*Kalispera*, Dhespinis Walker,' said the waiter, his face lighting up when he saw her. 'Good day?'

'Mmm!' she enthused. 'I took the boat trip out to all the different coves, as you recommended!'

'My brother—he look after you?' questioned Nico anxiously.

'Oh, yes—he looked after me very well.' In fact, Nico's brother had tried to take more than a professional interest in ensuring that she enjoyed the magnificent sights, and Catherine had spent most of the boat-trip sitting as far away from the tiller as possible!

'My usual table, is it?' she enquired with a smile, because Nico had gone out of his way to give her the best table every evening—the faraway one, which looked out to sea.

But Nico was frowning. 'Tonight it is difficult, *dhespinis*. The table is already taken. For tonight the man from Irlandia is here.'

Some odd quality changed the tone of his voice as

5

he spoke. Catherine heard reverence. Respect. And something else which sounded awfully like a grudging kind of envy. She looked at him with a lack of comprehension. The man from *where*? 'Irlandia?' she repeated.

'Ire-land,' he translated carefully, after a moment's thought. 'He arrive this afternoon and he take your table for dinner.'

It was ridiculous to feel so disappointed, but that was exactly the way she *did* feel. Funny how quickly you established little routines on holiday. Night after night Catherine had sat at the very end of the narrow wooden deck which made up the floor of the restaurant, so close to the sea that you felt as if you were almost floating over it.

You could look down over the railing and watch the slick black waters below as they licked against the supporting struts. And the moon would spill its shimmering silver light all across the surface—its beauty so intense that for a while Catherine was able to forget all about England, forget Peter and the always busy job which awaited her.

'Can he do that?' she pleaded. 'Tomorrow is my last day.'

Nico shrugged. 'He can do anything. He is good friend of Kirios Kollitsis.'

Kirios Kollitsis. The island's very own septuagenarian tycoon—who owned not only the three hotels, but half the shops in the village, too.

Catherine strained her eyes to see a dark figure sitting in *her* chair. They said that you could judge a woman by her face and a man by his body, and, though she couldn't see much in this light, it was easy enough to tell from the taut and muscular definition of a powerful frame that this man was considerably younger than Kirios Kollitsis. By about four decades, she judged.

'I can give you next table,' said Nico placatingly. 'Is still lovely view.'

She smiled, telling herself it wasn't his fault. Silly to cling onto a routine—even a temporary one—just because her world had shattered into one she no longer recognised. Just because Peter had gone and found the 'love of his life' almost overnight, leaving Catherine wondering wryly what that said about *their* relationship of almost three years standing. 'That would be lovely. Thanks, Nico.'

Finn Delaney had been slowly sipping from a glass of ouzo and gazing out at the sunset, feeling some of the coiled tension begin to seep from his body. He had just pulled off the biggest deal in a life composed of making big deals. It had been fraught and tight and nail-biting, but—as usual—he had achieved what he had set out to do.

But for the first time in his life the success seemed empty. Another million in the bank, true—but even that seemed curiously hollow.

The ink had barely dried on the contract before he had driven on impulse to the airport and taken the first flight out to the beautiful empty Greek island he knew so well. His secretary had raised her eyebrows when he'd told her.

'But what about your diary, Finn?' she had objected. 'It's packed.'

He had shrugged his broad shoulders and felt a sudden, dizzying sense of liberation. 'Cancel it.'

'Cancel it?' she'd repeated faintly. 'Okay. You're the boss.'

Yes, he was the boss, and there was a price to be paid for that position. With power went isolation. Few spoke to Finn Delaney without an agenda these days. But, in truth, he liked the isolation—and the ability to control his own destiny which went with that. It was only when you started letting people close to you that control slipped away.

He picked up his glass of ouzo and studied the cloudy liquid with a certain sense of amusement, feeling worlds and years away from his usual self. But then, this island had always had that effect on him. It had first known him when he had nothing and had accepted him with open arms. Here he was simply 'Finn', or Kirios Delaney.

Yet for a man known in his native Dublin as The Razor—for his sharp-cutting edge in the world of business—he would have been almost unrecognisable to his many friends and rivals tonight.

The fluid suits he normally sported had been replaced by a pair of faded jeans and a thin white shirt he had bought in one of the local shops. The top three buttons were left carelessly undone, veeing down towards the honed, tanned muscle of his chest. His thick, dark hair—as usual—was in need of a cut and his long legs were stretched out lazily beneath the table.

Tonight he felt like one of the fishermen who had dragged their silver shoals up onto the beach earlier.

It was a perfect night, with a perfect moon, and he sighed as he recognised that success sometimes made you lose sight of such simple pleasures.

'This way, Dhespinis Walker,' Finn heard the waiter saying.

The sound of footsteps clip-clopping against the

wooden planks made him look round almost absently, and his eyes narrowed, his heart missing a sudden and unexpected beat as a woman walked into the restaurant. He put the glass of ouzo down, and stared.

For she was beautiful. Mother of all the Saints! She was more than beautiful. Yet beautiful women abounded in his world, so what was different about this one?

Her long black hair tumbled in ebony waves over her shoulders and made her look like some kind of irresistible witch, with a face as delicate as the filmy dress which hinted at ripe, firm flesh beneath.

Yes, very beautiful indeed. His eyes glinted in assessment. And irritated, too. Her mouth was set and, very deliberately, she looked right through him as though he wasn't there. Finn experienced a moment of wry amusement. Not something which happened to him every day of the week. He spent his life fighting off women who rose to the challenge of ensnaring one of Ireland's most eligible bachelors!

He felt the stir of interest as she took her seat at the table next to his, mere inches away, and as the waiter fussed around with her napkin Finn was able to study her profile. It was a particularly attractive profile. Small, cute nose, and lips which looked like folded rose petals. Her skin was softly sheening and lightly golden, presumably from the hot Greek sun, and her limbs were long and supple.

The pulse at his temple was hammering out a primitive beat, and he felt the heated thickening of his blood. Was it the moon and the warm, lazy night air which made him look at a total stranger and wish he was taking her back to his room with him to lose himself in the sweet pleasures of the senses? Had the magic of the island made him regress to those instant clamouring desires of his late teens?

Catherine could feel the man's eyes scanning her with leisurely appraisal, and it felt positively *intrusive* in view of the fact that he was inhabiting *her* space. She studied the menu unseeingly, knowing exactly what she was planning to have.

Finn gave a half-smile, intrigued by the forbidding set of her body and the negative vibes she was sending out. It was enough of a novelty to whet his appetite.

'*Kalispera,*' he murmured.

Catherine continued to study her menu. Oh, yes, he was Irish, all right. The soft, deep and sensual lilt which was almost musical could have come from nowhere else. His voice sounded like shavings of gravel which had been steeped in honey—a voice Catherine imagined would have women in their thousands drooling.

Well, not this one.

'Good evening,' he translated.

Catherine lifted her head and turned to look at him, and wished she hadn't—because she wasn't prepared for the most remarkable pair of eyes which were trained in her direction. Even in this light it was easy to see that they were a deep, dark blue—as wine-dark as the sea she had idly floated in earlier that day. And fringed by thick, dark lashes which could not disguise the unmistakable glint in their depths.

He had a typically Irish face—rugged and craggedly handsome—with a luscious mouth whose corners were lifted in half-amused question as he waited for her to reply.

'Are you speaking to me?' she asked coolly.

He hadn't had a put-down like that in years! Finn made a show of looking around at all the empty places in the tiny restaurant. 'Well, I'm not in the habit of talking to myself.'

'And I'm not in the habit of striking up conversations with complete strangers,' she said blandly.

'Finn Delaney.' He smiled.

She raised her brows. 'Excuse me?'

'The name's Finn Delaney.' He gave her a slow smile, unable to remember the last time he had been subjected to such an intense deep-freeze. He noticed that the smile refused to work its usual magic.

She didn't move. Nor speak. If this was a chat-up line, then she simply wasn't interested.

'Of course, I don't know yours,' he persisted.

'That's because I haven't given it to you,' she answered helpfully.

'And are you going to?'

'That depends.'

He raised dark brows. 'On?'

'On whether you'd mind moving.'

'Moving where?'

'Swapping tables.'

'Swapping tables?'

Catherine's journalist training instinctively reared its head. 'Do you always make a habit of repeating everything and turning it into a question?'

'And do you always behave so ferociously towards members of the opposite sex?'

She nearly said that she was right off the opposite sex at the moment, but decided against it. She did not want to come over as bitter—because bitter was the last thing she wanted to be. She was just getting used to the fact that her relationship had exceeded its sell-by date, that was all.

She met the mockery lurking deep in the blue eyes. 'If you *really* saw me ferocious, you'd know all about it!'

'Well, now, wouldn't that be an arresting sight to see?' he murmured. He narrowed his eyes in question. 'You aren't exactly brimming over with *bonhomie*.'

'No. That's because you're sitting at my table.' She shrugged as she saw his nonplussed expression and she couldn't really blame him. 'I know it sounds stupid, but I've been there every night and kind of got attached to it.'

'Not stupid at all,' he mused, and his voice softened into a musical caress. 'A view like this doesn't come along very often in a lifetime—not even where I come from.'

She saw a star shoot a silver trail as it blazed across the night sky. 'I know,' she sighed, her voice filled with a sudden melancholy.

'You could always come and join me,' he said. 'And that way we can both enjoy it.' He saw her indecision and it amused him. 'Why not?'

Why not, indeed? Twelve days of dining on her own had left a normally garrulous woman screaming for a little company. And sitting on her own made her all the more conscious of the thoughts spinning round in her head—of whether she could have done more to save her relationship with Peter. Even knowing that time and distance had driven impenetrable wedges between them did not stop her from having regrets.

'I won't bite,' he added softly, seeing the sudden

sadness cloud her eyes and wondering what had caused it.

Catherine stared at him. He looked as though he very easily *could* bite, despite the outwardly relaxed appearance. His apparent ease did not hide the highly honed sexuality which even in her frozen emotional state she could recognise. But that was her job; she was trained to suss people out.

'Because I don't know you,' she pointed out.

'Isn't that the whole point of joining me?'

'I thought that it was to look at the view?'

'Yes. You're right. It was.' But his eyes were fixed on her face, and Catherine felt a moment halfway between pleasure and foreboding, though she couldn't for the life of her have worked out why.

Maybe it was because he had such a dangerous look about him, with his dark hair and his blue eyes and his mocking, lazy smile. He looked a bit like one of the fishermen who hauled up the nets on the beach every morning in those faded jeans and a white cotton shirt which was open at the neck. A man she would never see again. Why not indeed? 'Okay,' she agreed. 'Thanks.'

He waited until she had moved and settled in to the seat next to his, aware of a drift of scent which was a cross between roses and honey, unprepared for the way that it unsettled his senses, tiptoeing fingers of awareness over his skin. 'You still haven't told me your name.'

'It's Catherine. Catherine Walker.' She waited, supposing there was the faintest chance that Finn Delaney was an avid reader of *Pizazz!* magazine, and had happened to read her byline, but his dark face made no sign of recognition. Her lips twitched with amusement. Had she really thought that a man as masculine as this one would flick through a light-weight glossy mag?

'Good to meet you, Catherine.' He looked out to where the water was every shade of gold and pink and rose imaginable, reflected from the sky above, and then back to her, a careless question in his eyes. 'Exquisite, isn't it?' he murmured.

'Perfect.' Catherine, strangely disconcerted by that deep blue gaze, sipped her wine. 'It's not your first visit, I gather?'

Finn turned back and the blue eyes glittered in careless question. 'You've been checking up on me, have you?'

It was an arrogant thing to say, but in view of her occupation an extremely accurate one—except that in this case she had not been checking up on him. 'Why on earth should I want to? The waiter mentioned that you were a friend of Kirios Kollitsis, that's all.'

He relaxed again, his mind drifting back to a long-ago summer. 'That's right. His son and I met when we were travelling around Europe—we ended the trip here, and I guess I kind of fell in love with the place.'

'And—let me guess—you've come back here every year since?'

He smiled. 'One way or another, yes, I have. How about you?'

'First time,' said Catherine, and sipped her wine again, in case her voice wobbled. No need to tell him that it was supposed to have been a romantic holiday to make up for all the time that she and Peter had spent apart. Or that now they would be apart on a permanent basis.

'And you'll come again?'

'I doubt it.'

Her heard the finality in her voice. 'You don't like it enough to repeat the experience?'

She shook her head, knowing that Pondiki would always represent a time in her life she would prefer to forget. 'I just never like to repeat an experience. Why should I, when the world is full of endless possibilities?'

She sounded, he thought, as though she were trying to convince herself of that. But by then Nico had appeared. 'Do you know what you're going to have?' Finn asked.

'Fish and salad,' she answered automatically. 'It's the best thing on the menu.'

'You *are* a creature of habit, aren't you?' he teased. 'The same table and the same meal every night. Are you a glutton for stability?'

How unwittingly perceptive he was! 'People always create routines when they're on holiday.'

'Because there's something comforting in routines?' he hazarded.

His dark blue eyes seemed to look deep within her, and she didn't want him probing any more. That was *her* forte. 'Something like that,' she answered slowly.

She ordered in Greek, and Nico smiled as he wrote it down. And then Finn began to speak to him with what sounded to Catherine like complete fluency.

'You speak Greek!' she observed, once the waiter had gone.

'Well, so do you!'

'Only the basics. Restaurants and shops, that kind of thing.'

'Mine isn't much beyond that.'

'How very modest of you!'

'Not modest at all. Just truthful. I certainly don't speak it well enough to be able to discuss philosophy—but since what I know about philosophy could be written on the back of a postage stamp I'm probably wise not to try.' He gazed at her spectacular green eyes and the way the wine sheened on her lips. 'So tell me about yourself, Catherine Walker.'

'Oh, I'm twenty-six. I live in London. If I didn't then I'd own a dog, but I think it's cruel to keep animals in cities. I like going to films, walking in the park, drinking cocktails on hot summer evenings—the usual thing.'

As a brief and almost brittle biography it told him very little, and Finn was more than intrigued. Ask a woman to tell you about herself and you usually had to call time on them! And less, in some cases, was definitely more. His interest captured, he raised his eyebrows. 'And what do you do in London?'

She'd had years of fudging this one. People always tended to ask the same predictable question when they found out what she did: 'Have you ever met anyone famous?' And, although Finn Delaney didn't look a predictable kind of man, work was the last thing she wanted to think about right now. 'Public relations,' she said, which was *kind* of true. 'And how about you?'

'I live and work in Dublin.'

'As?'

Finn was deliberately vague. Self-made property millionaire sounded like a boast, even if it was true, and he had seen the corrupting power of wealth enough to keep it hidden away. Especially from beautiful women. 'Oh, I dabble in a bit of this and a bit of that.'

'Strictly legal?' she shot out instinctively, and he laughed.

'Oh, strictly,' he murmured, fixing her with a mock-grave look so that she laughed too. The laugh drew attention to the fact that she had the most kissable lips he had ever seen. He found himself wondering why she was here on her own.

His eyes skimmed to the bare third finger of her left hand. No sign of a ring, present or recent. He could see Nico bearing down on them, carrying their food, and he leant forward so that the scent of roses and honey invaded his nostrils.

'How long are you staying?' he questioned.

Still reeling from the pleasure of realising that she hadn't lost the ability to laugh, Catherine let her defences down—and then instantly regretted it. Because his proximity made her heart miss a beat she blinked, startled by her reaction to the warm bronzed flesh and dazzling blue eyes. Her emotions were supposed to be suspended, weren't they? She wasn't supposed to be feeling anything other than the loss of Peter. So how come desire had briefly bewitched her with its tempting promise? 'Tomorrow's my last day.'

Oddly enough, he felt disappointed. Had he hoped that she would be staying long enough for them to forge a brief holiday romance? He must be more stressed-out than he'd thought, if that were the case. 'And how are you planning to spend it? A trip round the island?'

She shook her head. 'Been there, done that. No, I'll probably just laze around on the beach.'

'I think I might join you,' said Finn slowly. 'That's if you don't have any objections?'

CHAPTER TWO

'I THINK I might join you,' he had said.

Catherine rubbed a final bit of sun-block onto her nose and knotted a sarong around the waist of her jade-green swimsuit, aware that her heart was beating as fast as a hamster's. She was meeting Finn Delaney on the beach and was now beginning to wonder whether she should have agreed so readily.

She let a rueful smile curve her lips. She was thinking and acting like an adolescent girl! She had broken up with her long-term boyfriend, yes—but that didn't mean she had to start acting like a nun! There was no crime in spending some time with an attractive, charismatic man, was there? Especially as she had barely any time left. And if Finn Delaney decided to muscle in on her she would politely give him the brush-off.

She scrunched her dark hair back into a ponytail and grabbed her sun-hat before setting off to find some coffee. The sun was already high in the sky, but the terrace was shaded with a canopy of dark, fleshy leaves and she took her seat, trying to imprint the scene on her mind, because tomorrow she would be back in the city.

'I see you with Kirios Finn last night,' observed Nico rather plaintively as he brought her a plate of figs and some strong black coffee. Every morning he tried something new to tempt her, even though she had told him that she never ate breakfast.

18

'That's right,' agreed Catherine. 'I was.'

'He like you, I think—he like beautiful women.'

Catherine shook her head firmly. 'We're just passing acquaintances who speak the same language,
that's all,' she said. 'I'm going home this afternoon—
remember?'

'You like him?' persisted Nico.

'I hardly know him!'

'Women like Finn Delaney.'

'I can imagine,' said Catherine wryly, thinking of
those compelling blue eyes, the thick, unruly hair and
the spectacular body. She might not be interested in
him as a man, but her journalistic eye could appreciate his obvious attributes.

'He brave man, too,' added Nico mournfully.

Catherine paused in the act of lifting her cup and
looked up. Brave was not a commonly used word,
unless someone had been sick, or fought in a war,
and her interest was aroused. 'How come?'

Nico pushed the figs into her line of vision. 'The
son of Kirios Kollitsis—he nearly die. And Kirios
Delaney—he save him.'

'How?'

'The two of them take scooters across the island
and Iannis, he crash. So much blood.' He paused. 'I
was young. They brought him here. The man from
Irlandia carry him in in his arms and they wait for
the doctor.' Nico narrowed his eyes in memory.
'Kirios Delaney had white shirt, but now it was red.'
And he closed his eyes. 'Red and wet.'

Oh, the power of language, thought Catherine, her
coffee forgotten. For some reason the stark words,
spoken in broken English, conjured up a far more
vivid impression of life and death than a fluent de-

scription of the accident could ever have done. She thought of the wet and bloody shirt clinging to Finn Delaney's torso and she gave a shiver.

'They say without Kirios Delaney then Iannis would be dead. His father—he never forget.'

Catherine nodded. No, she imagined that he wouldn't forget. A son's life saved was worth more than a king's ransom. But even if he hadn't acted as he had Finn Delaney was still an unforgettable man, she realised, and suddenly the casually arranged meeting on the beach didn't seem so casual at all.

She should have said no, she thought.

But her reservations didn't stop her from picking her way down the stone steps which led to the beach. When she had reached the bottom she stood motionless. And breathless.

The beach—a narrow ribbon of white bleached sand—was empty, save for Finn himself. His back was the colour of the sweetest toffee and the lean, hard body was wearing nothing but a pair of navy Lycra shorts. Catherine's mouth felt like dust and she shook herself, as if trying to recapture the melancholy of yesterday.

What the hell was the matter with her? Peter had been her life. Her *future*. She had never strayed, nor even looked at another man, and yet now she felt as though this dark, beautiful stranger had the power to cast some kind of spell over her.

He was lost in thought, looking out over the limitless horizon across the sea, but he must have heard or sensed her approach, for he turned slowly and Catherine suddenly found that she could not move. As if that piercing, blue-eyed stare had turned her to stone, like one of the statues which guarded Pondiki's tiny churches.

'Hi!' he called.

'H-hello,' she called back, stumbling uncharacteristically on the word. But didn't his voice sound even more sensual today? Or had the discovery that another man could set her senses alight made her view him in a completely different light?

Finn watched her, thinking how perfect she looked—as though she was some kind of beautiful apparition who had suddenly appeared and might just as suddenly fade away again. A faery lady. 'Come on over,' he said huskily.

Catherine found moving the most difficult thing she had ever had to do, taking each step carefully, one in front of the other, like a child learning how to walk.

Still, he watched her. No, no ghost she—far too vivid to be lacking in substance. The black hair was scraped back and barely visible beneath her hat, emphasising the delicate structure of her face, the wariness in the huge emerald eyes.

The swimsuit she wore was a shade darker than those eyes, and it clothed a body which was more magnificent than he had been expecting. The lush breasts looked deliciously cuppable, and the curve of her hips was just crying out for the lingering caress of a man's palm.

Realising that his heart was thundering like a boy's on the brink of sexual discovery, and aware that he must just be staring at her as if he'd never seen a woman before, Finn forced his mouth to relax into a smile as she grew closer.

'Hi,' he said again.

She felt strangely shy—but what woman wouldn't,

alone with such a man on a deserted beach? 'Hi.' She managed a bright smile. She wasn't a gauche young thing but a sophisticated and successful woman who was slowly recovering from a broken romance. And as soon as the opportunity arose she would tell him that she was interested in nothing more than a pleasant and companionable last day on Pondiki.

Finn smiled, so that those big green eyes would lose some of their wariness. 'Sleep well?'

She shook her head. 'Not really. Too hot. Even with the air-conditioning I felt as though I was a piece of dough which had been left in a low oven all night!'

He laughed. 'Don't you have one of those big old-fashioned fans in your room?'

'You mean the ones which sound as though a small plane has just landed beside the bed?'

'Yeah.' He wanted something to occupy himself, something which would stop him from feasting his eyes on her delicious breasts, afraid that the stirring in his body would begin to make itself shown. 'What would you like to do?'

The words swam vaguely into the haze of her thoughts. In swimming trunks, he looked like a pin-up come to life, with his bright blue eyes and dark, untidy hair.

Broad shoulders, lean hips and long, muscled legs. Men like Finn Delaney should be forbidden from wearing swimming trunks! More to distract herself than because she really cared what they did, she shrugged and smiled. 'What's on offer?'

Finn bit back the crazy response that he'd like to peel the swimsuit from her body and get close to her in the most elemental way possible. Instead, he waved a hand towards the rocks. 'I've made a camp,' he said conspiratorially.

'What kind of camp?'

'The usual kind. We've got shelter. Provisions. Come and see.'

In the distance, she could see a sun-umbrella, two loungers and a cool-box. An oasis of comfort against the barren rocks which edged the sand, with the umbrella providing the cool promise of relief from the beating sun. 'Okay.'

'Follow me,' he said, his voice sounding husky, and for a moment he felt like a man from earlier, primitive times, leading a woman off to his lair.

Catherine walked next to him, the hot sand spraying up and burning her toes through her sandals.

The sound of the sea was rhythmical and soothing, and she caught the faint scent of pine on the air, for Pondiki was crammed full of pine trees. Through the protective covering of her sun-hat she could feel the merciless penetration of the sun, and, trying to ignore the fact that all her senses felt acutely honed, she stared down instead at the sizeable amount of equipment which lay before her.

'How the hell did you get all this stuff down here?' she asked in wonder.

'I carried it.' He flexed an arm jokingly. 'Nothing more than brute strength!'

Memory assailed her. She thought of him carrying his wounded friend, his white shirt wet with the blood of life. Wet and red. She swallowed. 'It looks...it looks very inviting.'

'Sit down,' he said, and gestured to one of the loungers. 'Have you eaten breakfast?'

She sank into the cushions. She never ate breakfast,

but, most peculiarly, she had an appetite now. Or rather, other pervasive appetites were threatening to upset her equilibrium, so she decided to sublimate them by opting for food.

'Not yet.'

'Good. Me neither.'

She watched as he opened the cool-box and pulled out rough bread and chilled grapes, and local cheese wrapped in vine leaves, laying them down on a chequered cloth. With what looked like a Swiss Army knife he began tearing and cutting her off portions of this and that.

'Here. Eat.' He narrowed his eyes critically. 'You look like you could do with a little feeding up.'

She sat up and grabbed the crude sandwich and accepted a handful of grapes, preferring to look at the chilled claret-coloured fruit than meet that disturbing blue stare. 'You make me sound like a waif and stray!'

He thought she was perfect, but that now was neither the time nor the place to tell her. 'You look like you haven't eaten much lately,' he observed.

'I've eaten well on Pondiki,' she protested.

'For how long—two weeks, maybe?'

She nodded.

'But not before that, I guess,' he mused.

Well, of course she hadn't! What woman on the planet ate food when she had been dumped by a man? 'How can you tell?'

It gave him just the excuse he needed to study her face. 'Your cheeks have the slightly angular look of a woman who's been skipping meals.'

'Pre-holiday diet,' she lied.

'No need for it,' he responded quietly, his eyes glittering as he sank his teeth into the bread.

He made eating look like an art-form. In fact, he made eating look like the most sensual act she had ever seen—with his white teeth biting into the unresisting flesh of the grapes, licking their juice away with the tip of his tongue—and Catherine was horrified by the progression of her thoughts.

When she'd been with Peter she hadn't been interested in other men, and yet now she found herself wondering whether that had been because there had been no man like Finn Delaney around.

'This is very good,' she murmured.

'Mmm.' He gave her a lazy smile and relaxed back, the sun beating down like a caress on his skin. There was silence for a moment, broken only by the lapping of the waves on the sand. 'Will you be sorry to leave?' he asked, at last.

'Isn't everyone, at the end of a holiday?'

'Everyone's different.'

'I guess in a way I wish I could stay.' But that was the coward's way out—not wanting to face up to the new-found emptiness of her life back home. The sooner she got back, the sooner she could get on with the process of living. Yet this moment seemed like living. Real, simple and unfettered living, more vital than living had ever been.

Finn raised his head slightly and narrowed his eyes at her. 'Something you don't want to go back to?' he questioned perceptively. 'Or someone?'

'Neither,' she answered, because the truth was far more complex than that, and she was not the type of person to unburden herself to someone she barely knew. She had seen too much in her job of confidences made and then later regretted.

And she didn't want to think about her new role in life—as a single girl out on the town, having to reinvent herself and start all over again. With Peter away on assignments so much, she had felt comfortable staying in and slouching around in tracksuits while watching a movie and ploughing her way through a box of popcorn. She guessed that now those evenings would no longer be guilt-free and enjoyable. There would be pressure to go out with her girlfriends. And nights in would seem as though life was passing her by.

'I suppose I've just fallen in love with this island,' she said softly. Because that much was true. A place as simple and as beautiful as Pondiki made it easy to forget that any other world existed.

'Yeah.' His voice was equally soft, and he took advantage of the fact that she was busy brushing crumbs from her bare brown thighs to watch her again, then wished he hadn't. For the movement was making her breasts move in a way which was making him feel the heavy pull of longing, deep in his groin. He turned over onto his stomach. 'It's easy to do.'

Catherine removed a grape pip from her mouth and flicked it onto the white sand. 'And what about you? Will you be sorry to leave?'

He thought of the new project which was already mounting back home in Ireland, and the opposition to it. And of all the demands on his time which having his fingers in so many pies inevitably brought. When had he last taken a holiday? Sat in such solitude, in such simplicity and with such a—his heart missed another unexpected beat—such a beautiful companion? He pressed himself into the sand, ruefully observing his body's reaction to his thoughts and just hoping that she hadn't.

Her legs were slap-bang in front of his line of vision, and he let his lashes float down over his eyes, hoping that lack of visual stimulation might ease the ache in his groin. 'Yeah,' he said thickly. 'I'll be sorry.'

She heard the slurred quality of his voice and suspected that he wanted to sleep. So she said nothing further—but then silence was easy in such a perfect setting.

She feasted her eyes on the deep blue of the sea, and the paler blue of the sky above it. Remember this, she told herself. Keep it stored in your mind, to bring out on a grey wet day in England, as you would a favourite snapshot.

She flicked a glance over to where Finn lay, watching the rise and fall of his broad back as it became gradually slower and steadier. Yes, he was definitely asleep.

His dark tousled head was pillowed on hair-roughened forearms, and the image of the sleeping man was oddly and disturbingly intimate. Very disturbing. She found herself picturing his bronzed body contrasted against rumpled white sheets and the resulting flush of awareness made Catherine get abruptly to her feet. She needed to cool off!

The sea beckoned invitingly, and she pulled off her sun-hat and ran towards it, her feet sinking into the heavy wet sand by the water's edge. She splashed her way in, waiting until she was out of her depth before she began to strike out.

The sea was as warm as milk, and not in the least

bit invigorating, but the water lapped like silk over her heated skin. Catherine continued to swim quite happily in line with the shore, and was just thinking about going in when she experienced a gut-wrenchingly sharp spasm in her leg. She squealed aloud with the shock and the pain.

She tried to keep swimming, but her leg was stubbornly refusing to work. She opened her mouth to call out, but as she did salt water gushed in and she began to choke.

Don't panic, she told herself—but her body was refusing to obey her. And the more the leg stiffened, the more water poured into her mouth, and she began to flail her arms uselessly and helplessly as control slipped away...

Finn was lost in a warm world of sensation, inhabited by a green-eyed siren with a cascade of black hair, when his dream was punctured by a sound he could not recognise. His eyes snapped open to find Catherine gone.

Instinct immediately warned him of danger and he leapt to his feet, his blue eyes scanning the horizon until he saw the disturbed water and the thrash of limbs which told him that she was in the sea.

And in trouble.

He ran full-pelt into the sea, his muscular legs jumping the waves, breaking out into a powerful crawl which ate up the distance between them.

'Catherine!' he called. 'For God's sake, keep still— I'm on my way!'

She barely heard him, even though she registered the command somewhere in her subconscious. But her body was not taking orders from her tired and confused mind and she felt herself slipping deeper...

ever deeper…choking and gagging on the sour, salty taste.

'Catherine!' He reached her and grabbed hold of her, hauling her from beneath the surface and throwing her over his shoulder. He slapped the flat of his palm hard between her shoulder blades and she spat and retched water out of her mouth, sobbing with relief as she clung onto him.

'Easy now,' he soothed. 'Easy.' He ran his hands experimentally down over her body until he found the stiffened and cramped leg.

'Ouch!' she moaned.

'I'm going to swim back to shore with you. Just hold onto me very tightly.'

'You c-c-can't manage me!' she protested through chattering teeth.

'Shut up,' he said kindly, and turned her onto her back, slipping his arm around her waist.

Catherine had little memory of the journey back, or of much that followed. She remembered him sinking into the sand and lowering her gently down, and the humiliation of spewing up the last few drops of salt water. And then he was rubbing her leg briskly between his hands until the spasm ebbed away.

She must have dozed, for when she came to it was to find herself still on the sand, the fine, white grains sticking to her skin, leaning back against Finn's chest.

'You're okay?' he murmured.

She coughed, then nodded, a sob forming in her throat as she thought just how lucky she had been.

He felt her shudder. 'Don't cry. You'll live.'

She couldn't move. She felt as if her limbs had been weighted with lead. 'But I feel so…so *stupid*!' she choked.

'Well, you were a little,' he agreed gently. 'To go swimming straight after you'd eaten. Whatever made you do that, Catherine?'

She closed her eyes. She couldn't possibly tell him that the sight of his near-naked body had been doing things to her equilibrium that she had wanted to wipe clean away. She shook her head.

'Want me to carry you back to the lounger?'

'I'll w-walk.'

'Oh, no, you won't,' he demurred. 'Come here.' And he rose to his feet and picked her up as easily as if she'd been made of feathers.

Catherine was not the type of woman who would normally expect to be picked up and carried by a man—indeed, she had never been the recipient of such strong-arm tactics before. The men she knew would consider it a sexist insult to behave in such a way! So was it?

No.

And no again.

She felt so helpless, but even in her demoralised state she recognised that it was a pleasurable help-lessness. And the pleasure was enhanced by the sen-sation of his warm skin brushing and tingling against hers where their bodies touched. Like electricity.

'Finn?' she said weakly.

He looked down at her, feeling he could drown in those big green eyes, and then the word imprinted itself on his subconscious and he flinched. Drown. Sweet Lord—the woman could have *drowned*. A pain split right through him. 'What is it?' he whispered, laying her gently down on the sun-bed.

She pushed a damp lock of hair back from her face, and even that seemed to take every last bit of strength she had. But then it wasn't just her near escape which was making her weak, it was something about the way the blue eyes had softened into a warm blaze.

'Thank you,' she whispered back, thinking how inadequate those two words were in view of what he had just done.

A smile lifted the corners of his mouth as some of the tension left him.

Some.

'Don't mention it,' he said, his Irish accent edged with irresistible velvet. But he wished that she wouldn't look at him that way. All wide-eyed and vulnerable, with the pale sand sugaring her skin, making him long to brush each grain away one by one, and her lips slightly parted, as if begging to be kissed. 'Rest for a while, and then I'll take you back up to the hotel.'

She nodded, feeling strangely bereft. She would have to pack. Organise herself. Mentally gear herself up for switching back into her role of cool, intrepid Catherine Walker—doyenne of *Pizazz!* magazine. Yet the soft, vulnerable Catherine who was gazing up into the strong, handsome face of her rescuer seemed infinitely more preferable at that moment.

Peter? prompted a voice in her head. Have you forgotten Peter so quickly and replaced him with a man you scarcely know? Bewitched by the caveman tactics of someone who just happened to have an aptitude for saving lives?

She licked her bottom lip and tasted salt. 'You save a lot of lives, don't you, Finn Delaney?'

Finn looked at her, his eyes narrowing as her remark caught him off-guard. 'Meaning?'

She heard the element of caution which had crept

into his voice. 'I heard what you did for the son of Kirios Kollitsis.'

His face became shuttered. 'You were discussing me? With whom?'

She felt on the defensive. 'Only with Nico—the waiter. He happened to mention it.'

'Well, he had no right to mention it—it happened a long time ago. It's forgotten.'

But people didn't forget things like that. Catherine knew that *she* would never forget what he had done even if she never saw him again—and she very probably wouldn't. They were destined to be—to use that old cliché—ships that passed in the night, and, like all clichés, it was true.

He accompanied her back to the hotel, and she was glad of his supporting arm because her legs still felt wobbly. When he let her go, she missed that firm, warm contact.

'What time are you leaving?' he asked.

'The taxi's coming at three.'

He nodded. 'Go and do your packing.'

Catherine was normally a neat and organised packer, but for once she was reckless—throwing her holiday clothes haphazardly into the suitcase as if she didn't care whether she would ever wear them again. And she didn't. For there was an ache in her heart which seemed to have nothing to do with Peter and she despised herself for her fickleness.

She told herself that *of course* a man like Finn Delaney would inspire a kind of wistful devotion in the heart of any normal female. That *of course* it would be doubled or tripled in intensity after what had just happened. He had acted the part of hero, and there were too few of those outside the pages of romantic fiction, she told herself wryly. That was all.

Nevertheless, she was disappointed to find the small foyer empty, save for Nico, who bade her his own wistful farewell.

No, disappointment was too bland a word. Her heart actually lurched as she looked around, while trying not to look as though she was searching for anyone in particular. But there was no sign of the tall, broad-shouldered Irishman.

Her suitcase had been loaded into the boot of the rather ramshackle taxi, and Catherine had climbed reluctantly into the back, when she saw him. Swiftly moving through the bougainvillaea-covered arch, making a stunning vision against the riotous backdrop of purple blooms.

He reached the car with a few strides of those long legs and smiled.

'You made it?'

'Just about.'

'Got your passport? And your ticket?'

If anyone else had asked her this she would have fixed them with a wry look and informed them that she travelled solo most of the time, that she didn't need anyone checking up on her. So why did she feel so secretly pleased—protected, almost? 'Yes, I have.'

He ran his long fingers over the handle of the door. 'Safe journey, Catherine,' he said softly.

She nodded, wondering if her own words would come out as anything intelligible. 'Thanks. I will.'

'Goodbye.'

She nodded again. Why hadn't he just done the decent thing and not bothered to come down if that was all he was going to say? She tried to make light of it. 'I'll probably be stuck in the terminal until next week—that's if this taxi ever gets me there!'

He raised his dark brows as he observed the bonnet, which was attached to the car with a piece of string. 'Hmmm. The jury's out on that one!'

There was a moment's silence, where Catherine thought he was going to say something else, but he didn't. On impulse, she reached into her bag for her camera and lifted it to her eye. 'Smile,' she coaxed.

He eyed the camera as warily as he would a poisonous snake. 'I never pose for photos.'

No, she didn't imagine that he would. He was not the kind of man who would smile to order. 'Well, carry on glowering and I'll remember you like that!' she teased.

A slow smile broke out like the sun, and she caught it with a click. 'There's one for the album!'

He caught the glimpse of mischief in her green eyes and it disarmed him. He reached into the back pocket of his snug-fitting denims. He'd never had a holiday romance in his life, but...

'Here—' He leant forward and put his head through the window. She could smell soap, see the still-damp black hair and the tiny droplets of water which clung to it, making him a halo.

For one mad and crazy moment she thought that he was going to kiss her—and didn't she long for him to do just that? But instead he handed her a card, a thick cream business card.

'Look me up if ever you're in Dublin,' he said casually, smacking the door of the car as if it was a horse. The driver took this as a signal and began to rev up the noisy engine. 'It's the most beautiful city in the world.'

As the car roared away in a cloud of dust she clutched the card tightly, as if afraid that she might drop it, then risked one last glance over her shoulder. But he had gone. No lasting image of black hair and white shirt and long, long legs in faded denim.

Just an empty arch of purple blooms.

CHAPTER THREE

'CATHERINE, you look *fabulous*!'

Catherine stood in her editor's office, feeling that she didn't want to be there, but—as she'd told herself—it was her first day back at work after her holiday, so she was bound to feel like that. 'Do I?'

Miranda Fosse gave her a gimlet-eyed look. '*Do* you?' She snorted. 'Of course you do! Bronzed and stunning—if still a little on the thin side of slender!' She narrowed her eyes. 'Good holiday, was it?'

'Great.'

'Get Peter out of your system, did you?'

If Miranda had asked her this question halfway into the holiday Catherine would have bristled with indignation and disbelief. But the pain of losing Peter was significantly less than it had been. Significantly less than it should be she thought—with a slight feeling of guilt. And you wouldn't need to be an expert in human behaviour to know the reason why. Reasons came in different shapes and forms, and this one had a very human form indeed.

Catherine swallowed, wondering if she was going very slightly crazy. Finn Delaney had been on her mind ever since she had driven away from the small hotel on Pondiki, and the mind was a funny thing. How could you possibly dream so much and so vividly of a man you barely knew?

The only tangible thing she had of him was his

card, which was now well-thumbed and reclining like a guilty secret at the back of her purse.

'Got any photos?' demanded Miranda as she nodded towards the chair opposite her.

Catherine sat down and fished a wallet from her handbag. It was a magazine tradition that you brought your holiday snaps in for everyone else to look at. 'A few. Want to see?'

'Just so long as they're not all boring landscapes!' joked Miranda, and proceeded to flick through the selection which Catherine handed her. 'Hmmm. Beautiful beach. Beautiful sunset. Close-up of lemon trees. Blah, blah, blah—hang on.' Behind her huge spectacles, her eyes goggled. 'Well, looky-here! Who the hell is *this*?'

Catherine glanced across the desk, though it wasn't really necessary. No prizes for guessing that Miranda hadn't pounced on the photo of Nico grinning shyly into the lens. Or his brother flexing his biceps at the helm of the pleasure-cruiser. No, the tousled black hair and searing blue eyes of Finn Delaney were visible from here—though, if she was being honest, Catherine felt that she knew that particular picture by heart. She had almost considered buying a frame for it and putting it on her bedside table!

'Oh, that's just a man I met,' she said casually.

'*Just a man I met?*' repeated Miranda disbelievingly. 'Well, if I'd met a man like this I'd never have wanted to come home! No wonder you're over Peter!'

'I am *not* over Peter!' said Catherine defensively. 'He's just someone I met the night before I left.' Who saved my life. And made me realise that I *could* feel something for another man.

Miranda screwed her eyes up. 'He looks kind of familiar,' she mused slowly.

'I don't think so.'

'What's his name?'

'Finn Delaney.'

'Finn Delaney...Finn Delaney,' repeated Miranda, and frowned. 'Do I know the name?'

'I don't know, do you? He's Irish.'

Miranda began clicking onto the search engine of her computer. 'Finn Delaney.' A slow smile swiftly turned to an expression of glee. 'And you say you've never heard of him?'

'Of course I haven't!' said Catherine crossly. 'Why, what have you found?'

'Come here,' purred Miranda.

Catherine went round to Miranda's side of the desk, prepared and yet not prepared for the image of Finn staring out at her from the computer. It was clearly a snatched shot, and it looked like a picture of a man who did not enjoy being on the end of a camera. Come to think of it, he had been very reluctant to have *her* take his picture, hadn't he?

It was a three-quarter-length pose, and his hair was slightly shorter. Instead of the casual clothes he had been wearing in Pondiki, he was wearing some kind of beautiful grey suit. He looked frowning and pre-occupied—a million miles away from the man relaxing with his ouzo at the restaurant table with the dark, lapping sea as a backdrop.

'Has he got his own website, then?' Catherine asked, unable to keep the surprise out of her voice. He hadn't looked like that sort of person.

Miranda was busy scrolling down the page.

'There's his business one. This one is the Finn Delaney Appreciation Society.'

'You're kidding!'

'Nope. Apparently, he was recently voted number three in Ireland's Most Eligible Bachelor list.'

Catherine wondered just how gorgeous numbers one and two might be! She leant closer as she scanned her eyes down the list of his many business interests. 'And he has fingers in many pies,' she observed.

'And thumbs, by the look of it. Good grief! He's the money behind some huge new shopping complex with a state-of-the-art theatre.'

'Really?' Catherine blinked. He had certainly not looked in the tycoon class. Her first thought had been fisherman, her second had been pin-up.

'Yes, really. He's thirty-five, he's single and he looks like a fallen angel.' Miranda looked up. 'Why haven't we heard of him before?'

'You know what Ireland's like.' Catherine smiled. 'A little kingdom all of its own, but with no king! It keeps itself to itself.'

But Miranda didn't appear to be listening. Instead she was continuing to read out loud. '"Finn Delaney's keen brain and driving talent have led to suggestions that he might be considering a career in politics." Wow!' Her face took on a hungry look. 'Are you seeing him again, Catherine?'

'I—I hadn't planned to.' He had told her to drop by if ever she was in Dublin—but you couldn't really get more offhand than that, could you? Besides, if he had his very own appreciation society then she was likely to have to join a very long queue indeed!

'Did he ask you out?'

Catherine shook her head. 'No. He just gave me

his card and said to call by if I happened to be passing, but—'

'But?'

'I don't think I'll bother.'

From behind her spectacles Miranda's eyes were boring into her. 'And why not?'

'Millions of reasons, but the main one being that it's not so long since I finished with Peter. Or rather,' she corrected painfully, 'Peter finished with me. It went on for three years and I need to get over it properly.' She shrugged, trying to rid her mind of the image of black hair and piercing blue eyes and that body. Trying in vain to imprint Peter's there instead. 'A sensible person doesn't leap straight from one love affair to another.'

'No one's asking you to have a love affair!' exploded Miranda. 'Whatever happened to simple friendship?'

Catherine couldn't explain without giving herself away that a woman did not look at a man like Finn Delaney and think friendship. No, appallingly, her overriding thought connected with Finn Delaney happened to be long, passionate nights together. 'I'm not flying to Dublin to start a tenuous new friendship,' she objected.

'But this man could be a future prime minister of Ireland!' objected Miranda with unaccustomed passion. 'Imagine! Catherine, you *have* to follow it up! You're an attractive woman, he gave you his card— I'm sure he'd be delighted to see you!'

Catherine narrowed her eyes suspiciously. 'It isn't like you to play matchmaker, Miranda—you once said that single people gave more to their job! Why are you so keen for me to see Finn Delaney?'

'I'm thinking about our readers—'

Everything slotted into place. 'Then don't,' warned Catherine. 'Don't even *think* about it. Even if I was— even if I *was* planning to call in on him—there's no way that I would dream of writing up a piece about it, if that's the way your devious mind is working!'

Miranda bared her teeth in a smile. 'Oh, don't take things so seriously, girl! Why don't you just go?' she coaxed. 'Give yourself a treat for a change.'

'But I've only just got back from my holiday!'

'We can do a feature on the city itself—the whole world loves Dublin at the moment—you know it does! The single girl's guide! How about if we call it an assignment? And if you want to call in on Finn Delaney while you're there—then so much the better!'

'I'm not writing anything about him,' said Catherine stubbornly, even while her heart gave a sudden leap of excitement at the thought of seeing him again.

'And nobody's asking you to—not if you don't want to,' soothed Miranda. 'Tell our readers all about the shops and the restaurants and the bands and who goes where. That's all.'

That's all, Catherine told herself as her flight touched down at Dublin airport.

That's all, she told herself as she checked into the MacCormack Hotel.

That's all, she told herself again, as she lifted the phone and then banged it straight down again.

It took three attempts for the normally confident Catherine to dial Finn Delaney's number with a shaking finger.

First of all she got the switchboard.

'I'd like to speak to Finn Delaney, please.'

'Hold the line, please,' said a pleasantly spoken girl with a lilting Dublin accent. 'I'll put you through to his assistant.'

There were several clicks on the line before a connection was made. This time the female voice did not sound quite so lilting, and was more brisk than pleasant.

'Finn Delaney's office.'

'Hello. Is he there, please? My name is Catherine Walker.'

There was a pause. 'May I ask what it is concerning, Miss Walker?'

She didn't want to come over as some desperado, but didn't the truth *sound* a little that way? 'I met Finn—Mr Delaney—on holiday recently. He told me to look him up if I happened to be in Dublin and...' Catherine swallowed, realising how flimsy her explanation sounded. 'And, well, here I am,' she finished lamely.

There was a pause which Catherine definitely decided was disapproving, though she accepted that might simply be paranoia on her part.

'I see,' said the brisk voice. 'Well, if you'd like to hold the line I'll see if Mr Delaney is available...though his diary *is* very full today.'

Which Catherine suspected was a gentle way of telling her that it was unlikely the great man would deign to speak to her. Regretting ever having shown Miranda his photo, or having foolhardily agreed to get on a plane in the first place, she pressed the receiver to her ear.

Another click.

'Catherine?'

It was the lilting voice of honey pouring over shaved gravel which she remembered so well. 'Hi, Finn—it's me—remember?'

Of course he remembered. He'd remembered her for several sweat-sheened and restless nights. A few nights too long. And that had been that. He'd moved on, hadn't expected to hear from her again. Nor, it had to be said, had he particularly wanted to. The completion of one deal made room for another, and he had the devil of a project to cope with now. Finn dealt with his life by compartmentalising it, and Catherine Walker belonged in a compartment which was little more than a mildly pleasing memory. The last thing he needed at the moment was feminine distraction.

'Of course I remember,' he said cautiously. 'This is a surprise.'

A stupid, stupid surprise, thought Catherine as she mentally kicked herself. 'Well, you did say to get in touch if I happened to be in Dublin—'

'And you're in Dublin now?'

'I am.' She waited.

Finn leaned back in his chair. 'For how long?'

'Just the weekend. I…er…I picked up a cheap flight and just flew out on a whim.'

Maybe it wasn't the wisest thing in the world, but he could do absolutely nothing about his body's reaction. And his body, it seemed, reacted very strongly to the sound of Catherine Walker's crisp English accent, coupled with the memory of her soft, curved body pressed against his chest.

'And you want a guide? Am I right?'

'Oh, I'm quite capable of discovering a city on my

own,' answered Catherine. 'Your secretary said that you were busy.'

He looked at the packed page in front of him. 'And so I am,' he breathed with both regret and relief, glad that she hadn't expected him to suddenly drop everything. 'But I'm free later. How about if we meet for dinner tonight? Or are you busy?'

For one sane and sensible moment Catherine felt like saying that, yes, she was busy. Terribly busy, thank you very much. She need not see him, nor lay herself open to his particular brand of devastating charm. In fact, she could go away and write up Miranda's article, and...

'No, I'm free for dinner,' she heard herself saying.

He resisted a small sigh. She had been aloof on Pondiki, and that had whetted an appetite jaded by the acquiescence of women in general. For a man unused to having a woman say no to him, the novelty had stirred his interest. And yet here she was—as keen and as eager as the next woman.

But he thought of her big green eyes, hair which was as black as his own, and the small sigh became a small smile.

'Where are you staying?'

'MacCormack's.'

'I'll pick you up around seven.'

Catherine waited for him to say, Does that suit you? But he didn't. In fact, there was nothing further than a short, almost terse 'Bye' and the connection was severed.

She replaced the receiver thoughtfully. He sounded different. Though of course he would. People on holiday were less stressed, more relaxed. So was the fisherman with the lazy smile and sexy eyes simply a one-day wonder?

For her sanity's sake, she hoped so.

The morning she assigned to culture, and then she ate lunch in the requisite recommended restaurant. The rest of the afternoon she spent soaking up the city—marvelling at the shops in Grafton Street, studying the sparkling waters of the Liffey, just getting a feel for Ireland's beautiful capital city—before going back to the hotel to write up her copy.

It certainly has a buzz, she thought, as she reluctantly dragged her body from a bath which was filled right up to the top with scented bubbles.

She dressed with more care than usual. She wanted to appear all things. Demure, yet sexy. Casual, yet smart. To look as though she hadn't gone to any trouble, yet as though she'd stepped out from one of the pages of her own magazine! You ask too much of yourself, Catherine, she told herself sternly.

She decided on an ankle-length dress of cream linen, stark and simple, yet deliciously cut. Understated, stylish, and not designed to appear vampish. Not in the least.

Her black hair she caught up in a topknot, to show long jade earrings dangling down her neck, and at just gone seven she went down to the foyer with a fast-beating heart.

He wasn't there.

The fast beat became a slam of disappointment, and her mind worked through a tragic little scenario.

What if he had stood her up?

Well, more fool her for her impetuosity!

Catherine walked across the marbled space and

went to gaze at the fish tank. The exotic striped fish
swam in leisurely fashion around the illuminated waters, and she watched their graceful tails undulating
like a breeze on a cornfield. How uncomplicated life
as a fish must be, she thought.

'Catherine?'

She turned around, startled and yet not startled to
hear the rich Irish brogue which broke into her
thoughts, and there stood Finn Delaney—looking the
same and yet not the same. Some impossibly beautiful
and yet impossibly remote stranger. Which, let's face
it, she reminded herself, was exactly what he was.

He was dressed similarly to the shot she had seen
on the website, only the suit was darker. Navy. Which
somehow emphasised the blue of his eyes. And with
a silk tie, blue as well—almost an Aegean blue. The
tie had been impatiently pulled away from the collar
of his shirt so that it was slightly askew—and that
was the only thing which detracted from the formal
look he was wearing.

Even his hair had been cut. Not short—certainly
not short—but the dark, wayward black locks had
been tidied up.

Gone was the fisherman in the clinging, faded
denim and the gauze-thin shirt. And gone too was the
careless smile. Instead his luscious lips were curved
into something which was mid-way between welcoming and wary.

'Well, hi,' he murmured.

Oh, hell—if ever she'd wished she could magic
herself away from a situation it was now. What the
hell had possessed her to come? To ring him? To
arrange to meet him when clearly he was regretting

ever having handed her his wretched business card in the first place?

'Hi,' she said back, trying very hard not to let the rich Irish brogue melt over her.

He gave a little shake of his shoulders as he heard the faint reprimand in her voice. 'Sorry I'm late—I was tied up. You know how frantic Friday afternoons can be before the weekend—and the traffic was a nightmare.'

He was trotting out age-old excuses like an unfaithful husband! 'I should have given you my mobile number—then you could have cancelled.' She raised her eyebrows, giving him the opt-out clause. 'You still could.'

Finn relaxed, and not just because by offering to retreat she had made herself that little bit more desirable. No, the renewed sight of her had a lot to do with it. He *had* been regretting asking her to call by, but mainly because he hadn't imagined that she would. Not this soon.

Yet seeing her again reminded her of the heart-stopping effect she seemed to have on him. With an ache he remembered her in that stretchy green swim-suit, which had clung like honey to the lush curves of her breasts and hips. He remembered the heated cool of her flesh as the droplets of sea-water had dried on contact with his own. And the dark hair which had been plastered to her face, sticking to its perfect oval, like glue.

Yet tonight, in the spacious foyer of the up-market hotel, she couldn't have looked more different. She looked cool and untouchable and—perversely—all the more touchable just for that.

Her hair was caught back in some stark and sleek

style which drew attention to the pure lines of her features. The small, straight nose. The heart-shaped bow of a mouth which provoked him with its subtle gleam. High cheekbones which cast dark, mysterious shadows over the faintly tanned skin, and of course the enormous green eyes—fathomless as the sea itself.

'What? Turn you away when you've travelled so far?' he teased her mockingly.

She raised her eyebrows. 'From London, you mean, Finn? It's not exactly at the far end of the globe.'

'Is that so?' he smiled. 'Well, thanks for the geography lesson!'

His voice was so low and so rich and so beguiling that she thought he would instantly get a career in voice-overs if he ever needed money quickly. Though, judging by the information on the website, he wasn't exactly short of cash.

Reluctantly, she found herself smiling back. 'You're welcome.'

Finn's blue eyes gleamed. 'Do I take that to mean you don't want Finn Delaney's tour of Dublin's fair city?'

No. She meant that she was beginning to regret having come, but she understood exactly what had brought her so irresistibly. Or rather, who. In a plush Dublin hotel foyer Finn Delaney's attraction was no less potent than when he had hauled her flailing from the sea. When she had clung to his nearly naked body on a sun-baked Greek beach.

She swallowed. 'I thought we were having dinner. Not playing tourist.'

'Sure,' he said slowly. 'Are you hungry?'

'Starving.' It wasn't really the truth, nor even close

to it, but she was here now, and at least dinner would provide distraction techniques. She could busy herself with her napkin and sip at her wine and hope that the buzz of the restaurant would dilute his overpowering presence. Then maybe the evening would be quickly over and she could forget all about him.

'Then let's go.'

'Finn—'

The hesitant note in her voice stilled him. 'What?'

'You must let *me* buy *you* dinner.'

His eyes narrowed. 'Why?'

She shrugged awkwardly. Surely in some small way she could repay the debt she owed him, and in doing so give herself a legitimate reason for being here? 'I owe you. Don't forget, you saved my—'

'No!'

The single word cut across her stumbled sentence and in that moment she got an inkling of what it would be like to cross this man, was glad that she wouldn't.

'*I'm* buying dinner,' he said unequivocably. '*I* invited you and it's my territory.' His eyes narrowed. 'Oh, and Catherine—it was no big deal. You had a little cramp and I pulled you out of the water, okay? Let's draw a line under it and forget it, right?'

She wondered if there was anything more attractive than a modest hero, but she heard the determination which underpinned the deep voice and nodded her head with an obedience which was unusual for her. 'Right,' she agreed.

His face relaxed into a smile and his gaze was drawn to the direction of her feet. Flat heels, he noted. 'You wore sensible shoes, I see.'

He made her feel like Little Miss Frump! 'I didn't

wear spindly stilettos in case we were walking to the restaurant!' she returned.

'Good. Good because we are walking,' he replied evenly, though the thought of her wearing sexy high heels momentarily drove his blood pressure through the ceiling. 'Come on, let's go.'

They walked out into a warm summer evening, where the streets of Dublin were filled with people strolling with presumably the same purpose in mind.

'Have you booked somewhere?' asked Catherine.

Surely it would sound arrogant to say that he didn't need to? 'Don't worry, I've got us a table.'

He took her to St Stephen's Green—stunning and grand and as beautiful as anything Catherine had ever seen. And tucked away, almost out of sight of all the splendour, was a small restaurant whose lack of menu in the darkened windows spoke volumes for its exclusivity.

But they knew Finn Delaney, all right, and greeted him like the Prodigal Son.

'It's your first time here? In Ireland, I mean, and in Dublin in particular?' he asked, when they were seated at a window table which gave them a ringside seat for people watching. And people-watching was what Catherine normally loved to do. Normally. Except now she was finding her normal interest had waned and she was much more interested in watching just one person.

Trying not to, she shook her napkin out over her lap instead. 'Yes, it is.' Did he think she had flown out especially to see him? Some kind of explanation seemed in order. She shrugged. 'You said it was the most beautiful city in the world, and I thought I'd come and see for myself.'

He gave a low laugh. 'I'm flattered that you took my word for it.' Dark eyebrows were raised, and blue eyes sizzled into hers with a mocking question. 'And is it?'

'Haven't seen enough yet,' she said promptly.

'Haven't you?' His eyes were drawn to the curve of her breasts. 'Well, we'll have to see what we can do about that.'

CHAPTER FOUR

WHICH was how Catherine came to be sitting in Finn Delaney's sports-car late the following morning, with the breeze turning her cheeks to roses and the sky like a blue vault above her head.

'Don't forget to tie your hair back,' he had murmured as he had dropped her back at her hotel and bade her goodnight.

So she'd woven a ribbon into a tight French plait and was glad she had—because the wind from the open-top car would have left her hair completely knotted. A bit like her stomach.

'Where are we going?' she asked as she slid into the passenger seat beside him.

He turned the ignition key and gave a small smile. How cool she looked. And how perfect—with the amber ribbon glowing against her black hair. He couldn't remember the last time he had seen a grown woman tie a ribbon in her hair, and the result was a devastating combination of innocence and sensuality. 'To Glendalough. Ever heard of it?'

She shook her head. The way he said the name made it sound like music.

'Okay—here's your little bit of tourist information. It's a sixteenth-century Christian settlement about an hour outside Dublin—famous for its monastery. The name Glendalough comes from its setting—an idyllic valley in between two lakes.'

Idyllic.

Well, wasn't this idyllic enough? she wondered, casting a glance at the dark profile as he looked into his driving mirror.

Dinner had been bliss—there was no other way to describe it—though she supposed that this should have come as no surprise. Finn Delaney had been amusing, provocative, contentious and teasing, in turn. And if she had been expecting him to quiz her about her life and her loves and her career, she had—for once—been widely off the mark. He seemed more interested in the general rather than the specific.

Maybe that was a lucky escape—for she doubted whether he would have been so hospitable if he had discovered that she was a journalist. People had so many preconceived ideas about meeting journalists—usually negative—which was the main reason why Catherine had fallen into the habit of never revealing that she was a member of a despised tribe! At least, not until she got to know someone better.

No, it had been more like having dinner with the brightest tutor at university. Except that no tutor she had ever met looked quite as delectable as Finn Delaney. He had argued politics and he had argued religion.

'Both taboo,' she had remarked with a smile as she'd sipped her wine, though that hadn't stopped her from arguing back.

'Says who?'

'Says just about every book on social etiquette.'

'Who cares about etiquette?' he challenged, sizzling her with a provocative blue stare.

At which point she felt consumed by a feeling of desire so strong that it made her throat constrict with fear and guilt.

Surely it must be more than Finn himself that was having this effect on her? She'd met handsome, charming and successful men before—lots of them—but she couldn't remember ever being enticed quite so effectively.

And what about Peter? taunted the suddenly confused voice in her head. *Peter.* The man you expected to spend the rest of your life with.

Was the vulnerability which followed a break-up making her more susceptible than usual? Catherine squirmed uncomfortably in her seat, but Finn didn't appear to have noticed her self-consciousness.

Thank God.

Because he was looking at some squashy chocolate cake with a gleam of unfettered delight in the blue eyes.

'Wouldn't you just think that chocolate should carry a health warning?' he sighed.

'I thought it did—certainly if you eat too much of it!' She averted her eyes from the washboard-flat stomach.

He licked a melting spoonful with an instinctive sensuality which was making Catherine's stomach turn to mush.

'So everything in moderation, then? Is that right?' he observed softly, but the blue eyes were sparking with what looked like simple mischief.

'That wasn't what I said at all,' remarked Catherine tartly—but even so she could barely get her fork through her summer pudding.

Some men made deliberate remarks which were overtly sexual and which somehow made you end up being completely turned off by them. Whereas Finn made remarks which seemed to all intents and purposes completely innocent. So how come she didn't believe a word of the moderation bit? She'd bet that in the bedroom he was the least moderate person on the planet.

And Peter seemed a very long way away. In fact, the world seemed to have telescoped down into one place—and that was this place, with this man, eating a delicious dinner which was completely wasted on her...

The road to Glendalough passed through some of the most spectacular countryside that Catherine had ever seen.

'Oh, but this is glorious,' she sighed.

He shot her a faintly reproving glance. 'You sound surprised, but you shouldn't be. The beauty of Ireland is one of the best-kept secrets in the world. Didn't you know that, Catherine?'

And so were Ireland's men, if this one was anything to go by. 'I live to learn,' she said lightly.

And how he enjoyed teaching her, he thought, desire knifing through him in a way which made him put his foot down very hard on the accelerator.

She intrigued him, and he couldn't for the life of him work out why. Surely it couldn't *just* be a passing resemblance to a woman he had known so long ago that it now seemed like another lifetime. Or her cool, unflappable manner, or the way she parried his remarks with witty little retorts of her own, the way women so rarely did. But then, she did not know him, did she? Finn's reputation went before him in the land of his birth, and he was used to women—even intelligent ones—being slightly intimidated by that.

'Are you English?' he asked suddenly, as he slowed the car to a halt in Glendalough.

She turned to look at him. 'What an extraordinary question! You know I am!'

'It's that combination of jet hair and green eyes and pale skin,' he observed slowly. 'It isn't a typically English combination, is it?'

Catherine reached for her handbag, the movement hiding her face. Any minute and he would start asking her about her parentage, and she couldn't bear that. Not that she was ashamed—she wasn't. Of course she wasn't. But the moment you told someone that you might be descended from almost anyone but that you would never know—well, their attitude towards you changed. Inevitably. They pitied you, or looked at you with some kind of amazed horror, as if you were invariably going to be damaged by the circumstances of your upbringing.

'Oh, I'm a hybrid,' she said lightly. 'They always make for the most interesting specimens.' Her eyes met his in question. 'What about you, Finn?'

'Irish, true and true,' he murmured.

The expression in his eyes was making her feel rather dizzy, and her throat felt so dry that she had to force her words out. 'So when is my guided tour going to begin?'

'Right now.' He held the door of the car open, his hand briefly brushing against her bare forearm as he helped her out, feeling the shivering tension in response to the brief contact. Instinctive, he thought, and found his mind playing out wicked and tantalising scenes, wondering if she was an instinctive lover, if she gave and received pleasure in equal measure.

Through the backdrop of mountains she saw low streams with stepping-stone rocks, and Celtic crosses which were really burial stones. She stared hard at the primitive carvings.

'You don't like graves?' he quizzed, watching her reaction.

'Who does?' But the question still lay glinting in the depths of his blue eyes and she answered truthfully, even though it sounded a little fanciful. 'I guess that looking at them makes you realise just how short life is.'

'Yes. Very short.' And if his life were to end in the next ten minutes, how would he like to spend it? He stared at the lush folds of her lips and longed to feel them tremble beneath the hard, seeking outline of his. 'Let's walk for a while,' he said abruptly.

They walked until Catherine's legs ached, and she thought what a wimp living in a city had made her. Which just went to show that the machines at the gym were no substitute for honest-to-goodness exercise! 'Can we stop for a moment?' she asked breathlessly.

'Sure.'

They sat side by side on a large black rock in companionable silence and then he took her to a simple greystone building where refectory tables were laid out and lots of students sat drinking tea and eating big, buttered slices of what looked like fruitcake. It wasn't what she had been expecting.

'Ever eaten Champ?' he enquired, as they sat down.

She shook her head. 'What is it?' she asked.

'Potato.'

'Just potato?' She threw her head back and laughed. So much for eating out with a millionaire! 'You're giving me potato?'

He gave a slow smile. 'Well, no—there's chopped

shallots added, and it's served in a mound, and you melt a great big lump of butter in the centre. Try some.'

It was pure nursery food—warm and comforting, with a golden puddle of butter seeping into the creamy mashed potato.

'It's good,' said Catherine, as she dipped her fork into it.

'Isn't it?' Their eyes met in a long, unspoken moment. 'Where would the Irish be without the humble potato?'

'Where indeed?' she echoed, thinking how uncomplicated life felt, sitting here with him. For a moment all the stresses of Catherine's London life seemed like a half-remembered dream. There was a sense of timelessness in this place which seemed to give her a sense of being of this world and yet not of it.

And Finn seemed timeless, too—his clever eyes watching her, the tension in his body hinting at things she would prefer not to think about. Their mouths were making words which passed for conversation, but seemed so at odds with the unspoken interaction which was taking place between them.

After she had drunk a cup of tea as black as tar itself he leaned across the table towards her, smelling not of fancy aftershave but of soap and the undeniable scent of virile male.

'Would you like to see the Wicklow Bay?' he asked softly.

If he'd promised to show her the end of the rainbow she would have agreed to it at that precise moment. 'Yes, please.'

They drove through countryside as green as all the songs said it was, until Finn drew to a halt next to a spectacular seascape and switched the engine off. 'Let's get out. You can't appreciate it properly from here.'

They stood in silence for a moment, watching and listening as the waves crashed down onto the beach.

'There,' he murmured. 'What do you think to that?'

She thought of the view from her bedroom window back in Clerkenwell and how this paled in comparison. 'Oh, it's stunning!'

'But not a patch on Greece?'

She shook her head. 'On the contrary—it's just as beautiful. But wilder. More elemental.' Just like him, she thought, stealing a glance at him.

He stood like an immovable figurehead as he gazed out to sea, the wind whipping his black hair into dark little tendrils. He turned to look at her and something in the uninhibited pleasure in her eyes quite took his breath away.

'So, do you have a sense of adventure, Catherine?' he murmured.

'Why do you ask?'

'I'll guess you haven't been in the sea since your holiday?'

'Well, no. There isn't a lot of it in London!'

'And you know what they say about getting straight back on a horse after it's thrown you?'

'Just what are you suggesting, Finn?'

His eyes burned into her.

'Shall we let the waves catch us between the toes as we sink into the sand?' he asked, in a lilting voice. 'Take our shoes off and walk on the edge?'

It sounded unspeakably sensual, and unbelievably echoed the way she was feeling right then. On the edge. Yes. But the edge of what she didn't know.

'And you call *that* being adventurous?' she teased, because at least that way she could disguise the sudden helplessness she was experiencing. 'What a boring life you must have led!'

And she kicked off her sandals and took them in her hand, leaving her legs bare and brown as she looked at him with a touch of defiance. 'Come on, then! What are you waiting for?'

He was waiting for the ache in his groin to subside, but he gave a wry smile as he bent to roll his jeans up, wondering how she would react if he said what was *really* on his mind. That she might like to slip that dress right off, and her bra and panties, too, and go skinny-dipping with him and let him make love to her in the icy water? God, yes! Now that really *would* be adventurous!

Then he drew himself up, appalled. He didn't have sex in public with women he barely knew!

She ran ahead of him, wanting to break the sudden tight tension, and the sea was icy enough to achieve that. 'Yeow!' she squealed, as frothy white waves sucked up between her toes and rocked her. 'I'm going back!'

'*Now* who's the unadventurous one?' He held out his hand to her. 'Here.'

Feeling suddenly shy, she took it as trustingly as a child would, safe and secure in that strong, warm grasp. But a child would not have had a skittering heart and a dry mouth and a fizzing, almost unbearable excitement churning away inside her, surely?

'Blowing the cobwebs away?' he asked, as they retraced their steps.

'Blown away,' she answered. And so was she. Completely.

Her hand was still in his, and he guessed that to the eyes of an outsider they would look like a pair of lovers, killing time beautifully before bed.

He moved fractionally closer and whispered into her ear, as if afraid that the words might be lost on the wind. His whole world seemed to hinge on his next question and what her response to it would be. 'Would you like to see where I live, Catherine?'

She jerked her head back, startled. 'What. Now?'

He had not planned to say it. He kept his home territory notoriously private, like a jungle cat protecting its lair. In fact, he had thought no further than a scenic trip to Glendalough. But something about her had got beneath his skin.

He raised his eyebrows at her questioningly. 'Why not?' He looked at the goosebumps on her bare legs and arms and suppressed a small shiver as the tension began to build and mount in his body. 'You're cold. You look like you could do with some warming up.'

Catherine supposed that the drawled suggestion could have sounded like a variation on Come up and see my etchings, but somehow the rich, Irish brogue made it sound like the most wonderful invitation she'd ever heard.

He was right—she *was* cold. And something else, too. She was slowly fizzing with a sense of expectation and excitement—her nerve-endings raw and on fire with it.

Not the way that Catherine Walker normally behaved, but—so what? Surely it was just natural and acceptable curiosity to want to see his home? At least, that was what she told herself as she heard herself replying, 'Yes, I'd like that, Finn. I'd like that very much.'

CHAPTER FIVE

'SO THIS is where you live, is it?' asked Catherine, rather stupidly stating the obvious and wondering if she sounded as nervous as she suddenly felt.

What was she doing here, alone in a strange flat with this gorgeous black-haired and blue-eyed Irishman? Setting herself up for some kind of seduction scene? Waiting for Finn to put his arms around her and kiss her? To discover whether that kiss would really be as wonderful as she'd spent far too much time imagining?

And isn't that what you really want? questioned a rogue voice inside her head. Isn't that why your heart is pumping in your chest and your cheeks are on fire, even though you're supposedly cold?

Finn smiled. 'I bought it for the view.' But he wasn't looking out of the window.

'I can see why.' She swallowed, tearing her eyes away from that piercing sapphire gaze with difficulty.

The lit-up Georgian buildings in the square outside predominated, but she could see the sparkle of the Liffey, too, reflecting the darkening sky and the first faint gleam of the moon.

'Shall I make you something warm to drink?' he questioned softly.

She smiled. 'The cold's all gone.'

The walls of his huge flat seemed to be closing in on him, and he knew that if he didn't move he might do something both of them would regret. 'Then come outside, onto the terrace—you can see for miles.' He unlocked a door which led out onto a plant-filled balcony. 'The moon is huge tonight. Big as a golden dinner-plate and fit for a king.'

She thought how Irishmen had the ability to speak romantically without it detracting one iota from their masculinity. And he hadn't lied about the moon. It dazzled down on them. 'It looks close enough to touch,' whispered Catherine.

'Yes.' And so did she.

She forced herself to look at the pinpricks of silver stars, to listen to the muted sound of the city, knowing all the while that his eyes were on her, and eventually she turned to face the silent, brooding figure.

'It's lovely,' she said lamely.

'Yes.' He narrowed his eyes as he saw her shiver. 'You're cold again?'

'Yes. No. Not really.'

'Coffee,' he said emphatically. But he could see the tremble of her lips, and the tension which had slowly been building up inside him suddenly spilt over into the realisation that he could no more walk out into his kitchen and make her some coffee than he could resist what he was about to do next. 'But it's not coffee you want, is it, Catherine?' he questioned, and pulled her gently into his arms. 'Is it?'

Her world spun out of focus and then clicked back into perfection. 'Finn!' she said breathlessly. 'Wh-what do you think you're doing?'

He laughed softly at the predictable question, noting in a last moment of sanity that there was no reproach in it. 'Just this. What you want me to do. What those big green eyes of yours have been asking me to do from the moment I met you.' And he lowered his mouth, brushing his lips against the sudden wild tremble of hers.

She swayed against him, opening her mouth to his and feeling as though she had been born for this kiss, thinking that nothing had ever felt quite like this— not even with Peter.

Is this what all the books and magazines write about? she wondered dazedly. Is this why *Pizazz!* has such a massive and growing readership?

'Oh, Finn. Finn Delaney,' she breathed against the warmth of his breath, and the kiss went on and on and on.

He lifted his mouth away by a fraction, seeing the look on her face and feeling pretty dazed himself. As though he had drunk a glass of champagne very quickly, and yet he had drunk nothing stronger than tea. 'You were born to be kissed, Catherine,' he observed unsteadily.

'Was I?' she questioned, with equally unsteady delight.

'Mmm.' He pulled a pin from her hair so that it tumbled free, black as the sky above them. 'To be made love to beneath the stars, with the light of the moon gilding your skin to pure gold.'

'I've never been made love to beneath the stars,' she admitted, without shyness.

He smiled as he took her hand, raised it to his lips, his eyes unreadable. 'It's too cold out here, but you can see them from my bedroom.'

She didn't remember making any assent, only that her hand was moved from his mouth to his hand and that he was leading her through the splendour of his Georgian flat into his bedroom.

'See,' he said softly, and pointed to the huge windows where outside the night sky dazzled.

'It's like the London Planetarium!' she said. 'You're very lucky.'

'Very,' he agreed, but both of them knew he wasn't talking about the stars. 'You're a long way away, Catherine.'

'A-am I?'

'Yes, indeed. Come here.'

She knew a moment's apprehension as she walked straight into his arms. And now she *could* see his eyes, and read the hectic glitter in their velvet blue. What in the world was she *doing*?

But by then he was sliding the zip of her dress down in one fluid movement, as if he had done such a thing many, many times before. And Catherine supposed that he had.

'I should feel shy,' she murmured.

'But you don't?'

'You've seen me with less on than this.'

But underwear was always a million times more decadent than a bikini, however brief. 'So I have,' he agreed thickly, as he surveyed her lace-clad body. 'Only this looks a whole lot better.'

He bent his head to touch his lips against the tip of one breast which strained impatiently against the flimsy lace of her brassière.

And Catherine closed her eyes, giving herself up to sensation instead of thought. A soft, sweet aching overwhelmed and startled her, and she wound her arms tightly around his neck, as if afraid that he might suddenly disappear. As if this—and him—might be all some figment of a fevered longing. 'Oh, Finn,' she sighed.

He lifted his head and looked at her questioningly. 'Should we be doing this?' Her green eyes opened very wide.

He felt like saying that this was something she should have asked herself earlier than now, that his body was growing unbearably hard.

'That's up to you, sweetheart.' His mouth immediately stopped grazing the long line of her neck, the restraint nearly killing him. 'It's make-your-mind-up time. Stop me if that's what you want.'

Was he aware that he was asking the impossible?

'Do you want to?' he murmured.

'God, no. No,' she breathed. A thousand times no. She moved her mouth to rove over the rough shadow of his chin, her hands on the broad bank of his shoulders for support, her knees threatening to buckle.

He gave a low, uneven laugh as the moonlight shafted through the window and illuminated the ebony strands of her hair. Her undisguised need only fuelled him further, and he gave in to the overwhelming desire to possess her. His hand reached round to snap open her brassière, as though they were old and familiar lovers, and she clung to him wearing nothing but a tiny little thong.

'I want to make love to you, Catherine,' he said urgently.

She didn't reply, just burrowed her hands beneath his sweater, finding the silken skin there, her fingernails tracing faint lines against it, hearing him suck in a ragged breath.

'I want to make love to you,' he repeated. 'Come to bed.' He didn't wait for an answer, just led her over to the king-sized canopied bed and pulled back the cover. 'Get in, sweetheart,' he instructed shakily. 'You're shivering.'

Shivering? She felt in a fever of need, was glad to slip beneath the duvet—glad for its protection and for the opportunity to watch him throw his clothes carelessly to the floor, until he was completely and powerfully naked. All golden skin and dark shadows and hewn, strong limbs.

'Move over,' he whispered as he climbed in beside her, encountering the soft folds of her flesh, and he moved to lie over her. 'No, on second thoughts,' he drawled as the warmth of her body met his, 'stay exactly where you are.'

'Are you asleep?'

Finn opened his eyes. No, he hadn't been asleep. He had been lying there, alternating between revelling in the sated exhaustion of his flesh and wondering what the hell he had done. 'Not any more.' He yawned.

'Did I wake you?' She wondered if that sounded defensive, and then swiftly made up her mind that she was not going to lie around analysing what had happened. He had made love to her and she had enjoyed it. More than enjoyed it. End of story in this modern age. Not well-thought-out, not necessarily wise, but it had happened, and there was no point in trying to turn the clock back and regret it.

Finn smiled, his reservations banished by the sight of her wide green eyes and the dark, dark hair which tumbled down in disarray over her lush, rose-tipped breasts. He gave a rueful glance down at his already stirring body. 'Kind of.'

Catherine swallowed as she saw the involuntary

movement beneath the thin sheet and felt an answering rush of a warmth. Oh, God! How did he make
her feel the way he did? And then she looked at him,
every glorious pore of him, and the answer was there,
before her eyes.

To her horror she found herself asking the worst
question since the beginning of time. 'So how come
you've never married, Finn?'

He repressed a sigh. Silent acquiescence was what
his chauvinistic heart most longed for. He reached
and pulled her down against his bare chest. 'Is that a
proposal?' he teased. 'Because surely it's a little early
for that kind of thing?'

She felt her breasts pressing against him, but suddenly she wanted more than this. She had spent the
night making love to him. She knew his body. But
what did she know of the man himself? He might
have made her cry out his name time and time again,
but a girl had her pride.

'Are you always so evasive?' she teased.

'I am when my mind is on other things. Like now.'

'Finn!'

'Mmm?'

He was stroking her bottom now, running the flat
of his hand over it with the appreciation that a horse-
lover might give to a particularly prize filly. And
though her mind began to form a protest it was too
late, because he had slid his fingers right inside her
still-sticky warmth.

Her eyes opened very wide. 'Finn!' she said again,
only she could hear the helpless pleasure in her own
voice.

'What?'

'Stop it.'

'You don't want me to stop it.'

'Yes, I do!'

'Then why are you moving your hips like that?' he purred suggestively as his fingers continued to stroke and play with her.

'You know damned well why!' she moaned, feeling the sweet tension building, building.

'Still want me to stop?' He stilled his hand and looked at her half-closed eyes and parted lips.

She shook her head wildly. 'No!' she whimpered, and just the renewed touch of him was enough to make her splinter into a thousand ecstatic pieces.

He thrust into her warm, still-tight flesh, the sensation nearly blowing his mind, and his last thought before the earth spun on its axis was that nothing had ever felt this good. Nothing. He felt the violent beckoning of sweet release just as he heard her give another choked moan of disbelief, and then his blood thundered and he moaned.

She rolled off his sweat-sheened body and collapsed on the bed beside him. It took a moment for her breath to return to anything approaching normality. 'Wow,' she said eventually.

'Wow, indeed,' he echoed drily. But he felt shaken. Was it simply *because* they were virtual strangers that their lovemaking had been the best of his life? He stared sightlessly at the ceiling.

And now what? Catherine dozed for a moment or two, then opened her eyes again. 'I guess I'd better think about going.' She held her breath almost imperceptibly, wondering whether he would beg her to stay. She gave a half-smile. No, not beg. Men like Finn Delaney didn't beg—didn't ever *need* to beg, she would hazard.

'Must you?' he questioned idly.

Well, there she had it in a nutshell. He wasn't exactly kicking her out of bed, but neither was he working out a busy timetable for the rest of the day.

''Fraid so,' she fibbed. 'I have a plane to catch.'

'What time?'

'Five o'clock.'

He glanced at the wristwatch he had had neither the time nor the inclination to remove last night. 'It's only ten now.'

And?

'You'll have some breakfast first?' He turned onto his side and gave a slow smile. 'I make great eggs!'

He made great love, too. But she was damned if she was going to go through his thanks-very-much-for-the-memory routine. Dispatched with eggs and a shower, and perhaps another bout of uninhibited sex if she was lucky. Catherine Walker might have behaved recklessly last night, but at least she still had her pride.

And no way was she going to hang around like an abandoned puppy, desperate for affection!

'I'll skip,' she said casually, and slid her bare legs over the mattress. 'I never eat breakfast.'

'You should,' he reprimanded.

Perhaps she should. Like perhaps she should have thought twice about allowing herself to get into a situation like this.

'Coffee will be fine. Mind if I use the shower?'

'Of course not.'

How bizarre to be asking his permission for something like that when she had allowed him the total freedom of her body during that long and blissful night.

Had she just been feeling love-starved and re-jected? she wondered as she stood beneath the steam-ing jets of water in his typically masculine bathroom. And how often did he entertain women in such a spontaneous and intimate way?

It was a one-off for *her*, sure—but maybe she was just one of a long line of willing women who were so easily turned on by his captivating blend of Irish charm and drop-dead sexuality.

Catherine repressed a shudder as she dried herself. She didn't want to know.

She came out of the bathroom looking as cool and as aloof as a mannequin, and Finn blinked. To look at her now you would never have believed that she could be such a little *wildcat* in bed. He felt another tug of desire and despaired.

Catherine picked up her bag and went over to where he was standing by the window, watching her with an unreadable expression. She wondered how many hearts he had broken in his time. Scores, un-doubtedly—but hers would not be among them. She would extricate herself as gracefully and as graciously as possible.

'What about coffee?' He frowned.

She shook her head. She would not cling. Last night had just happened; she must put it down to ex-perience. And at least, she thought wryly, at least it had got Peter well and truly out of her system. 'I'll get some back at my hotel.' She gave him what she hoped was a cool, calm smile. 'Thanks for a great evening, Finn.' She raised herself up on tiptoe to kiss his cheek. 'A great night, I should say,' she added, braving it out.

'The pleasure was all mine,' he murmured.

Ruthlessly, she eradicated any trace of awkwardness or vulnerability from her voice, but it wasn't easy—not when confronted by the glittering blue eyes which reminded her of things which were making her pulses race. Even now. 'Bye, then.'

Once again her coolness intrigued him, particularly in view of what had happened—she was behaving as though she had just been introduced to him at a formal drinks party! Maybe she was trying to slow the pace down, and in view of the speed with which things had happened wasn't that the best thing to do under the circumstances? So why did he want to drag her straight back to bed?

He was just about to suggest running her back to her hotel when the telephone began to ring. He gave a small click of irritation.

'Answer it,' she urged, as this evidence of a life of which she knew nothing drove reality home. She was eager now to make her escape, to put it all down to a wonderful never-to-be-repeated experience.

'Don't worry, it's on the Ansaphone—'

It was also echoing out over the flat, and after his drawled and lilting message came the sound of a female voice. 'Finn, it's Aisling—where the hell were *you* last night?'

He leaned over and clicked off the machine, but by then Catherine was by the door, her features closed and shuttered.

'Look me up if ever you're in London,' she said, and walked out without a backward glance. She wondered who Aisling was, and where he was supposed to have been last night, before telling herself that her behaviour guaranteed nothing other than a night to remember—certainly not the right to question him.

Finn stood staring after her for a long, indefinable moment as the sound of the lift outside whirred into action, taking her out of his life just as quickly as she had burst into it.

And it occurred to him that he didn't have a clue where she lived.

CHAPTER SIX

CATHERINE spent the whole evening pacing the flat, tempted to smoke a cigarette—which she hadn't done in almost three years now. She kept telling herself that it had been out of character. True. Telling herself that it had been a terrible, terrible mistake. But unfortunately the jury was still out on that one.

Because the mind could play all kinds of tricks on you, and at the moment her mind seemed very fond of sending tantalising images of black hair, a bare, bronzed body and a pair of beautiful, glittering blue eyes. Images which kicked her conscience into touch.

She didn't want to think about him! Not when there was no future in it—and there was definitely no future in it. He hadn't exactly been distraught at the thought of her leaving, had he? Demanding to know her phone number and asking when he could fly out to London to see her?

But what did she expect? The pay-off for acting on instinct rather than reason was never going to be love and respect.

She forced herself to go through her photo albums and look at pictures of her and Peter, but instead of pain ripping through her there was merely a kind of horrified acceptance that Finn had been able to transport her to realms of fantasy which Peter never had.

So what did that say about their long-standing relationship? More importantly, what did it say about *her*?

She had only just sat down at her desk on Monday when there was a telephone call from Miranda.

'Can you get up here right now, Catherine? I want to talk to you about Dublin.'

'Sure,' answered Catherine, in a voice which was made calm only by sheer effort of will. 'I've written the piece.'

'Never mind about that,' Miranda answered mysteriously. 'Just get your butt up here!'

There was a quivering air of expectancy and excitement on the editor's face.

'Did you meet him?'

'Who?'

'Who? *Who?* Finn Delaney, of course!'

'Oh, him,' answered Catherine with monumental calm, though inside her heart was crashing painfully against her ribcage. She wondered what Miranda would say if she told her that she had spent most of her time in Dublin being made love to by Finn Delaney. Not a lot, most probably. Miranda had been a journalist for long enough not to be shocked by *anything*. Her throat felt too dry for her to be able to speak, but she managed. 'Er, yes, I saw him. Why?'

'And did he seem interested in you? I mean, like, *really* interested in you?'

It wasn't just the odd way that the last question was phrased, or that it was mildly inappropriate. No, something in Miranda's tone alerted Catherine to the fact that this was not simply idle curiosity, and she felt the first whispering of foreboding. She played for time. 'Interested in what way, exactly?'

Miranda snorted. 'Don't be so dense, Catherine— it doesn't suit you! Sexually. Romantically. Whatever you like to call it.'

'No comment.' But Catherine gave it away with the deep blush which darkened her cheeks.

Miranda looked even more excited. Everyone in the business knew what 'no comment' meant and immediately Catherine could have kicked herself for saying it. It implied guilt, and guilt was pretty close to what she was feeling.

'So he was?' observed Miranda.

'No!'

'I'd recognise that look on a woman's face anywhere—'

'What look?' asked Catherine, alarmed.

'That cat-got-the-cream look. The kind of look which speaks volumes about just how you spent your weekend!'

'Just leave it, Miranda, won't you?' Suddenly Catherine was feeling flustered, out of her depth. Her boss was the last person to make a value judgement about her behaviour, but what about the way she was judging *herself*? 'I don't want to talk about it!'

'Well, let me show you something,' said Miranda slowly, and picked up a clutch of photos which were lying on her desk, 'which might just change your mind.'

'If it's photos of Finn, you've already shown me—remember? I know he's loaded, and I know he's powerful and the next-best thing to sliced bread, but if you're looking for a kiss-and-tell story then you're wasting your time, Miranda.'

'No—look,' said Miranda with unusual brevity, and handed her one of the photos.

Catherine stared at it, and her blood ran cold as time seemed to suspend itself.

For it was like looking into a mirror. Seeing herself,

only not quite seeing herself. The same and yet remarkably different. She blinked. The woman in the photo had jet-black hair and huge green eyes, and a certain resemblance around the mouth, but there the similarities ended.

It was like comparing a piece of crude mineral deposit to the finished, highly polished diamond it would one day become.

Because the woman in the photo had all the pampered glamour of someone who spent absolute riches on herself. Someone who indulged, and indulged, and indulged.

'Who is this?' breathed Catherine.

'Deirdra O'Shea,' said Miranda instantly. 'Heard of her?'

'N-no.'

'Bit before your time, I guess—though I'd only vaguely heard of her myself. She's Irish—well, the name speaks for itself, doesn't it?—starred in a couple of forgettable films about ten years ago and has been living in Hollywood trying to make it big ever since but never quite managing it. She's your spitting image, isn't she?'

Something close to fear was making breathing suddenly very difficult. 'Why are you bothering to show me this?'

Miranda shrugged, and thrust another photo into Catherine's frozen fingers. 'Just that she was Finn Delaney's sweetheart.'

It was a curiously old-fashioned word to use, especially about a man like Finn, and it hurt Catherine more than it had any right to. 'What do you mean, his *sweetheart*?'

'He was smitten, apparently—completely and utterly smitten. They met before either of them had really made it—and you know what that kind of love is like. Fierce and elemental. Love without the trappings.' Miranda sighed, sounding for a moment almost wistful. 'The real thing.'

'I still don't understand what this has got to do with me!' said Catherine crossly, but she was beginning to get a very good idea.

'He's a notoriously private man, right?'

Catherine shrugged. 'Apparently.'

'Yet he meets you on a Greek island and tells you to look him up.'

'Lots of people do things like that on holiday.'

'And you fly out there and have some kind of red-hot weekend with him—'

'I didn't say that!'

'You didn't have to, Catherine—like I said, I can read it all over your face.' Miranda paused. 'Are you seeing him again?'

Now she felt worse than reckless—she felt stupid, too. 'I—hadn't—planned to.'

'He didn't ask you?'

No, he hadn't asked her. The truth slammed home like a blunt fist and defensiveness seemed her only rational form of protection. 'Miranda—what the hell is this all about? Some kind of Spanish Inquisition?'

'All I'm saying is that if he used you as some kind of substitute for the woman who broke his heart—'

Catherine opened her mouth to say that it wasn't like that. But what *had* it been like, then? He hadn't struck her as the kind of man who would normally make mad, passionate love to a complete stranger. A notoriously private man...

So what could have been his motivation?

She, at least, could blame her reeling emotions on having been dropped by Peter. But—dear God—had Finn Delaney spent the whole time imagining that she was *someone else*?

Her ego, already severely punctured, underwent a complete deflation.

When he'd told her she was beautiful, and how it was a crime against society for a body like hers to be seen wearing any clothes at all, had he been thinking about Deirdra? When he'd driven deep inside her, had he been pretending that it was another woman's soft flesh he was penetrating?

Inwardly she crumpled as she realised just what she had done. But most of all what *he* had done. He had used his Irish charm in the most manipulative and calculating way imaginable. He had guided her into his bed with all the ease of a consummate seducer, had made love to her and then let her walk out of his flat without a care in the world.

He hadn't even asked for her phone number, she remembered bitterly.

She came out of her painful little reverie to find Miranda's eyes fixed on her thoughtfully—with something approaching kindness in them. And Catherine was badly in need of a little kindness right then.

'Why don't you tell me all about it?' Miranda suggested softly.

Maybe if she'd eaten breakfast, or maybe if her body hadn't still been aching with the sweet memories of his lovemaking which now seemed to mock and wound her, then Catherine might have given a more thoughtful and considered response.

But memories of betrayal—her mother's and now

her own—fused into a blurred, salty haze before her eyes, and she nodded, biting her lips to prevent her voice from disintegrating into helpless sobs.

'Oh, Miranda!' she gulped. 'I've been so stupid.'

'Do you want to tell me what happened?'

She needed to tell *someone* about it. To unload her guilt. To make some kind of sense of it all. She shook her head. 'There's nothing to tell.'

'Try me.'

Distractedly, Catherine began voicing her thoughts out loud. 'Maybe it was a reaction to Peter—I *don't know*—I just know that I behaved in a way which was completely alien to me!'

'You slept with him?'

Catherine nodded. She supposed that was one way of putting it. 'Yes, I slept with him! I fell into his arms like the ripest plum on the tree. I spent the night with him. Me! *Me!* I still can't believe it!' Her voice rose in disbelief. 'I went out with Peter for three years and never even *looked* at another man.' But then, no man like Finn Delaney had come along for her to look at, had he? 'And before that there was only one significant other. I was too busy building up my career to be interested in men. And I've certainly never—*never*—been quite so free and easy. Not even with Peter.'

Especially not with Peter. Quite the opposite, in fact. Peter had been surprised that she had held out so long before letting them get intimate. He'd said it was a refreshing change to find a woman who played hard to get. But it hadn't been a game—it had been a necessity. Born out of a need for self-respect which her mother had drummed into her and a desire to have him respect *her*.

Which made her wonder what Finn Delaney must be thinking about her now.

'Maybe he has something special—this Finn Delaney.'

'Oh, he has something *special* all right!' burst out Catherine. 'Bucketfuls of charm and sex-appeal—and the ability to pitch it at just the right level to make himself irresistible to women!'

Miranda, not normally given to looking fazed, raised her eyebrows. 'That's some testimony, Catherine,' she murmured. 'I take it that he was a good lover?'

'The best,' said Catherine, before she had time to think about it. And with those two words she seemed to have managed to invalidate everything she had had with Peter, too. 'He was unbelievable.'

There was a long silence.

'You'll get over it,' said Miranda at last.

Catherine raised a defiant face, but her green eyes were full of a tell-tale glittering. 'I'll have to,' she said staunchly. 'I don't have any choice, do I?'

His face almost obscured by the creamy bloom of flowers and dark green foliage, Finn narrowed his eyes as he surveyed the names next to the doorbells.

Walker. Flat 3. He shifted the flowers onto one shoulder, as if he was winding a baby, and jammed his thumb on the bell.

Inside the flat, the bell pealed, and Catherine frowned, then stifled a small groan. Bad that someone should call unannounced after this week when she had lost almost everything. What had remained of her self-respect. Her pride. And now her job.

Miranda hadn't even had the grace to look ashamed

when Catherine had marched straight into her office and slammed the latest copy of *Pizazz!* on her desk.

'What the hell is *this* supposed to mean, Miranda?' she demanded.

Miranda's face was a picture of unconvincing innocence. 'You don't like the piece? I thought we did Dublin justice.'

'I'm not talking about the piece on Dublin and you know it, Miranda!'

'Yes.' Miranda's face turned into one of editorial defiance. 'The story was too good not to tell.'

'But there *was* no story, Miranda!' protested Catherine. 'You know there wasn't.' Except that there was. Of course there was. And it was the oldest trick in the journalist's book. Being creative with the facts.

The only facts that Miranda had gleaned from Catherine were that she had spent a wild night with Finn Delaney and that he had not asked to see her again. Miranda had discovered for herself that Catherine looked uncannily like an ex-lover of his, and from this had mushroomed a stomach-churningly awful piece all about Finn Delaney underneath Catherine's article on Dublin.

It described him as an 'unbelievable' lover, and hinted that his sexual appetite was as gargantuan as his appetite for success. It described the view from his bedroom in loving detail—and she didn't even remember telling Miranda about *that*! It did not actually come out and name Catherine as having been the recipient of his sexual favours, but it didn't need to. Catherine knew. And a few others had guessed.

But the person she had been astonished not to hear from was Finn Delaney—and she thanked God for the silence from that quarter, and the fact that *Pizazz!* didn't have a big circulation across the water.

'You deceived me, Miranda,' she told her editor quietly. 'You've threatened my journalistic integrity! I should bloody well go to the Press Complaints Commission—and so will Finn Delaney if he ever reads it and if he has an ounce of sense!'

'But it was in the public interest!' crowed Miranda triumphantly. 'A man who could be running a country—it's our *duty* to inform our readers what he's really like!'

'You don't have a clue what he's really like!' stormed Catherine. Though neither, in truth, did she. 'You've just succeeded in making him sound like some kind of vacuous stud with his brain stuffed down the front of his trousers!'

And with that Catherine had flung down her letter of resignation and stomped out of the office into an unknown future, her stomach sinking as she told herself that she could always go freelance.

The doorbell rang again.

Now, who the hell was bothering her at this hour in the morning? At nine o'clock on a Saturday morning most people were in bed, surely?

'Hello?' she said into the intercom, in a go-away kind of voice.

Downstairs, the petals of the scented flowers brushing against his cheek, Finn felt the slow build-up of tension. He had tried to pick a time when she would be in and it seemed that he had struck lucky.

His eyes glittered. He wanted to surprise her.

'Catherine?'

A maelstrom of emotions swirled around like a whirlpool in her befuddled brain as that single word instantly gave her the identity of her caller. But of course it would. She would recognise that rich Irish brogue from a hundred miles away, even if her guilty conscience hadn't been fighting a war with a suddenly stirring body.

Finn?

Finn?

Here?

He must have seen the article!

A fit of nerves assailed her. Catherine pressed her forehead against the door and closed her eyes. Oh, why the hell had she answered the wretched door in the first place? He knew now that she was here, and short of ignoring it and hoping he might go away...

She opened her eyes. Tried to imagine him shrugging those broad, powerful shoulders and just quietly leaving and failed miserably. She was trapped.

Presumably Finn Delaney had come here to wipe the floor with her. To tell her exactly what he thought of women who blabbed their tacky stories to middle-of-the-road magazines.

'Catherine?'

She tried to work out if he sounded furiously angry or just quietly seething, but the rich, lilting voice sounded nothing more than deeply irresistible.

'C-come up, Finn,' she suggested falteringly.

The words stayed in his mind as he rode up in the lift, and an odd sort of smile twisted his lips. Of course everything she said would drip with sexual innuendo—because it sure as hell was pretty much all they had really shared.

Sex.

But still he felt the unwilling burn of excitement just thinking about it.

Catherine had enough time to zip round her mouth with her electric toothbrush and then drag a comb through her long, mussed-up hair. The over-sized tee shirt which fell to an unflattering length at mid-knee she would just have to live with.

She cast a despairing glance in the mirror. At least she couldn't be accused of being a *femme fatale*.

Then her face paled as she heard the lift door open, and all flippancy fled as she remembered just why he was here. *Femme fatale,* indeed. As if he would look at her with anything but contempt after what had happened!

She opened the door before he had time to knock, and the first thing he thought was how pale her face looked without make-up. The second was that the baggy tee shirt did absolutely nothing to conceal the tight little buds of her nipples which thrust against the soft material. He felt himself harden.

'How lovely to see you!' she said brightly—which was true. Because he looked heart-stoppingly gorgeous in a pair of faded jeans and a sweater in a washed-out blue colour which made his eyes seem even more intense than usual. Her heart started crashing in her chest and she tensed in expectation, wondering how he was going to express himself.

Withering contempt? she wondered. Or blistering invective? But as she waited for the storm to rage over her, her pulse began to race in response to the confusing messages she was getting. He was carrying flowers. Strange, beautiful flowers, the like of which she had never seen before. With long white-green petals and dark leaves.

Flowers?

Finn gave a rueful shrug of his shoulders. 'Sorry.

It's a pretty unsociable hour to call, I know,' he murmured. 'And it looks like I just got you out of bed.'

She found herself blushing and hated herself for it. Why draw attention to a remembered intimacy which now seemed as false as a mirage? 'No, no—I've been awake for hours.' Which also was true; she certainly hadn't slept more than a couple of hours at a stretch since she had returned from her fateful trip to Dublin.

'Aren't you going to invite me in, Catherine?' His tone was as soft as the paw of a tiger moving stealthily through the jungle.

'You want to come in?' she questioned stupidly. Well, of course he did—no doubt a man of his status would object to a slanging match where the occupants of the nearby apartments were in danger of hearing!

He gave a half-smile. 'Is this how you usually react when lovers appear on your doorstep offering you flowers?'

He handed her the flowers but she barely registered their beauty—because all her attention had focused on that one hopeful word he had uttered.

Lovers.

That didn't sound past tense, did it? Which meant not one, but two things. That he couldn't possibly have read the article, and that possibly—just possibly—he wanted to carry on where they had left off in Ireland. But did *she*?

Of course she did! Just the sight of him was making her mind take flight into a flower-filled fantasy world where it was just her and Finn. Finn and her. Uttering a silent prayer of thanks, she swallowed down her excitement as she stared at the exotic blooms.

'They're for me?' she asked, even more stupidly.

He raised his eyebrows. 'Did you think I'd be so

insensitive as to turn up here carrying flowers for someone else?'

'I suppose not.' She smiled, hardly daring to acknowledge the growing pleasure which was slowly warming her blood, so that she felt as if she was standing in front of a roaring fire. 'Come in,' she said, and drew the door open. She thrust her nose into the forgotten blooms as the most delicious and beguiling scent filled her nostrils. 'These are absolutely gorgeous,' she breathed. 'Just gorgeous. And so unusual.' She turned wide green eyes to his. 'What are they?'

His voice was careless. 'Mock orange blossom.'

'You mean as opposed to real orange blossom?' she joked.

'Something like that.'

She'd never seen mock orange blossom on the stalls of her local flower market, but perhaps Finn Delaney had stopped to buy them in one of the more exclusive department stores. She smiled again, not bothering to hide her delight. 'I'll go and put them in water—please, make yourself at home.' Did that sound too keen? she wondered as she went off to the kitchen to find a vase.

Oh, who cared? Wasn't a man who turned up on your doorstep first thing on a Saturday morning bearing flowers being more than a little keen himself?

Maybe he felt the same as she did, deep down. That the time they had shared in Greece, and then in Dublin, hinted at a promise too good to just let go.

Humming happily beneath her breath, she filled a vase with water.

Finn prowled around the sitting room like a caged tiger, noting the decor with the eye of a man used to registering detail and analysing it.

The curtains were still drawn—soft gold things, through which the morning sun filtered, gilding the subdued light and giving the room a slightly surreal feel.

Lots of books, he noted. Run-of-the-mill furniture. Two fairly ordinary sofas transformed from the mundane by the addition of two exotic throws. A couple of framed prints and a collection of small china cats. Not enough to tell him anything much about the real Catherine Walker. His mouth flattened as she walked back into the room and deposited the flowers in the centre of a small pine coffee table. Their scent filled the room.

Now what? wondered Catherine. Were they going to carry on as if nothing had happened between them? 'Coffee?' she asked.

He shook his head and moved towards her, driven on by some primeval urge deep within him. His eyes were shuttered as he pulled her into his arms, feeling her soft flesh pliant against the hard lines of his body, which sprang into instant life in response. 'I haven't come here for coffee.'

She opened her mouth to protest that he might at least adhere to a *few* conventional social niceties before he moved in for the kill, but by then he had lowered his mouth onto hers, and she was so hungry for his kiss that she let him. How long had it been? Four weeks that felt like a lifetime...

'God, Finn—'

'What?' He cupped her breast with arrogant possession, liking the way that the nipple instantly reacted, pressing like a little rock against his hand.

To be in his arms once more was even better than she remembered, and the honeyed pleasure which was invading her senses was driving every thought out of her head other than the overriding one—which was how much she wanted this. Him.

'Mmm? You were saying?'

'W-was I? I can't remember.' Catherine's hands roved beneath the washed-out blue sweater, greedily alighting on the silken skin there. 'Oh, it's so good to see you.'

'And you, too. And this is certainly the kind of welcome I was hoping for.' His voice sounded thickened, slurred. He drew his mouth away from hers and his eyes were glittering with blue fire. 'My only objection is that I'm not seeing quite enough of you, Catherine. Don't you think it's time to remedy that situation?'

And with a single fluid movement he peeled the tee shirt off her body, over her head, and threw it to the ground, so that she was standing naked before him.

'Finn!' She felt the air cool her already heated body, but any consternation fled just as soon as he touched his lips to her nipple, and she began to shake as she clutched his dark head further against her breast. 'Oh, God!'

That shuddered cry of pure, undiluted desire fuelled his already overwhelming hunger, and he yanked his sweater over his head, kicked off his deck shoes, pulled roughly at the belt of his jeans and unzipped them. 'Take them off,' he commanded unsteadily.

On fire with her need for him, Catherine sank to her knees and slid the denim down over the hard, muscular shaft of his thighs, burying her head in the very cradle of his masculinity, her tongue flicking out to touch him where he was burningly hard. He groaned.

'Are you always like this?' he demanded, once the jeans were discarded, and he drew her down with an urgent need onto the carpet, their naked bodies colliding and merging with a mutual greed.

'Like what?' Hungrily she nipped at a hard brown nipple and he shuddered.

'So responsive.' So bloody easy to turn on, and so fiendishly good at turning *him* on until he thought he might explode with need.

Only with you, she thought, but that seemed too frighteningly vulnerable a thing to say. She licked instead.

He moved over her, his eyes burningly bright—a strange, shining combination of blue and black. In the heat of the moment his mind went blank and he forgot everything other than the sweet temptation of her flesh.

'God, Catherine, I want you so badly.' He slipped his hand between her thighs, where she was as wet as he had known she would be, and a wild kind of fever heated his blood. He moved and then groaned, then groaned again as he thrust into her, deep and hard and long, and she gave a low, exultant scream of pleasure.

'Is that good?' he ground out. 'Because—sweet God in heaven—it feels good to me!'

She gave herself up to the delicious rhythm, feeling control beginning to slip away.

'Is it, Catherine?' he urged, wanting to hear the surrender he could feel in her fast-shivering flesh. 'Is it good?'

Through dry lips she managed to say the very word

she had said to Miranda. 'Unbelievable,' she groaned, as he filled her and moved inside her. 'Unbelievable.'

It happened so quickly, and her orgasm seemed to make Catherine's world explode. For a moment consciousness actually receded, and she was lost in a dreamy, perfect world of feeling and sensation, then it slowly ebbed back and reality was just as good. She smiled. That was if reality was lying naked in Finn's arms with the whole day—maybe even the weekend—ahead of them.

And this time they would do things other than make love. She could cook him lunch—had she got enough food to produce something impressive?—and then afterwards she could take him to the park. Maybe an early film, and then supper... Sooner rather than later she was going to have to come clean about her job, and very probably the mix-up about the article, but she could deal with that. She was certain she could...

'Mmm,' she breathed in anticipation. 'Mmm!'

Her ecstatic response shattered his equilibrium and a sudden icy chill shivered its way over his bare flesh.

Finn withdrew from her and rolled away, and the physical deprivation of his presence made her whimper like a lost little animal.

'What are you doing?' she murmured sleepily, watching through half-slitted eyes the graceful, muscular body as he reached for his jeans.

'What does it look like? I'm getting dressed.'

He pulled the jeans back on and zipped them up before replying, and suddenly his face was shuttered. This was a new, hard Finn she didn't recognise, with a new, hard voice she didn't recognise either.

'Wh-where are you going?'

'I don't think that's really any of your business, do you?'

Catherine screwed up her eyes as she sat up, thinking that she must have misheard him—or that perhaps she had slipped unknowingly into a nightmare made uncannily real by his expressionless face. 'What?'

The movement which curved his lips was a bitter parody of a smile. 'Shall I repeat it for you in words of one syllable, Catherine?' he questioned cruelly. 'I said it's none of your business. Got that?' And he slipped his feet into the deck shoes, jerked on the blue sweater.

Her mind was spinning as it strove to make sense of this bizarre ending to what had just happened. Perhaps if she wasn't so befuddled by the aftermath of her orgasm then she might have made sense of it sooner. 'Finn, I don't understand—'

'Oh, don't you?' His mouth twisted and the blue eyes were as cold as ice. 'Then you can't be very good at your job, can you? If you lack the ability to understand the implication behind a simple sentence like that!'

The penny dropped. Her job, he had said. Yes, of course. Her job—her wretched, wretched job! Oh, God—he *had* seen the article! 'Finn, I want to explain—'

'Oh, please—spare me your lies. Just don't *bother!*'

Realising that she was completely naked, Catherine grabbed at her tee shirt and wriggled it over her head as she scrambled to her feet, aware of the movement of her breasts and aware too that Finn wasn't oblivious to their movement either. She turned to him with a face full of appeal, and suddenly nothing was more important than establishing the truth. 'You owe me the right to explain what happened,' she said in a low voice.

'I owe you *nothing*!' he spat back, and the temper which had been simmering away came boiling over, words spilling out of his mouth without thought or care. 'In fact, quite the contrary—I felt that in view of the fact I'd been paid nothing for an article about me which *I did not agree to*, then I should take my payment *in kind*!'

It took a moment or two for the meaning behind his words to sink in, and when it did Catherine felt sick. Physically sick. And even worse was the look in his eyes...

So here was the look of blistering contempt she had been anticipating at the very beginning but had conveniently forgotten when he had given her flowers and put his arms around her. And it was even worse than in her most fevered imaginings...

She swallowed down the bitter taste in her mouth, barely able to believe what he was implying. 'Y-you mean...you mean...you came here today *deliberately* to have sex with me—'

'Sure,' he answered arrogantly. 'It wasn't difficult—but why should it be? It was as easy as pie the last time.'

She wanted to hit him, to shout, to scream at him— but still she forced herself to question him, because surely there was some kind of ghastly mistake. 'To get your own back for some stupid magazine article?' she finished faintly.

'"Some stupid magazine article"?' Two high lines of colour ran across his cheekbones, and his Irish accent seemed even more pronounced. 'It may be just

some stupid article to you, sweetheart, but it has very
effectively sent my credibility flying!'

'You mean that you wanted to look whiter than
white because you hope to run for government?' she
demanded.

'That has nothing to do with it!' His voice became
a low hiss. 'Other people put labels on me that I do
not seek for myself! I couldn't give a stuff about politics, but I *do* care what my friends and family read
about me!'

And he fixed her with a look of such utter scorn
that Catherine actually flinched.

Her own look matched his for scorn now. 'And the
flowers? Such an elaborate masquerade, Finn,' she
said bitterly. 'Did you really have to go to so much
trouble to ensure my seduction? Did you think that
your powers of persuasion were slipping?'

'I never doubted that for a minute, sweetheart,' he
drawled, and then his eyes gleamed and his voice
softened. 'No, the bouquet was to send you a silent
message.'

She stared at him uncomprehendingly.

'Did you never hear of the language of flowers,
Catherine?'

The question and the way he asked it were so close
to the image of the poetic Irishman who had swept
her off her feet that for a moment Catherine was
lulled into imagining that the things he had said were
not real.

She shook her head.

'Every flower carries its own message,' he continued softly.

'And the mock orange blossom?' she asked shakily. 'What does that stand for?'

'Can't you guess?' He paused, and raised his dark eyebrows. 'Not got it yet, Catherine? Deceit,' he said finally, with a cruel, hard smile.

She supposed that as a gesture it deserved some kind of accolade, but it felt like a knife being twisted over and over in her gut.

'Just tell me one thing,' he said, and his eyes were piercingly clear. 'When you came to Dublin did your editor send you? Was it just coincidence that brought you? Or did she tell you to get something on me?'

Catherine opened her mouth. 'Well, she told me to, yes. But—'

'But what? The article just wrote itself, did it?' he questioned witheringly.

She wanted to say, It wasn't like that! But she knew that no words in the dictionary could ever make things right between them now.

'Please go,' she said quietly.

But he was already by the door. 'Nothing would give me greater pleasure,' he grated.

And with that he was gone.

CHAPTER SEVEN

THE moment the door had shut behind him, Catherine
snatched the flowers from out of the vase and took
them to the kitchen sink, where she squashed them
ruthlessly with a rolling pin, bashing and bashing at
them until they were made pulp.

That should relieve some of her pent-up frustration,
she thought, with a fleeting feeling of triumph which
evaporated almost immediately. Except that she
wasn't feeling frustrated—not in the physical sense,
in any case. No, her frustration was born out of the
random and cruel tricks of fate which had led her into
this situation. The man whom she had fallen for,
hook, line and sinker, would never trust her again.

But he didn't even give you a chance to explain
yourself, she reminded herself bitterly—and in the
heat of the moment she had forgotten to ask him
about Deirdra O'Shea. Finn Delaney himself was no
saint, she thought. And there had been a reason why
she had been so indiscreet with Miranda.

Tears began to slide down her cheeks just as the
telephone rang.

She snatched it up, despising herself for the eagerness which prompted her, thinking that maybe Finn
had had a change of heart—was ringing her to apol-
ogise for his unbelievably cruel behaviour.

'H-hello?'

But it was her mother. 'Catherine? Are you all
right?'

Catherine wiped the tears away with a bunched fist. 'Of course I'm all right, Mum.'

'Well, you don't sound it.' Her mother's voice sounded worried, but of course it would. Mothers were notoriously good at detecting when their daughters were crying, particularly when they were as close as Catherine and her mother. 'Have you been crying?'

'Not really.' Sniff.

'Not really?' Her mother's voice softened. 'Do you want to tell me about it?'

'I can't! You'll hate me for it!'

'Catherine, stop it. Tell me what's happened.'

Such was her distress that the story came tumbling out—or rather an edited version designed to cause the least hurt to her mother. Catherine did not mention that she barely knew the man, nor the shockingly short time scale involved. She just told her the simple truth of the matter, which was that she had leapt into a foolish and inconsidered relationship straight after Peter and that it was now over.

'Oh, Mum!' she wailed. 'How could I have done it?'

'You did it on the rebound,' her mother said firmly. 'Lots of people do. It isn't the end of the world! Just try to put it out of your mind and forget about it.'

'And I hadn't seen Peter for months and months!' Catherine found herself saying, which again was true. She didn't want her mother thinking that she was about to start taking lovers at the drop of a hat.

'I'm not making any value judgements, darling. I know the sort of person you are. I've never doubted you for a moment, and anyone who does needs their head examining!' she finished fiercely. 'Who is this man—is he married?'

Catherine heard the slightly raw tone. Even now her mother still hurt. She had had her own cross to bear. Loving a married man had brought with it nothing but pain and heartache. And a baby, of course. Mustn't forget the baby. For Catherine had been one of those fatherless children—a child who had never known her father. 'No, he's not married.'

'Thank God for that!'

'I shouldn't have worried you by telling you about it, Mum.'

'I'm more worried about the fact that you don't have a job any more,' her mother was saying. 'Any luck on the freelance front?'

'I haven't really been looking—'

'Well, better start, Catherine—you have to keep a roof over your head and food in your mouth and clothes on your back, remember?'

Oh, yes, she remembered all right. Independence had been another lesson drummed into her from an early age by a woman who had always had to fend for herself and bring up her child. Catherine's mother had initially been wary of her daughter's chosen career, seeing it as precarious—and for Catherine to now be freelance must be her idea of a nightmare.

'Oh, I'll find something—I've got plenty of contacts.'

'Why don't you come down this weekend? It'd be lovely to see you.'

Catherine hesitated, tempted. She couldn't think of anything nicer than to escape to her mother's tiny cottage, surrounded by fields and trees, with a distant peep of the sea. Under normal circumstances she would have been scooting straight out of the door to buy her ticket at the train station.

But these were not normal circumstances. No, indeed. Catherine cast a disgusted look down at her baggy tee shirt.

'No, Mum,' she replied. 'I have a heap of things to do here. Maybe next weekend.'

'All right, darling. You will take care of yourself, won't you?'

'Of course I will!'

Her mother's words came back to haunt her during the next few weeks as Catherine scouted around many publications angling for assignments. She had a mixed bag of luck. Some people knew her work and respected it, and were keen to hire her. But the market was full of freelance journalists—some of them talented and hungry and straight out of college—and Catherine knew that she was going to have to work very hard to keep up with the competition. Suddenly the staff job she had had at *Pizazz!* seemed terribly comfortable, and she wondered why she had bothered throwing it in.

As a defiant gesture it had been rather wasted. She had lost Finn anyway—though she reminded herself that he had never been hers to have.

And what else had her mother said?

'Take care of yourself.'

Had she known that the stress of everything that had happened would leave Catherine feeling distinctly peaky?

Stress had all kinds of insidious effects on the human body, she knew that as well as the next person. It played havoc with her appetite, for example. One minute she would be feeling so nauseous that just the thought of food would make her feel sick. The next she would be diving for the biscuit tin and thickly spreading yeast extract on a pile of digestive biscuits.

It wasn't until one afternoon when Sally—her best friend on *Pizazz!* and the only person she had kept in touch with from there—commented that she was putting on weight that Catherine's safe reality finally crumbled into dust.

She waited until Sally had gone and then shut the door behind her with a shaking hand. She went into the bathroom to stare at her white, haunted face with frightened eyes. Knowing deep down and yet denying it. Not wanting to know, nor daring to.

The thought that she might be pregnant simply hadn't occurred to her. But as she allowed the facts to assemble logically in her head she wondered how she could have been so stupid.

The next day she went through the rituals of confirmation, knowing that they were unnecessary, but until concrete proof confirmed her worst fears she might really be able to put it down to stress.

The blue line on the indicator was a fact. Just as was the faint tingling in her breasts. The missed periods. The nausea. The compulsive and compensatory eating. It all added up—and you wouldn't need to be Doctor of the Year to work out why.

Catherine sat back on her heels and took a deep breath, hugged her arms protectively around her heavy breasts.

Now what?

Her breathing short and shallow and low, she tried to flick her mind through her options. But nothing she thought of seemed to make any sense because it didn't seem real. It couldn't be real, could it?

She went into denial. Threw her energy into an

article on pet cemeteries and spent days researching it. Managed to agree to an almighty fee for a piece on London's newest wannabe club and spent a queasy evening in a smoke-filled room regretting it.

She denied it all over Christmas by wearing baggy jumpers and telling her bemused mother that she was trying to 'cut down' when asked why she wasn't drinking.

And still the days ticked by—until one morning, after dashing to the bathroom to be sick, she gripped the washbasin with still-shaking hands and stared at her white-green reflection in the mirror.

She was pregnant with Finn Delaney's baby!

A man who despised her, a man she barely knew— a man, moreover, who had walked out of her life with the clear wish of never setting eyes on her again.

She was going to have a baby.

And with that one focused thought all her options and choices dissolved into one unassailable fact.

She was going to have a baby.

She booked an appointment with her doctor, who raised her eyebrows questioningly at Catherine when she'd finished her examination.

'Yes, you're pregnant, though you're fine—fit and healthy.' The doctor frowned. 'You really should have come to see me sooner, you know.'

'Yes, I know.'

The doctor appeared to choose her words delicately. 'And you're going to go ahead with the pregnancy? Because if you're not...'

Catherine didn't even have to think about it. Some things you just knew, with a bone-deep certainty. She drew a deep breath, scared yet sure. Very, very sure. 'Oh, yes. Very definitely.'

The doctor nodded. 'How about the father? Will he be able to support you?'

Another pause. There was no doubt that he would be *able* to. But… 'I'm not expecting him to. We're not…together any more.' How was that for managing to make the truth sound respectable?

'But you'll tell him?'

Catherine sat back in her chair. 'I don't know.' She didn't feel she knew anything any more.

The doctor straightened the papers on her desk and looked at her. 'A man has a right to know, Catherine—I really believe that.'

Catherine walked back to her flat, scarcely noticing the light drizzle which slowly seeped into her skin and clothes. The doctor's question refused to go away. *Should* she tell him? Did he really have a right to know that he had fathered a baby?

She sat in the sitting room, nursing a cup of tea which grew cold and unnoticed, while the floor where she and Finn had made love seemed to mock her nearly as much as her idealistic thoughts.

Made love, indeed!

She might have been swept away with the passion of seeing him again, but Finn's seduction had been cold-blooded in thought, if not in deed.

And yet the responsibility was just as much his as hers, surely?

She could be proud and vow never to tell him that his child was growing inside her womb, but what of the child itself?

Was she going to subject him or her to a lifetime of what she had had to endure? The terrible insecurity of not knowing who your father was? Of growing up with one vital half of the gene jigsaw missing? And with her having to nurse some terrible, pointless secret?

So did she pick up the telephone and tell him? Or write him a letter detailing the consequences of their moment of madness? She winced as she attempted to compose a clumsy paragraph inside her head. Impossible.

The sun began to dip in the sky and she put the cup of untouched tea down on the coffee table as tears began to slide down her cheeks. She angrily brushed them away, her heart aching for the new life inside her. Why should her baby suffer just because two adults had acted without thought?

She needed courage, more courage than she had ever needed before, because there was only one way to tell him something like this.

Face to face.

CHAPTER EIGHT

'I'M SENDING Miss Walker through, Finn.'

'Thanks, Sandra.' Finn flicked off the intercom and waited, sitting very still behind the huge desk as the door to his office opened and Catherine walked in, an indefinable expression in her green eyes. She wore a black velvet coat—a loose, swingy sort of thing—and with its contrast against her pale face and black hair she looked liked a beautiful sorceress.

'Come in, Catherine,' he said evenly, and rose to his feet. 'Shut the door behind you.'

As if she needed telling! As if she wanted his assistant to hear what she was about to say to him—and the ensuing discussion which would inevitably follow it. She shut it.

'Sit down, won't you?' He sat down himself and gestured to the chair opposite his, but Catherine shook her head.

'I'll stand, if you don't mind. I've been cooped up on a flight and in a cab,' she said. And although she knew that the flutterings in her stomach were due to nerves, and not the baby, she wasn't going to risk sitting in front of him and squirming. She met his gaze. 'I'm surprised that you agreed to see me.'

'I'm surprised that you want to.'

In his unmoving face only his blue eyes showed signs of life. His features looked as cold and as motionless as if they had been hewn from rock as old as the stone of Glendalough, where he had taken her that day which now seemed an age ago. And it was. It had been a different Catherine who looked up and laughed into his eyes that day.

The Catherine who was here was on a mission. To give him the truth—a truth which she felt honour-bound to tell him. But wasn't it funny how you could practise saying something over and over again, yet when the opportunity came the words just wouldn't seem to come?

Finn watched her as he waited, thinking that somehow she looked different—and not just because her face was closed and wary and pale. No, there was something he couldn't quite put his finger on, something which alerted his sixth sense. The same sense which told him that a beautiful woman like Catherine Walker must have her pride. A pride which would have no time for a man who had acted as he had done. Yet she had phoned asking to speak to him. Personally and urgently.

'I'm all yours, Catherine,' he said, and then wished he hadn't, for the irony hadn't escaped him—nor her either, to judge from her brief, bitter smile.

No need to preface it with anything as humiliating as, Do you remember when we last met in London...? Such a distortion of the truth would only embarrass them.

'I'm pregnant,' she said baldly.

There was a long, long silence, but not a flicker of emotion crossed his face. 'I see.'

'It's yours!' she declared wildly, wanting to shatter the tense expectation in the air, to breathe some life into that unmoving face of his.

'Yes.'

Catherine stared at him, and delayed shock, together with his cold and monosyllabic reply, made her legs feel like water. She sank into the chair he had originally offered and stared at him with wide, uncomprehending eyes.

'You aren't going to deny it?'

'What would be the point? I can't imagine that I would be your first choice as father to your child. What we had between us hardly qualifies as the greatest love affair of all time, does it? So why would you lie about something as important as that? And if you aren't lying then the logical conclusion is that you must be telling the truth.'

It was a cold and analytical assessment and, oddly enough, seemed to hurt far more than if he had just lost his temper and flatly denied it—called her all names under the sun and told her to get out of his office and his life. For a start, it would have given her a let-out clause.

And it would have shown passion. Feelings. *Something* other than this cold and distant look in his eyes. As if he were a scientist surveying some rather odd-looking specimen in a test-tube. But then, what had she expected? 'You don't seem surprised,' she said heavily.

He shrugged. 'A simple case of cause and effect.'

'How very cynical, Finn.'

'Cynical, but true,' he mocked, then drew a deep breath as he thought back to that mad and tempestuous morning in her London flat. He gave a long and heavy sigh. 'That's what comes of forgetting to wear a condom, I suppose.'

Reduced to the lowest possible denominator.

Catherine flinched, as though he had hit her. And he might as well have hit her, the pain in her heart was so intense. She remembered the frantic way they had fallen to the floor, the wild hunger she had felt for him, and he, apparently, for her.

Yet he had come there that day with just such a seduction—if such a word could be used to describe something so basic—in mind. But he had not protected himself, and she had been too caught up in the mood and the magic—yes, magic—to notice.

She could deny it until she was blue in the face, but Finn Delaney had completely had her in his thrall. Then, and before. But now she saw the so-called magic for what it was—an illusion—like a trick of the light.

'Was your lack of care simply an omission on your part?' she questioned.

'What do you think?' he demanded. 'That I did it deliberately? That I somehow hoped for this particular little scenario?' His blue gaze bored into her. 'What was I *thinking*?' He gave a low, bitter laugh. 'That's the trouble, you see, Catherine—I wanted you so badly that I wasn't thinking at all.'

'A wanting fuelled by contempt,' she observed bitterly, noticing that he didn't deny it.

'And when is the—?'

His deep, musical Irish voice faltered just a little.

He stared down at the figures he had been working on, and she noticed that it was the first time he had let any emotion creep in.

He looked up again. 'When is the baby due?'

'They aren't sure.'

The blue gaze became more intense. Quizzical. Silently demanding some kind of explanation. And of course he was entitled to one. She was here, wasn't she? She had foisted paternity on him and with that he had earned certain entitlements.

'I wasn't really sure about my dates myself, that's all. June—they think.'

'June.' He stared unseeingly out at the panoramic view from the window. 'So I'm to be a father some time in June?'

'Not necessarily.'

Now it was *his* turn to flinch, the dark-featured face looking both pained and quietly thunderous, and she realised that he had grossly misinterpreted her words.

'No, no, no!' she defended instantly. 'I didn't mean *that*. What I mean is that you don't have to have anything to do with this baby. Not if you don't want to.' He had not sought fatherhood, and therefore he should not be shackled by it.

'So why exactly are you here, Catherine?' He narrowed his eyes at her thoughtfully. 'Is it money you want?'

His mercenary judgement was like a slap to the face, and Catherine blanched as she shakily tried to rise to her feet. But there seemed to be no power to her legs. How much more hurt could he inflict on her?

'How dare you say that?' she hissed with an angry pride. 'You may be a big, powerful, rich businessman, but if you think I've come here today begging—*begging* for your largesse,' she repeated on a shuddering breath, 'then you are very much mistaken, Finn Delaney!'

'So just what *do* you want? A ring on your finger?'

'Hardly!' she contradicted witheringly. 'Strange as it may seem, I have no desire to tie myself to a man who thinks so badly of me that he believes I would treat my child as a commodity! Actually, I came here today to tell you about the baby simply because I felt that as an intelligent human being you would want to accept your share of responsibility for what has happened.'

'Catherine—'

'No!' Anger was giving her strength—beautiful, restorative strength. 'You've made your views perfectly clear. Don't worry, I won't be troubling you again!'

'I guess you could always sell your story to the highest bidder,' he said consideringly, and then ducked instinctively as something whizzed across the room.

Catherine had picked up the nearest object to her on his desk, which happened to be a large and very heavy paperweight, and it flew a foot wide of him and bounced deafeningly against the wall, bringing a marvellous landscape painting shattering down beside it, the glass breaking into a million shards.

The office door flew open and Sandra, his assistant, ran in, her eyes taking in the scene in front of her with disbelief. 'Oh, my God! Is everything all right, Finn?' she asked, her soft Irish accent rising in alarm. 'Would you have me call Security?' She stared at a white-faced and mutinous Catherine. 'Or the police?'

But Finn, astonishingly, was laughing—a low, gravelly laugh.

He shook his head. 'No, no—leave it, Sandra,' he said. 'Everything's fine. Miss Walker was just getting in a bit of target practice!'

'But unfortunately I missed!' said Catherine, her voice tinged with a slight hysteria. Her chair scraped back as she struggled to her feet.

'That will be all, thanks, Sandra,' said Finn quickly.

Sandra gave him one last, mystified stare before exiting the room and shutting the door behind her, just as Catherine reached it.

But Finn was quicker, beside her in a moment, where he caught hold of her shoulder. 'You're not going anywhere!'

'Let go of me!'

'No.' He moved her away from the door and whirled her round. He could see that she was very, very angry indeed. 'You could have killed me, you know,' he observed slowly.

'I wasn't aiming at you!' she snapped. 'But I wish to God I had!'

'What, and leave your child without a father?'

'You're not fit to be a father!'

He saw how distressingly white her face was and his whole manner altered. No matter what his feelings on the subject, the fact remained that she was pregnant. With his baby. And this kind of scene could surely not be doing her any good.

'Come and sit down and have some tea.'

'I don't want any tea! I want to go home!'

'To London? I think not. You're in no fit state to be flying back today. Not in your condition.'

It was that time-honoured phrase which did it. Which finally broke down the barriers she had tried to erect around her heart. *In your condition.* Someone should have been saying that to her with tender loving care. Preferably a husband who adored her, worshipped the ground she walked on, wanted to rub the small of her back and wait on her. Not a man who had had sex with her as some primitive kind of revenge and got so carried away with himself that he hadn't stopped to think about the consequences.

Though neither had she.

And instead she was about to replicate exactly what she had spent her whole life vowing not to do. Becoming a single mother, with all the emotional and financial hardship which went with that role.

She thought back to her own childhood. Her mother doing two and sometimes three jobs to make ends meet, so that Catherine should never feel different from the other children. Of course, she *had* felt different—some of the other children had made sure of that—but she had always been fed and clothed and loved and warm enough.

She had prayed that her mother would meet someone, but when eventually she had he had regarded Catherine as an encumbrance. Someone who was in the way and would always be in the way of his new wife and himself. He hadn't been outwardly horrible to her, but she had seen the hostility in his eyes sometimes, and it had frightened her.

Her mother must have seen it, too—for one day she had greeted Catherine at the school gates, a little pale and a little trembling, and told her that she was no longer going to marry Johnny. Catherine had laughed with delight and hugged her mother, and they had gone out and eaten tea and scones in a small café. His name had never been mentioned again.

How often had she hoped to repay her mother for her hard work and sacrifice by providing lavishly for her as she became older? Hadn't she dreamed of being one of the most snapped-up journalists in the land? Of maybe one day even writing a novel—a novel which would be a bestseller, naturally. She would buy her mother's cottage for her, make her old age secure.

Instead of which she must now go and destroy her mother's hopes and dreams for her. And her own, too.

She wanted to go away and just howl in some dark and private corner, but she saw that Finn was effectively barring the door.

'Are you going to let me leave?'

'What do you think?'

She fixed him with an icy look. 'I could scream the place down—that would get "Security" up here in a flash—if they thought you were raping me!'

He opened his mouth to say something, but thought better of it. Now was not the time to make a cheap and clever remark. 'Sit down, Catherine.'

'No, I w-won't.'

'Sit *down*, will you, woman? Or do I have to pick you up and carry you?'

It was like a brand-new sapling trying to withstand the full force of a hurricane. Catherine gave a weary sigh. She could see that he meant business, and besides, sitting down was what she wanted to do more than anything else in the world. Though lying down would have been better. Much better.

She sat down in the chair and closed her eyes. 'Go away,' she mumbled. 'Leave me alone.'

'Your logic is failing you,' he said drily. 'This is *my* office, remember.' He flicked on the intercom again. 'Sandra, will you have us sent in some tea? Good, strong tea. Oh, and something to eat?'

'Cake, Finn? Your favourite chocolate?' purred Sandra.

'Something more substantial than cake,' he replied, with a swift, assessing look at Catherine's fined-down cheekbones. 'A big, thick sandwich with a bit of protein in the middle.'

'Did you not have your lunch, Finn?' giggled Sandra.

'*Now*, please, Sandra!' he snapped.

'Why, *certainly*!' his assistant replied, in a hurt and huffy voice.

His face was stern as he looked down at Catherine, who was still sitting in the chair with her eyes closed. 'Are you asleep?' he asked quietly.

'No. Just trying to block out the sight of your face!'

'And what if the baby looks like me?' he questioned. 'Won't that be a terrible problem?'

Catherine opened her eyes and steeled herself against the impact of his handsome, mocking features. 'I hope it's a girl,' she said frostily. 'Who looks as little like you as possible! And even if he or she *does* look like you—'

'Yes?'

'I'll still love them!' she declared fiercely. 'I may not have a lot to offer, but I can give this baby love, Finn Delaney! Now, are you please going to let me go? Or am I a prisoner here?'

He spoke using the soothing voice of a psychiatrist who was trying to placate an extremely mad patient. 'You're not going anywhere until you've calmed down.'

'Then get me as far away from you as possible—that's the only way to guarantee *that*!'

There was a light tap on the door. 'Come in, Sandra,' called Finn rather drily, noting how circumstances could change routine. Sandra never, ever knocked. But then he never, ever had women turning up at his headquarters hurling paperweights against the wall!

A frosty-looking Sandra deposited a loaded tray on the low table in one corner of the room.

'Will there be anything else, Finn?'

He shook his head. 'No—thanks, Sandra.'

'You're welcome.'

He couldn't miss the trace of sarcasm, but then maybe it wasn't so very surprising. Sandra had been with him for years, had seen him run his affairs with cool-headed acumen and detachment.

'Catherine?'

'What?'

'Do you take sugar?'

She almost laughed aloud at the irony of it all—until she remembered that it wasn't in the least bit funny. Her green eyes blazed with a kind of furious indignation, directed at him, but felt deeply by herself.

'What a funny old world it is, don't you think, Finn? Here I am carrying your baby, and you don't even know whether I take sugar in my tea! Or milk, either, for that matter!' she finished wildly, wondering if she could put these sudden, violent mood swings down to fluctuating hormones. Or the bizarre situation she found herself in.

'So, do you or don't you?' he questioned calmly. 'Have sugar?'

'Usually I don't, no! But for now I'll have two!' she declared, experiencing a sudden desire for hot, sweet tea. 'And milk. Lots of it.'

He poured the tea and handed her a hefty-looking sandwich.

'I don't want anything to eat.'

'Suit yourself.'

But the bread and the ham looked mouthwateringly

good, and Catherine remembered that she had eaten nothing since a midnight craving had sent her to the fruit bowl last night and she had demolished the last three remaining apples. Her stomach rumbled and her hand reached out for the sandwich. She began to eat, looking at him defiantly, daring him to say something. But to his credit he simply took his own tea and sat down in front of her.

He waited until she had finished, relieved to see that the food and drink had brought a little colour into her cheeks. 'So now what? Where do we go from here?'

'I told you—I'm going back to London.'

He shook his head. 'I don't think so,' he demurred. 'You can't just arrive on my doorstep like the good fairy, impart a momentous piece of news like that, then take off again.'

'You can't stop me!'

'No, I can't stop you. But you still haven't told me why you came here today.'

'I would have thought that was pretty obvious.'

'Not really. You could have phoned me. Or written me a letter.' The blue eyes challenged her. 'So why didn't you?'

What was the point of hiding anything now? If she hadn't kept her job secret then he probably wouldn't have given her his card, and she wouldn't have gone to see him, and then this would never...

But she shook her head. What was the point of wasting time by thinking of what might have been? Or what might *not* have been, in this case.

'I wasn't sure that you'd believe me.'

'You thought that seeing me in person would convince me?' He frowned. 'But why? You don't *look* pregnant—' With that she opened the buttons of her coat and stared at him defiantly. He stilled.

For there, giving a smooth contour to her slim body, was the curve of pregnancy, and Finn stared at it, utterly speechless.

'I just knew I had to tell you face to face, and show you that it's real, it's happening,' she said, meeting that shocked stare. 'Besides, it isn't the easiest thing in the world to write, is it?'

He forced himself to remember that she had betrayed him. 'Even for a journalist?' he questioned sarcastically.

'Even for a journalist,' she echoed, but she felt the prick of tears at the back of her eyes and bit her lip again, knowing that whatever happened he had to hear *this* truth, too. He might not believe her, but she had to tell him.

'Finn, my editor *did* send me to Dublin when she found out we'd met—and she *did* try to get a story on you. But I said no.'

'So the story was just a figment of my imagination?' he queried sarcastically.

'No, but I didn't write that piece about you, and neither did I receive any money.'

'Oh?' he queried cynically. 'So they just happened to guess what the inside of my apartment is like, did they? And the fact that you obviously rate me in bed?'

'I was upset, and I blurted a few things out to my editor, not expecting her to use them.'

'What very naive behaviour for a journalist,' he said coldly, but his heart had begun to beat very fast. If she had been tricked into giving a confidence, then didn't that put an entirely different complexion on matters? And didn't that, by default, make his subsequent behaviour absolutely intolerable?

'Oh, what's the point in all this?' she sighed. 'Don't worry about it, Finn. I'm not asking you to have anything to do with this baby.'

'But it's not just down to *you*, is it?' he asked quietly.

A cloud of apprehension cast its shadow. 'What do you mean?'

'Just that I want to,' he said grimly. 'This is my baby, too, you know, Catherine. By choosing to tell me you have irrevocably involved me—and believe me, sweetheart, I *intend* to be involved!

CHAPTER NINE

CATHERINE stared at Finn in shock and alarm.

'Well, what did you expect?' he demanded. 'That I would say, Okay—fine—you're having my baby? Here's a cheque and goodbye?'

'I told you—I did *not* come here asking you for money!' she said furiously.

'No? But you still haven't told me why you *did* come here.'

Catherine stared down at her lap, then looked back up at him, her eyes bright. 'Because I didn't know my own father.'

There was an odd, brittle kind of pause. 'You mean he died?' he questioned slowly.

She shook her head, met his eyes squarely. Defiantly. 'I'm illegitimate, Finn.'

'Come on now, Catherine,' he said gently. 'That isn't such a terrible thing to be.'

'Maybe not today it isn't—but things were different when I was a child.'

'Did you never meet him?'

'Never. I don't know whether he's alive or dead,' she said simply. 'He was married to someone, and it wasn't my mother. Like I said, I didn't know him and he didn't want to know me.' Her eyes were bright now. 'And I didn't want to inflict that on my own child.'

He caught a sense of the rejection she must have

felt, and again was filled with a pang of remorse. 'I'm sorry—'

'No!' Fierce pride made her bunch her fists to wipe away the first tell-tale sign of tears, and she set her shoulders back. 'I don't want or need your sympathy for my upbringing, Finn, because it was a perfectly happy upbringing. It's just—'

'Not for your childhood,' he said heavily. 'For my recklessness.'

Their eyes met. 'You don't have the monopoly on recklessness,' she said quietly. 'The difference is that our motivations were different. You came round hell-bent on revenge, and you extracted it in the most basic form possible, didn't you?'

Had he? Had he really been that cold-blooded? It was surely no defence to say that all he had planned to do was to deliver the flowers with a blistering denouncement, but that all rational thought and reason had been driven clean out of his mind by the sight and the touch and the feel of her. Was that the truth, or just a way of making events more palatable for his conscience?

'You have a very powerful effect on me, Catherine,' he said unsteadily. Because even now, God forgive him—even with all this going on—he was thinking that she looked like some kind of exquisite domesticated witch, with that tumble of ebony hair and the wide-spaced green eyes. Or a cat, he thought thickly. A minxy little feline who could sinuously make him do her will.

What kind of child would they produce together? he found himself wondering. An ebony-haired child with passion running deep in its veins? 'A very powerful effect,' he finished, and met her eyes.

She steeled herself against his charm, the soft, sizzling look in his eyes. 'Yes, and we all know why, don't we? Why I have such an effect on you.'

His eyes narrowed. 'You're attempting to define chemistry?'

'I'm not defining anything—I'm describing something else entirely.' She threw him a challenging look and he matched it with one of his own.

'Go on,' he said. 'I'm intrigued.'

'We both know why such a famously private man should act in such an injudicious way.'

That one word assumed dominance inside his head. It wasn't a handle which had ever been applied to him before. 'Injudicious?'

'Well, wasn't it? If you'd bothered to find out a little bit more about me then you would have discovered that I was a journalist and presumably would have run in the opposite direction.'

'You were being deliberately evasive, Catherine. You know you were.'

'Yes, I was. I always am about my job, because people hold such strong prejudices.'

'Can you wonder why?' he questioned sarcastically.

'But it all happened so quickly—there was no time for an extended getting-to-know-you, was there, Finn? Tell me, do you normally leap into bed quite so quickly?'

'Not at all,' he countered, fixing her with a mocking blue look. 'Do you?'

'Never.' She drew a deep breath, not caring whether he believed her or not. His moral opinion of her did not matter. He would learn soon enough that she intended to be the mother to end all mothers. 'But maybe you didn't *need* to get to know me.'

'Now you've lost me.'

'Have I? Well, then, let me spell it out for you! We both know that the reason you couldn't wait to take me to bed was because I reminded you of your childhood sweetheart!'

'My childhood sweetheart?' he repeated incredulously.

'Deidra O'Shea! Are you denying that I look like her?'

It took a moment for her words to register, and when they did his accompanying feeling of rage was tempered only by the reminder that she was pregnant.

'You have a look of her about you,' he said carefully. 'But so what?'

'So *what*?' Catherine turned a furious face to him. 'Don't you realise how insulting that is for a woman?'

'What? That I happen to be attracted to dark-haired women with green eyes? Where's the crime in that, Catherine? Don't you normally lust after men who look like me? Isn't that what human nature is all about? That we're conditioned to respond to certain stimuli?'

What would it reveal about her if she admitted that she didn't usually lust after men at all? That Peter had been the very opposite of Finn in looks and character. Peter didn't dominate a room, nor did his charisma light it up just as surely as if it had been some glorious, glowing beacon. Peter had not been able to make her melt so instantly and so responsively with just a glimmering look from his eyes.

'Did you pretend I was her?' she demanded heatedly. 'Close your eyes and think it was her?'

'But I didn't close my eyes, Catherine,' he answered seriously. 'I was looking at you all the time. Remember?'

Oh, yes, she remembered. She remembered all too well. The way his eyes had caressed her just as surely as his fingertips had. The things he had said about her body. He had compared her skin to silk and cream, in that musical and lilting Irish accent.

'And what about you?' he questioned suddenly. 'What's the justification for your behaviour? Was it perhaps a way of striking out at a man who had hurt you badly?'

Her mouth opened, but no sound came out.

'Peter,' he said deliberately. 'The man who left you.'

'How on earth did you find out about Peter?' she breathed.

'Oh, come on, Catherine! When the article was brought to my attention by my cuttings service, I had a check run on you. Suddenly everything made sense. Why a woman, seemingly so aloof, should go to bed with me without me really having to try. You wanted to get back at your ex-boyfriend, didn't you?'

She let him believe it. Because the truth was even more disturbing than his accusation. That she had been so besotted by Finn she had scarcely given Peter a thought. Didn't that fact damn her more than redeem her?

Catherine felt tired. Weary. Unable to cope with any more.

'Oh, what's the point in remembering? What's done is done and we just have to live with the consequences.'

'Don't go back to London today,' he said suddenly.

She looked at him. 'Can you give me a good reason why not?'

'You're tired. And we have things to discuss.' His blue eyes gleamed with resolve, and he continued in a quieter voice, 'Just as there are consequences to what happened between us, there are also consequences to your visit here. Come on.' He stood up. 'Let's go.'

'Go where?'

'I'll take you back to the flat. You can rest there, and then we can talk.'

It wasn't so much his strength or his determination which made Catherine weakly nod her head. She was pregnant, she told herself. She was allowed to be persuaded.

'Okay,' she agreed.

Finn stared out of the window at the distant waters of the Liffey—grey today, to match the sky. And to match his mood, he thought, with a heart which was heavy.

He turned silently to look at where Catherine lay, asleep on the king-sized sofa. She had been fighting sleep ever since he had brought her back here and at long last she had given up the battle.

Her hair lay in tousled silken strands of black, contrasted against a Chinese silk cushion, and her dark lashes feathered into two perfect arcs on her high cheekbones. She slept as peacefully and as innocently as a child, he thought. He stared at the curve of her belly as his thoughts repeated themselves in his mind.

A child.

A wild leap of something like joy jumped unexpectedly in his chest.

A child!

And not just any child. This was *his* child.

And, no matter what the circumstances, wasn't the procreation of life always a miracle? Didn't the tiny heart of his child beat inside this woman?

This stranger.

And yet he felt he knew her body more intimately than that of any woman who had gone before.

Catherine opened her eyes to find Finn standing, staring down at her. For a moment she was muddled and confused, wondering just where she was and what had happened. And then it all came back to her in one great jolting rush.

She was in his flat, and she had told him, and his reaction had been—unexpectedly—one of immediate acceptance, not suspicion.

She sat up and yawned. 'I fell asleep,' she said unnecessarily.

'You certainly did.' He glanced at his watch. 'For almost an hour. Looked like you needed it.'

An hour! 'Good grief.' She yawned again. When was the last time she'd slept so soundly in the middle of the day? Better start getting used to changes, she thought, as she ran her hand through her rumpled hair. She looked up into the imposing, impassive face. 'What are we going to do?'

He gave an almost imperceptible nod. *We*, she had said, acknowledging the power in a single word. He realised that already they were a unit. If you were lovers, even married, then no matter how long you were in a relationship a certain question-mark of impermanence always hovered unspoken in the air. But not any more. He and Catherine were fact. Chained together for the rest of their lives. The mother, the father and the baby.

'Tell me about what your life in London is like,' he said suddenly, and seated himself on the sofa opposite hers, stretching his long legs out in front of him.

Catherine blinked. 'Like what? You know where I live.'

'Yes. A one-bedroomed flat in the middle of the city. Not the most ideal place for bringing up a baby,' he observed.

She was intelligent enough not to argue with that. 'No,' she agreed quietly. 'It's not.'

'And your job?' he questioned. 'On *Pizazz!*.' He spat the word out as though it was a bitter pill. 'Will they give you paid maternity leave?'

Catherine hesitated. Of course. He didn't know— but then how would he? 'I don't have a job any more,' she said slowly, and saw his head jerk upwards in surprise. 'Or rather, I do, but it's certainly not one which will give me paid maternity leave. I'm…I've gone freelance,' she said at last.

'Since when?' he demanded. 'Since before you knew you were pregnant?'

'Of course! I'm not *completely* stupid!'

Guilt twisted a knife in his gut. 'You can't get another staff job?'

'Not like this! Who's going to take someone on at this stage of pregnancy? I can just see it now—Welcome, Catherine, we'd love to employ you. And, yes, we'd be delighted to give you paid leave in a few months' time!'

He studied her, trying to be dispassionate, to block out her blinding beauty. 'So how exactly are you planning to bring up this baby, in Clerkenwell, with no regular income?'

'I haven't decided.'

'You make it sound as though you have the luxury of choice, Catherine—which it seems to me you don't.'

'I'll think of something.' Her mother had managed, hadn't she? Well, *so would she*!

He looked at her closely, this beautiful woman he had been unable to resist, recognising that their lives would never be the same again.

'Where does your mother live?' he questioned, so uncannily that for one mad moment she wondered if he was capable of reading her thoughts.

'Devon.'

'Would you consider going there?'

Catherine shuddered. What, and let the village watch history repeating itself? The conquering daughter returning home vanquished, pregnant, and trying to eke out a living? Could she possibly land herself on her mother—who was happy with her independent life and her charity work? Would she want to go through the whole thing yet again?

'It would be too much for my mother to cope with,' she said truthfully.

That was one option dealt with. 'And do you know many people in London?'

She shrugged. 'Kind of—though I've only been there a couple of years. Colleagues, of course. Well, ex-colleagues, mainly,' she amended. And work friendships were never the same once you'd left a job, were they? Everyone knew that. 'I've got some good close friends, too.'

'Any with children?'

'Good grief—no! Career women to a fault.'

'Sounds a pretty isolated and lonely place for a woman to be child-rearing.'

'Like I said, I'll manage.'

His eyes narrowed. 'Commendable pride, Catherine,' he said drily. 'But it isn't just you to think about now, is it? Do you really think it's fair to foist that kind of lifestyle on a poor, defenceless baby?'

'You're making it sound like cruelty!' she protested. 'Lots and lots of women have babies in cities and all of them are perfectly happy!'

'Most probably have supporting partners and extended families!' he snapped. 'Which you don't!'

'Well—'

'And most do not have a credible alternative,' he said, cutting right across her protests. 'Like you do,' he finished deliberately.

There was something so solemn and profound in his voice that Catherine instinctively sat up straight, half-fearful and half-hopeful of what his next words might be. 'Like what?' she whispered.

'You could come and live here, in Dublin.'

She stared at him as if he had suddenly sprouted horns. 'Are you out of your mind?'

'I don't think that my thinking could be described as normal, no. Though that's hardly surprising, given the topic,' he answered drily. 'But it's certainly rational. Consider it,' he said, seeing her begin to mouth another protest.

'I have, and it took me all of three seconds to reject it!' she answered crossly, despising the sudden rapid race in her heart-rate.

'Listen,' he continued, as though she hadn't spoken, 'Dublin is a great city—'

'That's hardly the point! I can't live here with you, Finn—surely you can see that would be impossible?'

There was a long, rather strange pause. 'I wasn't suggesting that you live here with me, Catherine.'

Oh, if only the floor could have opened up and swallowed her! 'Well, thank God for that,' she said, rather weakly, and hoped that her voice didn't lack conviction. 'Where did you have in mind, then? Is there some home for unmarried mothers on the outskirts of the city?'

He had the grace to wince. 'I have a cottage by the sea. It's in Wicklow, close to Glendalough and a relatively short drive away. Fresh air and village life. It would be perfect for you. And the baby.'

It sounded like an oasis. 'I don't know.'

He heard her indecision and, like a barrister moving in for the kill with his closing argument, fluently outlined his case. 'You live on your own in London—what's the difference? And I can come and see you at weekends.'

Once again, she despaired at the sudden race of her pulse. He meant grudging duty visits, nothing else. She shook her head. 'No.'

'There are other factors, too, Catherine.'

She looked up, wishing that it wasn't such painful pleasure to stare into the eyes of the man who had fathered her child. 'Such as?'

'I have some friends who live there—Patrick and Aisling. I can introduce you to Aisling—she'd love to meet you, I'm sure. They've three children of their own—it would be good to have someone like that around.'

Aisling?

The name rang a bell and Catherine remembered

the morning she had left Finn's flat. A woman called Aisling had been talking on the answer-machine, asking where the hell he had been. She had assumed that it was someone he had stood up because he'd had a better offer.

'Do you know more than one Aisling?' she asked.

'No. Why?'

She shook her head. 'It doesn't matter.'

He carried on trying to sell the delights of Greystones, knowing that if she could see the place for herself she'd be sold. 'And my aunt lives there, too.'

'Your aunt?'

'That's right. She's…well, she's a very special lady.'

Catherine swallowed. She could just imagine what a protective relative would have to say about some conniving woman tricking her darling nephew into fatherhood.

'I don't think so, Finn,' she said uncertainly. 'Wouldn't everyone find the situation a little odd?'

'Well, of course they would. No one's ever heard me mention you before, and suddenly here you are—pregnant with my child!'

'Could do your street-cred a lot of harm?' she hazarded sarcastically.

'It's not my reputation I'm thinking about, Catherine,' he said softly. 'It's yours.' His eyes glittered as the spectre of responsibility reared its head. He did not balk it, but faced it head-on. 'There is, of course, one solution which would guarantee you all the respect a woman in your condition warrants.'

Utterly confused now, she stared at him in perplexity. 'What solution?'

'Marry me.'

There was a long, deafening silence and Catherine's heart clenched in her chest. 'Is this some kind of joke?' she demanded hoarsely.

He shook his head. 'Think about it, Catherine—see what sense it makes. It gives you security, for a start. And not just for you, for the baby.'

Perhaps someone else might have considered that offer in a purely mercenary way, but that someone else was not Catherine, with Catherine's experience of the world.

She had never thought about her own mortality much, but right now it was foremost in her mind. New life automatically made you think of the other end of the spectrum.

What would happen to her if she died suddenly? Who would look after and care for the baby? Not her mother, that was for sure.

But if she married Finn...

She stared at him with clear, bright eyes. 'And what's in it for you?'

'Can't a clever journalist like you work it out?' he answered flippantly, but then his voice sobered. 'As an ex-lover I can be sidelined, but as your husband I would have a say in the baby's life. It legitimises everything.' His eyes met hers with sudden under-standing. 'And didn't you say that you didn't want what you had to endure yourself for your baby? Whatever happens, Catherine, this child will have my name—and one day will inherit my wealth.'

'An old-fashioned marriage of convenience, you mean?'

'Or a very modern one,' he amended quietly.

It was a deliberately ambiguous statement. 'And what's that supposed to mean?'

'It means whatever you want it to mean. We can make the rules up as we go along.'

'And how long is this marriage supposed to last— presumably not for life?'

'Presumably not.'

'And if you want out?'

'Or you do?' he countered coolly.

'Either. If the situation between us is untenable in any way, then—'

'Aren't you jumping the gun a little? Why don't we save the big decisions until after the baby is born?'

He gave the glimmer of a smile, and Catherine felt her stomach turn over. Did he have any idea how that smile could turn a normally sensible woman's head? In spite of everything.

'What do you say, Catherine?'

She thought of going through it all alone, and suddenly felt the first tremblings of fear. For a moment she felt small and helpless and vulnerable—though surely that was natural enough?

While Finn was big and strong and dependable. It didn't matter what his feelings for her were, he would protect her, instinct told her that. And instinct was a very powerful influence where pregnant women were concerned.

She looked at him. He had stated that she didn't really have the luxury of choice, and in a way he was right. For what right-minded and responsible woman in her situation could give any answer other than the one which now came from between her dry lips.

'Very well, Finn. I'll marry you.'

CHAPTER TEN

AS WEDDINGS went, it was bizarre. The ceremony had to be quick and it had to be discreet—any sign of a hugely pregnant bride would have the press sniffing around in droves, and Finn didn't want that. Neither did Catherine.

And organising a wedding wasn't as easy as they made out in the films.

'Ireland's out,' he'd said grimly, as he replaced the telephone receiver. 'You need three months' written notice.'

'You didn't know that?' The question came out without her thinking.

'Why would I?' His eyes had sparked icy blue fire. 'I've never got married before.'

And wouldn't be now, she'd reminded herself painfully. Not if he hadn't been in such an invidious situation.

'It'll have to be in England, and I have to be resident for seven days prior to giving notice,' he'd said flatly. 'It's fifteen days minimum after that.'

He'd made it sound as if he was to undergo a protracted kind of operation. Catherine had turned away.

They'd flown back to England, where Finn had booked in to a hotel, and by some unspoken agreement they had not seen one another until the day of the wedding itself—although they'd had a few brief, uncomfortable conversations.

Catherine had spent the three weeks trying to behave as normally as possible—seeing her friends, trying to write—even once visiting her mother. And all the while her great big secret had burned so strongly within her that she was astonished no one else noticed.

When the day of the wedding finally dawned, her most overwhelming emotion was one of relief—that soon the subterfuge would be over.

Catherine glanced at her watch as she waited for her reluctant husband-to-be. She hadn't bought anything new—because that also seemed to go against the mood of the arrangement. Her favourite clingy violet dress made her look voluptuous, and she was grateful for the long jacket which covered most of the evidence.

But when she opened the door to him, her face drawn and tense, Finn felt his heart miss a beat.

'Smile for me, Catherine,' he whispered.

Obediently she curved her lips upwards into a smile, trying not to be enticed by the blue gleam of his eyes.

'You look like a gypsy,' he observed softly, as she pinned two large silver hoops to her ears.

'Is that bad, or good?'

'It's good,' he replied evenly, but he had to force himself to walk away and stare sightlessly out of the window. The trouble was that he still wanted her, and yet there now seemed to be an unbreachable emotional gulf which made intimacy out of the question. He glanced down at his watch. 'Almost ready to go?'

Nerves assailed her for the hundredth time that morning. He looked so devastating in his dark suit and snowy shirt that she was having difficulty remembering that this was all make-believe. He wasn't a *real* groom any more than she was a *real* bride. 'Finn, it's still not too late to back out, you know.'

'You want to?'

Of course she did. Part of her would have loved to be able to wave a magic wand and wish her old life back. While another part wished that this gorgeous man would sweep her into his arms and kiss all her make-up off and tell her that he couldn't bear *not* to marry her.

But of course he wouldn't. It wasn't that kind of deal. This was, to use her own expression—and it was one which had the power to make her giggle in a slight hysteria which she put down to hormones—a marriage of convenience. Modern or otherwise.

'Are you wishing it was Peter?' he asked suddenly.

'Peter?' To her horror she actually had to pause and think who he was talking about.

He heard the tone of her voice and his mouth thinned. That said a lot about her level of commitment, didn't it? 'Yeah, Peter—the man you went out with for—how long was it, Catherine? Four years?'

'Three.' She heard his disapproval and she couldn't bear that he might think she had just leapt from Peter's bed into his. 'We hadn't seen each other for six months before he ended it,' she said slowly. 'And I accepted that it was over.' She turned wide green eyes up to his. 'There was certainly no motive of getting my own back.'

'I see.' But he felt his body relax a little.

'And besides, what about you?' she challenged. 'Are you sorry that it's not Deirdra you're marrying?'

There was a pause. 'Deirdra's history.'

'That doesn't answer my question, Finn.'

He supposed it didn't. 'It happened a long time

ago.' He shrugged. 'We were both seventeen and discovering sex for the first time. It burnt itself out and then she went to Hollywood. End of story.'

He was describing first love, thought Catherine with a pang. And maybe for him—as for so many people—no one would ever live up to that idealised state. First love. There was nothing like it—even hard-bitten Miranda had said that.

'Oh, I see,' she said slowly.

He looked at her assessingly. 'Back out now, if you want to, Catherine.'

'No, I'm happy to go ahead with it,' she said.

'Well, you don't look it,' he said softly. 'You'll have to work harder than that to convince anyone.'

She fixed a smile to her glossy lips. 'How's that?'

'Perfect,' he answered, feeling an ache in his groin which he knew would not be satisfied by a traditional post-wedding night.

For directly after the ceremony they were taking the first flight back to Ireland. A car would be waiting at the airport and he was driving her to Greystones, to settle her into the house.

And after the weekend he would return to Dublin. Alone.

Finn thought how vulnerable she looked on the plane, shaking her head and refusing his offer of a glass of champagne, her face telling him that she had nothing to celebrate.

He had to keep telling himself not to be sucked in by a pair of green eyes and a rose-pink mouth, tell himself instead that Catherine Walker had a bewitching power which hid her true nature. And that beauty combined with burgeoning life could fool a man into thinking she was something different. And, while she might not have conspired to humiliate him publicly, she had still deliberately kept from him the fact that she was a journalist.

'Won't your mother think it strange that you didn't tell her about the wedding?' he asked, as the car left Dublin and began to eat up the miles leading towards the coast.

'Lots of people go away and get married without telling anyone these days.'

'She won't pry?'

'I'll have to tell her the truth—that I'm pregnant,' she said flatly. 'She'll understand.' Oh, yes—her mother would understand *that* all right.

'And when are you going to inform her that you've acquired a husband?'

Acquired a husband! He made it sound like something from a Victorian novel! 'When I'm…settled.'

'Soon?' he demanded.

She nodded. 'Once I've been at Greystones for a couple of days.' Catherine stole a look at Finn's dark profile. 'Have you told your aunt, or any of your friends?'

He shook his head, easing his foot down on the accelerator. 'They'd only have wanted to join in and make a big fuss of it.'

And, presumably, turn the day into something it wasn't.

But repeating her marriage lines after the registrar had made Catherine feel heartbreakingly wistful, and only the stirring flutter in her stomach had kept her voice steady enough to speak in a voice as devoid of emotion as Finn's.

'What a lovely couple you make!' the Registrar had

cooed, and then said with a twinkle, 'You may now kiss your wife.'

Finn had looked down at Catherine, a wry smile touching the corners of his lips as he saw the startled look which widened her green eyes. 'Mustn't disappoint, must we?' he'd murmured, and bent his head to brush his mouth against hers.

As kisses went, it had been almost chaste. Not deep and hungry and greedy, like the kisses they had shared before they had made love. But, in its way, the most poignant kiss of all—gentle and full of false promise. His lips were like honey and just the touch of them had sent little shivers of longing all the way down her spine. And yet it had mocked her with all that it could have been and was not.

Not for them the urgent and giggling drive to the nearest bed to consummate the marriage. Instead she would be delivered to a house which—although it sounded quite lovely—was to be hers alone during the week, while the baby grew inside her belly.

And after that?

Resisting the urge to wrap her arms around his neck, Catherine had pulled away, giving the watching registrar an awkward smile.

They arrived at Greystones late in the afternoon, through sleepy-looking streets and past stone houses. Finn's cottage stood at the far end of the small town, an unprepossessing low stone building which looked as though it had been there since the beginning of time.

'Oh, it's beautiful, Finn,' she said, breathing in the sea-air and thinking what a healthy place this was to be when she compared it to her tiny flat in London.

And she was healthy, too—the bloom of pregnancy making her face seem to glow from within. She looked both fragile and strong, and on an impulse Finn bent and scooped her up into his arms, his eyes glittering blue fire as he looked down into her face.

'What the h-hell do you think you're doing?' she spluttered.

'Bowing to tradition, as well as bowing my head,' he said softly, as he bent his head to carry her through the low door. 'By carrying you over the threshold.'

He placed her down carefully, seeming reluctant to remove his hands from her waist, and Catherine stared up into his face. 'Why did you do that?'

'It'll soon get round that I've married you. We ought to maintain at least a modicum of pretence that it's the real thing.'

She pulled away. It hurt just as much as it was probably intended to, and Catherine had to remind herself that she had walked into this with her eyes open. She had agreed to marry him for the sake of her baby and her baby alone—but that didn't stop her from having the occasional foolish fantasy, did it? Didn't stop her from wishing that they didn't have to go through a hypocritical stage-managed act just in case anyone happened to be watching them.

In an attempt to distract herself she looked around her instead. The cottage was comfortably furnished with squashy sofas, and paintings of wild and wonderful Wicklow were hung everywhere. But the walls were surprisingly faded—indeed, the whole room looked as though it could do with a coat of paint.

'Come through here,' said Finn, looking at the stiff and defensive set of her shoulders. 'I've something to show you.'

The smaller room which led off the sitting room looked similarly tired, but Catherine's attention was soon drawn from the state of the walls by a desk overlooking the big garden at the back of the house. Because what was on it stood out like a sore thumb. A desk with a high-tech computer, fax and telephone and state-of-the-art printer—all obviously and gleamingly new.

'For you,' he said simply.

Catherine looked longingly at the computer, which made her own look as if it had been invented around the same time as the wheel, then lifted her face up to him. 'Why?'

'A wedding present.'

'I've bought nothing for you—'

He shook his head. 'You write, don't you? I thought that as you were going to be living in a remote place you might as well have the most modern stuff on the market to keep you in touch with the big world outside.'

'I've brought my own computer,' said Catherine stubbornly.

'I imagined you would have done—but I doubt it has anything like the speed or the power of this one.'

She turned on him furiously. 'You don't have to *buy* me, you know, Finn!'

'For God's sake—do you have to be so damned defensive? You wouldn't *be* here if I had been thinking with my head instead—'

'You don't have to spell it out for me,' she said in a hollow voice, feeling quite sick. 'And there's no need for you to play the martyr, either.'

'I am not playing the martyr,' he retorted. 'I am just taking responsibility for your predicament—'

'Stop it! Just stop it!' she interrupted, even angrier now. 'I will not, *not* have this baby described as a "predicament". It wasn't planned, no—but it's happened and I intend to make the best of it. This baby is going to be a *happy* baby, whatever happens. And you shan't take the lion's share of the responsibility, either. We're both to blame, if you like.'

'Blame?' He gave an odd smile. 'Now who's using loaded words, Catherine?' But he forced himself to draw back, to blot out lips which when furiously parted like that made him want to crush them beneath his own. And to try to put out of his mind the fact that to spend the rest of the afternoon in bed might just rid them both of some of their pent-up anger.

And frustration, he thought achingly.

'Would you like to get changed?' he asked, eyeing the purple dress which clung so provocatively to her blossoming body and wondering how he was going to get through the weekend with any degree of sanity.

Catherine nodded. 'Please.'

'Come on, I'll show you upstairs.'

There were four bedrooms, though one was almost too tiny to qualify.

Finn put her suitcase on the bed of the largest room, which suddenly seemed like the smallest to her, when he was close enough to touch and she was beguiled by a faint, evocative trace of his aftershave.

'The bathroom's along the corridor,' he said quickly. 'You'll find everything you need.'

She had a quick bath and then struggled into her jeans, throwing a baggy jumper over the top. When she came downstairs she found that Finn had changed as well.

He saw her frowning. 'What's up?'

'My jeans won't do up!' she exclaimed, pointing at the waistband.

He hid a smile. 'That's generally what happens, Catherine. We'll have to buy you some pregnancy clothes—though God knows where around here!'

'Big tent-like dresses with Peter Pan collars!' she groaned.

'No, not any more,' he said knowledgeably.

Her eyes narrowed. 'How do you know that?'

'I remember Aisling telling me, the last time she was pregnant. Come on and I'll make you tea,' he said. 'And then I'll light a fire.'

She followed him into a kitchen which had most definitely not been modernised, and Catherine raised her eyebrows in surprise at the old-fashioned units and the brown lino on the floor. Even the ugly windows hadn't been replaced!

'How long have you owned this place, Finn?'

He turned the tap on and filled up the kettle, his back to her. 'It came on the market about five years ago.'

She heard the evasion in his voice and wondered what he wasn't telling her. She raised her eyebrows. 'It's not the kind of place I imagined you buying. It's…well, it's nothing like your place in Dublin.'

'No.' He had forgotten for a moment that she was a journalist, with a journalist's instinct for a story. *His* instinct would be not to tell it. But they were married now, even if it was in name only. And if she was going to give birth to his baby then what was the point in keeping everything locked in? 'It's where I was born. Where I lived until the age of seven.'

Catherine studied him. There was something else here, too—something which made his voice deepen with a bleak, remembered pain. She wondered what had happened to him at the age of seven.

He saw the question in her eyes and sighed, knowing that he had to tell her. She carried his baby, and that gave her the right to know about a past he had grown used to locking away. 'My mother died,' he said, in stark explanation, bending down to light the gas with a match.

'I'm sorry—'

'She'd been widowed when I was a baby—there was no one left to look after me and so I went to live with my aunt.'

'Oh, Finn.' Her heart went out to him, and she wanted to put her arms tightly round him and hug away his pain, but the emotional shutters had been banged tightly shut. She could read that in the abrupt way he had turned away, putting cups and saucers upon a tray with an air of finality. Catherine understood the need for defence against probing into pain. The time was not right—indeed, it might never be right. But that was Finn's decision, not hers.

'Have you such a thing as a biscuit?' she asked, with a smile. 'I'm starving!'

He let out a barely perceptible sigh. 'There's enough food to sink a battleship. I asked Aisling to come in and stock up on groceries. We don't have to go out all weekend, if we don't want to.'

Catherine's smile faded and she couldn't quite work out whether she felt excitement or terror. What did that mean? she wondered, with a slight tinge of hysteria. That play-acting as honeymooners was going to extend as far as the bedroom?

'Go and sit down, Catherine,' he commanded softly. 'And I'll bring this through.'

His face was unreadable in the dying light of the day, and rather dazedly Catherine obeyed him, sinking down onto one of the squashy sofas while she struggled not to project too much. There was no point in working out what she would do if he suggested bed when the circumstance might never arise!

He brought the tea in and poured her a cup.

'Is today a sugar day, or not?' he asked gravely.

She bit back a smile, stupidly pleased that he had remembered. 'Not. My cravings seem to have settled down into something approaching a normal appetite.' She waited until she had drunk some of the tea, then put the cup down. 'Finn?'

'Catherine?'

'How often do you come to stay here?'

'Not often enough,' he admitted. 'I keep meaning to spend weekends here, to get a breath of sea-air and a bit of simple living to blow the cobwebs away, but…' His words tailed off.

'But?'

'Oh, you know what it's like. Life seems to get in the way of plans.'

Yes, she knew what it was like—or rather what it *had* been like. But she was beginning a whole new life now, and a whole new future. And not just in terms of the baby. She was going to be living in Finn's cottage as his quasi-wife and she didn't have a clue about what role she was supposed—or wanted—to fulfil! Make up the rules as we go along, he had said, but surely that was easier than he suggested?

But for the baby's sake she cleared her thoughts of concern and settled down to drink her tea.

He saw the softening of her face, and the look of

serenity which made a Madonna of her, and found himself wondering how many different masks she wore. Or was her pregnancy just making him project his own idealised version of her as the future mother of his child? That she was soft and caring and vulnerable…rather than the cynical and go-getting journalist.

Life is evidence-based, Finn, he reminded himself grimly. Just think of the evidence. She wears different masks, that's all. Just as all women do.

He stood up. 'I'll light the fire,' he said shortly.

Catherine felt unreal and disconnected as he created a roaring blaze from the logs in the basket, and warmth and light transformed the room just as dusk crept upon the early evening air. The flames cast shadows which flickered over the long, denim-clad thighs and she remembered their powerful strength in different guises. Running through a Greek sea. Naked and entwined with hers.

He looked up to find her watching him, her slim body sprawled comfortably on the sofa, and the temptation to join her and to kiss her almost overwhelmed him. He knew that in her arms he could forget all his doubts and misgivings about the bizarre situation they had created for themselves.

But wouldn't being intimate with her tonight make a bizarre situation even more so? Confuse and muddy the waters?

He caught her eye but she quickly looked away, as if uncomfortable, and Finn was forced to acknowledge that things had changed, that there was no guarantee that Catherine wanted him in that way any more. Not after everything that had happened.

Later she unpacked, and Finn cooked them supper,

and afterwards they listened to Irish radio until she began to yawn and escaped to her bedroom. Her senses and thoughts were full of him. All she could think about was how much she wanted him.

And how much easier everything would be if she didn't.

But, after a surprisingly sleep-filled night alone on the big, soft feather mattress, the morning dawned bright and sunny. After breakfast Finn took her down to the beach to look at the boats and to walk along the sand, then afterwards to meet his aunt.

Her heart was beating nervously as they approached the house. 'What's her name?'

'Finola.'

'I bet she'll take an instant dislike to me.'

'Don't be silly, Catherine—she's hardly going to hate a woman I bring home and introduce as my wife, now, is she? She loves me; she wants me to be happy.'

Happy? What an ironic choice of word.

'So what's your definition of happiness, Finn?'

He stooped down for a pebble and hurled it out at the blue sea before turning to look at her with eyes which rivalled the ocean's hue.

'It's a way of travelling, Catherine,' he said slowly. 'Not a destination.'

So, was she happy at this precise moment? She thought about it. Actually, yes, she was. Though contented was probably a better description. She was healthy and pregnant and walking along a beautiful beach with a beautiful man. And if she defined happiness in a futile wish that their relationship went deeper than that, then she was heading for a big disappointment. You couldn't look for happiness in another person. First you had to find it within yourself.

She thought that to the outside world they probably made a very striking couple—both tall and slim, with matching heads of jet-black, and her gleaming and brand-new gold band proclaiming very definitely that she was a newly-wed.

But there were several giveaway signs that all was not as it appeared. Finn did not smile down into her face with the conspiratorial air of a lover, nor hold her hand as if he couldn't bear to let it go.

Not, that was, until they arrived at his aunt's house. Then he caught her fingers in his and squeezed them reassuringly. 'It'll be okay,' he whispered.

The door was opened by a grey-haired woman in her late sixties, whose faded eyes were a blue a few shades less intense than those of her nephew. She only came up to the middle of his chest, but she flung her arms around him all the same and Catherine's heart clenched as he hugged her back. She'd never seen him so openly affectionate and demonstrative.

'Why, it's the divil himself!' she exclaimed. 'Finn! Finn Delaney!' She fixed him with a look of admonishment, but anyone could see her heart wasn't in it. 'And why haven't you been round to see me sooner?' Without waiting for an answer, she moved the blue eyes curiously from Finn to Catherine. 'And who might this be?'

Catherine was feeling as nervous as a child on the first day of school, recognising how much this woman meant to Finn and desperately not wanting to start off on the wrong foot.

'I'm Catherine,' she said simply. 'I'm Finn's wife.'

CHAPTER ELEVEN

FINN'S wife.

The first and only time she had said it had been to
Finn's aunt, but she thought it often enough, running
the words sweetly through her mind like chocolate
melting over ice-cream.

She had thought it the first morning he had driven
back to Dublin, standing in the doorway just like a
proper wife, watching his car disappear over the horizon, leaving her alone with her thoughts and her
writing and her growing baby. And the big bed in
which she slept alone.

The car had become a distant dot and she'd slowly
closed the door on it, telling herself that she was glad
he had made no move to consummate the marriage.

It would have only complicated things. Made the
inevitable split more difficult—for her, certainly.
Because women grew much closer to a man when
they had sex with him. Even more so when that man's
child grew bigger with every day that passed.

But being off limits had forced them together in a
way which had its own kind of intimacy. For what
did you do when you were closeted together every
weekend and unable to do the one thing you most
wanted to do?

Well, they seemed to go for an awful lot of walks.
Brisk, bracing walks along the unimaginably beautiful
coastline. He would feed her cream and scones, and
afterwards take her back to the cottage and insist that

she put her feet up for the inevitable sleep which would follow. Sometimes she would wake up to find him watching her, the blue eyes so blazing and intent. And for one brief and blissful moment she would almost forget herself, want to hold her arms out towards him, to draw him close against the fullness of her breasts.

But the moment would be lost when he turned away, as if something he saw in her disturbed him, and she wondered if he felt uncomfortable with this masquerade of marriage. Did he find himself wanting to tell the aunt who was more like a mother to him that it was not all it seemed? That he had made her pregnant and was simply doing the right thing by her? Was he now perhaps regretting that decision?

He'd taken her to meet his friends who lived at the far end of the small town. Apparently he had known Patrick 'for ever', and Patrick's wife, Aisling, was an energetic redhead who squealed with delight when they told her the news.

'At last!' she exclaimed. 'You've done it at last! Oh, Finn—there'll be legions of women weeping all over Ireland!'

'And legions of men sighing with relief,' commented Patrick wryly as he reached into the fridge for a bottle of champagne.

'Shut up.' Finn smiled.

'So you went and got married *without telling anyone*?' Patrick demanded as he eased the cork out of the bottle. 'Even us?'

'Especially you,' murmured Finn. 'We didn't want the whole of Wicklow knowing!' He paused. 'Catherine's pregnant, you see.'

'Oh, Patrick,' said Aisling softly. 'Will you listen

to the man? ''Catherine's pregnant,'' he says. As if we didn't have eyes in our heads, Finn Delaney! Congratulations! To both of you!'

She hugged them both in turn and Catherine felt a great lump rise in her throat, glad to have her face enveloped in Aisling's thick-knit sweater. I don't deserve this, she thought. I can't go through with it. Pretending to these nice people that all is what it seems.

But she looked up, her eyes bright, and met a sudden warm understanding in Finn's, and she drew an odd sort of comfort from that.

'Will you look after Catherine for me while I'm away in Dublin, Aisling?' he said, his voice suddenly urgent.

'But I don't need looking after!' protested Catherine, slightly terrified that this attractive woman with the warm smile might ask questions which would be impossible not to answer truthfully.

'You can see me as much or as little as you wish to, Catherine—I won't mind in the least,' said Aisling firmly. 'But won't you be terribly lonesome with Finn away?'

'Catherine wanted peace and quiet,' put in Finn. 'So Dublin's out. And she wants to write.'

'Yes.' Catherine swallowed. 'I'm a journalist.'

'So I believe,' said Aisling lightly, leaving Catherine wondering whether she had read the article. But even if she had she didn't seem to hold it against her, not judging by the genuine warmth of her welcome, anyway.

A small boy came running in, closely followed by an older sister, his face covered in sand and the sticky remains of a crab. 'Jack Casey! Just what have you been doing to yourself?'

'He tried to eat the crab, Mammy!' crowed the little girl. 'Even though I told him not to!'

'And you just let him, did you?' asked her mother, deftly picking up a cloth and beginning to scrub at her protesting son. 'Does this not put you off what you're about to go through, Catherine?'

'Well, I'll have a few years to prepare myself,' said Catherine, as Jack deposited a chubby handful of shells into her lap.

'Jack! Please don't put sand all over Catherine's dress!' scolded Aisling.

'I don't mind—honestly, I don't.'

Finn sat and watched the interaction of everyday family life and felt a great clench of his heart. How easy and uncomplicated it all seemed on the surface. With Catherine sitting there laughing as a sticky hand was shoved towards her hair, which today she had woven into two thick plaits which fell over her breasts.

Pregnancy suited her, he thought unwillingly, and her growing body seemed just as sexy as the pre-pregnancy one had done.

Thank God he was going back to Dublin in the morning!

The weeks slid by and Catherine settled into her new life, taking to the slow, easy pace like a duck to water.

She rose early and walked along the seashore, tracing her route back via the shops, where she bought freshly baked bread and milk which tasted better than any milk she had ever drunk before.

Then she settled down to write, but found that her

writing had changed. She no longer had the desire nor the contacts to produce the punchy, easy-read features which had defined her career up until this point.

The flat in Clerkenwell was being rented out at an exorbitant fee, and so for the first time in her life there were no pressing money worries. She could enjoy her pregnancy and give in to what she most wanted to do.

She began to write a book.

'You're the only person I've told!' she said on the phone to her mother one night.

'What, not even Finn?'

'No. It's a surprise,' said Catherine truthfully. Or was she scared of trying and failing in his eyes?

'And when am I going to meet this husband of yours?' asked her mother. 'Everybody's asking me what he's like and I have to tell them that I don't know!'

This was a difficult one—more than difficult. Catherine had the means to fly her mother out—and knew how much she wanted to see her and how much her mother would enjoy life in the small Irish village. But—and it was a monumental but—how did she begin to explain the situation?

If her mother came she would either have to tell the truth or she would have to pretend, and she didn't know how long she could keep that up in front of the person who knew her so well.

For a start she and Finn would be expected to share a bedroom, and she knew for a fact that she couldn't do it. Couldn't sleep with him and not be climbing the walls with a terrible yearning to have him close to her in a way he did not want to be. It was bad enough on her nights alone, and the ones when he was sleeping just along the corridor—being in an enclosed space with a bed in it would be almost impossible.

'Soon, Mum,' she said lamely.

'If you leave it much longer, then I'll be a grandmother!'

And that might be the best solution all round. Wait until the baby was born and the disruption he or she would cause would detract from what was actually going on in Finn and Catherine's so-called relationship. And besides, no one expected a new mother to be energetically making love to her husband every night!

Having another person in the house would mean that Finn would be able to focus on the best thing to do. And so would she. They could come to an amicable agreement about access, and all the other things people had to discuss when they were no longer together.

Not that she and Finn had ever been together. Not really. Not in the true sense of the word, anyway.

But it was funny how you could grow close to someone, even though your head was telling you that it was sheer madness to do so. She didn't want to find him funny and sexy and engaging. She wanted to be able to pick holes in his character, to tell herself that actually he was a cold and power-hungry maniac and that she would never have been happy with him anyway.

But she couldn't.

She told herself that it was easy to get on well with someone over the course of a weekend—that if they lived together all the time they would irritate the hell out of each other. But she couldn't quite believe that, either.

Energy flowed through her like lifeblood. She wrote throughout the day, sometimes well into the evening, and when Finn rang she would tell him how her day had been. They would talk with an ease and familiarity which was poignant in itself.

One night she told him how she'd been over and helped Aisling with her baking, and that Aunt Finola had taken her to a bingo session at the church hall and Catherine had won an ironing board!

'What are you going to do with it?'

'I gave it to the priest's housekeeper. It seems silly to have two.'

'Could come in useful,' he said gravely.

'As an extra table, perhaps?' she suggested helpfully.

She told herself that of course it was easy to talk to someone on the phone, because you couldn't see the expression on their face or the look in their eyes. She told herself that it was important they remained on good terms because she would need to be in touch with Finn for the rest of her life. The baby would always connect them.

And she told herself that she would be okay when the day came—perhaps sooner than she would hope for—when he would tell her gently that the time had come for the parting of the ways. That they had done their best for the baby and now they were both free.

But she didn't want to be free. Or was that simply sneaky Mother Nature again—tying her emotionally to the biological father of her child?

It didn't seem to matter how much logic warned her that she mustn't embrace her new-wife role too enthusiastically, because try as she might she couldn't help herself.

Every Friday night she felt like a woman whose husband was coming home like a conquering hero. She would see the city-strain etched on his face as he opened the front door and she would pour him a gin and tonic—just like a real wife.

Finn found he couldn't wait to be out of the city on Friday nights, tying up his work as early as possible so that he could be roaring out of Dublin and heading for the sea.

His apartment now seemed very empty in a way that the cottage never did. But Catherine did girly things; maybe that was why. She put flowers in vases and she baked cakes. Any day now he was fully expecting her to have acquired a new puppy!

She's just playing another role—a domestic role this time, he told himself, as the glitter of the distant sea told him he was almost home. But surely she wouldn't be able to keep it up for ever?

He walked into the cottage one night and frowned. Something was different, and it took a moment or two to figure out what it was.

'You've painted the walls!'

'So I have.' She gave a serene smile as she walked over to the drinks tray, pleased with the soft-peach wash which had transformed the dingy room. 'Do you like it?'

He looked around, his expression closed yet edgy, trying to distract himself from the pink V-necked sweater she wore, which showed far too much of the heavy swell of her breasts and seemed far too provocative for a cold Friday night in Wicklow!

'You should have asked me first!' he ground out.

The smile died on her lips. 'I'm sorry, Finn,' she said stiffly. 'I was mistakenly using the place as my home, perhaps fooling myself a little too convincingly that we were a married couple!'

'Even if we were,' he came back bitingly, 'surely decorating is something a couple would discuss together?'

'I wanted to surprise you—'

'Well, you've certainly done that, Catherine!'

And then he turned on her, his blue eyes blazing with an anger which was surely disproportionate to the crime of painting a room.

'Don't you think that if I'd wanted it decorated I'd have done so before, myself? Don't you think I'd have had the best decorators in the damned country working for me?'

She slammed his gin and tonic down so hard that it slopped all over the sideboard, but she was too angry to care and Finn didn't seem to notice.

'Oh, I'm *sorry*! The best money can buy? Is that what you mean?' she questioned witheringly. 'Is that why you're so mad? Because I was stupid enough to do it myself? Because I picked up the paintbrush instead of snapping my fingers to get someone else to do it for me? Well, don't you worry, Finn Delaney— I happened to be very careful. And if I say so myself I did a *bloody good job*—even if you're too stupid and too arrogant to see it!'

And she stormed out of the room and up the stairs.

'Catherine, just you come right back here!'

'Go to hell! Except they'd probably turn you away!' she yelled back.

He took the stairs two at a time and reached her just as she was about to close the bathroom door, puffing and out of breath. She saw him coming and tried to slam it, but he stuck his foot in it.

'Get your foot out!'

'Not until you open it!'

'I want a bath!'

'And I want to talk to you!'

'Well, tough! If you want to complain about the wretched walls again, then don't worry—we'll go out in the morning and get some peat and rub it in. Then they'll look as dingy as before.'

He started to laugh, and she took the opportunity to push at the door again.

'Open the door, Catherine.'

'Open it yourself!' But she let go and he stepped inside, dwarfing the room with his powerful presence.

He saw the defiant yet defeated droop of her shoulders and something inside him melted. 'Oh, sweetheart, I'm sorry. I shouldn't have spoken to you like that!'

'You should have thought before you opened your stupid mouth! But you never do!'

'Yes, I should. And, no, I don't.' He gave a rueful smile. 'But I think we've already established that my thinking goes out of the window whenever you're around, Catherine!'

'Then maybe we should reconsider this whole stupid scheme!'

'You think it's stupid?'

'I think that we must be out of our minds to think we can go through with it, yes!'

'But I thought you were enjoying life down here—'

'Oh, you *stupid* man!'

He burst out laughing. 'You know, for a journalist, you're having terrible trouble with your command of the English language, Catherine. That's three times you've used the word ''stupid'' in as many—'

Her hand flew up to slap his face, but he caught it, using it to pull her right up close to him, and she saw that he was having difficulty controlling his breathing, that his blue eyes had suddenly darkened like the night.

'My, my, my, but you've a temper on you like a witch sometimes!'

'And is it any wonder, living with you?'

They stared at one another and the air was suddenly tight with tension.

'Do you know we're arguing like an old married couple?' he said unsteadily. 'You realise that we're getting all the worst bits out of marriage with none of the best bits?'

Something in his eyes was making her feel very dizzy. 'Finn?' she whispered.

'Catherine?' he answered unsteadily.

She knew that he was about to kiss her even before he moved. She could read it in the blue blaze of his eyes. And she opened her lips to greet his, not caring about the wisdom of it, only knowing that she had prayed for this moment ever since he had slipped that gold wedding band on her finger.

They kissed as if it was the first time, and in a way maybe it *was* the first time. This time they were not strangers, drawn together by a hunger which could not be denied. The hunger clamoured as ever before, but now they had a history—past and present and future all fusing together—made flesh by the baby which kicked in her belly.

He drew his mouth away and looked down into her

hectic green eyes, shaken by the power of that kiss. 'God, Catherine,' he said unsteadily.

Rocked by emotions she scarcely recognised, she shook her head. 'Just shut up and kiss me again.'

'Impatient woman,' he said, almost tenderly.

'Impatient?' she demanded incredulously.

'Shut up, Catherine.'

And their lips met again.

He ran his hand down over the fullness of her breast, alighting with possessive greed on the tight curve of her belly, and groaned against her lips as he felt the seeking urgency of her own.

'Catherine—sweet, beautiful, swollen Catherine— let me make love to you now.'

'Swollen' should not have sounded so erotic to her ears, but it did. More than erotic. But she was so aroused at that moment that if he had started reciting the telephone directory to her then it would have sounded like poetry.

She tore her mouth away with difficulty. 'Sweet heavens, Finn—I thought you'd never ask!'

Shakily, his hand traced the outline of her face. He cupped it between his hands and dropped soft kisses onto the pale silk of her skin. He wanted long, slow lovemaking, and he knew that he must be gentle with her, but—dear heaven—he felt so hard, so exquisitely hard, that if she had not been pregnant with his child then he might very well have pushed her to the floor and…

That particular memory drew him up with a jolt, and he allowed himself one fleeting and bitter regret that their child had not been conceived in love but in anger. But that did not matter now. What was done was done, and he now had the opportunity to make the kind of long, slow love which a woman like Catherine deserved.

'Come with me, sweetheart.'

'Where are you taking me?'

'Somewhere I should have taken you weeks ago.' It was a bed he wanted, and the nearest would do—which just happened to be Catherine's room. He spotted a filmy little thong protruding from the top drawer and gave a little shudder as he drew her into the circle of his arms. Could she still wear skimpy underwear like that, even though she was pregnant? He guessed that he was about to find out.

Still holding her with his hands, he pushed her away. 'I've never undressed a pregnant woman before,' he murmured.

'I should hope not!'

'I'll be very careful,' he promised, as he peeled her sweater over her head.

She looped her arms around his neck and followed with the nuzzle of her lips. 'Not too careful, I hope. And besides, it doesn't matter now!'

He smiled. 'That wasn't what I was talking about, and you know it. I meant because you're pregnant.'

'Pregnant women are very resilient—or hadn't you noticed?'

Oh, yes—he'd noticed all right. She wasn't one of those women who lay around like an invalid, expecting to be waited on. Why, just the other day he had had to forcibly remove a spade from her hand and tell her that it was too cold to be digging. She had become huffy and stomped off, and told him that it was a crime not to foster love on such a beautiful garden.

He sucked in a breath as her body was revealed to him. Her breasts were glorious, ripe and bursting as they pushed against ivory-coloured lace. And the matching lacy thong left very little to the imagination.

'God,' he moaned. 'I'd no idea that a pregnant woman could look so sexy!'

'Well, that's a relief,' she offered drily.

He unclipped her bra and the heavy breasts came spilling out. He bent his head and his tongue licked luxuriantly against one hard, dark nipple. Catherine clutched at him, dizzy with the sheer sensation of it.

'Finn,' she said weakly.

'Mmm?'

He tugged at the little lacy thong, sliding it down over her thighs, and laid his hand softly on the dark fuzz of hair which concealed the very core of her femininity. He felt her jerk with pleasure. Wanted to give her yet more pleasure.

He knelt in front of her as if in homage, then dipped his tongue to delve into her honeyed warmth. She clutched his head to her, catching sight of their reflected image in the mirror. The sight of it turned her on even more. It seemed outrageously provocative to see her naked, pregnant body and the dark-haired man working such magic with his mouth.

'I'd better get horizontal,' she groaned. 'Before I fall over.'

He lifted his head and saw the smoky look in her eyes. 'Yeah. I think you'd better.'

He carried her, protesting, but only half-heartedly.

'Finn, stop it—I'm much too heavy these days.'

'But I like it. I like carrying you.'

'I'd noticed!'

'And you're still light enough not to trouble me.'

'You're a very strong man, Finn Delaney,' she sighed.

'I know I am,' he teased.

But he felt as weak as a pussycat as he tore his clothes off and lost himself in the warmth of her embrace.

He kissed her long and hard, smoothing his hand reverentially over her belly, and was just about to move it along, down to the inviting softness of her thighs, when she shook her head.

'Wait,' she whispered.

'I don't think I *can*—'

'Your baby, Finn. He's going to kick.'

'How can you tell?'

'I just can—ouch!'

Finn felt the hefty swipe of a small heel as it connected with the flat of his hand, and he stared down into Catherine's eyes, more shaken than he would have imagined.

'You think it's a boy?' he questioned thickly.

'I think so.'

'How?'

'I don't know…I just… Oh, *Finn*!'

'Do you like that?'

He wasn't feeling the baby any more. 'Mmm.' She slipped her hand down luxuriously, to capture the silken-steel of him, exultant to feel him shudder helplessly beneath her caress. 'Do *you* like that?'

'It's not me I'm thinking of right now—I don't want to hurt you, Catherine.'

For a moment she closed her eyes. If only he knew that the only way he was going to hurt her was by leaving her. And this is only going to make it harder, whispered the voice of reason. You should stop it right now.

But how could she possibly stop him when she wanted him so badly?

'What shall we do?' he whispered.

For a moment she thought he was asking about their future—but his fingers were playing with her breasts, sending little shivers of exquisite sensation rippling like warm sun across her skin. 'You mean *how* shall we…?'

'Mmm.'

'Use your imagination, Finn—I'm as much of a novice at this kind of thing as you are. I—oh, *Finn*!' She gave an expectant wriggle as Finn turned her onto her side and began to stroke her bottom, the other hand sliding up around her waist and from there to cup a swollen breast. She felt him pressing against her, so hard and so ready.

He felt her heat, sensed her urgency. He would never normally have asked a woman if she was ready, but he needed to be sure. And not just because she was pregnant.

'Catherine?' he questioned unsteadily.

'Oh, yes, Finn. Yes!'

Her senses seemed more highly tuned than they had ever been, and she was not sure whether that was down to abstinence or pregnancy. But as he entered her Catherine's mind cleared and she identified the emotion she had not before dared analyse.

For it was love, pure and simple. She loved this man. This man who could never truly be hers. She closed her eyes tightly. Stopped thinking and started feeling. Less pain that way.

Afterwards they lay exactly as they were, like sweat-sheened spoons, their heartbeats gradually slowing along with their breathing.

He looped a careless arm around her belly and felt another kick. He smiled against her shoulder. 'Ouch, again!'

'You should feel it from inside!'

He levered himself up onto one elbow to stare down at her, brushing back a strand of black hair, his eyes serious. 'I'm sorry I snapped at you.'

'You were frustrated, I expect. Don't worry about it, Finn—so was I.'

His face darkened. 'You think that's what it was all about? Frustration?'

'I don't know, do I? I'm trying to be practical.' Trying not to read too much into this situation and having to fight very hard with herself not to. 'What was it about, if not frustration?'

He turned onto his back, noticing for the first time the old-fashioned embossed wallpaper which covered the ceiling. Would she have ripped *that* down, the next time he came home—and would it really matter if she did? 'You just happened to touch a raw nerve.'

'Because I went ahead and decorated without asking you? Because I took control away from you?'

Would it sound crazy to tell her? Was it crazier still to have her think that he was the kind of intolerant tyrant who insisted on being privy to every decision made inside the home?

He shook his head, wondering if she had become a journalist because she was perceptive, or whether perception had come as a by-product of her career. Or was this just what happened naturally when a man and a woman started living together—started to know one another inside and out? Surely it weakened your defences to let someone get inside your head? Strengthened the relationship, yes, but at what cost?

'What, Finn?' she persisted softly.

'More a case of burying my head in the sand, I guess. Arrested development—call it what you like. A crazy urge to hang on to the past—I'm not sure, Catherine.'

She rested her head on his shoulder. 'You're talking in riddles.'

He smoothed her hair absently. 'I never changed this house at all, you see. I wanted to have it exactly the way it was.'

She thought about this for a moment. 'Like Miss Havisham in *Great Expectations*, you mean?'

'Well, I haven't got a wedding dress covered in cobwebs, if that's what you're implying!' He wound a strand of hair around his finger. 'I suppose this place always represented where I came from. I felt it would be a kind of betrayal if I decorated the interior so that it looked like something you'd find in a magazine.'

'If you applied that theory to everything then we'd still be travelling by horse and cart,' she said reasonably.

He laughed. 'Perhaps.'

She looked at his pensive profile. Was it only in bed that a man like this let his guard down? 'You don't need material things to remind you of your roots, Finn,' she told him softly. 'The values you learned are what matters, and you keep those deep in your heart.'

He nodded. This felt close. Dangerously close. A warm haven far away from the rest of the world. He forced himself to return to reality—because reality was the one thing he was equipped to deal with. He turned to face her and ran a lazy finger down her side, enjoying her responsive shiver. 'So I guess this means we'll be sharing a bedroom from now on?'

It felt like one step forward and two steps back, and all her zing and fizz and exhilaration evaporated. The brightness dimmed and Catherine felt curiously and ridiculously disappointed at his matter-of-fact assessment. Until she reminded herself that nothing had changed—not really.

Their situation was no different from what it had been before, except that now sex had been introduced into the equation. She shouldn't start confusing post-coital confidences with real, true and lasting intimacy.

'I guess we will,' she said lightly. 'Now, are you going to go down and make me my supper? I have a ferocious appetite on me!'

'Ferocious, hmm?' He smiled as he swung his naked body out of bed and looked down at her. 'You know, Catherine, you're sounding more Irish by the day.'

She nodded. She needed to. Her baby was going to be born in Ireland and have an Irish father.

She, too, needed roots.

CHAPTER TWELVE

'CATHERINE! For God's sake, come in here and sit down.'

'I can't! I'm sorting out the kitchen cupboards!'

Finn levered himself up from the sofa and came and stood in the doorway, watching while she bent to work, wondering how a woman eight months into her pregnancy could possibly have such a delectable bottom. He walked over to where she crouched and cupped her buttocks.

'Finn, stop it—'

He bent his head to nuzzle her ear. 'Don't you like it?'

'That's not the point—'

'No?' He kissed the back of her neck. 'The point being what, precisely?'

'I told you—I'm trying to get everything sorted out for when the baby comes.'

'But the baby isn't due for another month,' he objected. 'And I'm flying to London tomorrow. Leave it, Catherine. You won't see me all week.'

'I don't see you all week as it is.' She straightened up with difficulty and allowed him to help her to her feet. 'So what's the difference?'

'A whole sea dividing us?' he teased. 'Won't you miss me?'

She wound her arms around his neck. 'A bit.'

He touched his lips to hers. 'Only a bit?'

Much, much more. 'Stop fishing for compliments!'

166

'Then come and sit down and have a drink and watch some television.'

She sank onto the sofa. 'What an exciting life we lead, Mr Delaney!'

'Are you complaining?' he asked seriously, as he handed her a glass of sparkling water.

'No, I love it,' she said simply. Just as she loved him. How cosy it all was on the outside. She took a sip and looked at him over the rim of the glass. She had been fidgety over the past few days. Perhaps it was because he was travelling to England. It *was* different, him being in London. A whole plane-ride away. Maybe now was the time to stop pretending that the future was never going to happen.

'Finn?'

'Mmm?'

'There are so many things we haven't discussed.'

'Such as?'

'Well, what happens when the baby's born. What we're going to do—'

'I thought we were taking it a day at a time?'

'And we are.' She drew a deep breath. 'But we can't go on like that for ever, can we?'

He put his glass down. 'I think we could.'

Her heart started beating frantically. 'You do?'

'I can't see any reason why not.' He smiled. 'My sweet Catherine! We've discovered that we like one another. That we can live together without wanting to throw things.' His eyes glittered. 'Thankfully, you seem to have got all that out of your system!' He smiled again as she giggled. 'See! We make each other laugh. We're compatible sexually—though that was never in any question, was it? That's not bad to be going along with.'

'And you think that's enough?'

He got up and threw a log on the fire, because the May weather had taken a sudden, unseasonable dip. It fizzed like a golden firework in the grate and he turned to look down at her, his face all light and shadows cast by the flicker of the flames.

'It's more than a lot of people have,' he said quietly. 'But you must decide whether it's enough for you. Whether you want to go chasing rainbows, or settle for giving this baby the security it deserves. Think about it, Catherine.'

Chasing rainbows. He made the search for love sound so insubstantial. And of course love had been the glaring omission from his list.

'And fidelity?' she asked, because that was more tangible than love.

'I could not tolerate infidelity,' he said slowly. 'And I would not expect you to either.'

Which was not quite the same as saying that the situation would never arise, was it? That if someone came along and captured Finn's heart he wouldn't be off?

'It's up to you, Catherine,' he said. 'The choice is yours. I'm being honest in what I'm offering you.'

Choice. There it was again, that infernal word he was so fond of using and which she was so wary of. Because choice meant coming to a decision, and there was always the chance that she would make the wrong one.

She could give her baby security—and not just the security of being legitimate and being cared for. The security of having a father around. A father who, she was certain, would love the baby as much as she did, who would be the kind of role-model that any small boy would give his eye-teeth for.

He was not offering her rose-tinted dreams and an impossibly romantic future together, but surely that was just practical. And honest, as he had said.

She considered the alternative. Going back out there as a single mother and consigning herself to a life alone with her baby. Or foolishly hoping that she might meet another man who would capture her heart as Finn had done—knowing, deep down, that no other man would ever come close to holding a candle to him.

If they had been different people, with different upbringings and in different circumstances, then both of them might have gone chasing those elusive rainbows.

But they were not different people. They were Finn and Catherine. And their pasts had made them into the people they were today. The past was powerful, she recognised—it sent far-reaching repercussions down through the ages.

'I'll think about it,' she said.

Their lovemaking seemed especially close that night, and they held each other very tightly afterwards for what seemed like a long time.

When Catherine went to the door to wave Finn off in the morning, her heart felt as heavy as the sky.

Finn glanced up at the leaden grey clouds and frowned. 'Feels like snow.'

'You can't have snow in May,' she protested.

'Who says we can't? One year we had a frosting in June!'

'You're kidding?'

'No, sweetheart, I'm not.' He caught her in his arms. 'You will take care, won't you?'

'Of course I will! What do you think I'm going to do? Start snow-boarding? Cross-country skiing?'

'I'm serious.'

She rose up on tiptoe to touch her lips to his. 'And so am I,' she whispered. 'I'll be fine. Ring me when you get to London.'

'Get Aunt Finola to move in if the weather turns bad or if you're worried. Or go and stay with Aisling and Patrick. When are you seeing the doctor next?'

'The day after tomorrow. Finn, stop fussing, will you? Just go!'

His mouth lingered on hers until he drew away reluctantly. 'Better go. Plane to catch.' He held her one last time. 'I'll see you Friday.'

Love you, she thought silently as his car roared away, and she shivered and shut the door.

He rang her from the airport. 'What's the weather like?'

She glanced out at the sky. 'Same.'

'I'll ring you just as soon as I get there.'

'Finn, what's wrong with you? Why are you so worried?'

'What's *wrong* with me? My wife's pregnant and I'm leaving the country! Why on earth should I be worried, Catherine?' he questioned wryly. But he *was* worried. Uneasy. Did every father-to-be feel like a cat on a hot tin roof at a time like this?

Catherine put the phone down and made herself some tea. She glanced at her watch to see that Finn's flight would now be airborne. Keep him safe for me, she prayed, while outside the sky grew darker and the first snowflakes began to flutter down.

It snowed all afternoon, becoming whiter and thicker, until the garden looked just like a Christmas card. Catherine had just lit a fire when there was a loud banging on the door, and there stood Aunt Finola, scarcely recognisable beneath hood and scarf, a rain-mac worn over a thick overcoat and countless sweaters!

'Come in.' Catherine smiled. 'What are you doing out on an afternoon like this?'

'Finn rang me,' explained Finola, shaking snow off her boots. 'Told me to drop in and keep my eye on you.'

'He keeps fussing and fussing!'

'He's worried about you. And the baby.'

'I'm fine.'

'Yes.' Aunt Finola sat down and held her hands out to the heat before sending Catherine a shrewd look. 'You're looking much better these days. Less peaky. More…at peace with yourself,' she finished.

It was an ironic choice of word. 'Well, I'm pleased that's the way I look,' said Catherine slowly.

'You mean it's not the way you feel inside?'

She hesitated. This was Finn's aunt, after all—and in some ways his mother, too. 'I'm fine,' she repeated carefully. 'Honestly.'

'Things seem better between you these days,' observed Aunt Finola carefully. 'You seem more relaxed these past few weeks. The two of yous seemed terrible tense a lot of the time before that.'

Catherine did some sums in her head, and blushed. Oh, God—was it that obvious? That the moment they had starting having sex their relationship had settled down?

'You really love my boy, don't you?' asked Aunt Finola suddenly.

Catherine met her eyes in surprise. But what was the point in lying to someone who loved him, too? Wouldn't she then be guilty of false pride? 'Yes, I love him. Really love him.'

'So why the long face?'

Catherine shook her head. 'I can't talk about it.'

'Well, maybe you can't—but I can. I don't know what went on before Finn brought you here, and I don't want to know, but I assume that he married you because you were pregnant.'

Catherine went very pink. 'Yes,' she whispered. 'Are you shocked?'

Aunt Finola gave a cross between a laugh and a snort. 'Shocked? I'd be a very strange woman indeed to have reached my age and be shocked by something like that! It's been going on since the beginning of time! But Finn's a good man. He'll care for you, stand by you.'

'Yes, but…' Catherine's words tailed away.

'You want more than that, is that it?' Finola nodded her head. 'Tell me, Catherine—is the relationship good, generally?'

'Very good,' Catherine realised, unconsciously beginning to list all the things he had said to her on the eve of his departure. 'We get on, we make each other laugh…' Her cheeks went pink again. 'Oh, lots of things, really. But—'

'But?'

It sounded so stupid to say it. 'He doesn't love me!'

Finola digested this for a moment or two in silence. 'Doesn't he? Are you sure?'

'He never says he does!'

Finola shook her head. 'Oh, you young women to-day!' she said exasperatedly. 'Fed a diet of unrealistic expectations by magazines and books! How many smooth-tongued chancers have you met for whom words are cheap—who tell you they love you one minute and are busy looking over your shoulder at another woman the next? It's not what you say that matters, Catherine, it's what you *do* that counts.'

'You mean you think that Finn loves me?'

'I've no idea what Finn thinks—he never lets me in. He's let no one in, not really—not since he lost his mother.' Her brow criss-crossed in lines of sadness. 'Think about it, Catherine. They'd been everything to each other and suddenly she was taken away, without warning. What child wouldn't have grown wary of love after something like that? Or of expressing it?'

Why had she never looked at it that way before? Her thoughts came tumbling out as words. 'You think I'm being selfish?'

Finola shook her head. 'I think you're not counting your blessings and thinking of all the good things you *do* have. Love doesn't always happen in a blinding flash, Catherine. Sometimes it grows slowly—like a great big oak tree from out of a tiny acorn. And marriages based on that kind of love are sometimes the best in the world. Solid and grounded.' She caught the look on Catherine's face. 'Which doesn't mean to say that they're without passion.'

No. It didn't.

'It all boils down to whether you want instant gratification or whether you are prepared to work for something,' finished Finola gently. 'It's not the modern way, I know.'

'An old-fashioned marriage?' questioned Catherine wryly.

'There was a lot less divorce in those days.' Aunt Finola shrugged. 'People stuck by each other through the good times and the bad times. For richer for poorer. In sickness and in health. Forsaking all others.'

'We got married in a register office,' commented Catherine absently.

'I know you did. But you still made vows, didn't you? Even if you didn't mean them at the time, that doesn't mean they can't be true in the future.'

Catherine nodded. 'Thank you.'

'For?'

'For talking sense to me. For making me realise what's important. I think I really needed to hear it!' She smiled. 'Shall I go and put the kettle on?'

'Now you're talking!'

By morning the world was silent and white, but at least the snow had stopped. Catherine got up as soon as it was light, peering out of the window at the frozen scene with pleasure—until she realised that the path to the gate was completely impassable. Someone could break their leg on that, she thought, especially if it became icy. And so, after a flurry of solicitous phone calls from Finn, Finola and Aisling, Catherine decided to clear the snow away.

She wrapped up warmly and set to work, and several people stopped to talk to her as she cleared the path—most of them asking when the baby was due.

'Not until June,' she told them.

'You've a bit of a wait, then!' said the postman's wife, who had six herself. 'The last month or so's always the worst!'

No one seemed to think it odd that a pregnant woman should be working physically, but that was because, Catherine realised, it wasn't. Not at all. And especially not in rural areas. For centuries women had been working in the fields until they had their babies, and what she was doing wasn't so very different. That morning she felt strong, capable and really *alive*—as if she could conquer the world.

The path was almost cleared when the first pain came, so sharp and so unexpected that Catherine dropped her shovel and held her hands to her tight belly, her breath coming in clouds on the frozen air.

It couldn't possibly be the baby, she reassured herself as the tight spasm receded. The baby wasn't due yet. These pains were nature's way of warning you what the real thing was like.

But the spasms continued throughout the night, and by three o'clock in the morning Catherine could stand it no longer and rang Finola.

'I think it's the baby!' she gasped. 'I think it's coming!'

'Jesus, Mary and Joseph! Don't do a thing. I'm on my way!'

'I couldn't do anything,' said Catherine weakly, and clutched at her middle. 'Even if I wanted to.'

Finola arrived and took one look at her. 'Let's get you straight up those stairs,' she said, 'and then I'm calling the doctor!'

'But I'm supposed to be having the baby in hospital!'

Aunt Finola snorted. 'And how do you suppose we're going to get you to hospital? On a sledge?'

Catherine giggled, and then groaned. 'Don't!' Her

mouth fell open. 'And Finn's supposed to be here! I want Finn here with me.'

'Finn's in London,' said Finola gently. 'Just think about him. Pretend he's here. He'll get here eventually.'

And so he did, by which time Catherine was propped up on the pillows, illuminated by the sunshine which was fast melting the snow, cradling a black-haired baby who was not as tiny as she should have been.

He burst in through the bedroom door, his face a stricken mixture of panic and joy, and was beside the bed in seconds, kissing her nose, her lips, her forehead.

'Catherine! Oh, sweetheart. Sweetheart! Thank God!'

Both Finola and Catherine heard the break in his voice and for one brief moment their eyes met across the room. The expression in the older woman's said as much as, Are you completely *mad*? and Catherine knew that she mustn't wish for the stars. Stars were all very well, but they were a million miles away. This was here. And now. Grounded and safe. Far more accessible than stars.

'You're okay?' he was questioning urgently.

'More than okay,' she said, with the first stirrings of a new-found serenity she suspected came hand in hand with motherhood.

'And is this my daughter?' he was saying in wonder as he stared down at the ebony-dark head and then slowly raised his head to look at his wife. 'My beautiful daughter.'

The soft blue blaze dazzled her, enveloped her in its warmth and wonder. 'Meet Mollie,' she said, and handed him the bundle who immediately began to squeak. 'Miss Mollie Delaney. She hasn't got a middle name yet—we hadn't agreed on one and I thought you might like to—'

'Mary,' he said firmly, as she had known he would. His mother's name.

Finn looked down at the baby in his arms.

'Hello, Mollie,' he said thoughtfully, and when he looked up again his eyes were suspiciously bright.

Aunt Finola made a great show of blowing her nose noisily.

He had come full circle, Catherine realised. Mollie had given him back something of himself. His own childhood had been snatched away from him by the death of his mother and now having his own baby gave him a little of that childhood back.

'What can I say, Catherine?' he said softly. 'Other than thank you.'

At which point his aunt got abruptly to her feet and glared at him. 'I'm off!' she said briskly. 'I'll be back tomorrow!'

After she had gone, the two of them just gazed at their sleeping infant for long, peaceful seconds.

He put the baby down gently in the crib and then sat on the edge of the bed, taking Catherine into his arms as though she was a fragile piece of porcelain which might shatter if he held her too hard.

'Catherine,' he said shakily.

She wanted him closer than this. 'I won't break, you know.'

He pulled her against him and kissed her then, soothed and excited her with just the expert caress of his lips. Catherine sighed with pleasure and then with slight irritation when he stopped, and opened her eyes to find him looking at her rather sternly.

'This changes everything, you know.'

'I know it does. No more sleep, for a start!'

But he shook his head. 'You know what I'm talking about, Catherine.'

That was just the problem. She didn't. Or rather, she didn't dare think about it. Hence her attempt at a joke.

His eyes were burning into her with such intensity—so blue, so beguiling. 'This baby cements what we have between us. You know that, don't you?'

It wasn't the most romantic way he could have put it, but then, whoever said anything about romance? She and Finn were about compatibility and maturity and making the best of a situation they had not chosen. And making the best of things was surely a sound bedrock from which to work?

She recognised, too, that Finn would do all in his power to make sure their relationship flourished—for the sake of Mollie if for nothing else.

She nodded, her eyelids dropping to hide her eyes, afraid that he might see traces of wistful longing there.

'Catherine,' he commanded. 'Look at me.'

She lifted her head and met the soft blue stare.

'Living with you is so easy,' he murmured. 'In so many ways.' There was a pause. 'You make me happy,' he added simply, and he lifted her fingertips to his lips and kissed them.

And if Catherine's heart ached to hear more then she was just being greedy. She made him happy—he had said so. And he made *her* happy. Which was more than most people had. Expecting those three little words said more about society's conventions and expectations than anything else. For how many people said 'I love you' and then proceeded to act as if they didn't? Why, Peter had said it, and then he had run off with someone else!

No, she would count her blessings—and they were legion.

They made each other happy.

Who could ask for anything more than that?

EPILOGUE

CATHERINE sighed a contented sigh. 'Not exactly a conventional honeymoon, is it?'

Finn glanced up from sleepy eyes. In the distance, the dark blue waters lapped rhythmically onto the sand. 'Well, it was never a conventional relationship, was it, sweetheart?' he asked sleepily.

'Finn Delaney, will you wake up and talk to me properly?'

He rolled over onto his back, screwing his eyes up against the bright sunshine, and gave a lazy smile. 'It's all your fault, Mrs Delaney—if you didn't make such outrageous demands on me every minute of every day, then I might be able to keep my eyes open!'

Catherine rubbed a bit more sun-cream onto her tanned arm. 'And you honestly think that Mollie will be okay?'

He propped himself up on one elbow. 'With your mother and Finola looking after her? And Aisling having to be forcibly restrained from dragging her off to the beach every second? Are you kidding, sweetheart? Sounds like bliss for a two-year-old, to me!'

'Mmm. I guess you're right.'

'And anyway—' he pulled her into his arms, feeling the stickiness of the lotion on her skin and pushing his hips against hers in a decidedly provocative way '—I thought we'd decided to do things more conventionally from now on?'

She kissed his neck. 'Mmm.' The church wedding had been conventional enough—even though she had balked at wearing full white bridal regalia. But the snazzy silk suit in softest ivory, purchased from a shop in Grafton Street, had certainly won Finn's approval! And so had the miniature duplicate she had secretly ordered for Mollie!

They had flown out to Pondiki that same afternoon, to discover that Nico had himself found a bride, and was soon to be a father!

Finn gazed at her. 'Are you happy, Catherine?'

'It's a way of travelling, Finn,' she reminded him. 'Not a—Finn!' For he had pulled her onto her back and was lying above her, his gorgeous face only an inch away.

'Are you?' he whispered, his breath warm against her face.

'Blissfully.'

And she was.

Finn now worked from home two days a week—though he claimed that she and his daughter distracted him far too much.

'So what?' she had asked him airily. 'You've enough in the bank, and a bit more besides!'

'Have you a shameless disregard for your future, woman?' he had demanded sternly.

Catherine's mother was a frequent visitor, and she and Finola had struck up a firm friendship.

'Would you ever listen to those two?' Finn would often say, when the rise of their laughter made Mollie giggle. 'What the hell do you think they're concocting now?'

And Mollie continued to thrive. The most beautiful child on the entire planet, as her adoring parents were so fond of saying when they looked at her sleeping every night.

Her early birth, while unexpected, had soon been explained by Catherine's gynaecologist. It seemed that Catherine really *had* got her dates wrong, and that Mollie had been conceived in Dublin, not London, which made her heart lift with pleasure.

'You know what that means, don't you, Finn?' she had asked him.

He certainly did. It meant that their child *had* been conceived in passion, not anger—thank God.

Catherine had abandoned the book she had been writing; she found motherhood much more rewarding. 'Doesn't mean that I'll never write again,' she'd told Finn. 'Just not now.'

And Finn had taken to helping her in the garden sometimes—a plot which she had so transformed that word had spread of its beauty through Wicklow and beyond. Last year she had opened it up to the public, charging entry to those who could afford to pay and selling tea and cakes to raise money for the local library.

Finn called it 'helping' her in the garden, but in reality he just planted things occasionally. Primroses and roses and hollyhocks, and an unusual variegated tulip. And a peach tree, and the arbutus which did so well in that part of Ireland and which was known affectionately as the strawberry tree.

She had leaned on her spade one day and looked at him. 'Odd choice of plants, Finn.'

'Mmm.'

Something in his tone had set her thinking, set a distant memory jangling in her head, and she'd gone to her computer that evening, when he had gone up to the pub for a pint with Patrick. She'd browsed through her search-engine and had looked up the language of flowers. And there it all was, in black and white before her eyes.

Primrose—fidelity.

Variegated tulip—beautiful eyes.

Peach tree—my heart is thine.

And most lovely of all was the arbutus, which meant esteemed love.

Her eyes had been moist when she'd opened the door to him later.

'You've been crying!' he accused.

'Oh, you stupid man!' she exclaimed, flinging her arms around him. 'Why didn't you tell me?'

'Tell you what?'

'The garden! All those things you planted and I never knew why! Why didn't you just come out and say so?'

'That I love you?' he said tenderly. 'Is that what you want to hear, my sweet, beautiful Catherine?'

'Of course it is!'

They ended up in bed, and afterwards she rolled over to lie on top of him, a fierce look in her eyes. 'Finn?'

'Catherine?'

'Did you ever give another woman flowers with a message?'

'Never.'

'So why me?'

He shrugged, and gave a contented smile which still somehow managed to be edged with sensuality.

'I never wanted to before.'

'Tell me you love me again,' she begged.

'I'll tell you that every day for the rest of our lives,' he promised.

He did. But Catherine had more than words to warm her. She had only to look out at her garden to see Finn's love for her growing every day.

PREGNANCY OF CONVENIENCE

by

Sandra Field

Although born in England, **Sandra Field** has lived most of her life in Canada; she says the silence and emptiness of the north speaks to her particularly. While she enjoys travelling and passing on her sense of a new place, she often chooses to write about the city which is now her home. Sandra says, 'I write out of my experience; I have learned that love with its joys and its pains is all-important. I hope this knowledge enriches my writing, and touches a chord in you, the reader.'

CHAPTER ONE

CAL FREEMAN turned the wipers on high and slid the clutch of his four-wheel-drive into a lower gear. Not that it helped. The snow blowing horizontally across the windshield enveloped him in a world of white, through which he could, occasionally, sight the tall poles that marked the edges of his narrow road across the prairie.

The visibility had been better on the northeast ridge of Everest, he thought semi-humorously. Although the cold was almost comparable. He would never have expected conditions like this in southern Manitoba, not even in January. His friend Stephen had been right to insist that Cal carry emergency supplies when he set off to visit the Strassens, whose isolated home was several miles from the nearest village.

That climb on Everest had been—literally—one of the high points of Cal's life. The struggle through the pinnacles, the bitter north winds, their decision to shoot for the top without oxygen…suddenly Cal snapped back to the present, his foot hitting the brake. What was that in the ditch to his left? A vehicle?

The snow whirled across the road like a phalanx of ghosts; he could see nothing but a smothering whiteness that mocked his normally acute vision. Slowing to a crawl, Cal peered through the glass. Perhaps it had been his imagination. After all, he and Stephen had stayed up late last night, catching up on the four-year gap since they'd last seen each other. And he'd drunk more than his fair share of that excellent Bordeaux.

No. There it was again, an angular shape skewed sideways into the ditch, hood tight against a telephone pole. Coming to a halt as close to the side of the road as he dared, Cal switched on his signal lights: not that he really expected to meet anyone else mad enough to be out in such weather. Then he hauled the hood of his down parka over his head and yanked on his gloves.

He wouldn't find anyone in the vehicle. Not in this bitter cold. But it was just as well to check.

As he stepped from the heated comfort of his Cherokee onto the road, the blizzard struck him with vicious force. The wind chill, he knew from the radio, was in the danger zone: frostbite on exposed skin within a couple of minutes. Well, he was used to that. He tucked his chin into his chest, fighting his way across the icy ruts in the dirt track, limping a little from an old knee injury. How ironic it would be if he, a world-renowned mountaineer, were to slip and break an ankle in one of the flattest places on the planet.

An irony he could do without.

The vehicle was a small white car. Bad choice, he thought trenchantly. And damn lucky the car hadn't slid completely into the ditch, in which case neither he nor anyone else would have seen it.

There was a brief lull in the wind. His heart skipped a beat. Someone was slumped over the wheel. A man or a woman? He couldn't tell.

Forgetting his knee, he lunged forward, adrenalin thrumming through his veins. The engine wasn't running; how long since the car had gone off the road? He scrubbed at the window with his gloved fist, and saw that the driver was a woman. Hatless, he thought grimly. Didn't she know better? Also, unless he was mistaken, unconscious. He grabbed the door handle, and discovered that it was locked. So were all the other doors. He pounded on the glass, yelling as loudly as he could, but the figure draped over the wheel didn't even stir.

Cal raced back to his vehicle and grabbed the shovel from the back seat. Then he staggered across the road again. Once again he banged on the window, but to no effect. Grimacing, he raised the handle of the shovel and hit the glass in the back window with all his strength. On the third try it shattered.

Quickly he unlocked the driver's door and pulled it open. Taking the woman by the waist, he lifted her awkwardly, trying to pillow her face in his shoulder. Once again he made the trip across the ice and drifts back to his vehicle. He eased her into the passenger seat, supporting her as best he could as he anchored her in place with the seat belt. Then he hurried back to her car, picked up her briefcase and threw it on the back seat of his four-wheel-drive. Clambering in on the driver's side, he turned the fan up to its highest setting, dragged off his parka and draped it over the woman's body, then tucked the synthetic silver emergency blanket around her legs. Only then did he really take a look at her.

The blizzard, the cold, the loud whir of the fan all dropped away as though they didn't exist. Cal's heart leaped in his chest. He'd never seen a woman so beautiful. So utterly and heartbreakingly beautiful. Her skin smooth as silk, her hair with the blue-black sheen of a raven's wing, her features perfect, from the softly curved mouth to the high cheekbones and exquisitely arched brows.

He wanted her. Instantly and unequivocally.

Cal swallowed hard, fighting his way back to sanity. Sanity and practicality. There was a bruised swelling on her forehead, where presumably she'd struck the windshield when the car had swerved into the light pole. Her face was as white as the whirling snow crystals, her skin cold to the touch, her breathing shallow. The most beautiful woman he'd ever seen? Was he crazy?

She was lucky to be alive. Besides, he didn't believe in love at first sight. A ludicrous concept.

So why was the hand he'd touched to her cheek burning as though it were on fire?

With an impatient exclamation, he checked the odometer. Less than three miles to the Strassens'. His best bet was to take her straight there. The sooner she was in a warm house and regained consciousness, the better. Unless he was mistaken—and he'd picked up a fair bit of medical expertise over the years—she was just concussed. Concussed and very cold.

He eased into first gear and out into the middle of the road, forcing himself to focus on staying between the ditches. He'd expected to arrive at the Strassens long before this; he hoped they weren't worried about him. His errand, after all, wasn't the most pleasant.

Dusk was falling, making the visibility even poorer. Snatching occasional glances at his passenger, whose head was now lolling on her chest, Cal shifted into third gear. A lot of the snow was being whipped from the fields, for there was nothing to stop the wind but the occasional line of trees along a creek. He'd always had plenty of respect for heights; he'd have more for flatness from now on, he decided with a wry twist of his mouth that simultaneously acknowledged he was concentrating on the weather so he wouldn't have to think about the woman.

She was probably married to a local farmer and had a clutch of raven-haired children. Why hadn't he checked to see if she was wearing a wedding ring?

What did it matter whether she was or she wasn't? The Strassens would know her name, they'd make the necessary phone calls, and she'd vanish from his life as precipitately as she'd entered it.

He'd seen lots of beautiful women in his life. Been married to one for nine years. So why had the startling purity of a stranger's profile, the elegance of her bone structure, affected him as though he were nearer his thirteen-year-old daughter's age than his own age of thirty-six?

Swearing under his breath as the gale flung snow across his path, Cal strained to see the poles along the road. He'd covered nine and a half miles since he'd left the main highway; if the Strassens' directions were right, he had another half a mile to go. Not for the first time, he found himself wondering about them, this elderly couple whose only son Gustave, a fellow mountaineer, had met his death on Annapurna just three months ago.

He, Cal, had come all this way to bring them their son's climbing gear and the few personal effects Gustave had had with him on his last expedition. An errand of mercy he'd be glad to have over and done with. His original plan had been to stay a decent length of time and then head back to the city tonight. But the weather was putting paid to that; he'd probably have to stay overnight. Not what he would have chosen, particularly as he'd never met Gustave Strassen.

An illusory gleam of lights caught his eye through the snow. That must be the Strassens' house. Now all he had to do was navigate the driveway.

Four minutes later, he was parked as near to the front door as possible. The house wasn't as substantial as he'd somehow expected. Leaving the engine running, he took the front steps two at a time and rang the doorbell.

The door opened immediately. A heavy-set man with a grizzled beard boomed, "Come in, come in out of the cold, you must be Mr. Freeman—what, no jacket?"

"Cal Freeman," Cal said rapidly. "Mr. Strassen, I have a passenger, a woman whose car went off the road. She struck her head, she needs attention right away—can I bring her in?"

The older man took a step backward. "A woman? Wha do you mean, a woman?"

What kind of question was that? "A young woman. O her own," Cal said impatiently, "and obviously unprepare for the weather. She ended up in the ditch. I'll go get her.'

"But we—"

Cal, however, had already turned back to his vehicle, the snow stinging his cheeks. Trying to keep the woman cov ered as best he could, he lifted her from the seat and wit his knee shoved the door shut. The wind seized the hoo of his parka and flung it away from her face. For a momen that was out of time he saw her lashes flicker—long dar lashes like smudges of soot. Her lips moved, as though sh were trying to speak. "It's okay," he said urgently "you're safe now, you don't have to worry." Then h headed up the steps again.

Dieter Strassen held the door open. But he was no longe smiling. He said, his accent very pronounced, "Tha woman is not welcome in my house."

Cal stopped dead, leaning back against the door to clos it. "*What* did you say?"

A strained voice spoke from behind Dieter. "Get her ou of here! I never want to see her again. Never, do you hea me?"

Cal knew instantly that this must be Maria Strassen Dieter's wife and Gustave's mother. Short, thin as a rail her hair in a gray-threaded bun skewered with pins. Wit a gesture that might have been funny had it not been s venomous, she thrust out one hand, palm toward Cal, a though she were about to push him physically back int the blizzard.

Him and his burden.

"Look," Cal said, "I don't know what's going on here but this woman needs help. She's concussed and she's cold

She needs some hot food and a warm bed. Surely you can provide those?''

With a depth of bitterness that shocked Cal, Dieter said, ''Better had she died.''

''Like our son,'' Maria flashed. ''Our beloved Gustave.''

Cal said flatly, ''How far is it to the next house?''

''Four miles,'' Dieter said.

''Surely you can see that I can't go that far,'' Cal said forcefully, shifting the weight in his arms. ''Not in this storm. I don't know who this woman is or what she's done to make you hate her, but—''

''If we hate her, Mr. Freeman, it is for very good reasons,'' Dieter said with something approaching dignity. ''You must allow us to be the judge of that.''

''She married our Gustave,'' Maria said icily. ''Married him and destroyed him.''

Cal gaped at her, the pieces belatedly falling into place. As though he had actually been picked up and moved, he found himself back in an alpine campsite overlooking the south side of Mont Blanc. Four weeks ago.

It was unseasonably warm for December, and Cal was in his bare feet, luxuriating in the damp grass beneath his toes after an arduous day hiking; he'd been testing some footwear for a friend who designed alpine boots. One of the guides who had just brought up a party of Germans and who had introduced himself to Cal as Franz Staebel, remarked, ''Gustave always liked to be in his bare feet after a climb...did you ever meet Gustave Strassen?''

''Oddly enough, no,'' Cal answered. ''Our paths nearly crossed several times but we never actually met...I was very sorry to hear about his death.''

''Ah, yes,'' Franz said, grimacing into the sun. ''He was an excellent climber, one of the best. Such a waste.'' With

sudden ferocity he banged an ice pick into the ground. "A
totally unnecessary waste."

"Oh?" said Cal, leaning back against the scaly trunk of
a rowan tree. "How so?"

"His wife," Franz said, pulling the pick out with a
strong twist of his wrist. "His wife, Joanna. She was pregnant, he'd just found out the day before. But there was a
good chance the baby wasn't his. She'd cheated on him,
had for years."

"Why did he stay with her, then?" Cal asked idly.

"You should have seen her. Beautiful in a way few
women are. And her body...Gustave was only human."
Moodily Franz kicked at a clump of grass he'd dislodged,
the pale sun gleaming in his red hair. "So Joanna and the
baby were on his mind that morning, the morning he attempted the rock ridge on Annapurna 3. And died in the
attempt."

As Cal knew all too well, distractions could be fatal on
the mountains, where a moment's misjudgment could send
a man to his death. "I'm sorry," he said inadequately. "I
hadn't heard about his wife before."

"She controlled the purse strings, too. A rich woman
who let Dieter be stuck with second-rate equipment, and
forced him to beg for sponsorships for his climbs. Ah, it
was bad. Very bad. How that man suffered."

"Where was he from?"

"Central Canada." Franz gave a bark of laughter. "The
prairies. Not a hill in sight. His parents live there still."

"I have a good friend in Winnipeg," Cal remarked.
"I've known him for years."

Franz sat up straight, dropping the pick on the grass.
"You do? Would you be interested in visiting your friend
and also doing a last favor for a climber who deserved
better than the fate he met?"

"What do you mean?"

"I have Gustave's gear back in Zermatt. I was going to mail it to his parents. But how much better if it could be delivered to them personally by a fellow mountaineer."

Cal said slowly, "I do have a week or so free early in the new year...after I bring my daughter back to school here in Switzerland. And it would be great to see Stephen and his wife again. Providing they're around."

"It would help the Strassens a great deal. Their hearts must be broken. Gustave's wife, she wasted no time after his death—she got rid of the baby. It could have been Gustave's child, that was certainly possible...in which case she got rid of the Strassens' grandchild, their only connection to their dead son." He spat on the grass. "I curse the day Gustave married that woman. She brought him nothing but grief."

"Mr. Freeman?" Dieter Strassen said, with the air of a man repeating himself.

With a visible start, Cal came back to the present; and to the simple and horribly unwelcome fact that the woman in his arms was the direct cause of a good man's death and the deep grief of that man's parents. "Sorry," he mumbled, and tried to pull himself together. There was no reason in the world for him to feel so massively disillusioned about a woman he hadn't even known existed half an hour ago. An unconscious woman, to boot, with whom he hadn't exchanged as much as a word.

"Mr. Strassen," he said, "I can see my arrival here is causing you and your wife great distress, and I apologize for that. But right now I don't see any way around it. I can't just dump her in the snow, no matter what she's done."

"So you know the story?" Dieter said sharply.

"Franz Staebel, the alpine guide who had your son's

gear, told me about your daughter-in-law a month or s
ago."

"Gustave thought highly of Franz." Moving like a muc
older man, Dieter turned to his wife. "Maria, we'll put he
in the back bedroom, it's the only thing we can do. She'
be gone by morning."

"Someone else can look after her," Maria said in a ston
voice.

Into the silence Cal said, "I will."

"That would be best," Dieter said with evident relie
"I'll show you the room, and in the meantime Maria wi
heat some soup for you. We are being bad hosts, M
Freeman." He gave a rather rusty bow. "Welcome to ov
home."

Two could play that game. "Thank you," Cal said, an
smiled at Maria.

Her response was as cold as a glacier. "That woman wi
leave here tomorrow morning," she said, "and she mu
never come back."

Cal's brain, which seemed to have gone to mush sinc
finding a raven-haired beauty on the side of the road, finall
made the connection. "Oh, of course—she'd just bee
here?"

"She had the audacity to bring us Gustave's silve
watch, his album of family photos. As though that woul
make us take her in. Forgive her for all that she's done."

"Now, Maria," Dieter warned.

"Our grandchild," Maria quavered, "she even destroye
our grandchild. Aborted it."

"According to Gustave, it might not have been h
child," Dieter said wearily, running his fingers through h
thatch of grizzled hair. "Gustave radioed a message out th
very day he died, Mr. Freeman. About the pregnancy an
his doubts. He wanted to divorce her." His gaze flicke
contemptuously over the woman in Cal's arms. "But h

knew that would mean no contact with a child who could be of our own flesh and blood.''

Maria bit off her words. "She took everything from us."

"Enough, now," her husband said. "I'm sure once Mr. Freeman has settled her, he'll be hungry."

"Please call me Cal...and some soup would be delicious," Cal said with another smile.

Maria turned on her heel in the direction of the kitchen. Dieter lead the way along a narrow hallway to a back annex of the house; the furnishings were sparse, Cal noticed, glancing into what appeared to be a formal parlor, everything immaculately tidy and painfully clean. The back bedroom was no exception. It was also very cold.

Dieter said, "You must excuse my wife, Mr.—Cal. She is very bitter, understandably so. I'll leave you to settle in, and whenever you're ready, please come through to the dining room."

Cal laid Joanna Strassen on the double bed, straightened, and said forthrightly, "Once she comes to, she'll need something hot to eat." And with annoyance realized he'd adopted the Strassens' habit of referring to Joanna Strassen as *she*. Never by name.

"I'll look after that. And I'll show you to your bedroom in the main house."

"I think I'd better stay here and keep an eye on your daughter-in-law," Cal said with a depth of reluctance that took him by surprise. But if he didn't look after her, who would? "After a blow on the head, it's always a good idea to be under supervision for at least twelve hours."

"Whatever you say," Dieter replied, and for a moment directed a look of such implacable hostility toward the unconscious woman on the bed that, even knowing the story, Cal was chilled to the bone. "There's extra bedding in the cupboard and the couch makes another bed," Dieter went on, just as though nothing had happened. "I'll see you in a few minutes."

As soon as the door closed behind him, Cal went into action. He drew the curtains against the snow that lashed the windowpanes, jammed the thermostat up several notches, and swiftly built a fire in the woodstove that stood in the corner. Touching a match to it, he watched briefly as the flames gained hold. Then he turned to the woman on the bed.

Joanna Strassen. Widow of Gustave. By all accounts an unfaithful and ungenerous wife, who apparently had destroyed her own child.

Nothing he'd learned made her any less beautiful.

CHAPTER TWO

CAL rubbed his palms down the sides of his cords, and with the same deep reluctance that he'd felt a few moments ago, approached the bed. Resting his palm on Joanna's cheek, trying to ignore the satin smoothness of her skin, he registered how cool she felt. He pulled off her gloves, chafing her cold fingers between his warmer ones. Ringless fingers, he noticed. Long and tapered, with neatly kept nails. She wore no jewelry, which rather surprised him. He met a lot of women, one way or another, and because he was rich and unmarried, spent a fair bit of energy keeping them at bay; most of them dripped with diamonds. So why didn't the wealthy widow, Joanna Strassen?

As though he had spoken her name out loud, she moved her head restlessly on the pillow, her lashes flickering. Her left hand plucked at his parka, trying to pull it around her chin. Then she gave a tiny moan of pain, a deep shudder rippling the length of her body.

Quelling an instinctive surge of compassion, Cal eased off her boots, practical low-heeled boots that looked as though they came from a factory outlet. Definitely not leather. This, like her lack of rings, seemed oddly out of character. Her tights were black, her plain sweater a deep blue. Her figure was just as much an attention-grabber as her face, he thought grimly, and almost with relief noticed that she was shivering. Hastily he pulled the covers from underneath her body, then tucked them around her.

The room was noticeably warmer, so much so that Cal stripped off his own thick wool sweater. Catching a glimpse of himself in the mirror by the door, he ran his fingers through his disordered hair, which was the dark brown of

17

polished leather. As for the rest, he'd always figured he had the right number of features in the right places and that was that. He'd never understood his appeal to women, blind to the unrevealing gray of his eyes, the strength of his chin and jaw, the flat planes of his cheeks and his air of self containment, which many might see as a challenge. He'd been rather less than amused just before Christmas, when he was trying to avoid the attentions of a local divorcée, to have his daughter Lenny say to him impatiently, "You don't understand why every woman you meet is after you? Get a grip, Dad. You're a hunk. Big-time macho man. You should hear the girls in my school go on about you."

"Oh no, I shouldn't."

Lenny had rolled her eyes. "You're also intelligent, rich, charming when you want to be, rich, and a famous mountaineer. Oh, and did I mention rich? I rest my case."

"Rich you got right," he'd replied. "The rest—forget it."

Lenny had laughed and cajoled him into helping her with some supplemental geometry, a subject that was as much a mystery to her as literature was a delight. Cal loved his daughter Lenny more than he could imagine loving anyone else in the world…more than he'd loved her mother for the last few years of his marriage, he could now admit that to himself. Although never to Lenny.

He should remarry. Settle down and provide a proper home for Lenny, add a woman's presence to her life. Trouble is, he didn't want to. Nor had he met anyone who gave him the slightest desire to embrace—for the second time—the state of holy matrimony.

If only he didn't travel so much; it made it more difficult with Lenny. He'd curtailed his mountain-climbing expeditions the past few years. But he also had to travel for his work. Cal had inherited money from his adventurous, immigrant father; after multiplying this money many times over in a series of shrewd investments, he'd purchased an international brokerage firm; then, later, a chain of prestigious auction houses in Europe and New York, dealing with antiques and fine art. Although computer technology had cut back a certain amount of travel, there was still no substitute for a hands-on approach to his various business concerns.

One more reason why Lenny was in a private school in Switzerland.

The woman on the bed gave another of those low moans. Cal came back to the present, thrusting a birch log into the heart of the flames, and turning his attention to the bed. Despite the heaped-up bedclothes and the warmth of the room, Joanna Strassen was still shivering. Moving very slowly, his eyes trained on her face, Cal lifted the covers and got into bed beside her. Gathering her in his arms, he drew the whole length of her body toward his.

She fit his embrace perfectly, as though she had been made for it. Her cheek was resting against his bare throat, her breath softly wafting his skin; he could feel her tremors, the small rise and fall of her breathing against his chest, and the firm swell of her breasts pressed to his rib cage.

His body's response was unmistakable. He still wanted her. No matter what she'd done.

Gritting his teeth, Cal thought about the ice ridges of Brammah, the ice cliffs of Shivling, the glaciers of Everest. All to no avail. Cursing himself inwardly, he then tried to imagine she was a fellow climber with hypothermia and that he was simply doing the medically correct thing.

Equally useless. Her skin was sweetly scented, her hair in its thick braid gleamed in the firelight as though the flames themselves were caught there, and each shiver that rippled through her slender frame he felt as though it were his own body. He'd been too long without a woman, that was his problem. After all, how long had it been?

If he had to struggle to remember, it had been altogether too long. Time he rectified that. Soon. And when better than now, with Lenny in school in faraway Switzerland?

There was that blonde in Manhattan, he'd met her at a

charity ball; she'd insisted he take her phone number, he must have it somewhere. She'd certainly given every signal that she was willing to climb into his bed, no question asked.

He couldn't even remember her name. Shows what kind of an impression she'd made.

There was also Alesha in Paris, Jasmine in Boston, Rosemary in London and Helga in Zurich. All of whom he'd dated; none of whom he'd slept with.

Joanna Strassen stirred in his arms. Hastily Cal eased his hips away from hers, wondering if her shivering had lessened slightly. The sooner he got out of this particular bed, the better.

The woman in Manhattan had had a diamond pin stuck through her left nostril. That he did remember. No wonder he hadn't phoned her.

A shudder suddenly ripped through Joanna's body. Her eyes flew open, wide with terror, and with a strength that shocked Cal she pushed hard against his chest. "No!" she cried. "No, I won't—" Then, with another of those racking shudders, she stared full at him. He saw her swallow, watched with a flash of admiration as she fought to subdue the terror that only a moment ago had overwhelmed her.

The terror that Gustave had come back from the grave to haunt her? His admiration vanished. But before he could speak, she muttered, "You're not Gustave...oh God, I thought you were Gustave." Her voice rose in panic. "Who are you? Where am I?"

"No," Cal said evenly, "I'm not Gustave. Gustave's dead, remember?"

Again terror flooded her eyes, eyes that were the sapphire blue of her sweater. As she pushed away from him, jerking her head back, she gave a sudden sharp cry of pain. Bringing one hand to her forehead, she faltered, "Please...where am I? I—I don't understand..."

No wonder Gustave Strassen had returned again and again to his faithless wife. If he, Cal, had thought her beau-

iful when she was unconscious, how much more so was
he with emotions crossing her face, with her eyes huge
nd achingly vulnerable in the firelight? He said with a
eliberate brutality that at some level he was ashamed of,
'You had an accident. You're at Dieter and Maria
trassens' house."

Her body went rigid with shock. Then she brought both
ands to her face, briefly closing her eyes. "No," she whis-
ered, "no…tell me that isn't true."

"It's true. Where else was I to bring you? They, I might
dd, were no happier taking you in than you are to find
ourself here."

"They hate me," she whispered, and for a moment the
lue of her irises shimmered with unshed tears. "I don't
vant to be here! Ever again."

Either she was an accomplished actress, shedding a few
ears to brilliant effect; or else everything he'd been told
bout her actions and character was inaccurate. Gustave,
ranz, Deiter and Maria; were all of them wrong? It didn't
eem very likely. Cal said coolly, "Little wonder they hate
ou."

She edged even further from him in the bed, her wince
f pain instantly disguised. "Who are you?"

"Fate?" he said, raising one brow.

"Stop playing with me," she pleaded, and again tears
limmered on her lashes. "Please…I don't understand
vhat's going on, you've got to tell me."

"I'm the guy who happened along the road after you'd
un smack-dab into a telephone pole. You should be thank-
ng me. With the car not running, you'd have frozen to
leath in short order."

"The car…" She frowned. "I remember now, I got into
he car and left here. It was snowing and windy, but the
oads are so straight, I was sure I'd be all right."

"It wasn't exactly the most intelligent course of action,"
Cal said bluntly.

"I couldn't bear to stay! And they wanted me gone, they

almost pushed me out the door. But once I was out on the road, I couldn't see where I was going and then suddenly that pole was right in front of me…the last thing I remember was turning off the ignition because I was afraid of fire.''

"One more dumb move to add to the rest."

"So they told you about me," she said quietly. "And you believe them."

"Is there any reason why I shouldn't?" Cal demanded, and discovered to his inner consternation that he did indeed want to be supplied with those reasons.

"Oh God…" she whispered.

She looked utterly forlorn. In one swift movement Cal rolled out of bed. "I'll go and get you some soup now that you're awake. Then I'll run a hot bath for you."

She tried to sit up, but a wave of dizziness forced her back to the pillow. "Just go away," she quavered. "Go away and leave me alone."

If only that were possible. "You don't like being confronted with the consequences of your actions, do you?" Cal said. "I suppose I should be congratulating you on having the rudiments of a conscience."

"Stop! Just stop—I can't take any more."

She did indeed look at the end of her tether. Cal bit his lip, feeling uncomfortably like the school bully that had made his life a misery when he was seven and small for his age. Now that he was six-foot-two and entirely capable of looking after himself, he made it a practice never to throw his weight around. Especially with a woman. On the other hand, he was damned if he was going to apologize. When all was said and done, nothing could bring Gustave back to life. And wasn't that the bottom line?

He said coldly, "I'll be back in a few minutes. The bathroom's through that door and if I were you, I'd stay in this part of the house. You're not welcome elsewhere."

"You think I don't know that?" she retorted with a flash of spirit.

"Yet you're the one who came here. Uninvited, I'm sure."

"If you think I'm going to justify myself to you, you're mistaken," she said bitterly, turning her face away from him.

The flickering gold light illuminated the exquisite curve of her cheekbone. Dragging his gaze away, Cal strode out of the room. In the hallway he stood still for a minute, trying to subdue the turmoil of emotion in his chest. What was the matter with him? Yelling at a woman with a concussion? Thoroughly disliking her and wanting to kiss her senseless all in the same breath?

Disliking her was fine. She was, after all, a liar and a cheat, according to people who'd known her intimately. But kiss her? Was he out of his mind?

Lots of women had deep blue eyes and long black hair. Grow up, Cal. Or, as Lenny would say, get a grip.

After checking with Dieter he made a couple of phone calls, to Stephen with his change of plans, and to the airport, where he discovered all flights were canceled. Maria had set a place for him at the plain oak table in the dining room. Mechanically he ate a bowl of delicious wild mushroom soup and some homemade rolls, along with a salad of fresh greens, making conversation with her and her husband as best he could.

At the end of the meal Cal said, "Gustave's things are in the back of my vehicle—would you like me to bring them in now, or tomorrow morning?"

"Tomorrow would be better," Dieter said heavily. "Today, already we have been through enough."

Maria said frostily, "I have put some soup on a tray. You will take it to her."

"Of course," Cal said. "That was delicious, Maria, thank you."

"We start our day early," Dieter added. "Living as we do so isolated, we keep to a strict routine. Breakfast at eight?"

''Thanks, that would be fine,'' Cal said, picking up the tray Maria had deposited on the table. ''I'll see you then.'

He walked back along the hallway, again glancing into the parlor. The only books were thick, leather-bound tomes, the photos on the wall were of grim-faced ancestors, and there wasn't an ornament in sight. Had the house always been this joyless? This austere? Had Gustave grown up in these stark surroundings, or were they a product of Dieter and Maria's middle age?

Either way, Gustave Strassen was beginning to have his entire sympathy.

When Cal went back into the bedroom, his socked feet soundless on the bare hardwood, Joanna Strassen was lying flat on her back, gazing up at the ceiling. Her brow was furrowed, as though she were in pain; the white pillowslips and her cheeks were exactly the same color. A floorboard creaked beneath his heel. She gave a visible start, just as quickly controlled; the face she turned to him was empty of expression.

He said, ''I'll help you sit up.''

''I can manage.''

''Don't be so dammed stubborn!''

Defiance flared in her eyes. But with that same super-human control, she subdued it. Where had she learned such control? And why?

And why did he care so strongly about the answers to his own questions?

As Cal put the tray down on the bedside table, she tried to struggle to an upright position, her lower lip clamped between her teeth. He'd been concussed once, on the Eiger, and it had left him with a splitting headache. He slid the pillows from behind her back, propping them against the headboard; then he put his hands under her armpits, lifting her whole weight.

The soft swell of her breast brushed his forearm, the contact surging through his body. Unceremoniously he pushed her back on the pillows, hearing her shallow, rapid breathing. He said with unwilling compassion, "I asked Maria for some painkillers, you'd better take one."

"They've probably got arsenic in them."

"I'll take one, too," he said dryly, "if that'll make you feel safer."

"I don't like taking pills."

"Is that how you got pregnant?"

He hadn't meant to ask that. He watched emotion rip across her face, raw agony, terrible in its intensity. As he instinctively reached out a hand in sympathy, she struck it away. "Just leave me alone," she cried. *"Please."*

She couldn't possibly have faked that emotion. The pain was real. All too real. He said flatly, "So you regret getting rid of the baby."

"Why don't you use the real word? Abortion. Because that's what you mean. And that's what Dieter and Maria think I did."

"That's certainly what they told me."

"And you believe everything you're told?"

"Why would they lie to me, Joanna?" Cal asked, and found he was holding his breath for the answer.

"Because no woman in the world would have been good enough for their beloved Gustave! I was their enemy from the very first day he brought me here."

Could it be true? Cal rested the tray on her lap and reached down to put more wood on the fire.

When he turned back, she was making a valiant effort to eat. But soon she pushed the bowl away. "That's enough," she mumbled, her lashes drifting to cheeks.

He took the tray from her, standing by the bed until her breathing settled into the steady rhythms of sleep. She'd stopped shivering, and there was the faintest wash of color in her cheeks. She was going to be fine and he was a fool to stay in this room overnight. How could he lust after a woman whose every word he seemed to distrust?

First thing tomorrow he'd organize a tow truck and see her on her way. Then he'd give the Strassens Gustave's gear and head for the airport. They'd rebooked him on a flight midmorning. Twenty-four hours and he'd have seen the last of Joanna Strassen.

It couldn't be soon enough.

Glancing at his watch, Cal saw to his dismay that it was scarcely eight o'clock. After leaving the bedroom, he checked out the tidy ranks of books in the parlor. He'd been meaning to read the classics, and apparently now was the time for him to start, he thought wryly, leafing through a couple of volumes of Dickens. Then Dieter spoke from the doorway. "Ah, I thought I heard you in here. Maria and I are not our best, Cal, you must forgive us. You have no suitcase, nothing. Please let us give you a new toothbrush, some pajamas."

Cal never wore pajamas. "That's very kind of you."

"Come through to the kitchen, and I will get them for you."

Maria was putting away the dishes. Cal said pleasantly, "Your daughter-in-law has no nightclothes—could I trouble you for something?"

Her lips thinned. Without a word she left the room, returning with a carefully folded pair of striped pajamas over her arm. "Give her these."

"We'll be gone by morning," he said gently.

"I regret the day our son first saw those big blue eyes of hers!"

Dieter came through the door, passing Cal towels, pajamas and toilet articles. "Thank you," Cal said. "I'll say good night now, I'm a bit jet-lagged."

He was actually distressingly wide awake, all his nerves on edge. Grabbing *War and Peace* from the shelves on his way by, he strode to the back bedroom. Joanna was still sleeping, her neck crooked at an awkward angle. For several minutes he simply stared at her, as though the very stillness of her features might answer some of the questions that tumbled through his brain. She was too thin, he thought. Too pale. Asleep, she looked heartbreakingly vulnerable.

Normally he was a fairly astute judge of character. But something about Joanna had disrupted his radar. One thing he did know: next time he was asked to do a favor for a dead mountaineer, he'd run a mile in the opposite direction.

He added more wood to the fire and settled down with his book. Two hours later, adding one name to his handwritten chart of the characters, he realized the fire had nearly died out. After he'd added some kindling and a small log, he turned around to find Joanna Strassen's eyes open, fixed on him. They looked almost black, he thought. Depthless and mysterious. Full of secrets.

He said heartily, "Sorry if I woke you. How are you feeling?"

"I have to go to the bathroom."

Moving very carefully, she sat up. Then she swung her legs over the side of the bed and pushed herself upright. Abruptly she brought her hand to her forehead, staggering a little. "I feel so dizzy…"

"Here," Cal said unwillingly, "lean on me."

She swayed toward him. He put an arm around her waist, furious with himself for liking her height, and the way her cheek brushed his shoulder. "Why don't you have a hot bath?" he added noncommittally. "It would relax you."

She stopped, looking him full in the face. "I won't relax until I'm on a plane heading east," she muttered. Then her jaw dropped. "My flight—I've missed it!"

"Everything's canceled because of the storm."

Agitated, she said, "It was a seat sale, will they charge me more?"

Franz had said she was miserly with her money. Is that why she wore no jewelry? "They won't. But if they did, surely you could afford it?"

Her eyes suddenly blazed like blue fire. "Oh, of course. I'm a rich widow. How stupid of me to forget."

He'd always liked a woman with spirit. Suzanne, his

wife, had made a fine art out of avoiding conflict. But then Suzanne had had something perennially childlike about her; she'd never matched him, adult to adult. When he'd married her, he'd been too much in love to understand that about her; or to anticipate how her behavior would affect him.

Suzanne had also lied to him frequently, with casual expertise. He'd gradually come to understand that she didn't lie out of malice, but simply because it was easier than owning up to responsibilities or consequences; after a while he'd stopped expecting anything more from her than a modicum of truth. While he certainly was intelligent enough to realize that every beautiful woman wasn't necessarily a liar, Suzanne's legacy, overall, had been a deep-seated reluctance toward any kind of facile trust. This trait had done well for him in the world of business. But as far as Joanna was concerned, was it doing him a disservice?

With an effort Cal came back to the present. "Maria's loaned you something to wear to bed. I'll get it for you."

As she supported herself on the frame of the bathroom door, he passed her the pajamas. Automatically she took them, the fingers of her other hand digging into the wood: for a moment Cal wondered if she was going to faint. He grabbed her around the waist. "What's wrong?"

"How she hates me," Joanna whispered, and suddenly flung the pajamas to the floor. "Don't you see? They're Gustave's pajamas! She knew I'd recognize them."

Cal said evenly, "You hated Gustave. Didn't you?"

"I no longer loved him. If that's what you mean."

"I'm not sure it is."

"You won't believe me when I say this, because your mind's made up about me. But a long time ago I realized that to hate Gustave would destroy me."

Hate was horribly destructive: Cal was certainly sophisticated enough to know that. He said provocatively, "So you destroyed him instead?"

She sagged against the door frame. "Can one person destroy another? Doesn't destruction come from within?"

Again, Cal could only agree with her. Into his silence, Joanna added fiercely, "So you think I could destroy you? And how would I go about doing that?"

"Like this," said Cal, putting his arms around her and kissing her full on the mouth.

She went rigid with shock, her palms bunched into fists against his chest. Then she wrenched her head free, her breasts heaving under her sweater. "Tell the truth—it's you who wants to destroy me," she cried. "But I won't let you, I'll never let a man that close to me again."

What the devil had possessed him to kiss her like that? And why, when she was glaring at him as though he was the Marquis de Sade, did he want to kiss her again? But differently this time, not out of anger but out of desire.

The bruise on her forehead standing out lividly, she backed into the bathroom and slammed the door in his face. The lock snapped into place. If she'd taken the prize for stupidity by attempting to drive a small white car through a blizzard, he was now a close second. Kissing Joanna Strassen had been the stupidest move he'd made in a dog's age.

But he'd liked kissing her. More than liked it. It had inflamed every one of his senses.

When he left Winnipeg, he was headed to Boston on business. He'd give Jasmine a call. Wine her and dine her and take her to bed. That's what he'd do. And the sooner the better.

In fact, he might even phone her from here. Yeah, he might just do that.

Picking up Gustave's pajamas from the floor, Cal put them on the dresser. He could hear water running in the bathroom. He hoped to God Joanna wouldn't slip or faint in the bathtub.

He'd broken a car window already today. He could always break down the bathroom door.

That would really impress Maria.

Somewhat cheered, Cal picked up *War and Peace* again. He had the whole night. He might as well get on with it.

Half an hour later, Joanna opened the bathroom door. She was fully dressed, her cheeks pink from the heat. Cal said calmly, "You can have these," and passed her the new pajamas Dieter had given him.

"They're yours," she said inimically.

"They're Dieter's. I never wear pajamas."

"And where are you planning to sleep?" Her nostrils flared. "Do you know what? I don't even know your name."

"Cal," he said, and held out his hand, adding ironically, "Pleased to meet you."

She kept her own hands firmly at her sides. "Answer the question."

"On the couch. Unless you'd rather have it. It'll be too short for me."

"As far as I'm concerned you can sleep outdoors in a snowdrift."

For the first time since finding her in the car, Cal's smile broke through. "That's not very nice of you. I did, after all, save your life."

"And would you have, had you known who I was?"

"Of course I would. What kind of a question's that?"

She chewed on her lower lip. "Thank you," she said grudgingly. "I guess."

"Put on your pajamas and go to bed," Cal ordered. "Before you fall flat on your face."

She was scowling at him as though her one desire was to strangle him with the pajamas. Cal quelled an inappropriate urge to laugh his head off. He'd give her one thing: she sure didn't back down.

She shut the bathroom door smartly in his face. He remade the bed, stoked the fire, and went back to his book. Considering the disruptive effect a black-haired woman was having on his life, he was getting quite interested in the doings of Pierre, Natasha and Prince Andrew. He'd have to tell Lenny. She'd be impressed.

The door opened again. As Cal glanced up, *War and Peace* fell from the arm of his chair to the floor with a resounding thump. Dieter was a big man: his pajamas were far too large for Joanna. Even though she'd buttoned them to the very top, her cleavage was exposed, a soft shadow in the V of the neckline; the blue cotton hinted at her breasts. The sleeves fell over her fingertips, and she'd turned up the cuffs of the trousers. Cal found himself staring at her bare feet, which were narrow and high-arched. Then his eyes of their own accord found her face again.

She had freed her hair from its braid, so that it rippled down her back. Under his scrutiny, she was blushing as though she were as innocent as his own daughter.

Which, of course, she wasn't.

Slowly Cal got to his feet.

CHAPTER THREE

As JOANNA took a nervous step backward, Cal stopped
dead in his tracks. He'd been going to kiss her again; that
had been his intention. A repeat of a less than clever move.

He said roughly, "Will the light bother you if I read for
a while?"

"No," she stumbled, "no, of course not."

"I'll probably wake you up a couple of times in the
night—that's standard practice after a bump on the head."

"Oh." She swallowed, the muscles moving in her throat.
"I don't think that's necessary, I feel much better."

"Let me be the judge of that."

For a moment he thought she was going to argue with
him. But then the flare of temper died from her eyes. She
got into bed, pulled the covers up to her chin and turned
her back to him. Within a very few minutes, Cal could hear
the gentle rhythm of her breathing, and realized he'd been
reading the same paragraph over and over again.

Swearing under his breath, he forced himself to read on.
Before he made up a bed on the couch at eleven-thirty, and
again at two in the morning, he checked her pulse and the
dilation of her pupils, both times without waking her. But
at five, when the beam of his flashlight fell on her face, her
eyes jerked open, full of terror. Like those of a rabbit who
sights the talons of an owl seconds before they strike, Cal
thought, and said with swift compassion, "It's okay, I'm
just checking to see you're all right."

She sank back on the pillow, her pulse hammering at the
base of her throat. "Is that the wind I hear?" she whispered.

"Yeah."

"I've got to get out of here today!"

"It'll die down soon," he said without much conviction; if anything, the storm had increased in intensity in the night.

"I can't stay here any longer."

She'd spoken in such a low voice he had to strain to hear her. She looked at the end of her tether, as though at the slightest provocation she would start to weep and be unable to stop. "I want to leave here, too," Cal said dryly. "But unfortunately neither one of us can influence the weather."

"To be here," she faltered, "don't you see, it brings it all back, all those terrible, wasted years. And the baby...I can't bear to think about the baby."

The fire had died down; he and Joanna were isolated in the small circle of his flashlight, darkness and the cry of the wind pressing in on all sides. Cal had never seen such desolation on a woman's face; it cut him to the heart. Clumsily he sat down on the bed and put his arms around her.

For a few seconds she yielded, her forehead burrowed in his shoulder, her spine a long curve of surrender. Through the thin cotton of his shirt, he felt tears dampen his skin, and realized she was weeping without a sound. "Did you really abort the baby?" he asked with sudden urgency.

"I didn't! I swear I didn't. It didn't matter that I no longer loved Gustave, I'd have loved the baby...I already did love it."

He wanted to believe her—God, how he wanted to! So what was holding him back?

Her hair smelled enticingly of hyacinths, and the soft weight of her breasts against his chest—bare where his shirt was open—filled Cal with a fierce surge of desire. He fought to subdue it. Was he about to take Gustave's widow to bed in Gustave's house? What kind of a man would that make him? In a harsh voice he scarcely recognized as his own, he said, "I don't know who the hell to believe—you or your dead husband's parents."

She flinched as though he'd physically struck her. Then she pulled free of him, swiping at the tears on her cheeks with the back of one hand. "You can keep your sympathy," she said stonily, "I as good as killed Gustave and I certainly killed the baby. Oh, and I was promiscuous, let's not forget that."

"I'm not sure sympathy's what this is about," said Cal, and kissed her hard on the mouth.

It was as though the flames suddenly rekindled in the hearth, lapping him in their fiery dance. He'd never felt such raw, basic hunger in his life. His arm tightened around her waist. Her ribs were a taut curve, her hair tumbling over the hand that was pressed to her back. Then her lips, warm and soft, yielded so suddenly and so ardently to his kiss that he'd have sworn she was enveloped in the same fire. He thrust with his tongue and fumbled for the buttons on her pajamas.

She struck him hard on his bare shoulder with her bunched fist and yanked her head free. "Don't!"

His arms aching with emptiness, Cal snarled with no subtlety whatsoever, "You kissed me back."

"All right, so I did. So what?"

"You've been widowed three months and you kissed me as though it's been three years."

"For the space of five seconds, I kissed you."

"Franz said you were promiscuous."

"Franz? I'd hardly call him a reliable witness."

She had a point, Cal thought reluctantly. He knew nothing about Franz. Had never met him before that day on Mont Blanc.

"Anyway," Joanna went on, "what about you? Why would you want to kiss me? You've made it all too clear

ou don't believe a word I've said. Which means you think
'm responsible for Gustave's death, and—'' momentarily
he faltered ''—the loss of the baby, as well.''

Cal had no answer for her. When he was blinded by lust,
ow could he possibly discern the truth? But if he really
lid disbelieve her, he was kissing a woman he should de-
pise.

He'd loved Suzanne when he married her, he'd never
een unfaithful to her, and anyone he'd taken to his bed
ince her death he'd at least liked. He pushed himself up
rom the bed, noticing with one small part of his brain that
oanna's cheeks were still streaked with tears and that the
ruise on her forehead was now a lurid mix of purple and
ellow. ''Let's just call it temporary insanity,'' he said
ersely. ''On both our parts.''

''It's not going to happen again!''

He could see the hard jut of her nipples beneath her
acket. ''You don't have a worry in the world,'' he grated.
'I'm going back to sleep. Alone. And we'd better hope the
weather improves.''

''It's got to,'' she said with an edge of real desperation.

He felt exactly the same way. Although he was damned
f he was going to tell her that. He'd already made enough
of a fool of himself, no point in adding to it. ''Are you
warm enough?'' he asked curtly.

''Yes. Thank you.''

He flicked off the flashlight and lowered his body onto
a couch that was at least eight inches too short for him. He
lidn't care what the weather was doing, he was out of here
once it was daylight. And he wasn't taking Joanna Strassen
with him.

Daylight was chinking through the dark brown curtains
when Joanna woke up. She lay still for a moment, totally
lisoriented, wondering why her head hurt and why the

wind was howling so ferociously that the house creake
under its onslaught. Then it all came flooding back. He
disastrous and ill-thought-out attempt at reconciliation wit
Dieter and Maria. Her precipitate departure yesterday af
ternoon and the way the car had slid so gracefully an
inevitably into the telephone pole. Her return to conscious
ness in this room, the waves of dizziness and pain, th
gradual realization that she was back in the one place i
the world she'd hoped never to see again.

And then there was her rescuer.

It wasn't chance that she'd left him to the last. Had sh
ever laid eyes on a man so magnetic, so masculine, so self
assured? So guarded, so reluctant to trust her? Wh
couldn't she have been rescued by a country farmer in
three-ton truck, with a plump, friendly wife and a kitche
smelling of borscht and freshly baked bread?

Cal was his name. And that was all she knew about him

Except for the inescapable fact that his two brief kisse
had melted the very bones of her body.

She had to get out of here. Soon. Sooner. Soonest.

Cautiously Joanna sat up. In the dim light, she could se
Cal stretched out on the couch, his feet dangling over th
edge, his neck stuck at an awkward angle. A blanket hal
covered his long body. He was still sound asleep.

He'd saved her life. If he hadn't come along, she'd have
frozen to death.

She shivered, knowing that in spite of all the unhappines
of her marriage, and the acute pain of the last few months
she was deeply glad to be alive. So she had much to than
him for, this dark-haired stranger with eyes as gray and
depthless as a winter sea.

If only he didn't share Dieter and Maria's opinion of he
character. Which was, to put it mildly, rock-bottom. Why
that should hurt her so badly, she didn't understand. He

was a stranger, chance-met and soon to be forgotten. So why should it matter what he thought of her?

Not liking her own thoughts, Joanna got up as quietly as she could, parted the curtains and peered outside. Her heart sank. All she could see was the driven whiteness of snow; all she could hear was the howl of the wind. It was worse than yesterday, she thought numbly. But she had to leave. She had to.

From behind her Cal said with a lack of emotion that infuriated her, "Looks like we'll be stuck here today, too."

She whirled, frightened that she hadn't heard him get up, let alone cross the room. He was standing altogether too close, his crumpled shirt unbuttoned from throat to navel, his cords creased from sleeping in them. The sheen on his tousled hair reminded her of mahogany; her mother had left her a beautiful little mahogany end table. Then he yawned, and the corded muscles of his belly tightened; all his muscles were truly impressive, she thought wildly.

"I'm leaving here this morning," she spat. "You can do what you like."

"And how are you going to leave?" he said mockingly. "Your car's wedged to a telephone pole three miles down the road, and I'm not driving you anywhere, not in this." He lifted one brow. "Unless you think Dieter will lend you his car?"

So angry she could barely talk, she seethed, "I will not stay one more hour in a house where everyone—including you—thinks I'm a cold-blooded, immoral bitch!"

"I'm not—"

As if he hadn't spoken, she swept on, "I made the biggest mistake in my life—apart from marrying Gustave, that is—to fly out here with belongings of his I thought his parents should have. To believe that now he was dead, maybe we could somehow make peace. I sure go to the top of the class for naiveté."

"Naive isn't exactly the word I'd use for you."

"But you know nothing about me, Mr. Cal whatever-your-name-is. Only what you've been told. *You're* the one who's naive. You believe Dieter and Maria, who thought the universe revolved around Gustave. And you believe Franz, who hero-worshiped him and made one heck of a lot of money out of him into the bargain. Three cheers for you."

She was being very childish, she thought in a sudden wave of exhilaration. And it felt extremely good. She added peevishly, "What *is* your last name? And what are you doing here? You don't look the type to be a friend of the Strassens."

"Cal Freeman," Cal said, and watched her closely.

Her brow furrowed. "The name's familiar...but we've never met, I'd have remembered you."

"I'm a mountaineer."

She paled. "That's where I've heard your name—Franz was telling us once about the team you took up Everest."

"Franz gave me Gustave's climbing gear to bring to the Strassens."

She clutched the bedpost, her voice ragged. "Did you know Gustave?"

"No. But I'd heard of him, of course. I was sorry to hear he'd died."

"Play with fire," she said unsteadily, "and sooner or later you get burned."

The words were out before he could prevent them. "You being the fire?"

She raised her chin. "No, Cal. The mountains. The mountains that I grew to hate because they destroyed any chance I might have had of happiness."

"So you think all mountaineers are irresponsible dare-devils?"

"You're darn right I do."

He tapped himself on the chest. "Not this one."

Her eyes seemed to have glued themselves to the taut skin over his breastbone, with its tangle of dark hair. "Then you're the exception that proves the rule," she said, and couldn't have disguised the bitterness in her tone.

"Gustave was a mountaineer when you met him."

"And I was nineteen. Young enough to find both him and the mountains romantic."

It was an entirely plausible reply. Feeling frustrated and unsure of himself, Cal ventured, "You were jealous of the mountains?"

"I suppose I was," she said wearily. "Are you married, Cal? Does your wife hate it when the mountains take you away from her?"

Years ago, whenever Cal used to go on an expedition, Suzanne would fly to Paris and indulge in an orgy of shopping. He'd sometimes thought it would have suited Suzanne very well to have been left a wealthy widow; she'd have had the fun of spending his money without the bother of a relationship with a real, flesh-and-blood man. "That's none of your business," he said tersely.

"I beg your pardon," Joanna retorted. "So you can ask questions but I can't?"

Cal said impatiently, "I'm not spending the entire day trading insults with you."

"No, you're not. You're moving into the other part of the house, where you can spend the day with Dieter and Maria." With a flick of malice, Joanna added, "Have a good one."

Curiosity overcoming everything else, Cal asked, "Has this house always been so bleak and bare?"

"Ever since I've been coming here." Joanna bit her lip. "I'm sure it wasn't easy for Gustave, growing up with such strict, joyless parents. At first I tried to be understanding, but that wore thin after a while."

Wishing with fierce intensity that he'd just once met Gustave Strassen so he could have formed his own opinion of the man, and wishing with equal intensity that he could spend the entire day in bed with Gustave's widow, Cal said harshly, "If you'll excuse me I'm going to have a shower, get breakfast and check the weather report. Then I'll bring you something to eat."

"Bread and water?"

"Don't be ridiculous."

"It's not so ridiculous. Because I'm a prisoner in this room, aren't I?"

She was. No question of it. And he along with her. "Pray for sunshine," Cal said ironically, and headed for the bathroom.

It would have given Joanna enormous satisfaction to have thrown her pillow at his retreating back. Or drummed her heels on the cold hardwood and screamed out all her frustration. She did neither one. Cal Freeman already thought she was the equivalent of pond scum. A tantrum would really finish her off.

Why did she care what he thought?

So he had a great body. More than great, she thought, her mouth dry. And she'd be willing to bet he was quite unaware of the effect of his physique on a woman who, apart from that one time a few months ago, hadn't been to bed with anyone for at least four years. Including her lawfully wedded husband, Gustave Strassen.

Not that Cal would believe that.

Cal Freeman. She'd heard about him over the years. That spectacular ascent of the northeast ridge of Everest. His climbs on the Kishtwar range and the Kongur Massif. His heroic rescue of two French climbers in the Andes. Gustave had never encouraged talk about Cal Freeman; Gustave had always wanted to be the center of attention, another facet of his character that a love-blind nineteen-year-old had totally missed.

How ironic that Cal should have effected another rescue, this time of Gustave's widow, from a blizzard on the prairies.

Hurriedly Joanna got dressed; she was already heartily sick of her blue sweater. Then she braided her hair, made the bed, drew the curtains, and undid her briefcase. If she was to be stuck here for the morning—beyond the morning, she refused to look—she might as well get some work done.

So when Cal emerged from the bathroom, his hair still damp, she had her laptop set up and was frowning at the screen. He said, "I'll be back in half an hour with your breakfast."

She nodded without raising her eyes. He added, an edge of steel in his voice, "Where I come from, you look at someone when they speak to you."

"I'm working—can't you see?"

"According to Franz you've got lots of money. So what kind of work do you do that's so important that you can't even be civil?"

This time her head snapped up. "What I do with all the spare time I have as a stinkingly rich widow is none of your business."

"Don't push your luck, Joanna," Cal said with dangerous softness.

He hadn't yet shaved; the dark shadow on his jawline did indeed make him look dangerous. But Joanna had done a lot of growing up since she was nineteen. "And what happens if I do?"

"I wouldn't advise you to ask that question unless you're prepared for the answer."

Although her pulse was beating uncomfortably fast, she said with credible calm, "He-man stuff."

His words had an explosive force. "Do you have any idea how beautiful you are? Especially when you're in a rage."

A blush scorched her cheeks. "Don't change the subject!"

"Oh, I don't think I am." He gave her a grin she could only call predatory. "I'll be back."

The bedroom door closed behind him. Joanna let out her breath in a long sigh. She wasn't normally argumentative, nor was she overly aware of the male half of the species: if Gustave had been anything to go by, she was better off alone. But Cal Freeman seemed to destroy all the self-sufficiency she'd striven to achieve over the long years of her marriage.

Her first resolution, she thought fiercely, was to work all morning. And her second, to ignore the dark-haired man who was virtually her jailer.

She turned her attention back to the screen, and by sheer stubbornness managed to immerse herself in revising the tenth chapter. Her New York agent had already found a publisher for this, her second novel; she was determined it wasn't going to bomb, as could so often happen with second novels. Especially after all the critical attention the first one had gained.

It seemed no time before Cal opened the door, carrying a tray. Quickly she closed the file; she had no intention of him finding out about her other life as a writer. She said casually, "That smells good."

"I cooked the eggs myself," Cal said. "Didn't want Maria pouring hot pepper sauce all over them."

She steeled herself against the laughter lurking in his gray eyes. "What's the weather forecast?"

"Like this all day. Wind dying around midnight, the plow should come through during the night, and I've ooked a tow truck first thing tomorrow. No flights out of Winnipeg today.''

''Oh, that's just wonderful,'' said Joanna, fighting down a wave of panic that was out of all proportion.

Cal's eyes narrowed. ''I'm going out to my vehicle to bring in Gustave's gear,'' he said coldly. ''I'm presuming you don't want any of it?''

She flinched. ''No,'' she said in a low voice. ''I don't need a harness or a set of ropes to remind me of Gustave.''

Cal plunked the tray down on the table. The trouble was, she fascinated him with far more than her incredible beauty. Anger, sadness, frustration, terror, she'd shown them all; and now he had to add a kind of dignity that he could only respect. ''Eat your breakfast,'' he ordered. ''Any complaints about the eggs can be directed to the chef.''

She suddenly grinned. ''I'm hungry enough they could be as tough as climbing boots and I wouldn't complain.''

Her smile was full of mischief. Turning away so he wouldn't grab her with all the subtlety of a caveman, Cal said brusquely, ''I'll be back with your lunch.'' Then he wheeled and left the room.

The next couple of hours were far from pleasant for Cal. Maria's iron facade wasn't equal to seeing her son's climbing gear; Dieter openly had tears in his eyes. Against his will, Cal's anger toward Joanna was revived; although he was honest enough to admit some of that anger should be directed toward himself for letting her get past his defences so easily. Eventually the Strassens disappeared to their own room; around noon, his eyes tiring from the fine print of *War and Peace,* Cal took himself to the kitchen and produced some untidy but interesting sandwiches for himself and Joanna. Picking up hers, he headed back to the bedroom.

He could be very soft-footed when he chose to be. Not

stopping to analyze just why he should want to take Joann
by surprise, Cal padded into the bedroom they'd shared la
night. She was scowling into her laptop computer, totall
focused on what she was doing. He couldn't help admirin
her concentration, for Joanna Strassen definitely didn'
want to be here: that much he did believe. Suzanne, unde
similar circumstances, would have been indulging in a ma
jor sulk. But Joanna was being…stoic, he thought. Stoicis
was right up there in his list of virtues.

She'd fastened her hair in an untidy mass on top of he
head; skewering the shiny black coils was a yellow penci
As he watched, she leafed through a black-covered journa
to her left, read half a page intently, and began rummagin
through the papers on the table, muttering something unde
her breath.

Cal said lightly, "What's your problem?"

She jumped, knocking several papers to the floor. "D
you get a kick out of creeping up on people?" she de
manded. "Where the *hell* is my pencil?"

"In your hair," he said amiably.

Her scowl deepened. "I've been doing that for years—
never think to look there and don't you dare laugh at me.'
Her gaze dropped to the plate in his hands. "You expec
me to eat those?"

He glanced down. The tomato slices had skidded, th
lettuce was falling out, and he'd been so generous with th
egg salad that each sandwich bulged bounteously. Like
pregnant woman, he thought. "I couldn't care less if yo
eat them or not! After Dieter and Maria saw Gustave's gea
they were very upset, and I sure as heck wasn't going t
ask either one of them to make your lunch."

Joanna pushed back her chair, stood up and marched
over to him. Her chin high, she said, "I'm sorry they'v
lost their son. Truly I am. But Gustave was a disaster wait-

ng to happen—far too taken up with his own ego to be
alf the climber they thought he was.''

''If he'd just found out you were pregnant and he wasn't
ure who'd fathered the child—that's completely irrele-
ant?''

''He knew who the father was. Trust me.''

Why couldn't he trust her? She wasn't Suzanne: or even
emotely like Suzanne. Deliberately needling her, Cal said,
'How could he have known? There are a lot of men in
Europe.''

''And according to Dieter and Maria I've slept with most
f them.'' She gave an unamused laugh. ''I'd like to know
when I'd have found the time.''

Suzanne still on his mind, Cal said with a touch of bit-
erness, ''Some women can always find time for what they
want to do.''

Joanna said very softly, ''Why don't you stick to stuff
you know something about? Because you know what? I
hate generalizations almost as much as I hate false accu-
ations.'' Putting her head to one side, she examined him
with a clinical detachment Cal thoroughly disliked. ''Oddly
enough, I'd have thought you were too intelligent for either
one.''

Normally, Cal would have thought the same thing.
Pushing his luck, he said, ''So whose baby was it,
Joanna?''

''Gustave's. Of course.''

Of course. Cal dumped the tray on the coffee table. ''I'll
bring you dinner around six-thirty,'' he muttered, and
marched out of the room to find his book. The fact that
Joanna was every bit as complex as some of the characters
both incensed and confused him. For a man who'd made
his first fortune by the time he was twenty-three, he was
behaving like an idiot. A total Neanderthal.

Going back into the kitchen, Cal picked up his own sandwiches, sat down in the bleak parlor, and opened *War and Peace*. He wasn't going to think about Joanna Strassen until suppertime.

Not once.

CHAPTER FOUR

JOANNA ate her sandwiches, which were as tasty as they were messy, did some energetic stretches, and saw with true despair that somehow these two tasks had only passed thirty-nine minutes. Had a day ever been so interminable? Had she ever wished so passionately to be elsewhere?

She picked up her pile of papers, forcing herself to enter that other world of the imagination; and hour by slow hour the afternoon passed. But by six o'clock Joanna was desperate to escape the confines of the bedroom. She marched up and down, counting the turns under her breath, pumping her arms vigorously. She should exercise more often; she hadn't really regained her strength since losing the baby.

Her eyes filmed with tears. Joanna scrubbed them away. The past was over. Over and done with. Tomorrow when she left here, she must put it behind her. She had a teaching job that paid the bills, she had her all-important vocation as a writer, and she had two good friends back home in the little university town of Harcourt, Nova Scotia. She was extraordinarily lucky.

As she blinked the last tears away, Joanna became aware that for the past few minutes a man had been speaking on the other side of the closed bedroom door. Cal. She'd know his voice anywhere. She crept closer to the door, unashamedly listening. He was on the phone, she realized, and strained to hear.

"I'm glad we've been able to talk," he was saying, "whatever did people do before long distance? And of course I want you to be happy...no, I'll be going on to New York, there's an auction of Chinese jade there next

47

week...I know, darling, I know. But it's not much longer and then we can be together in the summer...okay, you'd better go. I'll call you tomorrow when I get to Boston. See you soon, sweetheart. 'Bye.''

The receiver was replaced with a soft click. Joanna straightened, her heart thumping. So Cal Freeman was either married or otherwise taken; and the woman in question was unhappy without him. Yet the only time he was willing to spend with her was the summer. Were all mountaineers the same? Demanding untrammeled freedom, but at the same time wanting the little woman to keep the home fires burning?

How his voice had softened when he'd called her *sweetheart*. Almost as though he'd meant it, Joanna thought cynically. Because this was the man who'd kissed her, Joanna as though she were the only woman left on the surface of the earth.

Another man who believed words were as disposable as empty oxygen tanks. Worse, another mountaineer whose middle name was infidelity.

Who *was* the unknown woman he'd been talking to? Was she beautiful? Was she his wife? Or his mistress?

Then another voice spoke in the narrow hallway. "Ah...there you are, Cal. Maria is making dinner, she's feeling a little better now. Why don't you join me for a drink? And tonight you must sleep in the guest room, you'll be much more comfortable there."

"I would certainly prefer that," Cal said loudly, so loudly that Joanna shrank back, her cheeks hot. He couldn't have known she was listening...could he?

"Did you get your connection without any trouble?"

"Yes, thanks. Clear as a bell. It's so important to keep in touch, isn't it, when you—"

His voice was suddenly muffled as the door to the main house swung shut. Joanna wandered over to the window.

staring into the snow and the endless darkness. There was no reason for her to feel so suddenly, acutely and miserably lonely. No reason at all.

Joanna woke early. She lay very still and realized she was listening to silence: the wind had died. She sprang out of bed and pulled back the curtains on a world of sculpted snowbanks and fading stars in the vastness of a prairie sky.

She could leave today. Leave and never come back.

For a moment she rested her forehead against the cold glass. Maybe coming here hadn't been such a terrible mistake, after all...for hadn't she, in the past couple of days, somehow severed the last of her ties to Gustave? Hopefully he really was part of her past now, this man she had once passionately loved; and it was in the past that he must remain.

Quickly she showered, toweled her hair dry and dressed. Then she closed her mind to everything but chapter eleven, and got to work. An hour later, Cal tapped on the door. "Are you awake, Joanna?"

"Come in," she said crisply.

He was wearing the same heavy sweater and thick cords; his hair shone with cleanliness, and he was clean-shaven. The cold white light from the window threw shadows over the jut of his cheekbones and the strong line of his jaw; his eyes were an unfathomable gray. Power was what he exuded, she decided, her mouth suddenly dry. The power of a man who'd met challenges that would have defeated a lesser man; the power of a man used to command. Certainly his masculinity would never be called into question. Sexy didn't even begin to describe him.

"Why are you staring at me?" he demanded.

"Trying to figure out what makes you tick."

The last thirty-six hours had disabused Cal of any notions

that he knew what made him tick. "You can keep you
pretty nose out of my business," he retorted.

"Good morning to you, too," she said cordially.

He jammed his hands in his pockets. "The road's
ploughed, and the tow truck's taking your car back to the
airport…you managed to damage the radiator, so you can'
drive it. Anyway, it's full of snow because I had to break
one of the windows. The driver will leave your suitcase
with the rental agency."

"It's only a small overnight bag," Joanna said, biting
her lip. She had no idea what a tow truck cost, but she was
willing to bet it wouldn't come cheap. With luck she could
squeeze the bill onto her Visa and stay under her limit. But
the insurance she'd purchased on the car was five-hundred-
dollar deductible, she realized with a cold sinking in the pit
of her stomach.

"What's the matter?" Cal rasped.

She blurted, "How much does a tow truck cost?"

"A couple of hundred, probably."

She'd definitely be over her limit. But there was about
four hundred in her savings account, she could access that
at the airport. Then she realized Cal was speaking again.
"Sorry?" she muttered.

"Supposedly you've got lots of money."

"Suppositions can lead you badly astray."

"Supposedly you were too cheap to buy proper equipment for Gustave. Which supposedly had something to do
with what happened on Annapurna."

Enough, thought Joanna in a flood of pure rage. More
than enough. In fact, a great deal more than enough. "Just
you listen to me, Cal Freeman! I had money when I married
Gustave, quite a lot of money. He spent it, every single
cent, going to the Alps and the Andes and Nepal and China.
Plus he spent it on women, don't let's forget that—so many
women I lost track. And I was too stupid, too trusting, too

naive, to realize what he was doing until it was too late. Yes, he had second-rate equipment by the end. But that wasn't my fault, it was his. *His,* do you hear me?"

"I should think Maria and Dieter can hear you," Cal said in a peculiar voice. "Are you trying to tell me you're broke?"

"That's precisely what I'm telling you. That, and the simple fact that I'm sick to death of being accused of causing my husband's death." Her voice suddenly cracked. "My husband's and my unborn child's."

She swung around to face the window, furious with herself for crying and too proud to let Cal see the tears trickling down her cheeks. Then she felt his hand fall heavy and warm on her shoulder. She whirled, striking it off, her eyes blazing. "Don't you dare touch me!"

"Don't cry, Joanna...please," Cal said, a note in his voice that was new to her.

"I'll cry if I want to," she retorted and made a dive for the box of tissues on the table. She blew her nose hard. Tears or no, she felt better right now than she'd felt since she arrived here two days ago. She'd been behaving with entirely too much restraint; losing her temper had felt just fine. And if Mr. Cal-Almighty-Freeman didn't like it, too bad.

"Either you're telling the truth, or you're an extremely good actress," Cal said slowly.

"Oh, in between my affairs with all the men in Europe, I went to drama school—did I forget to mention that?"

"They hate you, Dieter and Maria."

"They hate life," she said pithily. "Life, laughter, fun, passion, red roses and sunsets—you've seen their house and don't get me going."

"They loved their son."

"Love's a word capable of many interpretations. Surely you're old enough and savvy enough to have learned that.

Not, of course, that I'm interested in your thought pro cesses.''

"Did you ever love your husband?" Cal asked in th same infuriatingly level voice.

"Falling in love with Gustave was the biggest mistak of my whole life," she snapped, adding with complete un truth, "Look, Cal, I don't care whether you believe on word I've said to you or not. What I do care about i whether you'll drive me to the airport—or do I have to cal a cab?"

"I'll drive you. We'll leave in half an hour. I'll brin; you something to eat right away."

He turned on his heel and left the room. Joanna sagge into the nearest chair. Losing her temper had felt wonderfu in the moment, she thought ruefully, but it had sure taker the good out of her. And it hadn't accomplished anything Cal, she was almost sure, still didn't believe one word she' said.

Which hurt. Rather a lot.

Cal pulled up outside the terminal building. "I'll leave yor here and park in the rental area. See you in a few minutes.'

"Fine," Joanna said briefly. For the past two hours, nei ther she nor Cal had said anything beyond commonplaces She hurried inside the terminal, dismayed to see the crowd of delayed passengers and the length of the lineups. She had to get out of here today. She couldn't afford a night in a hotel.

Planting herself at the end of the line, she took out paperback novel. Half an hour passed, during which she shuffled in small stages closer to the counter. Then from the corner of her eye she saw Cal duck under the tape. She closed her book. How appropriate that they say goodby here in a crowd of strangers, she thought. For hadn't each of them remained a stranger to the other?

Cal said curtly, "I'm on a flight to Boston that leaves in an hour, I was lucky to get it."

Boston. The woman he'd called *sweetheart*, hadn't he said he'd phone her from Boston? Was that where she lived?

"Where are you headed?" Cal finished.

Joanna clutched her book to her chest; she was using her ticket as a bookmark. "I reckon I'll go to Hawaii—spend some more of my money."

"Where do you live, Joanna?"

"You don't need to know that."

"For some reason that escapes me," he said in a savage whisper, "I do."

"Too bad."

"In that case I guess I'll just have to stay by your side all the way to the counter."

"Cal," she seethed, "go to Boston. Go to hell for all I care. After today we'll never see each other again—and never's too soon for me. In other words, get lost!"

"I don't think I'm quite ready to do that."

She couldn't lose her temper again. Not twice in one day. The woman ahead of her was listening with unabashed interest, and the couple behind her, who'd been bickering ever since they'd joined the lineup, had fallen silent. To get a lesson from the professionals, Joanna thought wryly. And would it really matter if Cal found out she was flying to Halifax? She didn't live there, and she certainly wasn't going to give him her address. "Do what you like," she said with assumed indifference. "I'd hate for you to miss your plane, though."

"You let me worry about that."

Ostentatiously she reopened her book and began to read; and in fifteen minutes, with Cal so close to her the elusive tang of his aftershave teased her nostrils, she reached the counter. "Halifax?" the man said, and consulted his computer. "First flight I can get you on is at three-thirty, via Toronto, getting into Halifax at seven forty-six."

Joanna gave him a brilliant smile. No hotel. No more bills added to her overloaded credit card. "That's wonderful, thank you," she said, and a few minutes later had her boarding card. She marched away from the lineup, glanced at her watch and said levelly to the man glued to her side, "You'd better go through security—they won't wait for you."

Cal pulled a piece of paper from his pocket and thrust it between the pages of her book. Then he took her by the shoulders, his fingers digging through her coat. "I've given you a phone number where I can always be reached, plus my e-mail address." He hesitated, then went on with a raw honesty that took her aback, "I know this makes no sense, Joanna...but please give me your address. We're not finished with each other and don't ask me to explain that because I can't."

"You're wrong and the answer's no."

"We met under the worst of circumstances, and initially I had no reason to disbelieve Franz, or Dieter and Maria."

"Why don't you try believing me?"

Cal winced. Suzanne had spoken just like that after any number of escapades. And of course he'd learned not to believe her.

He'd hesitated too long. Joanna said coldly, "Go catch your plane. Why would I want to keep in touch with someone who thinks I've done nothing but lie to him since we met? You're really no different from Gustave's parents."

"You sure know how to flatter a guy."

Her question came from nowhere. "Cal, are you married?"

"No," he said curtly.

So the woman on the phone was his mistress. But a man wasn't labeled promiscuous if he had more than one woman on the go. No, he was admired. He was envied, not despised.

Joanna took a deep breath. "I know you saved my life—if you hadn't come along, I'd have frozen to death. I haven't really thanked you for that." She looked him right in the eye. "I do thank you. From the bottom of my heart. But as for the rest, we have nothing to say to each other."

"Then let me at least say this," he grated. Before she realized his intention, he slid his arms around her, pulled her hard against the length of his body, and kissed her with passionate intensity.

For a few seconds Joanna was so shocked that she was rigid in his embrace. But the heat of his lips, the sureness with which he moved his mouth against hers, the first thrust of his tongue, made her head swim and her body spring to life. She clutched his sleeves so she wouldn't fall, and kissed him back as though she'd never kissed a man in her life before, as though he were the first and she as innocent as a virgin.

Her pulse was racing; her breasts were pressed hard against his chest, and even through her coat she could feel his arousal. Desire, that had lain dormant in her for so many years, unfurled like the petals of a flower, encompassing her in the fiery beauty of her body's truth. She wanted Cal. Wanted him fiercely, urgently and now.

As she opened to him, her tongue meeting his with unbridled generosity, he strained her closer. His kiss deepened, until she swore she could feel the pounding of his heart in the thrumming of her own blood. It was a kiss she wanted to last forever, she thought dazedly, twining her arms around his neck, discovering with a small leap of surprise the warmth of his nape, the thick silkiness of his hair. From a long way away she heard a raucous laugh. Closer, a woman's voice said, "Oh, Mabel, aren't they cute?"

"Just like in the movies," the unknown Mabel breathed. "Airports are such fun, you never know what you're going to see next."

Cute, thought Joanna dimly. *Cute?*

Then Cal pushed her away so suddenly that she staggered. His chest heaving, he said in a voice she'd never heard him use before, "For someone who hates making a spectacle of himself, I seem to be excelling myself. Goodbye, Joanna Strassen. Don't spend all your money in Hawaii, will you?"

"I won't. And I'll only have affairs with half the men there," she said faintly, and watched him wheel and stride toward the escalator that led to security. A tall, broad-shouldered man wearing a down parka. A man who with one kiss had made nonsense of the celibacy she'd lived with for so long.

A man who couldn't decide whether she was telling the truth or acting her head off. Who had a mistress he called *sweetheart.*

A man she was never going to see again.

Thank heavens she hadn't given him her address. Because she couldn't afford to see him again. One more unfaithful mountaineer in her life would be one too many.

Her nose in the air, Joanna walked past Mabel and her friend, both of whom had blue rinses and were smiling at her with misty sentimentality. The rental agency was at the other end of the airport. She headed in that direction, clutching her paperback to her chest. Dealing with a broken radiator, a smashed window and a tow truck would bring her back to earth in a hurry.

A good thing, too.

CHAPTER FIVE

A STUPENDOUS view, a full stomach, and the company of a good friend: what more could a man want?

He could want Joanna Strassen, thought Cal grimly.

Four months since he'd seen her and he still couldn't get her out of his mind. Wasn't she the reason he was here, sitting on the front deck of Ludo Galliker's chalet, which faced the three snow-draped peaks of the Eiger, the Mettenberg and the Wetterhorn, along with their mighty glaciers? His old friend Ludo, retired now from guiding groups up these same peaks, from whom he, Cal, had learned so many of the basics all those years ago.

He'd driven the crowded highways from Lenny's school near St. Gallen all the way to the tourist trap of Grindelwald just to see Ludo. For old times' sake, certainly. But also to ask him a question. A crucially important question.

Ludo came out on the deck, bearing a carved antique tray on which was a full bottle of plum brandy and two small glasses. He glanced over at the peaks, which the setting sun had tinged with rose. "Many years have gone by since our first abseil on the Eiger," he said. "Do you remember the first time your father brought you here? What were you, fourteen? But even then, strong as a man and oh, so determined." He chuckled. "Not for you the easy routes, the safe ones."

For a couple of hours, as the light faded from the meadows around the chalet and the level of brandy slowly sank in the bottle, the two men reminisced about some of their favorite climbs. Because Ludo was one of the few people who had known Cal's flamboyant, affectionate father, Cal always enjoyed these visits, and now felt a twinge of conscience that he hadn't come here more often: Ludo wasn't getting any younger.

Not that Ludo would ever admit that. His shock of white hair seemed imbued with its own energy, and his laugh was as robust as ever. But Cal had noticed each time Ludo lowered himself into his wooden chair, he'd moved carefully; his weathered hands were knotted with arthritis.

The first stars pierced the alpine sky. Into a gap in the conversation, Cal said casually, "Did you ever come across a climber called Gustave Strassen, Ludo?"

Ludo drained his glass, and refilled it. "Why do you ask?"

"A few months ago, I met his widow."

"Ah...I, too, met her. Twice, some years ago. What did you think of her?"

"I asked you about her husband. Not about her."

"So you did. Humor an old man, Cal. Give me your impressions of Joanna Strassen."

Ludo's homemade brandy had defeated more than one seasoned mountaineer; Cal said indiscreetly, "So beautiful I can't get her out of my mind."

"So bedworthy, you mean?" Ludo said dryly.

"That, too. But not just that. Intelligent, fiery-tempered. Yet according to Gustave's parents, she has the morals of an alley cat."

"An alley cat? What does that mean?"

"Sleeps around," Cal said pungently.

Ludo delicately raised one brow. "So did she or didn't she get into *your* bed?"

"Didn't," Cal exploded, "and what the devil's the alcohol content of this stuff we're drinking?"

"My secret," Ludo said with a smug smile. "Tell me how you met her."

Briefly Cal described his errand to the prairies, the storm,

he car in the ditch. "A guide I met on Mont Blanc said
she denied her husband equipment that might have saved
his life, and that she cheated on Gustave for years. Then,
according to Gustave's parents, after he died she even
aborted a child that might have been his," he finished, and
heard pain underlying the anger in his voice.

Since last January, he'd done his level best to forget
Joanna Strassen. He'd dated Jasmine in Boston, taking her
for a very expensive dinner and then leaving her—to their
mutual surprise—at the door of her condo. He'd dated
women in New York, London and Zurich, beautiful, intelligent women who'd left him stone-cold. He'd led an expedition to Patagonia in March. He'd visited Lenny in
February, April, and May, yesterday attending a performance of her school play. And none of it had worked. A
tall, enigmatic woman with a sheaf of blue-black hair and
eyes the vivid blue of delphiniums had haunted him, day
and night. Although the nights, he admitted savagely, were
the worst. By far.

Ludo said matter-of-factly, "And you believed these
people? Gustave's parents and the guide?"

"At first I did. Why wouldn't I?"

"Even after you'd spent some time with Joanna, you still
believed them?"

"I don't know!" Cal exclaimed in utter frustration. "I
wanted to believe her, you don't know how I wanted to.
But from the first moment I saw her, she knocked me right
off balance—I didn't know which way was up."

Ludo raised his brows. "How about listening to a different version? That Gustave cheated on Joanna. That he
spent her money as though it were water in a mountain
stream, never to run dry. That he had an ego as big as the
Eiger, a heart cold as the Aletsch glacier."

"And whose version is that?" Cal said carefully, noticing that his fingers weren't quite steady as he put his glass down on the tray.

"My version. And you know me for an honest man."

"You knew Gustave?"

"I came across him eight years ago when he was newly married, him and his beautiful wife. Because you are right, she is beautiful beyond any words that I could find. And in those days, so in love, so blind to the man Gustave really was, that it hurt me to see it."

Cal poured himself another glass of *Pflümli*. He wasn't going anywhere tonight, and if he had the granddaddy of all hangovers tomorrow, that was the least of his worries. "You're saying the fault was all Gustave's?"

"Yes. I met them again, five years ago, at the cheese festival in the Justistal valley. She was trying to behave as though nothing was wrong; he was throwing his weight around, flirting with anything in skirts, and, according to report, bedding any who were willing. He was a bad man, Cal. And not even a very good climber. What saved him all those years were the guides he chose. He paid them well—from Joanna's money—and depended on them to keep him out of trouble. I, for one, wasn't surprised when he fell on Annapurna. Only surprised it had taken that long."

Cal said quietly, "My God...she'll never forgive me."

"For believing what everyone else told you about her?"

"Believing it. Throwing it in her face. Refusing to admit the evidence that was in front of my eyes that she was different."

"If you're in Grindelwald and she's in Canada, it will certainly be difficult for her to forgive you."

"If she were standing right here in front of me, she wouldn't forgive me."

"The first step is to ask her for forgiveness."

"Canada's a big country and I don't even know where he lives."

"I'm sure if you can track down a Vermeer that's been lost for three hundred years for one of your auctions, you can find this one woman," Ludo said with heavy irony.

"You think she'll talk to me after all the things I said?" Cal demanded in a cracked voice.

"Why is Lenny going to school in Switzerland, Cal?"

His brain whirling, Cal stared at his old friend. "What's that got to do with Joanna Strassen?"

"Answer the question."

"I thought it best for her. I'm away a fair bit, she's thirteen and needs female company—"

"She needs a mother."

"You can't just order one of those whenever it suits you!"

"Go and find Joanna Strassen. Lenny doesn't like her new school, you told me that while we were eating dinner."

"She's homesick. She'll settle down."

"You're paying huge fees at this so-elegant school so you can shirk your responsibilities to your daughter."

Cal said tightly, "Go easy, Ludo."

"You're in love with Joanna Strassen."

"Dammit, I'm not!"

"I think you are. I've known you for years and your father before you. He was a one-woman man—never looked at anyone else after your mother died. And you're the same. It's just that you've never found the right woman. You might have thought Suzanne was the one for you—but I knew better. Suzanne wasn't in any way a match for you. But Joanna—ah, Joanna Strassen is more than your match."

"Joanna Strassen thinks I'm worse than the dirt under her feet. And with good reason."

"Then you'll have to change her mind, won't you?"

"Are you saying I should *marry* her?"

"I do believe I am…I think a little chestnut torte would go well with the last of the brandy, what do you think?"

Cal rested his forehead on his hands. "It's true, isn't it? She never cheated on Gustave. I think part of me knew that all along."

"Never. I would swear to that in a court of law."

"So it must have been his child she was carrying. She told me she loved her unborn baby…so what happened to it?"

"I don't know the answer to that question. So why don' you ask her? She's the one who knows."

"Yeah," said Cal. "Just like that. You might as well suggest we scale the Matterhorn before breakfast."

With a heartless laugh Ludo levered himself up from his chair. "But you've always loved a challenge, haven' you?"

He'd rather climb the Matterhorn, before or after break fast, than face Joanna Strassen, thought Cal. He knew where he was on the Matterhorn. Knew the dangers. A woman like Joanna was unknown territory.

She'd been faithful to her husband through the most dif ficult of marriages. Faithful to Gustave and truthful to Cal.

Somehow he had to find her. Find her, ask her to forgive him, and take her to bed.

And if that wasn't a challenge, he didn't know what was

But marry her? What would he do that for? Because Ludo was wrong. Dead wrong. He, Cal, wasn't in love with Joanna Strassen.

No way.

"Apple tree," Joanna said slowly, standing under a haze of sweetly scented pink blossoms. "The apple tree is in bloom."

The small crowd of students surrounding her dutifully

stared up at the tree, which was loud with the buzzing of bees. "Apples," Luis said. "No apples. Not yet no apples."

"Not yet any apples," Joanna smiled. "In the autumn, there will be many apples on the tree. Do you understand, Luis?"

"In spring the tree is very beautiful," Sanches said, his voice without expression.

Joanna smothered a sigh. Sanches had the best grasp of English of all her foreign students, and not a scrap of poetry in his soul.

"Exquisito," said Angelica, *"sí perfumado."*

"Exquisite," Joanna responded, "so fragrant."

"Fray-grant," Angelica repeated, inhaling the scent of the clustered petals with a beatific smile.

They were grouped on the slope in front of the arts building on a sunny afternoon in early June; whenever possible, Joanna conducted her classes outdoors. Harcourt, in Nova Scotia's Annapolis Valley, was at its best in June: the fresh green leaves, the blossoming orchards, the birds in their bright plumage flitting among the trees.

It beat the prairies in January.

She didn't want to think about the prairies. In January or in June. She hadn't heard a word from Gustave's parents, not that she'd expected to. As for Cal Freeman, she'd forgotten him.

Or, to be more truthful, she wished she had.

"Bzzz?" said Rodrigo, and flapped his arms.

"Bee," Joanna said. "Bumblebee. Oh, and look, a bird in the branches of the tree...*un pájaro en las ramas de los árboles.*"

They were wandering in the general direction of the parking lot, where her plan was to talk about cars. Absently she noticed a bright red minivan pull into the lot allocated to the registrar; she'd had dinner with the registrar a couple of times recently, it was funny he hadn't mentioned he was buying such a splashy new vehicle.

Not that she'd encouraged him to confide in her. Even though he was a nice man. A very nice man, compared to Cal. She heaved a sigh. She'd really only gone out with the registrar because her two best friends, Sally and Dianne, were insistent she have some kind of social life that included the male of the species.

She didn't need men. Sally and Dianne were mistaken.

And then a man climbed out of the front seat of the minivan, and her heart lurched in her breast. It wasn't the registrar. It was Cal. Cal Freeman.

But it couldn't be. Not here. Just because she'd had some of the most graphic and erotic dreams in her life about that particular male didn't mean he was in Nova Scotia, walking across the grass toward her.

"The bird is yellow," said Sanches. "The bird sings."

"Canary," Luis said triumphantly.

Dazedly Joanna dragged her eyes away from the man who was undoubtedly Cal Freeman. The bird was a goldfinch. "Not a canary," she stumbled, "we don't have wild canaries here."

"A man walks by the grass," Angelica said, giving Cal a thoughtful glance.

"Across the grass," Joanna corrected automatically, and made a valiant effort to pull herself together. "I don't want to talk to him, I'll send him away."

"Tall," said Angelica, smoothing her jet-black hair. "And very…*guapo,* how do you say in English?"

"Handsome," Sanches supplied.

"*Por Dios,* why you send him away?" Angelica asked.

Cal was now within earshot, Joanna realized, her mouth dry. He looked wonderful, his loose-limbed stride, his powerful shoulders and flat belly, the sun caught in his thick dark hair. He was smiling at her. Smiling as if no one else in the world existed but her.

As though this were all happening to another woman, she watched him close the distance between them, his eyes pinioning her to the spot. Then he put his arms around her and kissed her full on the mouth.

Nothing had changed. Absolutely nothing. She still wanted him with every fiber of her being; and fought against a response as inevitable as the unfolding of apple blossoms to the heat of the sun. She jammed her fists against his chest and shoved hard, pulling her mouth free at the same time. "Stop it!" she gasped. "Can't you see I'm teaching?"

Cal looked around with leisurely interest. Angelica visibly preened, Luis gave him a comradely grin, while Sanches regarded him with the detached curiosity of a scientist examining a laboratory specimen. "And what are you teaching, Joanna, my darling?"

"I am not your darling! I'm teaching English as a second language and will you please leave immediately."

Ignoring this in a way that infuriated her, Cal said, "Are you explaining the beauties of springtime to them?"

"I was. Until you came along."

"Then let's give the lesson a boost," he said, smiling at her with such warmth that her heart flipped in her breast. "You look quite astonishingly beautiful, by the way." He glanced around. *"Bella. Muy bella."*

Blushing fierily, Joanna scowled at him. She was wearing purple walking shorts, a crisp white shirt with the sleeves rolled up, and thin-strapped sandals. She'd gained a little weight the last few months, and because she'd planted a garden at her rented cottage, her face and legs were lightly tanned. Then Cal reached over and plucked the pencil from her hair, which she'd gathered in a loose knot on her crown. "So you still do that," he said softly. "I don't think I've forgotten anything you did or said the whole time we spent together.''

Joanna finally found her voice. ''Cal,'' she said strongly. ''I haven't forgotten anything you said, either. Which is why I'm not falling into your arms, surprise, surprise. And now I have a job to do. Vamoose. Get lost. Take a hike. Go!''

''Get lost?'' Luis repeated, puzzled, looking at the broad expanse of clipped lawn. ''Here *es difícil* to be lost, no?''

''She means she'd like me to fall off the tip of the Matterhorn,'' Cal explained with a fiendish grin. ''But, Joanna, *querida,* you can't have a lesson about springtime without including *amor. Te quiero. Te amo. Estoy locamente enamorado de ti.*''

''You don't! You aren't! Cal—''

But Cal had swept her into his embrace and was waltzing her around on the uneven slope, singing a bawdy Spanish bar song at the top of his lungs. A song that brought the faintest of smiles to even Sanches's lips. Then, coming to such a sudden halt under the apple tree that she was thrown against his chest, Cal addressed the fascinated students. ''Flowers are one of the many ways to a woman's heart,'' he said. Breaking a branch from the tree, he bowed from the waist and presented it to Joanna with another wicked grin. ''Do not scorn me, fairest of the fair, for I am sick with love.''

''You'll get fined for vandalism and it would take ten orchards of apple trees to make me spend even a minute of my time with you!''

''She's rejecting me,'' Cal said to Luis. ''As we say here, she's playing hard to get…shut up, Joanna, you're interrupting the lesson. But do I accept defeat? No, I do not. Since candlelight, wine and a band of Gypsy violinists aren't immediately available, I'll have to improvise. *Improvisar.*'' He dropped to his knees in front of Joanna and clasped her hands. "'Come live with me and be my love,'" he intoned. "How's that for starters?" Then he further spoiled the effect by winking at her. "In fact, you can marry me if you like."

She hardened her heart against the laughter gleaming in his gray eyes. "I don't like."

Angelica said with a practiced pout, "Our teacher, she is *loca, muy loca.* A man such as this…one could wait forever for such a man."

Cal didn't even look around. "If you were to marry me, dearest Joanna, it would solve several of my problems. And yours too, I'd be willing to bet. I have a lot of money, *querida.* Quite an astonishing amount of money. Think of the fun you could have spending it."

As it happened, in the last few months Joanna had taken enormous pride in earning her own money and paying her own bills. No inheritance from her parents to smooth her path. No husband to reduce her to penury. Just what she herself was earning and choosing to spend. She glanced around and said sweetly, "What he means is that when flowers, candlelight and wine fail, a man waves his cash in front of a woman so that she'll succumb to his many charms. Of course, if he'd had any charms to start with, he'd already have succumbed."

"Oh, Joanna," Cal said, getting to his feet and brushing off the knees of his trousers, "how can you be so cruel?"

"It's easy, believe me."

"Then," said Cal to Luis, "as a last resort, there's always sex. *Sexo. Comprendes?*"

"Cal Freeman, I'll—"

But Cal had already enveloped her in his arms. Her last thought was how white his teeth were against his tanned skin. White and predatory. Then she stopped thinking altogether.

Ten seconds—or could it have been ten minutes?—later,

Cal released her. The small crowd of students clapped loudly, Luis producing a piercing wolf whistle. Joanna gaped at them with the air of a woman who had no idea where she was. Not even at the Winnipeg airport had Cal kissed her so comprehensively, with such single-minded passion and such total possessiveness.

She'd liked it. Who was she kidding? She'd adored it. She'd succumbed.

Her shirt was rucked out of her waistband, and her hair had fallen loose of its pins to tumble down her back. How had that happened? Looking from Luis to Angelica to Sanches, she said fiercely, "Sex and liking are not always related. Let alone sex and love. Or sex and marriage. Remember that. And now we're walking over to the parking lot where we'll finish the lesson by talking about cars. Mr. Freeman will not be joining us."

Disdaining to tuck in her shirt or fix her hair, she put words into action. The students followed her, chattering to each other in Spanish. She should have prevented this; they were supposed to use only English during the lessons. But she didn't have the nerve to face them yet, let alone chide them. Besides, if she turned around, she might see that Cal was following them.

And if he was, what would she do? Scream at him like a shrew? Beg him for another of those glorious kisses? Oh God, what was wrong with her?

How could she be filled with joy, rage and desire simultaneously?

How could she have responded to him when she hated the ground he walked on?

CHAPTER SIX

WHEN Joanna eventually reached the parking lot, she saw to her infinite relief that Cal was still standing under the apple tree. He hadn't followed them. He'd taken the hint. Quelling a pang she refused to call disappointment, she tried to gather her wits. The rest of the lesson wasn't as coherent as she might have wished; but it was a small miracle that she could put words together in one language, let alone two. Finally the clock on the bell tower struck four. With a bright smile she said, "That's all for today. See you Thursday afternoon, we'll meet in the classroom at two-thirty."

Angelica said with the utmost seriousness, "You give me this man's telephone number?"

"I threw it away," Joanna replied truthfully; at the Winnipeg airport she'd tossed the piece of paper Cal had given her into the nearest waste bin. "Anyway, the last I heard, he's got a woman and she sure isn't me."

"Que lástima."

"A pity, indeed," said Joanna, and watched her students wander off, talking animatedly among themselves. About her, she'd be willing to bet, and with no surprise turned around to find Cal striding toward her across the grass. No point in running or trying to hide. He'd only follow.

So she held her ground, her heart thudding in her chest. His play-acting under the apple tree had been all very amusing; but why was he really here? When he was close enough to hear her, Joanna said coldly, "You could have gotten me fired with that little exhibition. Is that what you want? Or do you even care?"

69

He'd thrust his hands in his pockets and was standing a careful distance away from her. "I haven't seen you fo the better part of five months and I got carried away," he said. "I'm not going to apologize for that. But I do owe you an apology for something much more important. Ten days ago I was in Switzerland, where I visited my old friend Ludo Galliker—he's a guide who knew Gustave, and who met you at least twice. He straightened me out on a numbe of things. He told me Gustave was the one doing the cheating in your marriage. And spending all your money into the bargain. Joanna, I'm so sorry I believed Gustave's parents and Franz, rather than you. More sorry than I can say.'

His voice was raw with sincerity, his gaze not faltering from hers. "Oh," she said blankly.

"I don't know what held me back from trusting you— although maybe, in a crazy way, it was your astonishing beauty. I was so bowled over by you, so off kilter, that my judgment was way off, too. Which is no excuse for the way I behaved, I know."

"I don't really—"

"I can't make reparation for what I did," Cal went on "Can't ask you to forgive me. But I don't want to jus vanish from your life, either. I'd like us to start over, as though January never happened. Because I can't get you out of my mind—and I'll be honest, I've tried. Tried very hard."

"Cal," she said deliberately, "what about your mistres in Boston?" And saw, to her great satisfaction, that fo once she'd knocked him off balance.

"I don't have a mistress in Boston."

Her eyes narrowed. "Oh yes, you do—you talked to he on the phone at the Strassens', you called her *darling* and *sweetheart* and said you'd be together in the summer... heard you. How dare you kiss me the way you did, and tel me you want to start over when there's another woman in your life?''

"The only person I talked to at the Strassens' was Lenny."

"So who's Lenny? Another of your women?''

"Lenny's my daughter. My thirteen-year-old daughter.''

Joanna's jaw dropped. "Your *daughter?*"

"She goes to school in Switzerland. I try and phone her every couple of days. I'm a widower, Joanna…my wife died six years ago. I'm not involved with anyone, haven't been for some time."

Joanna gaped at him, quite unable to think of anything to say; the odd thing was that she believed him immediately. And of all the emotions seething in her breast, sheer relief was uppermost. Relief that Cal hadn't been cheating on her. That he was free.

Free? she thought. Free for what?

Relief was instantly eclipsed by fear. She wasn't going to get involved with Cal Freeman. One charismatic mountaineer in her lifetime was enough for any woman. She couldn't afford to make a second mistake. The results were too painful, too all-encompassing. Too costly in all senses of the word.

So Gustave wasn't really in her past, she thought unhappily. She'd been fooling herself back in January to think she'd exorcised him merely by visiting his parents. The scars he'd left on her psyche were too deep to be so easily removed; maybe she'd carry them for the rest of her life.

She said with careful truth, ''Thank you for coming all this way to apologize for not believing me, Cal. And for explaining about your daughter. It makes me feel better about you—that you weren't cheating on another woman when you kissed me. But that's it. I have nothing else to say to you. Anyway, I have to go now, I'm meeting a friend in a few minutes."

As Cal took a step closer, she instinctively shrank back. He stopped dead in his tracks; he looked appalled. "Joanna, are you afraid of me?"

Afraid of what happened to her when he kissed her: yes. "I'm rebuilding my life. And it doesn't include you."

"But there's something between us—admit it."

"Sure—it's called *sexo,*" she flashed. "Let me tell you this much—in the last four years, I made love with Gustave exactly once, which is when I got pregnant, and I haven't made love with anyone else. Surely I don't need to spell it out any clearer than that?"

"Dammit, it's more than deprivation!" Cal exploded. "In January I thought that's what I was suffering from, too. But ever since I met you, I haven't wanted to be within ten feet of another woman. I can't explain it. I only know it's true."

She hadn't wanted to be with the registrar, admirable man though he was. In fact, he'd bored her to distraction. She pushed this thought back down where it belonged. "I'm sure you'll get over it," she said.

"I'm not nearly as sure as you seem to be. Give us another chance—that's all I'm asking. At least let me take you out for dinner this evening."

With the sense that she was making one of those decisions that would affect the rest of her life, Joanna said tersely, "No. Thank you."

"*No?* Is that all you can say?"

"It's a perfectly good word. Even if you have difficulty understanding it."

"I have difficulty believing you can't see what's in front of your nose! Come on, Joanna, admit the truth. There's a huge attraction between us, and we'd be fools to turn our backs on it. And I refuse to call it nothing but lust." His smile was ironic. "Even though I've had more X-rated dreams in the last few months than in the rest of my life put together.''

Two nights ago, she'd been rolling around in an alpine meadow with Cal, as naked as the day she was born. A fiery blush mounted her cheeks. Cal said, his grin cracking his face, "So I'm not the only one. Thank goodness for that.''

"It is lust," she said furiously. "And even if it weren't, are you totally oblivious? Do you think I'd risk getting involved with another sexy mountain climber? I did that once, and it was a disaster. I'm not nineteen anymore, I'm twenty-eight—I've learned a thing or two. I'll never get involved with you. Never."

"I am not Gustave Strassen," Cal said tightly.

"I'm happy here," she said wildly. "I'm paying my own way, getting rid of my debts, making new friends and spending time with old ones. The last thing I need is a man in my life. And if you can't get that through your head, then you're not half as smart as I think you are."

"Life moves on—that's something *I've* learned in the last few years. You can choose to go with it. Or you can close yourself off from it."

"Keep your fancy philosophizing, I don't need it. Any more than I need you. The answer's no, Cal. No, no, no— why don't you get it?"

Then, from the corner of her eye, Joanna saw a tall blond woman emerge from the side door of the arts building. With huge relief she said, "There's Sally, I've got to go. I don't want you in my life…it's that simple. Thank you for apologizing and goodbye."

She wheeled and ran across the pavement, waving at Sally. Sally and Dianne were her two best friends; they'd been a trio at high school and now they were together again. Safe and undemanding friendships. She didn't need Cal. Who was neither safe nor undemanding.

"Hi, Sally," she called breathlessly. "Let's go to the S.U.B. and get a milkshake, I've had the day from hell."

"Who's the guy?" Sally asked. "Pretty darn cute."

"I'll tell you about him if you promise you won't ever mention his name again."

"Hmm," said Sally. "Maybe. Give, Joanna."

Without a backward look, Joanna headed for the Student Union Building. She was finished with Cal. Now that he'd apologized, she'd be able to forget him. Really forget him. She said rapidly, "When I was out west in January taking Gustave's personal effects to his parents, that man you just saw—well, I guess he saved my life. And now he's come back to haunt me."

Sally took her by the arm and steered her past the S.U.B. "This calls for a beer—we're going to the pub," she announced. "Why didn't you tell me and Dianne about this when you came back?"

"Because I wanted to forget about it. About him."

"Listen, I may have only gotten within forty feet of him, but that's one sexy dude."

"Sexy," Joanna said bitterly. "You can have him. He's all yours."

"From the look of him, he's not interested in anyone but you."

"He doesn't understand no. It's not a complicated word but he has a problem with it. A serious problem. Sally, I'll tell you what happened out west and you can pass it on to Dianne, and that's the end of it. *Hemos terminado.*"

"I'm meeting Dianne for supper at Tonio's Pizza, then we're going to the movies. Why don't you join us?"

And have the inquisition continue? "No, thanks, I'm going home, I've got a stack of papers to mark," Joanna said, pushing open the door to the student pub. Quickly she found a table and sat down facing her friend. "Now pay attention, because I'm only going through this once."

"You're being extremely belligerent," Sally said, her sky-blue eyes resting on her friend's flushed face. "That guy sure has gotten to you. Unlike Eugene."

Eugene was the registrar. "I'm not ready to date," Joanna said shortly. "It's too soon."

Sally signaled the waitress, ordered two chilled beers, and said, "Give, Joanna Strassen. And I want all the details."

"You're clean out of luck," said Joanna, and found she was blushing again. Fortunately it was dark. She fished in her wallet, paid for the beers, and began to talk. And all the while, as she spilled out the tale of that disastrous visit to the prairies, was achingly aware that she'd just sent Cal away. Definitively and definitely away.

He wouldn't be back. He was too proud a man for that. This time, it really was goodbye.

His jaw clenched, Cal watched Joanna run across the pavement, her bare legs flashing in the sun, her sheaf of black hair skimming her back. Away from him. Away from him for good.

To her, he was just one more mountaineer. To be avoided at any cost. Like an avalanche. Or a crevasse deep as the one on the Western Cwm.

Time to go home, he thought. Go home and lick his wounds.

But where was home? The farm in Vermont, notable for Lenny's absence? His flat in Paris? His condo in New York? All equally luxurious and equally empty.

Lonely? Him? He was completely self-sufficient, had been for years.

No, she'd said. No. A short and unequivocal word.

He fumbled in his pocket for the keys of the red minivan, which he'd rented at the Halifax airport. He'd find a phone in town and make a reservation to fly back to New York tonight. There was an auction there the day after tomorrow, of stringed instruments, including a rare Stradivari cello from the early seventeen hundreds. He should be there. He would be there.

No use staying here.

His gut felt hollow, and his hands were cold. What was wrong with him? So she'd said no. So what? She was just a woman, and it wasn't as though females weren't thick on the ground.

She was the only woman he'd ever met that he knew—knew in his bones—he had to take to bed if he was to have another moment's peace. The two of them naked, body and soul.

And explain that, Cal Freeman.

He couldn't. But it was true. Of course he'd wanted to bed Suzanne, he'd been young and in love. But he'd felt none of the desperation, the fierce compulsion, that drove him toward Joanna. None of the life-or-death intensity.

So was he going to turn tail and run, back to the Jasmines and Aleshas who until now had been enough for him?

When he'd told Joanna about his daughter, she'd been relieved. More than relieved, he'd swear to it. Up until then, she'd obviously assumed he was taken. Involved with a woman in Boston: and consequently unfaithful. Betraying another woman's trust. Like Gustave.

But now she knew better.

Today everything had all happened too fast. Too publicly. He'd been a fool to have kissed her under the apple tree, but she'd looked so beautiful, so familiar, so... essential. He raked his fingers through his hair. Damned if he was going to turn tail and run for the airport. He didn't want Alesha or Jasmine. He wanted Joanna. And he was going to do his level best to get her.

Plan B, he thought. Sit in his van and watch the main gates of the university, and pray that Joanna left for home that way. And if she didn't, then tomorrow he'd go to her office and he wouldn't leave until…until what, Cal? Until she called campus security and had him forcibly ejected?

If he could climb Everest, he could surely persuade one woman to have dinner with him.

For the next hour Cal sat in his van, drumming his fingers on the wheel, failing utterly to concentrate on a copy of the local paper he'd been given on the plane. The sun disappeared behind a tower of dark-edged cumulus; the sky darkened, suiting his mood exactly. Not once in his life had he waited for a woman like this. They'd always flocked to him, and over the years he'd come to take this for granted.

Was it only Joanna's beauty that had him by the throat? Or was it more? The stoicism he'd sensed in her, the dignity, the intelligence. Her loyalty to a husband who hadn't deserved it.

What had happened to the baby she was carrying?

She hadn't had an abortion; he'd swear to that.

Fifty-five minutes he'd been waiting, and it felt like forever. The wind had come up, petals whirling to the ground around the apple tree whose branch he'd broken off. And then he saw a woman in purple shorts come down the hill on a bicycle, concentrating on keeping her balance in the wind. She braked at the main gate, turned right and headed into town.

His heart pounding, Cal turned the key in the ignition and drove after her. All along the main street, he kept a couple of cars between his van and her bike. Thunder rolled in the distance, overriding the sound of the traffic. She pedaled past the last of the stores and neatly shingled houses of the town; farms replaced them, massed purple clouds casting a lurid light over the vibrant green of the hayfields. Head down against the wind, Joanna cycled another mile before turning down an unpaved lane edged with orchards of apple trees in full bloom.

With dramatic suddenness, lightning forked in the sky, bathing the blossoms in eerie blue-white. In a clap of thunder worthy of a horror film, the storm broke. Rain hit Cal's windshield with a rat-tat like bullets, pinged off the leaves, bounced in the dirt; a rain so heavy he had to slow down. He put on his turn signal and followed Joanna down the lane. No point in secrecy now. Pressing his palm on the horn, he drove past her, and pulled up at the edge of the ditch. Jumping out, he waved her down.

She slewed to a stop in the greasy mud, putting her sandal down in a puddle that he was quite sure she hadn't even noticed. Over the drumming rain and seethe of wind, she cried, "You follow me any further down this lane and I'll call the police!"

He grabbed her by the elbow, the feel of her slick, wet skin rocketing through his senses, and yelled back, "I'll put your bicycle in the van and drive you home."

She shook free. "I'm not afraid of a thunderstorm!"

The next bolt of lightning didn't even make her flinch. With a big grin Cal hollered, "You don't need to be afraid of me, either."

"I'm more afraid of drowning in this puddle than I am of you."

"Fine," Cal said, and took the bike by the handlebars. "The passenger door's unlocked."

"I'm not going anywhere with you!"

Her hair was wrapped around her throat in soaked black strands; he said with all the intensity he was capable of, "I'm the one in danger of drowning. In your eyes, in your beauty and defiance and courage."

She swallowed hard. "I—"

"If you don't want me to touch you, or kiss you, I won't. I swear I won't."

"That's not—"

"Not what, Joanna?" he said with sudden gentleness,

or weren't her eyes blurred with something other than
ain?

"You do scare me," she blurted.

"I don't mean to."

A rainsquall lashed at her cheeks. Staring straight at him,
he quavered, "You don't just scare me—you terrify me.
thought Gustave was part of my past. But he isn't. I can't
fford to get hurt again, Cal, I just can't, don't you *see?*"

She was being as honest as she could be, he thought, and
ought down the impulse to take her in his arms, hold her
ight to his chest and never let her go. "I don't want to
urt you or frighten you," he said hoarsely.

Her eyes dropped. "It's all too soon," she whispered.

Thunder rattled the sky like a band of percussionists.
Raising his voice, he said, "At least let me drive you home.
You're soaked."

With the faintest of smiles she said, "So are you."

Rain was trickling down the back of his neck, plastering
is shirt to his chest. He grinned at her. "Get in. I'll throw
your bike in the back."

For a long moment she stood still. Cal held his breath,
oping she couldn't see the banging of his heart under his
vet shirt. Then she relinquished her hold on the bike,
urned and climbed into the red minivan. Cal let out his
ent-up breath in a long sigh. So far, so good. The next
tep of Plan B was to convince her to have dinner with
im.

After he'd put the bike in the van, he, too, climbed in,
avoring his left knee, the one he'd injured three years ago
n a fall on the south ridge of Kongur. It always bothered
im in wet weather. Joanna's hand was resting on the door
andle; she looked very much like a woman about to
change her mind. He said calmly, "How far do I have
o go?"

She bit her lip. "Half a mile. It's a white-painted cottage on the right."

Cal eased his foot onto the accelerator and concentrated on his driving, for the van seemed to be intent on finding every pothole and mud slick on the road. As he went around the last corner, the rain lessened as dramatically as it had started. The road opened into a field beyond which was a magnificent panorama of the bay and the far red cliffs. On the expanse of open water, the waves curvetted like white-maned stallions. As lightning split the sky, he said inadequately, "That's quite the view."

"I'm very lucky to have found this place...the owners are on sabbatical for eight months."

The cottage, white-shingled, was surrounded by a tall hedge of old-fashioned lilacs; it had a front porch, a fieldstone chimney and a small vegetable patch. It was like a miniature version of his property in Vermont, Cal thought with a quickening of his pulse. Joanna would like "Riversedge." Not for her the safe little bungalow in town. He said, "I'll get your bike."

"Thanks," she said with notable brevity.

He wheeled the bike to the front of the cottage, trying to disguise his limp, and hefted it onto the porch. Then he said without emphasis, "May I come in?"

She was facing him in the open front door, her eyes as dark as the massed thunderclouds. "You're awfully wet," she said reluctantly. "But I don't—"

"I've got dry clothes in my suitcase in the van. At least let me change before I drive to the airport."

She frowned at him. "Well, all right. But—"

As another rainsquall whipped across the bay toward the cottage, Cal headed for the van. He grabbed his bag, climbed the porch stairs and pulled the screen door open, stepping inside. Joanna was standing only four feet from he door, her gaze far from friendly. "The bathroom's over here," she said.

"You go first, you're wetter." He grinned. "And muddier."

As she glanced down at her bare legs, which were liberally splashed with red clay, he added solemnly, "Did you ever think of a career in modelling?"

"Not skinny enough and I'm too old."

"Your body's perfect and you're just the right age," Cal said huskily.

She gave a hunted look around the small room and said breathlessly, "I won't be long."

"Put on a dress," he said deliberately, "we'll go to that inn that overlooks the bay. The one with the fabulous scallops and the famous raspberry flan."

"I can't afford even one scallop in that place, let alone a plateful!"

"I'm paying. Part of the apology."

"One thing about you, you're persistent."

"You're worth being persistent for. Lousy grammar, but you get my drift."

"Dinner," Joanna said with an edge of desperation. "Just dinner."

"That's all I'm offering," he countered, a gleam in his eye. "Take your time, Joanna, I'll make a reservation for an hour from now."

She glanced at his soaked knit shirt. "They have a dress code, you have to have a proper shirt and tie."

"Don't you worry, I won't disgrace you."

She made a rude noise, turned on her heel and scurried into her bedroom; emerging a few minutes later with clothes over her arm. Then she vanished into the bathroom.

Cal twisted his shoulders to rid them of tension. His shirt was clammy against his skin, the rain was drumming on the roof, and he felt wonderful. He checked the number in

his wallet, picked up the phone and made a reservation a
the inn; then he went out to the van and brought in hi:
luggage. Finally, he looked around the room with frank
curiosity.

Simple furnishings, colorful braided rugs, a stone fireplace, and in the far corner a desk with a computer. He
wandered over to it, remembering how single-mindedly
Joanna had concentrated on her laptop in the back bedroon
at the Strassens'. A neat pile of galley proofs sat by the
computer, a title page on the top. "*A Time for Wild Swans,*
by Ann Cartwright," he read.

Cal stood still, his brain racing. Ann Cartwright's firs
novel had come out two years ago, to much critical acclaim.
he'd read it en route to an auction in Tuscany, and found
its combination of poetic intensity and stark emotion very
moving. So was Joanna Strassen the author of that novel?

The words at the bottom of the title page leaped out a
him. Copyright: Joanna Strassen.

His intuition, that had refused to allow him to forget her.
had been dead-on. Her intelligence, her anguish and fiery
temper, her complexity, he'd known them already from he
book.

She was as different from Suzanne as a woman could
be. And she'd agreed—if with no enthusiasm whatsoever—
to have dinner with him.

Then his mind made another leap: one by one the
thoughts clicked through his brain. Lenny loved poetry and
adored reading novels. Lenny needed a mother, as Ludc
had so cogently pointed out. Who better than Joanna?

Add to that the fact that Joanna was presumably teaching
at the university to keep her head above water: critically
acclaimed first novels didn't often translate into money in
the bank. Besides, she'd mentioned debts, undoubtedly
Gustave's. So Joanna needed money. He, Cal, had money.
More than enough for both of them. He could marry her

solve all his problems with Lenny, and give Joanna the
time to write without having to worry about paying the rent.

He could take her to bed.

Isn't that what he'd wanted since the first moment he'd
gazed into her unconscious face on the snowswept prairie?

Adrenaline surging through his veins, Cal strode over to
the window, staring unseeingly at the wet, windswept orchard. Joanna as his wife. Yes, he thought. Yes.

CHAPTER SEVEN

JOANNA twisted around to make sure the label wasn't showing on her dress. She felt as uncertain and shy as if this were her first date. I'm a twenty-eight-year-old widow, she thought. Cal Freeman is just a man, and we're only going out for dinner. I'm not marrying him, for heaven's sake.

I'm not marrying anyone. Ever again.

Somewhat heartened, she decided her deep red lipstick looked fine with the dress, an indigo calf-length shift slit to the knee; what she didn't see was how the simplicity of the dress artfully called attention to her figure, to the coil of silken hair at her nape, to the elegant line of her brow and the haunting shadows under her cheekbones. She was, instead, rather pleased that her eyeshadow and mascara had gone on so smoothly, considering that her fingers had felt all thumbs. She slipped on her sandals, inserted antique silver earrings from Tibet into her lobes, and gathered up her small evening purse.

There. She was ready.

Time to face Cal.

She walked out into the living room and said coolly, "I've put towels on the shelf. I hope I haven't been too long?"

He'd been staring out the window. He turned around and she saw with a jangling of her nerves the utter stillness that seized his tall frame. Only his eyes moved, flickering up and down her body.

With a huge effort Joanna kept silent, forcing herself to breathe through the tightness in her chest. Finally Cal said, a note in his voice new to her, "Joanna, I—you're so ut-

84

terly beautiful, I don't know what to say. Only that I'll be the most fortunate man in the whole dining room. Hell, the most fortunate man in the province." His smile was crooked. "How about the continent, the world and the universe?"

Tears pricked at her lids. Gustave had always denigrated her beauty, perhaps hoping to subjugate her that way. "Thank you," she mumbled. "I hope you're not cold, waiting in your wet clothes."

"I'm fine. Five minutes."

He picked up his bag and walked past her into the bathroom. Slowly she let out her breath. She was playing a dangerous game, she knew that. Because hadn't part of her hoped Cal would take her in his arms and kiss her as he'd kissed her in the orchard a few hours ago?

Hoped? Craved would be a more accurate word, she thought crazily. The mere thought of kissing Cal spread an ache of desire through her body. Desire such as she hadn't felt for years. If ever.

She couldn't give in to it. Couldn't, wouldn't, mustn't.

Focus on the scallops, she told herself. Scallops, raspberries and small talk. That's all she had to do. Surely she could manage that.

To her ears came the buzz of Cal's razor. A small, intimate sound, that made nonsense of her resolutions. As did their table at the inn half an hour later, a table set apart from the others, overlooking the water and softly bathed in candlelight. And then there was Cal. His lightweight suit fit him to perfection, subtly emphasizing the strength of his shoulders, his lean belly and long legs; while his silk shirt and tie breathed money and the power that money conveys.

But Cal's power came from within, Joanna thought unwillingly. Nothing to do with his clothes or his money, and everything to do with a confidence and masculinity that were bone-deep. "Something to drink?" he said.

"I'll have wine with the meal," she replied, adding unwisely, "I need my head clear when I'm with you."

"That's encouraging," he said dryly.

Quickly they dealt with the menu and the choice of wine. The waiter brought delicious crunchy rolls, hot from the oven. Going on the attack, Joanna said, "I noticed you're limping."

"A fall in a slide on the Kongur massif. It only bothers me in damp weather."

She said with hostile emphasis, "I long ago decided that all mountaineers have a death wish."

His jaw tightened. "You can count me out on that one."

"Then why do you risk your life time and again?"

So she wanted warfare, did she? "For glory, of course," he said fliply.

Her nostrils flared. "It's a real question, Cal."

He put down his knife. "For a whole lot of reasons. Pushing myself to my limits, and beyond. Trying to align myself with the mountain, so that we're allies, not opponents. Craving the elemental beauty of snow, ice, sky and rock, and the utter silence of the peak. Where you're always alone, no matter who's with you." He ran his fingers through his hair. "That'll do for a start."

And those accomplishments, she thought with an inward shiver, were surely a major source of his power. She said sharply, "You didn't mean to tell me all that."

"I never talk about that stuff. I just do it."

"Not even to your daughter? To Lenny?"

"Lenny's never asked…I don't really know how she feels about me climbing." He gave an exasperated sigh. "Which is something else I've never told anyone."

All Joanna's resolutions to keep her distance flew through the window. "Why me?"

He said obliquely, "I saw your manuscript on the desk. I know you're Ann Cartwright."

"Darn it," she muttered, "I'd forgotten about the proofs." Then her eyes widened. "You think I'm pumping you," she said, horrified, "so that I can use you in a book?"

"No, Joanna, I don't mean that at all. I read your first book, I know you're capable of understanding what I'm getting at with the mountains."

Briefly she closed her eyes. "Gustave climbed for glory. He was always trying to beat the other guy, to conquer and be lionized."

"And you didn't intend to tell me that."

Her smile was twisted. "The plan was to keep you at arm's length emotionally and physically," she said glibly.

He leaned forward, his eyes like gimlets. "Neither one is possible with you and me."

She dragged her gaze away, and to her infinite relief saw the waiter approach with the wine. Once he'd left, Cal raised his glass. "To us," he said.

"To me and to you," she flashed.

"Two separate entities, is that what you mean?"

"Precisely."

"But I refuse to accept that."

"You may not have any choice."

"I've read your book—it was a fine book, by the way, full of nuance and hard-earned wisdom. So I know you're a risk-taker. You were pushing your limits with that book just as I push mine on the ridges and ice fields."

She took a long drink of her wine, savoring its aftertaste. "It's one thing to push limits at the computer. Another to push them in bed. Because that's what we're talking about."

He laughed, his teeth very white. "I like you," he said spontaneously. "You say it like it is. Sexual attraction is most certainly a big part of what's going on."

"The answer's no," she said very quietly.

"Did Gustave damage you that much?" he asked, equally quietly.

She raised her chin. "Yes, he did."

For a moment Cal's features were suffused with an anger all the more powerful for being contained. "Bastard," he said.

"Not really," she responded wryly. "After all, you met his parents."

"Yeah..." His smile was wry. "Odds are they're legally married, wouldn't you say?"

"Definitely." As the waiter brought their salads, she deftly changed the subject. "Tell me about your daughter."

"Lenny? Thirteen years old, acts nine some days and twenty others. Skis competitively, writes poetry, reads voraciously, takes in every stray animal in miles, one day she wants to be a vet, the next day she's going to be president and run the country right..." He smiled ruefully. "Don't get me started."

"What grade is she in?"

"She's going to school in Switzerland this year."

"Oh? Why?"

"I'm often away, with my job or on an expedition. I felt it was better for her to be in an all girls' school with female teachers." He moved his shoulders restlessly. "But she doesn't like being away from home—we live by a river in Vermont."

"How could you send her away?" Joanna demanded, glaring at him. To have a child and then send her thousands of miles across the ocean to go to school? What kind of a father was he?

"I thought it was for the best. And, of course, the skiing there is out of this world."

"There's more to life than mountains, Cal. Why don't you get married and provide her with a mother and a proper home?"

So Joanna was the one to bring the subject up. His nerves tightened. "I should get married, I know I should."

Discovering she didn't want to picture an unknown woman living with Cal, sharing his bed and his life, Joanna snapped, "Why don't you? I'm sure you must meet lots of women."

"Never found the right one."

His flippancy infuriated her. Patches of pink staining her cheekbones, she retorted, "If I had a daughter, I'd want her with me. Especially at thirteen, that's such a vulnerable age."

"Joanna, what happened to the baby?"

The color drained from her cheeks. Her lashes flew down to hide her eyes, her fingers tightening around the stem of her glass. Cal said abruptly, "I'm sorry, I shouldn't have asked."

His question had come out of the blue. Yet wasn't her vehemence about Lenny's exile a direct result of her own experiences? And didn't she, deep down, want Cal to think well of her? To know the truth about the loss of her child? Joanna said rapidly, her voice purged of emotion, "Gustave came to visit me last July. I hadn't seen him for a couple of years—ever since the money ran out. He was full of contrition. He'd had a near escape on those rock towers in Patagonia and it had changed him, he said. He swore he'd be a better husband, that he'd be faithful to me, and that he loved me."

Absently she twirled the glass on the linen tablecloth, her thoughts a long way away. "I no longer loved him. I hadn't for months...there'd been too many betrayals. But this time he was so sincere, so sorry for the way he'd behaved in the past that I felt I had to try again—I took my marriage vows very seriously, you see. I know that's old-fashioned, but that's the way it was."

She glanced up. Cal's eyes were trained on her face, his

big body very still. "We went to bed together," she said flatly. "I completely forgot I hadn't been using birth control pills, what was the point of using them, Gustave hadn't been home for ages—so I got pregnant." She stared fixedly into the pale gold wine, shot through with candlelight. "As it turned out, Gustave's visit had nothing to do with contrition. My great-aunt Lucy had died and left me some money...he stayed around long enough to get his hands on it and then he took off. To organize the Annapurna expedition, so I found out later."

"Joanna..."

Cal rested his lean fingers on her hand, stilling its restless movements. She stared down at the narrow ridge of scars on his knuckles, feeling the warmth of his skin seep into hers. "I was three months pregnant when Gustave radioed me from the second base camp on Annapurna, it was the first time I'd talked to him since his visit. He needed more money, that was the reason for getting in touch...but I didn't have any to give him. Anyway, I told him about the baby." Keeping her words steady with an effort, she went on, "The very next day Gustave was killed in a fall. Franz, of course, blamed me totally."

"And then?"

"I was in our Toronto condo when I got the message, dressing to go out and do a couple of errands before I settled down to write. For some reason I decided after the phone call that I should still do the errands. So I set off anyway. There'd been a heavy frost that night. Crossing the park, I slipped and fell." In a ragged voice, she finished, "Because of the fall, I lost the baby...I should never have gone out, I don't know why I did, it was such a stupid thing to do."

"You were in shock, Joanna. Not thinking straight."

She couldn't bear the compassion in his voice. "I should have stayed home!"

He stated the obvious. "So you blame yourself."

She nodded miserably, tapping her fingernails against the heavy crystal. "Wouldn't you?"

"You did the best you could. For years you did your best. What more can any of us do?"

"I suppose so," she mumbled. "I'm sorry, Cal, I didn't mean to dump all this on you."

"You're not dumping, you're sharing some hard truths with me...which in a way is quite a compliment."

She gave him a faint smile. "Well, that's one way of looking at it."

"I'm sorry you lost the baby," he said gently.

Only Sally and Dianne knew how much she'd longed for that baby, despite the fact that she no longer loved the man who'd conceived it; and how cruel a blow her loss had been. She pulled her hand free, saying with attempted lightness, "It's over and done with, isn't it? Here comes the waiter. It might be ten years before I eat here again, I'm determined to enjoy every bite."

Cal sat back. So the confidences were over, he thought; and knew that in a very short time he'd learned a lot about Joanna, about her vulnerabilities and her strengths. The only unpalatable fact—apart from the fact that he couldn't wipe the floor with Gustave Strassen—was that she in no way had connected Cal's need for a wife with herself.

So what was the next step in his plan? Charm her, he decided. Relax her so that she let down her guard. He topped up her wineglass and lifted his salad fork. "Did you do much traveling with Gustave?"

"In the early years, yes," she said, and went on to describe some of her experiences in Tibet and southern Switzerland. From there they moved to Cal's job, then on to movies and politics. The candle was replaced with a fresh one. Joanna's unabashed enjoyment of the scallops and then of an Amaretto chocolate mousse touched Cal;

most of his dates took these small luxuries for granted. Bu Joanna, from the things she'd let drop, was living on th edge of poverty and had been for some time. That' change, he vowed, and as their coffee was poured decide the moment was right to raise Plan C.

He said casually, "How long since you've had a vaca tion?"

Joanna laughed. "Vacation? What's that?"

"I have a proposal. Hear me out before you say any thing."

Her smile had faded and she was looking at him warily There was a small smudge of chocolate on her lip; Ca reached over, smoothing it away, and saw her eyes darke and her mouth tremble. "In a couple of weeks," he said "I'm bringing Lenny back home to Vermont for the sum mer holidays. I'd like to treat you to a few days i Switzerland. You can fly over, I'll meet you in Zurich, an we'll drive to my chalet in Appenzell and then get Lenny She'd like you, I know she would. And not just becaus you're a famous novelist."

"Hardly famous," Joanna said, her head whirling. Onc again Cal had knocked her off balance. That streak of fir on her lip, and then an invitation that could mean only on thing. An affair. In which he'd foot the bill. "I can't d that," she muttered.

"Why not? You told me earlier you'll soon be finishe with this group of students. So it's an ideal time for you t take a break."

"Cal, I don't have any money," she said with barel controlled impatience. "The royalties on my first book an the proceeds from the sale of the condo went to pay of some of my debts. My salary's a pittance. I'd scarcely b able to buy an ice cream in Switzerland, and I certainl won't accept money from you."

"I don't see why not."

"Just because you're rich, you can't buy me!"

He said evenly, "You'd sleep in the guest room, Joanna."

"You're all heart," she snapped. Perhaps she'd misjudged him about the affair. But what matter if she had? He had only to kiss her, and she'd climb into his bed quicker than you could say traveler's check. And that was the real reason she couldn't go anywhere near Switzerland.

"I'm asking a favor of you, that's all," Cal persisted. "I'd like you to meet Lenny, give me some advice. There are times she scares me half to death—I don't have a clue how to handle a teenage girl."

"And you think I have?"

"At least you've been one," he said with that crooked smile that always made her want to smile back.

"I can't go," she said with utter finality. "It's out of the question."

His eyes hardened. "Come on, Joanna, do I have to spell it out? It's payback time. I saved your life in January and now I'm asking a favor in return."

Her chin snapped up. "So you're a businessman to the core! Cost and benefit. That's a pretty crude way to treat another human being."

"It's not as though a trip to Switzerland would be any hardship," he said curtly.

For a treacherous moment Joanna allowed herself to imagine the alpine meadows, the astonishing physicality of the peaks, the tolling of cow bells and the flowers that tumbled from the window boxes. She desperately needed a holiday; and she'd always loved Switzerland, even in the worst of times with Gustave. Besides, she'd never been to the northeast; she and Gustave had always used Geneva as their home base, not Zurich. "I'm not going," she repeated, and drained her coffee cup.

"That I saved your life means nothing to you?"

"What do you want, a medal?"

"I want you to meet Lenny, tell me if you think sh
should stay in Switzerland next year or come home. That'
all."

He wasn't going to give up. Gripping the edge of th
table, Joanna said, "Let's be honest, Cal. You've kisse
me, you know what happens when you do. Even if yo
promised me you wouldn't as much as touch me the whol
time I was with you, I wouldn't trust that promise. So that'
one more reason I won't go to Switzerland."

In a biting voice he said, "First, you're equating me wit
your husband, which is something I thoroughly dislike
Second, you're not being entirely truthful. It's yourself yo
don't trust. You want me just as much as I want you an
don't bother denying it—I've held you in my arms, I know
what I'm talking about."

His accuracy only made her angrier. "I'm not going!"
she announced. "How many times do I have to say that
Drop it, it won't fly."

"We'll drop it for now. But I'm not through."

"*No* is a word you sure have trouble with."

"Whereas you have trouble with *yes*. You're afraid o
coming to life again, that's your problem. I wouldn't hav
thought you were a coward—but I guess I'm wrong."

So angry she could scarcely speak, Joanna flared, "I wa
married to a man who deceived me financially and sexuall
for years, and who persisted in risking his life and the live
of others so he could get to the top of any peak that at
tracted his fancy. And now you're recommending I get in
volved with another mountain climber—namely you? Giv
me a break."

"Stop labeling me! I'm a hell of a lot more than someon
who just climbs mountains."

Suddenly exhausted, Joanna said, "Cal, I don't want t
fight with you like this. You did save my life and I'm s

rateful to you. But that doesn't mean I'll do whatever you sk.''

Cal shoved his credit card in the folder with the bill and ignaled to the waiter. "Let's get out of here.''

They sat in silence until the bill was returned. Then oanna said with deadly politeness, "Until you broached our crazy idea about Switzerland, I enjoyed myself very much. Thank you.''

"I'll take you home.''

"You're being a sore loser!''

"Oh, I haven't lost yet,'' he said softly, and gestured for er to precede him out of the dining room.

Joanna sat in a stony silence all the way back to her ottage. Cal pulled up as near to the front walk as he could; efore she could unlatch her door, he slid to the ground nd was striding around to open it for her. She climbed own, horribly aware of how close he was standing, the ulk of his body obscuring the garden behind him. She tepped back a pace, felt the heel of her sandal sink into he damp earth, and said frostily, "Good night.''

And then he did what all evening had been inevitable: e took her in his arms, fastened his mouth on hers and issed her as though she were the woman he'd been waiting or all his life. Kissed her with such raw hunger that she urrendered without a murmur. More than surrendered, she hought dimly: and knew she was meeting him on his own erms, hunger for hunger, demand with demand.

Her arms were around his neck, holding him so tightly hat her breasts were strained to his chest. The heated thrust f his tongue made her moan with pleasure; like a reed to he wind she was pliant in his embrace. His hands were lasping her waist, smoothing her hips, pulling her so close hat his arousal inflamed her, made her ache and throb with esire.

She'd never wanted Gustave so instantly, so fiercely. Her

whole body was on fire for Cal, desperate to be possesse
by him; she whimpered his name, felt his lips slide dow
her throat and bury themselves in the hollow where he
pulse was frantically racing. Then with one hand he cuppe
the soft weight of her breast, kneading it with exquisi
gentleness. As her nipple hardened to his touch, she hear
him mutter, ''Joanna, you're so beautiful, I want you s
much.''

She raised his face to hers, so he could see the desir
naked in her eyes, and for a long moment in the blossom
scented darkness of the lane they gazed at each other,
gaze every bit as intimate as his caresses. Then Cal leane
forward, letting his lips wander from her forehead to he
eyelids, across her cheekbones to her mouth again, a trai
of delicious sensation that made Joanna tremble like a lea
to the breeze.

As his kiss deepened, she abandoned herself to it, he
hands drifting from his nape to his waist, searching out th
long indentation of his spine, the taut muscles over his ribs
then, daringly, the hard jut of his hipbones. He rubbed him
self against her until she was enveloped in nothing bu
need. Then he said hoarsely, his breath warm on her cheek
''Let's go inside…I want to make love to you.''

Wasn't that what she wanted, too? Hadn't she discovere
in Cal's arms in the last few minutes a woman she hardl
recognized, passionate, wanton and hungry? She opene
her mouth to say yes, and saw behind his head the soli
outline of her little cottage, which had brought her suc
solace in the last few months. Her home. Her refuge. He
place of safety.

She was going to risk all that for a tumble in bed wit
a man she scarcely knew? A man used to women fallin
into his arms? In a voice she wouldn't have recognized a
her own, she said, ''We can't! We're not in love, we can'

ust fall into bed because of—of lust. Because that's what
t is. Nothing to do with feelings. Or real connection.''

''Maybe this is how we find the connection,'' he said
uskily, nibbling at her lips with exquisite persuasiveness.

''And maybe it isn't—what then?'' In sudden despair she
oushed herself away from him. ''This is exactly what I did
when I was nineteen—fell into Gustave's arms. And paid
'or it for the next nine years.''

''How about this scenario? You fall into my arms and
we find out it was the right thing to do?''

''And then you leave for Everest or Annapurna and I
tay here worried sick about you? No, Cal, I've done that
ill too often, and I hated it.''

''What if I quit the mountains?''

''What are you saying? Quit something that's so impor-
ant to you?'' She stepped back, staring into his shadowed
'eatures with strained intensity. ''You're surely not in love
with me?''

''No,'' he said levelly, ''I'm not.''

So the scene in the orchard had been nothing but play-
acting. Just as she'd suspected. ''If you quit the mountains,
you'd resent me, I know you would. Maybe in a different
ifetime something would have worked out between us. But
n this lifetime, there's just too much against it. And I'm
iot into casual affairs, I never have been.'' She smoothed
ier dress down, her heartbeat still racketing in her chest.
'Look, it's late and I have to teach tomorrow morning.
Thank you for dinner, and good luck with Lenny. Drive
:arefully, won't you?''

He said without inflection, ''I'll call you in a week about
Switzerland. Think about it, Joanna. Are you going to live
n Gustave's shadow for the rest of your life?''

''It's not that simple!''

''I think it is.'' He gave her an abrupt nod, turned on his
ieel and strode to the far side of the van. He was limping

very slightly, she noticed with the only part of her brain that seemed to be working. Limping from an injury on the mountains.

Swiftly he reversed, and without a backward look drove away up the lane, the sound of the engine gradually diminishing until silence claimed the night again.

Joanna stood still. A week wouldn't make any difference. She wasn't going anywhere with Cal Freeman; and the sooner he accepted that, the better.

She wasn't a coward. She was just being sensible. Adult. Responsible. All the things she hadn't been at nineteen.

CHAPTER EIGHT

FOUR days later, Joanna parked her bicycle outside Sally's bungalow. Geraniums and lobelia lined the walk with pink, red and blue; orange California poppies and huge purple and yellow irises flanked the front door. Sally opened the door. "Hi, Joanna, Dianne's already here. We're out back on the patio. Like my garden?"

"It's very cheerful."

"I did get a little carried away. I'm sort of hoping the Liatris won't bloom until the poppies are done."

Liatris was magenta. "Hey, it's all nature," said Joanna. "I brought a bottle of wine."

"Great, thanks. The barbecue's on."

Sally's bungalow was as untidy as her garden was colorful. She coached basketball at the university and was steadfastly in love with a man called Albert who lived with his mother. As they emerged into the sunshine on the patio, Joanna blinked against the light. "Hi, Dianne."

Dianne was short, plump, and indolent, married to Peter, a marine biologist who was out at sea most of the summer. She waved her wineglass at Joanna. "You look gorgeous as usual," she said, without a speck of envy. Then her gaze sharpened. "Although do I detect circles under your eyes? What's up? The students getting to you?"

Joanna hadn't been sleeping well ever since Cal had left. "You know how it is," she said lightly. "They've suddenly realized our time's nearly up and they want to cram the entire English language into the last three lessons."

Dianne taught French at summer school. "I understand totally," she said, and proceeded to tell a very funny story about a champion football player who'd flunked French twice already. In the meantime Sally grilled chicken and produced a Caesar salad from the refrigerator, which they followed up with one of Dianne's luscious, calorie-loaded desserts. Joanna sat back with a sigh. "Butterscotch cream pie, food for the gods. Good thing I'm biking home.. Dianne, I forgot to ask how your sister is? You mentioned last week she might be having some tests."

Dianne's face clouded. "She got the results yesterday. She has thyroid cancer, they're going to operate next week."

"Cancer? How serious is it?"

Dianne's smile was wobbly. "Well, if you've got to get the big C, this is the kind to have. Slow-growing and easily contained. She'll have radiation afterward."

"You should have told us sooner," Sally said, distressed. "Here we were going on about Albert's mother and the perils of buying plants that don't turn out the right color...I'm so sorry she's sick."

"I planned to tell you, I just didn't want to put a damper on the meal. And I talked to Peter last night, he'll be home next week when Sara's scheduled for surgery. So that's good."

"You just never know, do you?" Joanna said, grimacing. "You chug along day to day doing all the stuff that has to be done, and then something like this happens."

"It does make you think," Dianne agreed. "Sara's always been so healthy, I guess I took that for granted."

They talked back and forth, getting more details of the treatment. Sally said finally, "*Carpe diem* isn't such a bad idea, is it? You know, I really wonder sometimes if I shouldn't break my engagement to Albert. When he told his mother he and I were going to spend a week at the beach in July, she promptly had an asthma attack. Now

here's a woman who's as tough as a carthorse, she'll prob-
bly outlive me.''

Dianne laughed. ''You could try. Breaking it, I mean.
Maybe it would shake him up.''

''He can be so sweet,'' Sally said in exasperation. ''Men!
Why is it we can't live with them or without them? By the
way, Joanna, what happened with that gorgeous hunk called
Cal?''

''Sally told me about him,'' Dianne chimed in.

''Nothing,'' Joanna said.

Sally gave a rude snort. ''Come clean.''

Over the years the three had exchanged many confidences, and had never had a trust betrayed. Confident that
they would share her views, Joanna said easily, ''We had
dinner together. He wants me to spend some time in
Switzerland with him. Ostensibly to meet his daughter, who
goes to school there. But really for a quickie affair.''

''When are you leaving?'' Dianne asked.

Joanna raised her brows. ''I'm not. I said no.''

''You *what?*'' Sally squeaked.

''But why?'' Dianne demanded.

''I'm not going to take off into the wild blue yonder with
a man I don't know from Adam!''

''I saw him,'' Sally said. ''His kind are rare on the
ground. Especially in Harcourt.''

''He saved your life,'' Dianne said. ''You owe him.''

''You'd be crazy to turn him down.''

''Out of your mind.''

''Anyway, you really need a holiday.''

''We'll lend you some money so you can go.''

''Sure we will, great idea, Di.''

Joanna covered her ears. ''Stop it, you two! I'm not go-
ng!''

''We think you should,'' Sally said firmly. ''You should
isten to us.''

"You don't love Gustave anymore," Dianne put in. "So that's not an issue."

"But Cal's another mountaineer," Joanna protested.

"Come off it, Jo, you can keep him away from a few mountains," Sally said. "I mean, look at you, you're drop dead gorgeous—and the man definitely had eyes in his head."

"But—"

"Time you broke loose, Joanna," Dianne announced. "Sally and I have been worried about you, wondering how you'd ever meet anyone in Harcourt. If even half of what Sally told me is true, this is quite a guy. Go for it."

Abruptly Sally sobered. "You know, there's another issue here. Even if you don't want to marry again, you do want a baby. We've always known that, ever since high school."

Joanna gaped at her. It was true. She'd wanted to have children for as long as she could remember.

"So here's your chance," Sally went on. "Go to Switzerland, get pregnant and come home."

"We'll knit you booties," said Dianne. "Pink ones and blue ones."

"*You'll* knit her booties," Sally said. "I'll buy her those cute little sleepers that babies seem to need. Green and yellow," she finished thoughtfully.

"Stop!" Joanna said wildly, grabbing her scalp with both hands. "You must be drunk, both of you—I can't go off to Switzerland to make a baby!"

"Stone-cold sober and of course you can," Sally said.

"And have a bit of fun in the process," Dianne added naughtily. As Joanna blushed scarlet, she added, "So you're not immune to him. Thank heavens, there's hope for you."

Remembering that impassioned embrace outside her cot

age, Joanna wailed, "He just has to look at me and I melt.
Me. Who's not into affairs."

"I'll drive you to the airport," Sally said.

"And we meant what we said about the money," Dianne
seconded.

Joanna's throat tightened. "That's so sweet of you. Both
of you. But I—"

"You can't go asking him for money every time you
want to buy chocolate," Dianne said. "They make the best
chocolate in the world in Switzerland."

"You could bring us back some," Sally teased.

"If I go," Joanna said weakly.

"When you go," her two friends chorused.

"But I've never had an affair in my life," Joanna
blurted, "I wouldn't know how to behave."

Dianne rolled her eyes. "Just let nature take her course.
Although there's no harm in taking a sexy nightgown to
help her along."

With a quick glance at Joanna's flushed cheeks, Sally
said, "How about you both help me load the dishwasher?"

Joanna surged to her feet and started gathering plates.
What was she thinking of, even to hint that she might go
off to Switzerland to meet Cal? Let alone get pregnant.

The party broke up half an hour later; all the way home,
as the light on her bike picked out a small circle of pavement, and then the ruts in the lane, Joanna thought about
babies. Rather than about sexy nightgowns.

She'd been a much-loved only child who'd longed for a
sister or a brother, and who'd played, very traditionally,
with dolls. She'd taken a baby-sitting course as soon as she
was old enough, and in her late teens got summer jobs at
play schools. She'd assumed that she and Gustave would
start a baby once the honeymoon was over; and had battled
with the bitterest of disappointments when he'd made it
brutally clear he didn't want children.

He'd always begged the question before they were married, and in that tempest of longing and misplaced romanticism that had mesmerized her from the first moment she'd met him, she'd ignored this warning signal. After their marriage, Gustave had been unequivocal. *A couple of squalling brats? Not part of my life plan.* And then, as the months and years went by, she'd gradually become aware that she wasn't the only woman he was sleeping with. Tears, accusations, rage, none had had any effect. Or rather, they had had an effect: they'd driven her husband from her bed altogether.

She'd sometimes wondered if she'd outgrow this deep need to have a child. But she hadn't. If anything, as the years ticked by, the need grew stronger. She'd be twenty-nine her next birthday. Time was running out.

Joanna wasn't blind to reality. Having a baby wouldn't combine easily with writing; it would limit her options for part-time jobs and a social life. But none of this made any difference. She longed to be a mother, in a way that made nonsense of all her qualms.

The loss of the baby eight months ago had cut her to the quick. No matter that she hadn't loved the baby's father, her pregnancy had been the answer to a lifelong dream.

Tonight, hearing about Dianne's sister, she'd realized something else: that there were no guarantees. *Carpe diem* Sally had said. Should she, Joanna, go to Switzerland, have an affair with Cal, and if she became pregnant, rejoice?

Could she do that?

Could she afford not to?

In the air-conditioned cool of Zurich's Kloten Airport, Cal was waiting at the arrivals gate. He was casually dressed in cotton trousers and an open-necked blue shirt. But he didn't feel casual. Anything but.

Joanna was due through the gate at any moment.

Would he ever forget that phone call, a few days ago, when she'd agreed to come to Switzerland? Even though she said she could only get away for four days because of her next group of students, the upsurge of pleasure he'd felt had been out of all proportion. But when he'd asked her why she'd changed her mind, she'd been downright evasive.

Well, he had four days to find out.

Was Plan D to seduce her?

Slow down, Cal. One thing at a time.

The first passengers trickled through. Over the babble of languages around him—Swiss-German, Italian, English, French—he swore he could hear the pounding of his own heart. Then he saw a tall, black-haired woman walk through the gate and hesitate for a moment, glancing around her as warily as a wild creature in an unfamiliar and threatening environment.

She was wearing raspberry-colored pants with a long, loose jacket over a purple camisole. Her hair was pulled back in a severe style that emphasized her stunning cheekbones and slanted blue eyes; she looked both ravishing and remote. With a clenching of his nerves, Cal raised one hand in salute, easing his way through the crowd toward her.

She saw him immediately, and with none of her usual grace took a couple of steps toward him. Like Marie Antoinette on the way to the guillotine, Cal thought. "Joanna...lovely to see you," he said, contenting himself with kissing her on both cheeks, European-style. Her skin was cool; close up, her eyes were filled with primitive terror.

Terror? Did she regret her decision already?

"Jet-lagged?" he said lightly.

"Mmm...I didn't sleep well on the overnight flight to London. Then I had three hours in Heathrow, and now here I am. Not even sure what time of the day it is."

"We'll take it easy today, we don't have to get Lenny until tomorrow. Let's go find your bags."

He threaded her hand through his arm; her fingers were ice-cold. At the baggage carousel, Cal turned to face her. "Wishing you weren't here?" he asked, and watched her lashes flicker.

"I—"

"I'm very happy that you're here. You're on holiday, and all I want is for you to have a good time."

She made an indeterminate noise, staring absorbedly at his watch. "Is that Swiss?"

"Yeah." He tilted her chin with his fingers so she had to look at him. "Are you hungry?"

She swallowed, panic flaring in her irises. "I—plane food scarcely qualifies as food, does it?"

What the hell was going on? Apart from his hormones going on a rampage. That was a given. "I figured you might want to eat. So I made a reservation where we can sit outdoors and watch the world go by. Then we'll drive to my chalet near Appenzell and you can put your feet up and relax. The view's incredible and you won't have a thing in the world to do."

"Sounds great," she mumbled. "Oh look, there's my bag."

Cal picked it up, then guided her outdoors to the parking lot. He kept a sleek gray Jaguar for his use in Switzerland; as she settled herself on the leather seat, Joanna said, "You own this?"

"It's easier to keep a car here than rent one each time."

"I'll pay for lunch," she said edgily.

"You will not, and what's going on?"

"You paid my airfare, you don't have to pay for my meals, as well."

"You're here as my guest. And that's that."

Her lips were stubbornly set; he wanted to kiss them so

badly that he had to force himself to look away. Taking a couple of deep breaths, he set out to charm her, describing local landmarks as they drove into the city; earlier, Joanna had told him she'd never visited this part of the country. Flags snapped in the breeze. The River Limmat glittered under a cloudless sky, white swans drifting elegant and aloof on its polished surface. Rather like Joanna, thought Cal, and parked by the stone abutment. "We'll walk from here. Those spires are the cathedral, the Grossmünster, one of the best-known landmarks..." He kept talking, steering her toward Bahnhofstrasse, known as the most expensive street in Europe. He could sense her relaxing, her eyes wide as she took in the elegant stone facades of world-famous banks. Blue and white trams glided past stores offering designer jewelry, the latest in haute couture, leather handbags and handmade shoes. He said dryly, "You notice I'm not offering to buy you a present."

Her smile was almost natural. "Not even that taffeta gown with a waistline too small for Tinkerbell? I could wear it to weed the garden." Then she averted her eyes from an exquisite negligee displayed in solitary splendor behind plate glass, gazing instead at a trio of business-suited bankers. So was she as achingly aware of him as he of her? Cal wondered, and decided he wouldn't ask.

He'd like to buy her that negligee. Then he'd like to remove it from her body with leisurely sensuality...

He walked a little faster. Their table with its pristine linen cloth overlooked the river. Joanna watched the passersby with obvious fascination, tucking into a fondue made of three Swiss cheeses, accompanied by Kirsch. She followed this with a rich pastry drizzled with milk chocolate and filled with whipped cream. "Luscious," she said, licking her lips. "We'd better go for a brisk walk after this or I'll be asleep on my feet."

Obligingly he took her on a tour of the narrow streets of

Niederdorf, on the other side of the river, where she admired the medieval guild halls, the baroque Rathaus, and the galleries and boutiques of the Old Town; she bought chocolates for Sally and Dianne, carefully counting out her money. Under the shadow of the Fraumünster with its delicate spire, she gave a sigh of repletion. "I'm feeling better," she said. "But, you know, I'm really anxious to see the countryside, Cal."

"Then let's go," he said promptly, and again tucked her arm into his.

For a moment her fingers were rigid on his bare flesh. Then a flock of pure white gulls rose into the air from the river, and her eyes followed them, her fingers loosening. He had to make love to her while she was here, Cal thought, his mouth dry; but how could he, if she was this uptight?

Jasmine, Alesha and the rest had left him in no doubt that they were willing. Easy come and easy go, he thought grimly. Whereas Joanna knocked him off balance every time he looked at her and he had no idea in the world what she was thinking. Or feeling. Lenny, had she known about all this, would no doubt tell him it served him right.

Maybe Joanna was afraid to touch him. Afraid of the power of her own desire and where it might take her.

Maybe.

They drove east out of Zurich, Cal turning off as soon as possible onto lesser-traveled roads that wound through rolling green hills dotted with the sleek brown Simmental cows, brass bells jangling around their necks. Groves of dark evergreens climbed the slopes, amid whitewashed farmhouses and red-roofed barns. Cal talked on about the history of the area, and the prevalence of small family farms with their long-rooted traditions, finally stopping in exasperation to say, "I sound like a tour guide, for Pete's sake. Joanna, how *are* you?"

She sat up straight, giving him a wary glance. "Tired. Not quite here—jet travel's too fast, the rest of you has to catch up." She added less audibly, "Not at all sure I should be here."

"You're acting like I'm going to jump on you the minute we get to the chalet."

"Are you, Cal?"

"Dammit, no!" he exploded, and wondered who he was trying to convince, her or himself.

"Oh, look," she exclaimed as they turned a sharp corner, "mountains!"

A not very subtle change of subject from a woman entirely capable of subtlety. And he'd just publicly declared that he wasn't going to jump on her. So how was he going to seduce her if he couldn't even touch her? And what was wrong with him anyway? He was acting like a twelve-year-old instead of a grown man of thirty-six who knew the score. Or until today he would have thought he knew the score. "The highest one's called Säntis," he said, "we get a nice view of it from the balcony of my chalet."

Nice. A word he loathed.

Fifteen minutes later they drove through the little town of Appenzell, with its brightly painted, decorative houses, its window boxes crammed with geraniums, and its quaintly carved signs. A mile out of town, Cal took a driveway that wound up the hillside to a gabled wooden chalet. More window boxes, the blatting of the white goats that belonged to a villager, and a view that indeed he loved, for as always the mountains beckoned to him. "Well," he said tritely, "here we are."

The rest of the evening would long remain in his memory as one of the most excruciating in his life. He showed Joanna to the spacious guest room, the open window filled with the scent of roses that grew against the fence. He produced a credible meal of farmer's sausage and *rösti*, crusty potato cakes, along with a salad from his neighbor's garden. He talked. My God, how he talked. He even made her laugh once or twice. But by the end of the meal she was openly yawning. "Cal, I'm sorry. But I didn't sleep well last night, and I feel like I've been up forever."

"There's lots of hot water," he said, "feel free to have a shower. And get up whenever you feel like it in the morning." He leaned over and chastely kissed her on the cheek, keeping his arms at his sides with an effort that knotted his shoulders with tension. She stepped back faster than was necessary, smiled in his general direction and vanished down the hallway.

Seduction? That was the joke of the century. Plainly she was regretting her decision to come here; even more plainly, she was giving him the message that an affair was out of the question. So had he dreamed that kiss outside her cottage, the passionate generosity of her response, her shallow breathing and heated skin?

Whether he'd dreamed it or not, it was obviously a thing of the past. Not to be repeated. Joanna had come to Switzerland to admire the scenery, meet Lenny and take home some Swiss chocolate. Have a well-earned holiday, exactly what he'd promised her. And that, Cal Freeman, was that.

CHAPTER NINE

JOANNA woke at six-thirty in the morning, after a solid eight hours of sleep. She'd left the curtains open, and the pale pink light of dawn flooded the room. She got up and looked out. Wraiths of mist blanketed the valley; the early sun gilded the hills and the distant peak of Säntis. Somewhere close nearby a cow was chewing the cud, its bell a rhythmic accompaniment. The roses smelled delicious.

Without stopping to think, she pulled on some jeans and a sweatshirt, ran a brush through her hair and laced her sneakers. Then she crept down the hall and out the front door onto the veranda, where she filled her lungs with clean country air. Purposefully she set off down the driveway, goats scattering at her approach.

After her grand resolution to have an affair with Cal and start a baby, she'd spent the night alone in her double bed sleeping like a baby.

She wasn't even sure he wanted an affair. He'd acted more like her uncle, or a brother. Kissing her on the cheek, never once putting his arms around her, and talking nonstop. Speech could be a very neat ploy to keep someone at a distance and avoid all the essentials.

But then she hadn't been exactly honest when he'd asked her how she was. Asked with the kind of intensity that meant he'd really wanted an answer.

Tired, she'd said. Not really here. What she should have said was that her plan to get pregnant, which had seemed quite manageable in Sally's back garden with a bottle of wine on the table and Sally and Dianne encouraging her,

111

had revealed itself as utterly outrageous in the antiseptic cleanliness of the Kloten airport when face-to-face with the putative father.

She should never have come here. Just wait until she saw her two friends again. Friends, huh. Friends didn't talk you into nonsensical projects that you couldn't possibly carry out.

Cal didn't want her anymore. Had no plans to jump on her, to use his phrase. And wasn't that what really rankled? Although *hurt* would be a more accurate word for the way she felt.

She took a little path that meandered along the slope, yellow and white daisies nodding good morning to her. So was she going to spend this brief holiday bemoaning her undesirability? Or was she going to enjoy herself as much as she could?

The latter, Joanna thought valiantly, and concentrated on the stretch of her leg muscles and the pastoral beauty of her surroundings. An hour later, feeling wide awake and very hungry, she let herself in the front door as quietly as she'd exited. Cal must still be sleeping. She padded toward the bathroom in her socked feet, hoping she could find something for breakfast in the kitchen without having to open every cupboard.

The bathroom door swung open and Cal stepped out. With a tiny shriek of alarm, because she'd thought she was the only one up and about, Joanna walked right into him. Into his bare chest, into the towel swathed around his hips.

Into his waiting arms.

Heaven, she thought. Sheer heaven. And felt his arms tighten around her, fasten on her as if she were his heart's desire. He muttered her name, burying his face in her hair, raining kisses on her throat, pushing her shirt aside and tracing the line of her collarbone with his lips. Her whole body was engulfed in a wave of desire so primitive, so fierce, that she forgot everything but the delicious sensuality of Cal's mouth on her flesh.

She put her arms around his shoulders, caressing the tautly flowing muscles, the hardness of bone, the heat of his skin that smelled of pine-scented soap and of the man himself. As he pulled her roughly to his hips, she felt that other hardness with every nerve of her body. She wanted him. Here. Now. She wanted to know him in all the ways a woman can know a man, completely and without holding back anything of herself.

"Cal," she whispered, "oh, Cal, make love to me…"

He raised his head, his eyes boring into hers. "I want to. More than I can say…are you sure, Joanna?"

Her eyes shining, she said, "More sure than I've ever been of anything in my life."

He said roughly, "You're so honest. So generous."

"I thought last night you didn't want me anymore."

His laugh was wry. "I was thinking exactly the same about you."

"You *were?*"

"But I was wrong?"

That he should need reassurance moved her deeply. "We were both wrong," she said softly, and guided his hand to her breast. "Touch me, Cal…"

She hadn't bothered with a bra when she'd gone outside so early. She watched his face change as he traced the soft swell of her breast to its tip; then his mouth plummeted to hers as imperiously as an eagle falls from the sky.

She met him more than halfway, parting her lips to the demands of his tongue, making her own demands in a way new to her and utterly liberating.

Even now, before she'd made love with Cal, she somehow knew that he would welcome everything she was willing to give. So she opened to him, trusting him with both body and soul; as his hand roughly pushed aside her sweatshirt to smooth her bare skin, she said with only a touch of shyness, "This isn't fair."

He glanced at her, his smile weakening her knees. "What's not fair, darling Joanna?"

"You're only wearing a towel. But I've got clothes on. I happen to be a thoroughly modern woman who believes in equality."

"Plus the towel's slipping."

She looked down, blushed and said lamely, "So it is."

"In the interests of equality," he said, "I should take you to bed and remove every stitch you're wearing."

"Sounds like a plan," she said with a brilliant smile.

He swung her into his arms; as she linked her fingers around his nape, she said, "You have little black flecks in your eyes."

"I could drown in yours," Cal said. "Or clothe myself in your hair."

Shaken, she felt tears prick her lids. "That's a lovely thing to say."

He pushed at his bedroom door with his knee, kissing the sweep of her cheekbone. "I want you to know one thing—I'm not taking you to bed to have a casual affair. I don't know what you are to me—I'm being honest here— but there's something between us, I'd swear to it."

But Joanna didn't want talk. Especially talk about the future. She reached up, kissing him with lingering pleasure on the mouth, and saw the gray of his eyes darken to a storm of longing. Then he stooped, lowering her onto the crumpled sheets on his bed. "Last night I dreamed about you…and now you're here. In my bed."

"It's where I want to be," she whispered.

He dropped the towel to the floor. Fully naked, he leaned over, one hand on either side of her, and kissed her with passionate intensity. She pulled him down, exulting in his weight, his closeness, his very obvious hunger for her.

heir tongues danced, his tracing the soft curve of her ower lip, then plunging to taste all her sweetness. Her heart acing in her chest, she pressed the softness of her breasts gainst the hard wall of his chest.

He muttered, "You did say something about too many lothes, didn't you?"

She laughed, a carefree ripple of pure happiness. "What re you going to do about it?"

He raised himself on his palms. "Let me show you." hen, with barely restrained impatience, he tugged at the em of her sweatshirt, raising it so the twin peaks of her reasts shone like ivory in the room's pale light. For a long noment he was silent. Then he said huskily, "I can't be-ieve how exquisite you are. Tell me I'm not dreaming, oanna."

"I'll show you," she said, and with a lithe twist of her ody, sat up, pulling the shirt over her head.

Her hair, black as night, slid like water over her breasts, oth hiding and revealing them. Cal took them in his hands, easing the pink buds of her nipples, running his mouth over he firm rise of her flesh until she whimpered with mingled leasure and need. Then he eased her back on the pillows, is fingers pulling down the zipper on her jeans and draw-ng them over her hips.

His eyes were fastened on her face. As he let his finger-ips drift down her thighs, she gasped with delight, her hips rching upward. Lifting her in his hands, he stroked with ips and hands the arc of her rib cage, the curve of her vaist and flare of her hips. Then he lowered his weight nto her, his chest hair abrading her breasts, his arousal eated and silky between her thighs.

He was ready for her. More than ready. What a fool he'd been to think he no longer wanted her, when every uance of touch and impetus of desire now assured her of he contrary. As she moved her hips below him, aching to gather him in, words suddenly flashed across her mind. *I'm getting what I came here for: an affair with Cal. A possible pregnancy.*

The baby I've always wanted.

A baby had been the last thought in her mind the last few minutes. Briefly she turned her head away, closing her eyes, feeling as though someone had thrown ice-cold water in her face. As he'd carried her into his bedroom, Cal had been honest with her about his feelings. But she was about to deceive him. Use him for her own ends. Could she do that? Return truth with lies?

"Joanna, what's wrong? Did I hurt you?"

There was such concern in Cal's voice that of all Joanna's emotions, shame was uppermost. She couldn't do it. Much as she longed for a baby, she couldn't lie to Cal either in words or actions. He deserved better of her than that. She stammered, "I—I have something to tell you."

He reared up on his elbow, smoothing her hair from her face, tension tightening his jaw. "What is it, sweetheart?"

Sweetheart... She said rapidly, before she could lose her courage, "The reason I changed my mind about coming to Switzerland to see you—Cal, I'm so ashamed of myself."

"Tell me, Joanna."

She bit her lip. "Ever since I was a kid, I've wanted to be a mother. To have a child of my own. But Gustave didn't want children, although he didn't tell me that until after we were married. And on my next birthday I turn twenty-nine. So I decided I should come here and have an affair with you and perhaps I'd get pregnant—oh, God, it sounds so sordid, I'm sorry..."

His eyes narrowed. "What made you confess? Because I might as well tell you, birth control was the last thing on my mind."

"I couldn't use you like that," Joanna said in a low voice. "Or deceive you. It would be wrong."

He tilted her chin to the light, his gaze pinioning her to the bed. "So was all that an act?" he said harshly. "You were just pretending desire, so you could start a baby?"

"No!"

"Are you sure?"

"Cal, I swear to you I wanted you more than I ever wanted Gustave. I can't explain it, I don't understand it—but it's true. You think I'd have gone to bed with you otherwise?"

"I don't know...after all, what do I really know about you?"

The words poured out. "I've never gone to bed with anyone other than Gustave. I hated sex with him almost from the beginning, he was as selfish in bed as out. I couldn't have got this close to you without wanting you, of course I couldn't." She paused, frowning. "It would be like trying to write a book whose story I'd stolen from someone else, that didn't spring from my own imagination. Don't you see? Anyway," she added with a flare of spirit, "if I'd only cared about getting pregnant, all I had to do was keep my mouth shut."

He let out his breath in a small sigh. "I suppose so."

"I'm really sorry about all this," Joanna said painfully. "I'm going to get on the first plane out of here—I should never have come, I must have been out of my mind. And the last thing I should do is meet Lenny, that would be a disaster."

But Cal, she suddenly realized, wasn't listening; he had the air of a man who was thinking hard and fast. She sat up, grabbing for her shirt, wishing he'd pull the sheets over the sculpted lines of his torso with its pelt of dark hair and elegant curve of ribs. Confession or no, she still wanted him: her whole body was an ache of unfulfilled desire.

Not that she was going to tell him that. One confession before breakfast was more than enough.

He said in a peculiar voice, "You know, this could al
work out for the best."

"I don't see how," she said. "I'm going home, Cal
Today."

"You could have a baby, Lenny could have a mother
and as for me—why, I could wake up every morning to
find you in my bed."

A cold fist clamped around Joanna's heart. "What are
you talking about?"

"Marriage," he said.

"*Marriage?*" she squawked.

"That's right. You and I. We'll get married. I'd be de
lighted to make a baby with you...and Lenny would love
to have a brother or sister, she doesn't really like being an
only child. I know she'll like you. She can come back to
live in Vermont because you'll be living there, too, so that
solves the problem of her homesickness. And you won'
have to have part-time jobs because I'll pay off all you
debts and support you—so you can write all the time. I
works out perfectly, Joanna."

"But I don't want to get married!"

"Of course you do. You want a baby, don't you?"

"Haven't you heard of single mothers?"

"Not a good idea if there's a viable alternative," Cal
said confidently. "Much better for the child to have two
parents. That's one of the main reasons I've wanted to re
marry, to give Lenny a stepmother."

A viable alternative. As if he were discussing the stock
market, not the state of holy matrimony, thought Joanna in
true fury. "You're not hearing me," she said crisply. "You
might want to remarry. But I don't."

"I keep telling you I'm not Gustave!"

"Maybe not. Although how would I know until it's too
late? I didn't find out what Gustave was like until after I
was married to him."

"Then we'll live together for a while, if that'll make you feel better."

He had an answer for everything. Feeling beleaguered and horribly unhappy, Joanna hauled her sweatshirt over her head, saying in a muffled voice, "I'll probably never remarry. But I certainly won't marry another mountaineer. So that's that. Now let's phone the airline and have breakfast."

As she emerged from the folds of her shirt, she saw with another rush of fury that Cal was laughing at her. He said, "You look like a bantam rooster, all your feathers ruffled. Joanna, stop and think for a minute. All three of us—four, when our baby's born—can have what we want. It's so simple."

Our baby... Joanna smothered a pain so sharp that she almost cried out. She said in a hostile voice, "You know one thing that's wrong with this scenario? It's all about convenience. Nothing to do with feelings."

He rapped, "Don't tell me you didn't have any feelings when I was kissing you!"

"Love, Cal," she fumed, "I'm talking about love. You don't love me and I don't love you. So we can't possibly get married."

"You, I presume, were in love with Gustave when you married him...as I was in love with Suzanne. Gustave took you to the cleaner's, and Suzanne sure did the same to me. The kind of agreement we'd have would be much better than all this talk about love. Because that's all it is. Talk."

Joanna didn't have to be a mind reader to hear the pain underlying Cal's declaration. "How did Suzanne take you to the cleaner's?"

As he restlessly moved his shoulders, the muscles rippled across his chest. "She never grew up," he said. "She didn't want children, Lenny was a mistake. She just wanted me to climb mountains, play the stock market and leave her free to shop. Paris, London, New York, those were Suzanne's playgrounds, and in my heart I knew she wouldn't have been unhappy if I'd never come back from one of my expeditions. She'd have much preferred being a rich widow than a rich man's wife—all the fun and none of the responsibility.'' He added with a wry twist of his mouth, ''She also lied to me as often as she told the truth—one more reason I had trouble believing you back in January. I was like you, too young when I married to know the score.''

So Cal's marriage had been, in its way, as much of a wasteland as her own. ''I'm sorry,'' Joanna muttered inadequately.

''It's in the past. Over and done with.''

She wasn't so sure about that. ''Either way,'' she said carefully, ''I can't marry you. Not to have a baby, not for convenience, not for Lenny's sake. It wouldn't work, I know it wouldn't—I've had one bad marriage, I don't need another.''

''You're making a big mistake, you know that?''

''It's time you added the word *no* to your vocabulary!''

He grated, ''I've already told Lenny you'll be with me today, and you're not going to disappoint her. So you'll stay until Saturday as planned.''

Saturday was an aeon away, and how could she bear to be with Cal yet unable to make love with him? ''Tell her I had to fly home for an emergency,'' Joanna cried.

''I won't lie to my daughter for you or anyone else.''

She flushed. ''So I've got to act as though I'm delighted to be with you from now until Saturday? What's that if not a lie? She's smart, she'll know something's wrong.''

''The more I listen to you, the more I think you were acting your head off in bed. So to act delighted for a couple of days shouldn't be any problem.''

He couldn't have said anything more calculated to hurt

"And a happy vacation to you, too," she retorted, swung her legs off the bed and got up. "I'm going to have a shower."

Cal, who had somehow maintained a formidable dignity while stark naked, made no move to stop her. Joanna stalked to the bathroom, locked the door and stared at herself in the mirror. So Cal thought she'd been faking desire: one lie on top of another. And once again, she'd been thwarted in her longing for a child.

She mustn't start to cry: because she might never stop. Joanna turned the water on cold and stepped in the shower. If she were writing this scene, there'd be a fadeout, and she'd find herself at the airport on Saturday without having to live through the intervening four days. She'd edit them out.

But unfortunately this was reality. She had to go out to the kitchen, eat breakfast with Cal and drive to Lenny's school.

How was she going to make small talk with Cal after her confession and his ridiculous proposal? And what if she really liked Lenny?

More to the point, Joanna thought, shivering as the cool water ran down her spine, how was she going to keep her hands off Cal?

Next time Dianne and Sally had an idea, she was going to run to her cottage, lock herself in and hide under the bed.

Bed...that word again.

A word she couldn't separate from another three-letter word. Cal.

CHAPTER TEN

SUNLIGHT filtering through handmade lace curtains, the scent of newly mown grass, the plaintive bleating of goats and the faraway clang of cow bells: the setting was idyllic, Cal thought, gazing out of the kitchen window at the blindingly white snow on the mountains. And he wished he were a thousand miles away.

With Joanna a thousand miles in the opposite direction.

Then the skin on the back of his neck prickled as he heard the pad of her approaching footsteps. He turned to face her. Her hair, whose midnight sheen had lain like silk over her naked breasts, was now held with a clasp on her nape; she was wearing a simple cap-sleeved dress the blue of the lobelias in his window boxes, sandals on her bare feet. Steeling himself, knowing it would be all too easy to refrain from admitting the truth, he rasped, "I shouldn't have said that about you acting in bed. I don't think you were."

Joanna stopped dead in her tracks. "You know what? You have a singular talent for taking me by surprise."

"Well, that's something," Cal said wryly.

"I was definitely not expecting you to apologize."

"I didn't apologize. I made a retraction."

"Oh, pardon me," she snorted.

He was starting to enjoy himself; especially when she added, "I certainly wasn't. Acting, I mean."

Her cheeks were fuchsia-pink. "You're sure not indifferent to me," he said slowly. "Guess I should be glad of that."

She was frowning at him. "I just figured something

122

out—I really hurt your feelings, didn't I? When I said I wouldn't marry you.''

Hurt, anger, frustration, desire: what hadn't he felt? ''I don't like rejection,'' Cal said. ''Who does?''

''You're not used to it,'' Joanna said shrewdly.

The words fell from his tongue without conscious volition. ''Suzanne never really liked sex. For her, it was part of the bargain—I got to have sex, she got to spend money.''

''So sex is a loaded issue for you, too. Truly I wasn't acting, Cal.''

''We'd better eat,'' he said brusquely. ''I don't want to be late for Lenny.''

She glanced at the table. Muesli, fresh strawberries and slices of cantaloupe, chocolate-coated croissants and a pot of delicious smelling coffee; she felt her throat tighten. In a rush she said, ''Gustave never once retracted anything he said, and he certainly never got breakfast for me—that was woman's work. And now I really will shut up.''

She plunked herself down at the table and reached for the pot of coffee at the same time as Cal. Briefly his hand overlaid hers; she stared with fascination at the tendons and white-scarred knuckles. He said in a strangled voice, ''You've got to stop doing that.''

''I took a cold shower—not that it did any good.''

''It'd take a couple of glaciers to cool me down.''

''Swimming in the Atlantic in January.''

''Scaling an Antarctic crevasse.''

She chuckled. ''I'm not *that* sexy. Pour the coffee…maybe caffeine will help.''

Since when had he laughed with a woman as much as with Joanna? And she was indeed that sexy. ''Did you know muesli was a Swiss invention?'' he said.

''I know it's very good for you, and if I eat a bowlful I can justify stuffing myself with croissants.''

He grinned. "A woman called Heidi makes them. Her husband yodels, just to complete the stereotype."

She helped herself to cereal and fruit, and for several minutes they chatted about the local economy. Then Joanna asked, taking a second croissant, "What have you told Lenny about me?"

"That you're the writer Ann Cartwright and the widow of a mountaineer. That's about it."

Lenny had been extremely curious about Joanna; but the more questions she'd asked, the more Cal had clammed up. He added, "Lenny writes poetry. I'm not sure which scares me more, poetry or puberty. Her real name's Ghislaine, by the way. But she started calling herself Lenny when she was three, and it stuck. Suzanne always called her Ghislaine, and made her wear frilly dresses...to this day, Lenny's something of a tomboy."

"I'm looking forward to meeting her," Joanna said. For wouldn't she learn more about Cal by seeing father and daughter together?

As though he'd read her mind, Cal said evenly, "I'm not retracting my proposal of marriage."

Her knife clattered on the plate. "Stop it, Cal."

"We get along well, we're attracted to each other and we could help each other out. Aren't those better reasons for marriage than undying love?"

The croissant suddenly tasted like paper. Joanna drained her coffee and stood up. "I'm going to clean my teeth. Then I'm ready to go."

"Think about it, Joanna. Think very hard."

"I bet sheer stubbornness got you to the top of all those mountains," she said nastily.

His jaw tightened. "I don't want us sniping at each other in front of Lenny."

"I'll be as sweet and gooey as a chocolate croissant."

"I mean it!"

"I promise that the—the impasse between you and me will not spoil your visit with your daughter."

"You're every bit as stubborn as I am."

"But not as arrogant."

"You're twice as sexy," he said, and watched unwilling amusement flicker across her features.

"I couldn't possibly be," she said, and fled the room.

They left ten minutes later, driving the short distance to St. Gallen through the lushly green countryside, then taking the narrow streets with care. The fifteenth-century houses, built to encircle the abbey, were lavishly decorated with gilt and brightly colored paint, full of Gothic charm. The abbey was famous for its sacred art and magnificently appointed library; the tolling of bells echoed among the rooftops. Lenny's school was just north of the town; a crowd of girls were gathered on the wide stone steps, and as Cal pulled up, one of them detached herself and came running down the steps toward them. Swiftly Cal got out of the car.

Lenny had a cap of gleaming brown hair, braces and Cal's gray eyes: that much Joanna saw before the girl flung herself into her father's arms. "Hi, Dad, great to see you, I'm so glad it's the last day of term and I can wear real clothes, not a uniform, and I've got a favor to ask you."

Cal swung his daughter into the air. "Great to see you, too. You're a half an inch taller than last time."

"For sure? I thought I was going to be short forever."

"Forever's a long time, Lenny," Cal said, and put her down on the ground again.

None of this was acting, either, thought Joanna; the affection between the two of them was very real. Her throat choked with emotion. Lucky Cal. If his marriage had been far from ideal, at least he had Lenny.

Then Cal said, "Joanna's in the car."

Hastily Lenny smoothed down her hair and tugged at her T-shirt. Oh, no, Joanna thought, she's nervous. Neophyte poet meets critically acclaimed author. She climbed out of the car and walked around to meet Lenny, her hand held out. "Hello, Lenny," she said with a warm smile, "I've heard so much about you. I'm delighted to meet you."

Lenny gulped. "Hello, Mrs. Strassen."

"Unless your father objects, I'd much prefer to be called Joanna."

"Fine with me," Cal said.

"Good," said Joanna. "You must be happy to be heading home, Lenny."

"I miss the farm, and my horse and the dogs and cats. And Dad, too, of course."

She, Joanna, by agreeing to marry Cal, could put an end to Lenny's homesickness. She said quickly, "You must tell me more about your horse…I used to have one when I was growing up."

"Horses were in your book."

"I have a feeling a lot of my childhood was in that book," Joanna said dryly. "A bit like undressing in public. Your father told me you write. If you like, we can talk about that, too."

"Oh, I'm not a real writer. Not like you."

"Everyone has to begin somewhere. And who says you're not a real writer?"

Lenny hesitated. "Me, I guess."

"Inner critics are the very worst kind."

Lenny was now gazing at Joanna with something like hero worship. Not quite sure how to deal with this, Joanna heard Cal ask, "What was the favor you wanted, Lenny?"

"My best friend Jan had to go home a week ago because she had the flu really badly. She's better now and wants me to go and stay overnight at her house before I go home. Her parents say it's okay. Can I, Dad?"

"Isn't that in Zermatt?"

"It's not that far."

"I'd have to see if we could get hotel rooms."

Joanna bit her lip, feeling suddenly frightened. If they went to Zermatt, it would mean another night in Cal's proximity, without the safety of Lenny's presence. Then Lenny said, "I bet you could—you've got all sorts of connections in Zermatt. There's a phone just inside the main door, Dad."

Cal's gaze met Joanna's and held it; she had no idea what he was thinking. He said abruptly, "That okay with you, Joanna?"

"Fine," she said brightly.

He took the steps two at a time. Lenny said, "Dad's kind of famous in Zermatt—he rescued four climbers who got in trouble on the north face of the Matterhorn when the weather changed. Dad went with the rescue helicopter and got them off the ledge, it was just about a blizzard. Dad hates to talk about stuff like that."

So Cal took risks. Big risks. No reason why that should upset her, all mountaineers took risks, it went with the territory. That he should be courageous in the service of others, Joanna chose to ignore. Discovering she didn't want to talk about Cal to Cal's daughter, Joanna said weakly, "I see," then changed the subject with a gaucheness rare to her. "What's your horse's name?"

Lenny chattered on for five minutes about all the animals on the farm; then Cal reappeared. "We're all set," he said, "let's get your luggage, Lenny."

The journey to Zermatt was so beautiful that Joanna ran out of superlatives. They drove due south at first, skirting the Austrian border and that of the little principality of Liechtenstein; then they turned west, following the Vorderrhein River past magnificent vistas of the Glarner Alps. They stopped for lunch by a tumbling mountain stream, its turquoise meltwater icy cold; a magpie scolded them from the spruce trees, the high peaks clothed in wisps of cloud. The Rhône valley led them further west until again they headed south along the Vispa. Dark chalets houses as blindingly white as the snow on the mountains of Valais, the steep rocky gorge at Stalden; and then, finally, the short train trip to Zermatt.

"Jan'll meet us at that little café, Dad, on the main street," Lenny said as they disembarked. "We're early though."

"We'll check in at the hotel first. Then we'll have time for a glass of wine at the café," Cal said. "Or else tea and pastries. Joanna has a sweet tooth too, Lenny."

Lenny had relaxed during the drive, Cal had noticed; and now was chatting to Joanna as if she'd known her for years. His intuition had told him that the two of them would like each other; he'd been right. Somehow he had to convince Joanna to marry him. Or at least live with him. She was a perfect choice from every angle that he could think of; he refused to believe that a few mountains and the ghost of her husband could get in the way. Or her insistence that the two of them should be madly in love with each other.

Love couldn't be trusted. They both knew that.

Once they'd checked in, they walked back to the café. Lenny and Joanna were ahead of him, Joanna's long, lightly tanned legs gleaming in the sunlight, her dress gently outlining the curves of hip and waist; her hair hung like a dark waterfall down her back. God, how he wanted her!

Tonight he'd be alone with her in the hotel. Was he going to move to Plan D? Do his level best to seduce her?

A horse-drawn carriage clopped past, and two of the ubiquitous electric taxis whizzed by. At the café, the roar of the river overlaid the guttural Swiss-German dialect; as they were led to their table, they could see the jagged tooth of the Matterhorn's summit rising from its wrap of cloud.

Then a man's voice called, "Cal, how are you? I didn't know you were in the area."

"Rudolf, good to see you—we just arrived," Cal said. 'It's been a while...join us, why don't you?"

Rudolf, it transpired, was a member of the mountain rescue patrol; his eyes were very blue in his weatherbeaten ace. "You must come and see our new helicopter, Cal," e enthused, "the very latest in technology. One of these days they won't even need pilots. Would the ladies excuse you for a short while?"

Lenny grinned, clearly entranced by Rudolf's courtly bow. As for Joanna, the less time she spent with Cal, the better. Being with him was like being presented with the biggest chocolate croissant in Switzerland and then being told you mustn't touch it. "Okay by me," she said.

"Sure," said Lenny. "Here's Jan's phone number, Dad. 'll be back at the hotel around nine tomorrow because the whole family has to go to Geneva in the morning."

"Have a good time," Cal said, kissing his daughter on he cheek. "Joanna, you'll be all right for a while?"

"I'll do some window-shopping," she said. "Why don't we meet at the hotel at seven?"

He leaned over and kissed her on the cheek, too. Subduing her shiver of response, she smiled at him sweetly. 'Take your time, I'll enjoy being on my own."

His eyes narrowed. "I'll be back before seven."

As the two men threaded their way through the tables, Joanna noticed how women's eyes followed Cal's progress. And why not? He carried himself with an easy assumption of masculine power coupled with a kind of animal grace that was incredibly sexy. Why would she be the only one to notice him? He'd have no trouble finding a second wife and a mother for Lenny; the women would line up from here to the tip of the Matterhorn.

Joanna came back to earth with a bump as Cal's daughter said rather too casually, "Have you known Dad for long?"

"We met in January. But we've really seen very little c each other," Joanna said repressively.

"Oh." Lenny hesitated. "He never goes on holiday witl anyone. Except me. So I kind of thought—"

"Lenny," Joanna said gently, "I think your father tol you I'm a widow. My husband was also a mountaineer, h died on Annapurna last October. I don't really want to ge involved with anyone right now."

Lenny's delicate features were screwed up in thought "But maybe later?"

"I don't think so. You see, I found it very difficult bein married to someone who was, in effect, married to th mountains. I was always afraid that he'd be killed...an then he was. So I'm not likely to choose another moun taineer for a husband—if that's what you're getting at.' She smiled into Lenny's gray eyes. "Or maybe I'm jump ing the gun. I just don't want you pinning your hopes o something that's not going to happen."

Lenny said naively, "I like you. Lots of adults say thing like, *you wouldn't understand* or *you're much too young dear*. You treat me like I'm grown up. Do you have an kids?"

Joanna fiddled with her cutlery. "No."

Lenny said with another of those outbursts of honesty "I wish Dad would quit climbing. I get scared, too. Ever time he goes. Although I've never told him because I don' want him to stop because of me. If you know what mean."

"I know exactly what you mean."

Lenny frowned. "You know, it's funny but I don't re member my mother worrying much. She used to sing around the house when he was gone. And go out shopping lots. She was awfully pretty, not like me. She used to cal me her little brown sparrow."

Joanna swallowed a rush of anger toward the unknowr

Suzanne. She said calmly, "You'll be a Ghislaine before long, Lenny, you wait and see. Your eyes are beautifully shaped, and once your braces are gone and your face fills out a little, you'll be stunning."

"*Me?*"

"Yes, you."

"Wow." Lenny sat up a little taller. "But you're more beautiful than anyone I've ever seen...I'll never look like you."

"Nor should you—you'll look like yourself."

To Joanna's great relief, a tall red-haired girl suddenly hailed Lenny from the far side of the café. "Oh, there's Jan," Lenny said, and waved; Jan's parents were standing in the background. Lenny gave Joanna a blinding smile. "Thanks for telling me all that stuff. Maybe if we both work on Dad, he'll quit climbing." Then she grabbed her overnight bag and hurried to meet her friend.

Joanna watched them leave. So Lenny wanted Joanna as a stepmother; and hadn't wanted to hear how impossible that was. The trouble was, Joanna would love to be Lenny's stepmother; she'd warmed to Cal's daughter from the start.

One more reason she should never have come to Switzerland.

Joanna read for a while, drinking herbal tea and nibbling on yet more pastries. Time for a walk, or else she wouldn't fit into this dress anymore. Determined not to think about either Cal or Lenny, Joanna set off. The crowded main street fascinated her, with its classy boutiques where she did indeed just window-shop; she browsed happily in a bookstore for the better part of an hour, and avoided the shops carrying climbing equipment, although she couldn't as easily avoid all the climbers, some with harnesses and grappling hooks dangling from their waists. If it hadn't been for Gustave's climbing gear, she would never have met Cal...

She soon discovered the winding back lanes, where geraniums and fuchsias cascaded from the window boxes of the little chalets; after exploring there, she passed some more souvenir shops, wincing at the ubiquitous silhouette of the Matterhorn on everything from T-shirts to teapots; wandering further, she found herself at the gates of a cemetery.

A special cemetery, set apart for all those who had died on the mountain that dominated the skyline. Most of them men, many of them young.

As Gustave had been young. As Cal was young.

Cal. She gazed at the rough carving of a coil of rope on one of the headstones. What if something happened to Cal on his next expedition? What if he never came back?

How would she bear it?

She rested her fingers on the rough stone. She'd never see him again. Lenny would be left an orphan, and she, Joanna, would be—her thoughts slammed to a stop. Distraught? Bereft? Filled with a far deeper grief than the pain she'd felt for Gustave? Gustave had never honored the mountains with a matching honesty and integrity of his own. But Cal always would.

I'm not in love with Cal.

I can't afford to be in love with him.

I am in love with him.

CHAPTER ELEVEN

JOANNA stood very still, the headstone warming to her touch, her heart thumping as though she'd been running through the streets of Zermatt. Had she done what she'd sworn she'd never do, fallen in love again? With another mountain climber?

The thought of Cal being buried by an avalanche, lying broken-boned in a crevasse, or falling from a sheer rock face to his death: she knew too much about the very real dangers, and her imagination could supply the rest. Each of the infinite possibilities filled her with horror.

No, she thought frantically. Not Cal.

The stones, humped and weathered, wavered in her glance. The heat of the sun and the glancing shadows mocked her: for hadn't the cruelest of jokes been played on her? Once again she'd fallen in love with a mountaineer, a man in love with danger. But she could never tell him so, and she couldn't possibly live with him.

She had to get out of here. Her dark glasses hiding her eyes, Joanna stumbled out of the cemetery and back onto the street. She'd go to the hotel, where she could be alone. Out on the street like this, there were too many people and too much noise; and she herself was too far from home and all that was familiar and safe.

Blind to the allure of the boutiques, doing her best to avoid pedestrians, she took a wrong turn and found herself in the back streets again. Suppressing a whimper of pure distress, she stopped, trying to orient herself. The hotel should be to her right.

She hurried across the road, a couple of minutes later

seeing, far down the street, the elegant facade of their hotel. What she wanted to do more than anything was bury her face in her pillow and cry her eyes out. She couldn't do that: Cal was far too discerning. However, she could soak in a hot bath. Not exactly a cure for heartache. But it would have to do.

A woman pushing a baby carriage passed just in front of her, the baby peacefully sleeping, one little fist curled into its cheek. Like a knife to the heart, Joanna realized something else: that to bear Cal's child, loving him as she did, would make her the happiest woman on earth.

But she couldn't. Cal didn't love her, and he'd never agree to her raising his child on her own.

Tears filmed her vision. Frantic for privacy, Joanna lunged across the road toward the hotel, not even seeing the electric taxi racing up the hill. A horn assaulted her eardrums. Someone shouted a warning. She glanced sideways and made a leap for the sidewalk. But her toe caught on the curb. She tumbled forward, her knees and palms slamming onto the cool concrete. For an instant, she felt nothing. Then pain ripped along her nerves.

"Madame, permettez-moi…"

"Give the lady a hand up, now."

A small crowd had surrounded her. Italian and German added themselves to the chorus, and a man started lifting her to her feet. And then she heard the voice she least wanted to hear. *"Joanna…*what happened? Here, I'll look after her, thanks for your help."

Arms went around her, lifting her. Cal's arms. It was both agony and bliss to be held by him. The brass-ornamented doors swung open and closed behind her. An attendant offered more help in a tactful murmur, and then blessedly she was in the elevator, the doors smoothly shutting out the rest of the world. She faltered, "Let me down, it's nothing—"

"You've removed a fair bit of skin from one knee and I'm not putting you down until we get to our suite."

"I just want to be by myself," Joanna wailed, and to her horror started to sob as though her heart were broken. Cal tucked her head into his chest, marched down a paneled corridor and inserted a card into double doors that were painted with sprightly scenes of a medieval garden. Inside, he carried her straight to the bathroom, whose spotless mirrors presented Joanna with several reflections of a black-haired woman with bleeding knees in the arms of a tanned, broad-shouldered man. The woman was crying. Copiously.

Between sobs, she said fiercely, "Cal, go away!"

"No."

"I don't want you here."

"Too bad," he said, and lowered her into a gilt-edged chair covered with exquisitely embroidered tapestry. Then he reached up and pulled off her sunglasses. "What's the matter?" he said so gently that her eyes filled with tears again. "Don't cry, Joanna, I hate to see you cry."

"I feel so s-stupid, falling like that on the street."

"You don't know another soul here except me and Lenny, and we won't tell her a thing," he said comfortingly, meanwhile searching in his first-aid kit for disinfectant and filling the sink. "This probably reminds you of when you fell on the ice and lost the baby."

"Yes...yes, it does." Grateful for his understanding, she wrinkled her nose as he applied disinfectant; it stung enough to take her mind off everything else. She snuffled, "I won't be able to wear shorts for days."

"I'll order room service for dinner—a fall like that can leave you shaken up."

Cal was kneeling at her feet, smoothing on antibacterial cream, his lean fingers very gentle. His hair shone like polished leather under the lights; at the open neck of his shirt she could see the tangled pelt on his chest. She was stabbed

by a desire so strong that she felt almost faint; of its own
accord, her hand reached out and very lightly stroked his
hair.

At that precise moment Cal looked up. She snatched her
hand back. "I wasn't—"

He said hoarsely, "Joanna…sweetheart."

He lifted her to her feet, wrapped her in an embrace that
felt like heaven on earth, and kissed her. Kissed her as he
always kissed her, with passion and a desperate hunger that
more than matched her own.

Afterward, she dimly remembered being carried into his
bedroom with its huge bed and blue velvet drapes. She was
never quite sure how they both got out of their clothes; but
she did remember the heat of his naked skin on hers, his
weight pressing her into the mattress. He muttered, "I'll be
careful of your knees, my darling." And then neither of
them said anything for quite a while.

Clinging to him as though she might fall were she to let
go, Joanna ran her fingers the length of his spine, caressing
his tautly muscled shoulders, kissing his mouth, his throat,
his chest, and all the while achingly aware of his own ex-
plorations. Her breasts felt swollen, the nipples so sensitive
that she cried out as he laved them with his tongue. Then
he moved lower, parting her thighs, seeking out her other
sensitivities. She was more than ready for him, engulfed in
a storm of longing that would brook no delay. As a deep
throbbing seized her, she felt him slide into her waiting
warmth, filling her, so that her whole body was locked to
his. Again she cried out his name.

His own throbbing leaped to meet hers, his face con-
vulsing. But his eyes held hers, feeding on her release, allowing her to share his own so that she fell headlong into
a pleasure that was overwhelmingly intense, an intimacy
greater than she'd ever known. Nothing else in the world

existed but Cal and herself, joined in the most primitive way possible.

Her heart was hammering in her ears: or was it Cal's heart? They were indistinguishable, she thought with sudden fierce possessiveness; and smiled at him with all her newly discovered love. "Oh, Cal," she said breathlessly, "I've never in my life been swept away like that."

"Nor I," he said huskily. "But it all happened too quickly, I shouldn't have been so—"

"I wasn't exactly telling you to slow down," she said. "No buts...it was perfect."

He gave her a lingering kiss. "How are your knees?"

Her laugh cascaded like sunlight on water. "Knees? What knees?"

But then, as though it were she who had fallen into a crevasse, she remembered her impetuous dash across the road, and her sudden fall. She sat bolt upright, her eyes wide with distress. "I know I'm the one who started this, you were so close and I wanted you so much—I just had to touch your hair, I couldn't stop myself. But I didn't plan it, truly I didn't."

Cal hesitated infinitesimally. "Plan it?"

"To get pregnant," she cried. "I'm not on the pill, and we didn't use any protection. But I swear it wasn't a setup."

"I didn't think you planned it," he said slowly, adding with the crooked smile she loved so much, "surely you've heard of spontaneous combustion?"

If anything, her distress deepened. She'd sworn to keep her distance from Cal and here she was naked in bed with him. That couldn't be called keeping her distance. And for all his endearments, she knew he didn't love her. He didn't believe in love. She pushed away from him, hauling the sheets up to cover her nudity. "We shouldn't have done this," she burst out.

"Joanna, we both wanted to. We're adults, neither of us involved with anyone else."

"Involved," she repeated bitterly. "What a cold-blooded word that is."

"Then if you prefer, we're neither of us in love with anyone else," he blazed. He reached for her, grasping her by the elbows and drawing her nearer to his body. "And now we're going to do it again. Taking our time."

To her utter consternation, desire spread a slow ache through her body. Already she wanted to make love with him again, she thought sickly, and struck him away. "You just don't get it, do you? I won't have an affair with you, Cal!"

"Then marry me."

The force of his will smote her like a blow. But that was all it was. Willpower. A rational list of all the reasons why she should marry him.

Nothing to do with love.

"I can't marry you. Or have an affair with you." Desperate to escape, she slid from the bed, grabbed her clothes, which were scattered all over the carpet, and clutched them to her chest. "There's nothing more to say, except I'm sorry we went to bed together, we shouldn't have...I'll see you in the morning."

With the speed and litheness of an athlete, Cal also stood up. He said with dangerous softness, "I won't force you, it's not my style. And I won't beg. Any more than I'll tell you I love you when the words are meaningless. But be very careful here, Joanna. You'd be a fool to deny what's between us."

"Sex. That's all it is."

"It's more than that, and you know it. It's some kind of elemental attraction that I've never felt before and that I don't understand—but I'm willing to go with it. All I'm asking is that you do the same."

"And what happens if I do?" she flashed. "Will you
cancel your next expedition? Or will you head off to
Annapurna leaving me home in dread of every phone
call?"

"I don't take unnecessary risks on the mountains! I've
turned back far more times than I've reached the summit—
I'm not into the do-or-die stuff, believe me."

Which was, she realized, another source of his power:
that he was confident enough of his masculinity to know
when to turn back. "I won't do it to myself again," she
said flatly. "For me to have an affair with you would be
like heading for the summit in the worst blizzard of the
century."

"For you to deny what's between us is to stay stuck at
the base camp for the rest of your life."

"There's a difference between cowardice and learning
from experience!"

"I said I wasn't going to beg, Joanna—and I'm not."

"I can't take this anymore," she said raggedly. "I'll
meet you downstairs in the lobby at nine tomorrow morning."

Head held high, her clothes trailing on the floor in a loose
bundle, she walked away from him; and with each step felt
as though her heart were being torn in two.

She could have spent the night in his arms; he wanted
her to, and didn't she crave to with every nerve in her
body?

But at what cost?

Her bedroom adjoined the palatial living room; she
opened the door and closed it behind her, the click of the
latch as definitive as the final sentence of a book.

The End.

And what a horribly unhappy and ambivalent ending, she
thought. But I can't edit it. It has to stay the way it is.

Sinking down on the bed, Joanna pressed her hands to

her face. Her skin smelled elusively of Cal. With a smoth
ered cry of despair, she closed her eyes; never in her lif
had she felt so alone.

Cal woke in the middle of the night from a restless slee
punctuated with nightmares. The cry he'd heard—was tha
part of his dream or had it been real?

He lay still, eyes wide open, and heard it again. It wa
coming from Joanna's room, he realized, and surged to hi
feet. There couldn't be a break-in, the security in the hote
equaled that of the Zurich banks. But if someone was i
her room, he'd flatten the bastard first and ask question
afterward.

He flung the door open and stood still, his eyes adjusting
to the darkness. The room was empty but for Joanna; she
was lying in a tangled heap of bedclothes and even as he
watched, she gave another of those cries of utter desolation

Pierced to the heart, he sat down on the bed and gathered
her into his arms, cradling her head to his bare chest. He
nightgown, a concoction of silk and lace, was calculated to
drive any man out of his mind. "Wake up, sweetheart,'
he urged, "you're having a bad dream."

Her eyes flew open, full of primitive terror. "Cal?" she
whispered, pushing herself away from him. "*Cal?* Bu
you're dead, I just identified the body…"

She thrust her fist into her mouth, biting hard on the
knuckles. "It was in the morgue…they'd called me
Gustave had fallen from the Matterhorn. So I went there
But when they showed me the body, it wasn't Gustave. I
was *you*…"

"I'm right here, Joanna," Cal said matter-of-factly. "I
climbed the Matterhorn in my twenties and have no desire
to climb it again. It was a dream, that's all. You're awake
now and everything's okay."

"A dream," she repeated, as he reached over and moothed her fingers flat.

"I was awake and I heard you cry out."

Her shoulders sagged. "What are we going to do, Cal? can't be around you like this, it's too painful."

Suzanne had never showed him her pain; perhaps she'd ever allowed herself to feel any. Even her final illness had een as swift and deadly as a heart attack, with no time for er to talk about her feelings. But Joanna was as open with er emotions as with her desire. Something tight-held hifted in Cal's chest; his one desire to comfort her, he said, 'Just let me hold you for a while. Until you go back to leep."

When he drew her toward him, she surrendered with a iny sigh. The softness of her breasts heated his rib cage, er breathing teasing his shoulder with its elusive warmth. Iis reaction was entirely predictable, he thought ruefully. 3ut he mustn't make love to her again. Because she was ight: last time they'd used no protection.

If she got pregnant, surely she'd marry him.

He tried to banish these words. But they insisted on staying in the forefront of his mind. Were they true?

She'd said she'd raise a child on her own, as a single mother. But confronted with something other than theory— vith a positive test result, with bodily symptoms and an ictual delivery date—wouldn't Joanna think differently? Wouldn't she realize that an unborn child deserved two parents?

She placed a high premium on love. Just yesterday morning, in Appenzell, she'd said she didn't love him. Would hat keep her from marrying him?

His thoughts were whirling in his head like a squirrel on a wheel. He tried to subdue his body's rampant response o her closeness, shifting a little so she wouldn't be aware of it. Then she looked up, her features a soft blur in the dim light. "You tear me apart, Cal...right now all I wan is for you to make love to me. And yet we mustn't."

Only wanting to remove the strain in her voice, he kisse her awkwardly on the forehead. Then he started rubbin her shoulders, back and forth in a soothing rhythm. Sh cuddled into him with another of those small sighs, her hai lying like a length of dark silk over his forearm. Its scen reached his nostrils, mingling with the warm fragrance c her skin. Again he shifted a little. He'd pushed himself t his limits more than once in his life: but to hold Joanna i his arms and not make love to her was probably a greate challenge than any.

You can do it, he told himself. Sure you can.

Her hands, which had been cold when he'd first sat o the bed, had warmed now, curled into his chest like tw small, trusting animals.

He couldn't abuse that trust. His shoulders tight wit tension, his breathing shallow, Cal sat as still as he could One leg was doubled under him, the cramping almost relief because it took his mind off everything else. He dropped his cheek to the top of her head, letting his gaz roam around the room.

The red numbers on the digital clock by her bed change with tantalizing slowness. Then, to his infinite relief, he realized Joanna had fallen back to sleep, her breathing sub tly deeper and more relaxed.

He was safe. He'd wait a few more minutes, then he' get out of here. With any luck she wouldn't even remembe this in the morning. In fact, he hoped to heaven she wouldn't.

Making love with her earlier had blown his mind Technique, timing, finesse, they'd all gone out the window eclipsed by a raging hunger that—he now realized—had deep down, frightened him. Because he'd been out o control.

Just as well Joanna had fallen asleep, he thought with a touch of grimness. These were deep waters that he'd do well to beware. Deeper than he'd expected. Far deeper; and more dangerous.

All he wanted was a good mother for Lenny, and a bedmate for himself. A companion. Certainly Joanna would never bore him; she was like the mountains in that respect.

What he didn't need was some kind of cataclysm in his life. Like falling in love. He'd done that once; and it hadn't worked. He wasn't about to do it again.

Besides, what was the point of falling in love with a woman who'd made it all too clear she didn't love him?

CHAPTER TWELVE

TEN minutes had passed since Joanna had fallen asleep. Moving very carefully, Cal pulled his thigh free, wincing as the circulation started up again. Then he eased her body down to the mattress. She murmured something in her sleep. Her hair slithered down his arm, running through his fingers and sliding onto the sheet. He'd like to see it in moonlight. He'd like it spread across his pillow every morning when he woke up.

With an exclamation of disgust, Cal straightened his other knee, the injured one that sometimes gave him trouble. As he rubbed it absently, Joanna twisted toward him, draping an arm over his other thigh; he was only wearing briefs. Her cleavage was a dark shadow; the swell of her hip made his fingertips itch to caress her. Then her eyes drifted open. He held himself like a statue, not even breathing.

"Cal?" she said softly, stroking his thigh with her hand, then resting her cheek against it. "To wake up and find you here...you feel so warm. So wonderfully familiar."

Go back to sleep, he thought, agonized. Because I can't take this anymore.

Then she pushed herself up on one elbow, smiling at him, her lips a soft, seductive curve, her eyes almost black. And Cal lost it. He plunged for her mouth. Taking her face between his palms, he kissed her as though there was no tomorrow. Only now.

Her response, fiery and overwhelmingly generous, inflamed every one of his senses. His control began to slide away from him, faster and faster. Slow down, he thought,

urgently. This time you can woo her, give her all the pleasure you're capable of.

Impregnate her?

He shoved that thought back where it belonged. This was
about something else. Possession, certainly. Hunger, yes.
But even more, it was about Joanna's needs. Wanting her
happiness and fulfillment more than his own. Wanting to
heal some of the wounds Gustave had dealt her.

With a feeling that he was scaling a peak he'd only
dreamed of, and for which he might not be prepared, Cal
gentled his kiss, wrapping her hair around his fingers. His
tongue laved her lower lip. He drew her closer, the silk of
her gown cool to the touch, her skin just as silky, infinitely
desirable.

She felt fluid in his arms, pliant. Again forcing himself
to move slowly, he pushed the straps of her gown from her
shoulders, stroking the delicate bones, dropping his lips to
trace their hollows and curves. Then he followed the sweet
rise of her breast to its tip, her sharp indrawn breath all the
encouragement he needed.

She found his own nipples, tangling her fingers in the
rough hair on his chest. Suddenly impatient, she tugged at
her gown, pulling it over her head and tossing it aside. Then
she moved her hands lower down his body; with something
of the same impatience, he rid himself of his briefs. She
encircled him, his involuntary throb of response making her
smile with a pride that touched him to the core. "Do that
again," he whispered.

Then she lowered her head to take him in her mouth, her
tongue circling where her fingers had been until he wondered if he could die from sheer pleasure. "You'd better
stop," he gasped. "Besides, it's your turn, my darling."

He laid her back on the bed, her hair a black swirl, and
rested his weight on her, kissing her lips, the long tendons
of her throat, the swollen peaks of her breasts. Drinking in

her beauty, from the taut belly to the nest of dark hair a
the juncture of her thighs, he covered her with his kisses
setting his seal upon her, the seal of possession. She
writhed beneath him, her hips lifting to take him in, he
breath coming in short gasps as he played with the sof
petals of wet, warm flesh where she was most sensitive t
his touch.

But Cal was in no hurry. He rolled over, carrying he
with him, her body boneless in his hands. Then he lifted
her to straddle him, taking care not to jar her sore knee. A
he slid into her, her face changed. She said urgently, "Now
Cal, now…"

He thrust upward, clasping her around the waist, the firm
rise of her breasts as erotic as the host of other sensation:
that claimed him in all their inexorability. But even then
he was stroking her between the thighs with all the skill a
his command, watching the tension gather in her face. Her
head bowed, she gasped his name, then cried out in a pas
sion of release.

Only then did Cal allow himself his own release, a
abyss of mingled pain and pleasure that carried him deeper
and further than he'd ever been before. Distantly he was
aware of her heels gripping his thighs, her hands smoothing
the tangle of hair on his chest. And realized he'd beer
saying her name over and over again, wanting time to stop
with Joanna and him as one.

With exquisite grace, she lowered herself to lie across
his chest; and in another of those pangs of tenderness, Cal
felt the racing of her heart against his breastbone. He
wrapped his arms around her. "Darling Joanna…"

She made a tiny sound of pure contentment. "I know
you're not supposed to make comparisons," she murmured
drowsily, "it's not good etiquette. But you took such care
of me—that's never happened to me before."

Gustave, in other words, had looked after himself rather

han his wife. In bed as well as out. Cal said, "Suzanne never liked sex. Too messy, too real, too—naked, I suppose."

"Were you faithful to her, Cal?"

"Yeah...part of the deal."

She raised her head. "So you liked what we did?"

There was a touch of uncertainty in her voice. "Liked it?" he repeated. "Oh, yes, I liked it. The earth moved, isn't that the current cliché? Well, let's say the Matterhorn moved."

"Just the Matterhorn? Not the entire Alps?"

He wanted to say, *Next time we'll go for the Alps.* But something stopped him. "How about the Himalayas?" he offered, and heard her chuckle sleepily. Again she rested her cheek on his chest, closing her eyes with a sigh of repletion. Cal lay very still. Within moments she was asleep again, the fingers of her left hand curved to his ribs, of her right curling around his shoulder.

This was what he wanted. Joanna in his bed. Making love with her, sleeping with her, waking in the morning to find her in his embrace.

He was happy, Cal thought incredulously. Filled with happiness, pure and simple. Light-headed with happiness. Wasn't that partly why he climbed, in search of a joy he'd never found in the arms of a woman?

Until Joanna.

What if she were pregnant? What then?

Joanna woke gradually, to a delicious lassitude and the heat of a man's thigh lying against her own. An arm lay heavily across her hip. In a flash it all came back to her: the tumultuous love-making in Cal's bedroom, her flight to her own room, the nightmarish images of a dead climber who was the man she loved...and then that other, dreamlike lovemaking, slow and infinitely erotic.

Only a few hours ago, she'd sworn she wouldn't have an affair with Cal. And now she'd woken in his arms.

He was a wonderful lover, passionate and attentive, totally focused. She'd never felt such a pitch of arousal, or such incredible fulfillment.

And now it was over. Lenny would be back this morning, and two days from now she herself would get on a plane to fly to London. How long before she'd wonder if she really had dreamed this night in Cal's arms?

Her lashes flickered. Again they'd used no protection. And it was—she'd known this before she left home—the most fertile part of her cycle.

Perhaps she was pregnant.

The mere possibility filled Joanna with a tumult of emotions, so that she could scarcely breathe. Hope like sunshine after a storm, joy like an opening rose; and the utter despair, the blighted rose, of knowing that the father of her child would never fall in love with her. Wouldn't allow himself to.

Valiantly she pushed all the emotions down. She couldn't afford them. Not now. Not when she had to spend the day with Cal and Lenny. Besides, it was very unlikely that she was pregnant. Raising herself cautiously, she peered at the digital clock beside the bed.

Eight forty-five. She blinked, wondering if she were dreaming again. But even as she watched, the last number changed. Eight forty-six.

Lenny was due back at the hotel at nine. With a yelp of alarm, Joanna scrambled out of bed. Cal turned over in his sleep, reaching for her. Then his eyes opened, and he stretched luxuriously. "Joanna?" he mumbled. "Come back to bed."

"It's quarter to nine! Lenny'll be here any minute."

He reared up on his elbow, raking his hair back. "Are you kidding? I never sleep past seven."

"You just did. I'm going to have a shower."

She ran for her bathroom and locked the door. After the quickest shower on record, she hurried back into the bedroom, which was mercifully empty, and dressed in her tunic top over a camisole, along with loose trousers that hid her scraped knees. Her hair she gathered in a knot on the back of her head; huge purple and pink earrings would, she hoped, distract from the faint blue shadows under her eyes.

Not once did she look at the bed.

Her sandals were in the living room. She pulled them on and slapped on some makeup to the sound of Cal's razor. "I'll meet you in the dining room," she called, and ran for the elevator.

So when Lenny appeared in the archway of the elegant dining room, with its splendid view of the hooked Matterhorn, Joanna was peacefully reading a book. As Lenny sat down across from her, Joanna said smoothly, "Your father should be down any minute. Did you have a good time with Jan and her family?"

Then, with a lurch of her heart, she saw Cal come through the archway and stride toward their table. Formidable, she thought. That was the word that most truly applied to him. And braced herself to act like a platonic friend and not the woman who'd spent a night of passion in his arms.

He hugged his daughter, smiled at Joanna as impersonally as if she were indeed nothing but a friend, and said cheerfully, "I'm starving. Have you eaten, Lenny?"

And somehow that set the pattern for the next three days. It would have been very difficult for Joanna to have staved off advances from Cal; it was totally disconcerting to have him act as though she scarcely existed. Nevertheless, she stayed close to Lenny, who, not very subtly, kept trying to leave the two adults alone. Cal smiled a lot, with the air of a man having a pleasant holiday with his much-loved daughter and a female acquaintance who just happened to have joined them.

They hiked around the Saas villages, discovering a path set with fifteen white chapels, sighting the glacier and the peak of the Dom; every mountain seemed a cruel reminder to Joanna of what she couldn't have. They stayed in a delightful chalet that night. The next morning, they drove to Montreux, eating lunch on the shore of Lake Geneva, the patio of the restaurant surrounded by rose-pink camellias and the rustle of palm trees. Lenny, who had been exposed to Byron in her English class, wanted to see the Château de Chillon; after a short boat trip, Joanna saw the towers and high windows of the castle, where a sixteenth-century prior had been chained for six years in an underground dungeon. Lenny had a ghoulish wish to see the dungeon; Joanna stayed behind in the Great Hall with its magnificent frescoes.

She had no desire to see a dungeon. For wasn't she a prisoner? she thought painfully. A prisoner of her past. And surely Cal was the same. Long ago, he'd fallen in love with a woman who, by all accounts, had both used and disdained him. So he'd lost faith that real love could exist between a man and a woman.

Tomorrow couldn't come soon enough.

Cal drove fast all the way to Bern, where they stayed in a charming centuries-old hotel. As soon as they'd eaten a late dinner, Joanna gave an exaggerated yawn. "I'm off to bed," she said with a smile that felt as though it was stretching every muscle in her face. "See you both in the morning."

She ran upstairs, bolted herself into her room, and fell into bed. All she had to do was keep Cal at bay for one more day. Then she'd be safe.

Not that she'd had to keep him at bay: he'd made no attempt to be alone with her. Was he biding his time? Was he so scrupulous a father he wouldn't allow even the slightest hint to his daughter that he could be involved with Joanna? Or had he—since she'd surrendered so ardently to him—lost interest in her? Perhaps she was like the Matterhorn, she thought with a nasty jolt: once climbed, he'd lost interest in it.

She slept fitfully, went for an early and solitary walk in the lanes of the old city, where the ubiquitous clock faces did little to comfort her, and was back for breakfast before Lenny was up. Cal was sitting alone in the dining room. Steeling herself, she went to join him.

He looked at her unsmilingly. "Lenny'll be here any minute," he said in a clipped voice. "I've purposely kept my distance the last few days, Joanna. It seemed the best way to handle the situation with Lenny around—we sure as hell couldn't sleep together. But once you've finished with your next group of students, I want you to visit us in Vermont. You can get a feel for the place...see us on our home turf."

"Do you love me, Cal?" she said deliberately.

His jaw hardened. "I told you how I feel about love. It doesn't last."

"Then the answer's no—I won't come to Vermont."

"Do you love me?"

She should have seen that coming. She said, choosing her words, "I, too, have learned that falling in love doesn't guarantee happiness. We're both prisoners. Just like that man Bonivard in his underground dungeon."

"What if you're pregnant?"

"I doubt that I am."

"Answer the question, Joanna."

"I'll manage."

Sheer fury darkened his eyes. "You'll manage," he repeated in a savage whisper. "This isn't just your child we're talking about—it's mine, too."

"Perhaps you should have thought of that before you made love to me."

"You said it wasn't a setup!"

"It wasn't. You were there, you know what happened.'

He grasped her wrist with punishing strength. "If you're pregnant, you must let me know."

"You're hurting," she seethed. "Let go!"

With insulting speed he let her hand drop back on the cloth. "You'll let me know, Joanna."

"All right," she snapped, "I will."

He leaned back in his chair. "Smile," he said mockingly, "Lenny's coming."

"It's a wonder to me no one's ever pushed you off a mountain face."

"I'll have to make sure I never take you climbing," he said with a lazy grin that she itched to remove from his face. "Hello, hon," he added, "how did you sleep?"

Lenny smiled at Joanna. "Dad took me for an ice cream after dinner, down by the river. We saw all these incredible clocks with bears on them, you should have come Joanna."

Joanna produced some kind of reply, and buried her face in the menu. Only seven more hours, she thought. Then she'd be winging west to London, where she'd make he connection for the transatlantic flight. Back home.

Those seven hours, which began in Bern and ended in Zurich, were never very clear in Joanna's mind. They drove through the Jura, with its ripening vineyards, sloping farms and sleekly handsome horses. Lunch, a meal for which Joanna had no appetite, was in Solothurn near the cathedral. Her nerves were tightening to an unbearable pitch; just to glance at Cal filled her with an agony of regret. Yet she was sure she was doing the right thing: a clean break now was better than prolonging a relationship that was doomed to be one-sided.

They skirted Zurich, driving straight to the airport. Once Joanna had checked in, Lenny said overly brightly, "Goodbye, Joanna…please come for a visit."

Joanna kissed the girl on the cheek. "It was lovely to meet you, Lenny," she said evasively. "Good luck with your writing."

But Lenny could be as persistent as her father. "Be sure and give Dad your address. Then I can send you some of my poems, that'd be okay, wouldn't it?"

"Yes," Joanna said weakly, "that would be fine."

"I'm going to get a magazine, Dad, I'll be over at that kiosk."

So what Joanna had hoped wouldn't happen had happened: she was alone with Cal. She said rapidly, "My box number is 183, in Harcourt."

"And I already have your phone number." He rested his hands on her shoulders; to her overwrought imagination, they felt heavy as boulders. "Marry me, Joanna."

As she flinched, shaking her head, he added with ruthless certitude, "I'm not going to go away."

"You've got to."

"I'll call in a month or so to find out if you're pregnant. Lenny really likes you, you know that."

She said in a low voice, gazing at the buttons on his shirt, "I beg you not to use Lenny as a weapon…if you have any feelings toward me at all, just let me go."

"Oh, I have feelings toward you."

He didn't look remotely loving, she thought with an inward shiver. He looked more like he hated her. "I have to go through security," she said jaggedly, "I want to pick up a couple of bottles of Swiss wine in the duty-free."

He glanced over his shoulder; Lenny was absorbed in reading a magazine, her back to them. Taking Joanna in his arms, Cal lowered his head and kissed her with a powerful mix of fury, possessiveness and passion.

For a moment Joanna was petrified. Then her fighting spirit rose to the surface. She could go out with a bang or a whimper, she thought, and kissed him back with all her pent-up frustration and unhappiness. But all too quickly those emotions turned to desire, a desire she was helpless to resist. Melting into his arms, she laced her hands around his neck and surrendered herself to a tide of sensation.

Abruptly Cal pushed her away. His eyes like stones, he rasped, "You have feelings for me and don't bother denying it. I'll be in touch." Then he strode across the terminal toward the kiosk.

Joanna took her boarding pass and passport out of her bag with fingers that were shaking like poplar leaves, and followed the signs to security.

Security. What a laugh.

But at least she was going home. Home where she belonged.

CHAPTER THIRTEEN

EARLY August, and one of those days that proved summer a misnomer. Joanna came out of the doctor's office and started walking along Harcourt's main street, her head bent against the wind and rain. She'd planned the appointment so that no matter what she found out, she wouldn't have to go back to the campus and face any of her students or co-workers. So now all she had to do was get her bicycle from the car park where she'd locked it to the bike rack, and cycle home.

The weather perfectly suited her mood. The last few weeks had been the worst in her life: worse than last October when she'd miscarried; worse even than that long-ago summer when she'd finally realized that Gustave had no intention either of being faithful to her or of giving her a baby.

She missed Cal unrelentingly, his absence like a gaping wound in every moment of every day. Not that she was allowing her misery to show. Rather, she was carrying on with her classes, seeing Sally and Dianne, shopping, going to the occasional movie, working in her garden. Just like normal.

Except that nothing about her days—or nights—felt normal. Not even now, when Cal had at last stopped phoning her. Three times in the first week after she'd returned from Switzerland it had been his voice on the end of the line when she'd picked up the phone. So she'd threatened to change to an unlisted number, and the phone calls had stopped.

But now she had to phone him.

Raindrops were clinging to the handlebars of her bike. She undid the padlock, got on the bike and turned onto the street. The swish of the tires on the road was oddly comforting; she had to pay attention to the puddles and the oncoming traffic, and that, too, was a good thing. Then on the lane it was a question of avoiding the worst of the mud.

It had been raining the day Cal had come to Harcourt, and followed her down the lane; the day he'd kissed her by the apple tree in front of all her students.

Cal. Father of her child.

For, of course, she was pregnant. She'd been almost certain she was for the last three weeks, and today's visit with her doctor had confirmed it. At long last she was to realize her desire to become a mother.

So why wasn't she delirious with joy? Hadn't she gotten exactly what she'd wanted when she'd gone to Switzerland to be with Cal?

She wobbled down the rutted lane, the leaves on the hedges flailed by the wind, clouds skudding across the sky. When she'd set off for Switzerland, she'd only planned on getting pregnant; not on falling in love with Cal. Or had she already fallen in love with him and simply not realized it, blind to all the signs? Either way, it made no difference. He had feelings for her. So he said.

Sexual feelings, she thought. The possessiveness of a powerful male. But not love.

She couldn't marry him. And that was the stance she had to stick to when she phoned him this evening.

Her little cottage was dank and chilly. She flipped on the electric heat, made herself some supper, and did her best to ignore the pile of papers on one side of her desk: poems that Lenny had sent her. Astonishingly good poems, given Lenny's age and lack of experience. Lenny had ended her last letter to Joanna by saying that her father was stomping around the house like a bear with a head cold and she hoped

Joanna would come for a visit soon: a naive comment that had caused Joanna to wish Lenny would stick to writing poems, rather than letters.

Cal hadn't written to her. But then, why would he?

The clock crept toward six, when the phone rates went down. At two minutes past six, Joanna picked up the receiver and dialed Cal's number, praying that he'd answer rather than Lenny, simultaneously praying that he was in Kathmandu.

"Cal Freeman," he said, sounding very business-like.

She took a deep breath, realizing in a panic that she should have rehearsed what she was going to say. "Hello?" Cal repeated sharply.

"Cal, it's Joanna."

There was a noticeable pause. Then he said in a voice like surgical steel, "Are you pregnant?"

How typical of the man that he go straight to the essentials, she thought in a spurt of rage. "Yes."

Another pause, so long that she couldn't bear the silence. "I just found out today," she added.

"I'm coming up to see you."

"No! No, you mustn't."

"Joanna, I'm the father of your child. We have to talk about the future. When we'll get married."

Her palm wet on the receiver, she said, "We're not getting married."

"I'm not having a child of mine brought up in penury."

She played her trump card. "My second novel was accepted last week by a major publishing house in New York. I'm getting a six-figure advance. So I don't need your money."

"I guess I should be congratulating you on two fronts," he grated. "You achieved your aim in coming to Switzerland and you're obviously launched on a very successful career. But you'll forgive me, I'm sure, if I say I don't feel congratulatory.'' His breathing harsh, he went on, ''Okay, we'll skip the money angle. You think I'm going to put up with my son or daughter being brought up illegitimate? Do you know how cruel kids can be in the schoolyard—is that what you want?''

''Of course not.'' Her brain seemed to be on hold; she faltered. ''You knew I wanted to get pregnant. You shouldn't have made love with me.''

''You think I had a choice?''

She knew exactly what he meant. ''Even the second time, we didn't use protection.''

''Did it ever occur to you that I thought about that at the time, and was stupid enough to believe you'd marry me if you got pregnant?''

It hadn't occurred to her. ''That *was* stupid of you.''

''I'll book a flight as soon as I get off the phone. I can be there tomorrow.''

''Cal, you're not invited! I don't want to see you. Tomorrow or next week or next year. I'm on my own with this baby and that's the way I want it to be.''

''But it's not the way I want it to be.''

''If you come up here harassing me, I'll move in with my friends. Or I'll report you to the police.''

''You hate me, don't you?'' Cal said in a voice empty of emotion. ''You're right, I am stupid—it took me this long to see it.''

''Of course I don't.''

''So what is this, some kind of posthumous revenge on Gustave?''

Worse and worse. ''I don't play games like that.''

''Then what kind of game are you playing?''

''It's your old problem, Cal—you don't want to hear the word *no*. No, I don't want to see you. No, I don't want your money. No, I don't want to marry you.''

''Yet you want my child.''

"I've wanted a child for as long as I can remember."

"A child. Any child will do. Thanks a lot, that really makes my day."

"Oh, stop!" she cried. "You're poisoning everything. I won't marry you—I won't!"

An inimical silence echoed down the line. "And that's your final word?"

"Yes," she said; and wondered how one small word could make her feel so horribly unhappy.

"In that case, I'll speak to Lenny this evening," Cal snarled, "and tell her I don't want her communicating with you anymore. And you won't get in touch with her, do you hear me?"

What had she expected, that she'd be able to cut her ties with Cal and keep them with Lenny? Have her cake and eat it, too? "Very well," she said tightly.

"Goodbye, Joanna."

The connection was cut with a decisive click. Joanna dropped the receiver as if it were red-hot, sank into the nearest chair and gazed unseeingly at the wall.

An hour after Cal finished talking to Joanna, the phone rang again. He snatched it up, convinced she'd changed her mind, his heart racing as if he were twenty-thousand feet up a mountainside. "Joanna?"

"Cal? This is your old friend Ludo Galliker. I am calling you from Grindelwald."

Not Joanna. Well, of course not. She wasn't the type of woman to say she never wanted to hear from him again and then pick up the telephone half an hour later. "Ludo," Cal said, trying to pull himself together. "How are you?"

Really original, Cal. Brilliant.

"I am well, thank you," Ludo said with the formality that he favored when on the phone. "I thought I should get in touch with you…in case you hadn't heard about Tony Mason.''

Tony had been on the Everest and Kongur expeditions with Cal: an experienced and canny climber, whose store of off-color stories had often entertained them in their tents high on the ridges. ''What's wrong?'' Cal asked, apprehension stretching nerves already pulled taut.

''An icefall on Brammah. I only heard because my nephew was on the same expedition. It happened two days ago.'' He went on to give a few technicalities about location.

''I'm so sorry,'' Cal said. ''He was a great guy—and such a good climber.''

''Good climbers die, bad climbers survive, sometimes it's just a matter of luck…you are in the wrong place at the wrong time and no skill in the world can save you,'' Ludo said. ''That's one reason I do very little climbing now. Lady Luck—isn't that what you Americans call her?—she doesn't like to be pushed too far.''

Cal knew there was more than an element of truth in this. On several of the expeditions he'd been on, luck had run out for one or more of the climbers, men whose judgment and skill he had deeply respected. He said heavily, ''I'm glad you let me know.''

There was a brief pause. ''If you don't mind me asking,'' Ludo said, ''did Joanna Strassen forgive you?''

''I asked her to marry me. She won't.''

''Ah…so the wounds went deep from Gustave—I'm not surprised,'' Ludo said, adding dismissively, ''Well, it was worth a try. And it's not the end of the world, there are lots of other women.''

Cal didn't want any other women. ''Yeah,'' he said, ''of course there are. How's the arthritis?''

They talked a few more minutes, then Cal hung up. His own luck had run out today, he thought. He'd been so sure

Joanna would marry him if she were pregnant. But he'd been wrong.

Maybe he'd been wrong about her all along. Maybe she'd simply used him for her own ends, and now that she'd gotten what she wanted, he was of no further good to her. Useless as a frayed harness.

He sure hadn't realized what Suzanne was like when he'd first met her; he'd been blind as the proverbial bat.

But he'd been in love with Suzanne. He wasn't in love with Joanna.

Distantly he heard the sound of a vehicle on the gravel driveway: Lenny, back from practising for the local horse show next week. He'd better start acting like a human being.

"Dad?" she called. "Hey, guess what, Dad?"

Lenny would soon have a half sister or brother, he thought. But he couldn't tell her that. Now or ever. He called back, "I'm in my study."

She burst in the door, her cheeks pink with excitement. "I jumped Lara twice over the water hazard, and she did just fine. Then we topped four feet six on the bars."

"That's great," Cal said.

"And I had a letter from Joanna today, critiquing my poems, she thinks some of them are good." Lenny gave a sigh of pure bliss. "What a fab day."

He'd better tell her now. What was the point of delaying it? He said, "Lenny, there's something I have to tell you."

Lenny's smile died. She said slowly, "You don't look so hot. What's up?"

"I'd rather you didn't get in touch with Joanna again. And I've told her the same."

"Why not?" Lenny asked blankly.

"I'd hoped she might marry me, but she won't," Cal said, trying to erase any trace of feeling from his words. "So I think it's better we cut the connection completely."

"It's because you're a mountaineer—that's why she won't marry you."

"She doesn't love me," Cal heard himself say, and instantly wished it unsaid. Love. He didn't believe in it. Except for his love for Lenny, of course.

"She's scared to. Her husband was a mountaineer, she told me about him, he was killed on Annapurna...if you quit climbing, I bet she'd reconsider. She liked you, I could tell."

"I don't think it's that simple."

"Why don't you stop climbing?" Lenny blurted. "You've done all the big ones."

Cal said reluctantly, "I just had a call from Ludo that one of my climbing buddies was killed in an icefall on Brammah a couple of days ago."

"Oh." His daughter's face was suddenly pinched. "So when are you going again, Dad?"

Soon. The sooner the better. "I don't know, I haven't—"

"I wish you'd quit, too," Lenny said almost inaudibly.

"Lenny—did you say what I thought you said?"

"I've wanted you to quit for ages!"

"You do? You've never said so before."

"It's like Joanna said," Lenny went on in a strained voice. "Always waiting for a phone call, afraid to pick it up, knowing people die just because they're on the mountain. Is that what happened to your friend?"

"Yeah...but Lenny—"

Lenny's jaw set mulishly. "Anyway, I don't want to stop writing to Joanna! I really like her, and I'm sure she likes you. If only you'd give up climbing, I bet she would marry you."

"Lenny, I don't often lay down the law. But this is one case where I'm going to. I don't want you to keep in touch with Joanna."

Tears filmed Lenny's gray eyes, that were so like his own. "So climb your stupid mountains, see if I care!" After this unusually childish outburst, she ran from the room. A couple of moments later Cal heard her bedroom door slam.

How could he quit climbing? And what if Lenny disobeyed him and somehow found out about Joanna's pregnancy? For which he was at least half responsible.

What would he do then?

He rued the day he'd driven along a prairie road in a blizzard and stopped to rescue a stranger. A woman who'd turned his life upside down. A woman who didn't want to live with him, even though he was the father of her child. Was he going to spend the rest of his life hankering after a black-haired beauty who had all kinds of hang-ups about love and children and mountains?

It's not the end of the world, there are lots of other women... Was Ludo right?

CHAPTER FOURTEEN

AUGUST was passing, progressively more hot and humi
Physically Joanna was feeling very well; emotionally sh
was a basketcase. The latter she kept to herself as best sh
could. Last night over chips and salsa she'd told Sally an
Dianne about her pregnancy, certain that they'd support h
in her wish to be a single mother. But neither of them ha
Worse, they'd argued with her vociferously. So she'd ha
a rotten night's sleep, and woken from a dream in whic
Cal's arms were wrapped around her.

Her bed had been empty, her heart one big ache.

Five in the afternoon. Yesterday her classes had finishe
for the summer. She'd weeded the garden, trimmed th
hedge, oiled her bicycle and vacuumed the cottage. He
advance check wasn't due for another two weeks, so sh
couldn't go shopping. And there were still four hours t
pass before she could reasonably go to bed. Then her ea
pricked up. Wasn't that someone coming?

Her nerves clenched with terror. What if it were Cal?

She looked out the window. Two cars, Sally's an
Dianne's. Not Cal.

Never again Cal. Wasn't that what she'd told him? An
he'd listened. Obviously. He hadn't phoned her. Or writte
He had enough money to buy a helicopter—a whole fle
of helicopters—and land in her back garden. He hadn
done that, either.

Unlike her, he must have moved on. He was probabl
already dating someone else, a thought that made her s
acutely unhappy she could hardly bear it.

One car door slammed, then the second. Joanna walke

ut onto the porch. "Hi, there," she said, rather proud of
ow normal she sounded. "Why both cars?"

"You'll see," said Dianne. "Do you have any of that
crumptious iced tea you make?"

"I do."

Sally plunked herself down on one of the wicker chairs
n the porch. "I'd like some, too. With an extra slice of
emon."

"Is this a deputation?" Joanna asked shrewdly. "Be-
ause if it is, you're wasting your time."

"Iced tea," said Dianne. "Move it."

Rolling her eyes, feeling minimally better, Joanna headed
or the kitchen. When the three of them were settled on the
orch with tea and cookies, Dianne said, "I had a call from
ny sister this morning. All her latest tests are good, and
he prognosis is almost certainly for a full recovery."

"Oh, Dianne," Joanna exclaimed, "that's wonderful
ews, I'm so happy for her. And for you."

"We were both bawling like babies," Dianne admitted.

"So she's been given a second chance," Joanna said;
nd heard the words echo in her head.

"Precisely," said Dianne. "Which is why we're here."

Sally chimed in, "Once we've drunk our tea, Dianne's
riving me home and you're taking my car and going to
Vermont."

"I'm *what?*"

"You're going to see Cal and tell him you'll marry
im," Dianne said. "This is *your* second chance."

Sally said, "You can't let a few chunks of rock called
he Alps stop you from being happy."

"Because you're not happy."

"The last rose of summer," Sally echoed.

"Not even a rose," Dianne said. "Pickerel weed."

"You're in love with Cal and—"

"How did you know?" Joanna interrupted. "I've neve said that to either one of you."

Dianne raised elegantly plucked brows. "It sticks out a over. Just look at you, you're a wreck."

"I'm not!"

"You are," Sally and Dianne chorused.

Joanna, to her horror, put her head in her hands an started to weep. She cried for quite a while, her two friend patting her back and murmuring soothing phrases, then sup plying her with tissues to blow her nose. She wailed, " miss him so! All I want all day is just to see him and touc him and hear his voice."

"Well, of course you do," Dianne said. "You love th guy."

"I just couldn't bear it if he was k-killed. Like Gustave.'

"So you're going to be miserable for the rest of you life just because he's a mountaineer?"

"I am miserable," Joanna admitted, rather redundantl given her red nose and tear-streaked cheeks.

"And knowing you," Sally said, "you're in love fc life."

"So we've put maps in the car, and a few treats, and it' full of gas. The rest is up to you."

"But," Sally said smugly, "we expect to be invited t the wedding."

Again Joanna's eyes filled with tears. "He doesn't lov me! He doesn't believe in love."

"Then it's up to you to make him."

"If anyone can, you can."

Joanna gave one last snuffle. "I don't know about that.'

"We do."

"I do know one thing—I've got two good friends," Joanna quavered. "Even if they are nosy and dictatorial."

"That's us," Dianne said. "Now we're going, so tha

ou can pack and get ready and leave early in the morn-
ng."

"One more thing," Sally interjected. "I dated someone
lse last week. Twice. In the last four days Albert's ar-
anged for a live-in companion for his mother and he's
ented his own apartment."

Helplessly Joanna began to laugh. "Oh, Sally, that's
vonderful."

"So don't you dare suggest you can't make Cal Freeman
it up and take notice."

"All right," Joanna said meekly. "I won't."

Both of her friends hugged Joanna. "Have a fantastic
ime," Sally added. "I don't need the car for a whole week.
But I bet it won't take that long."

They drove away up the lane, Dianne beeping the horn
o the rhythm of the wedding march. Joanna gazed at
ally's neat little blue car sitting in her driveway. She was
oing to Vermont. Apparently. First thing tomorrow morn-
ng.

What if Cal were away? Climbing a mountain? Or stay-
ng at a luxury resort with a gorgeous blonde?

She ran in the house and dialed his number. After three
ings, Joanna heard his deep baritone say, "Cal Freeman."

She banged the receiver on the hook. He was there. The
est was up to her.

Maybe the gorgeous blonde was in Vermont with him.

If Cal was with someone else, and she, Joanna, drove all
he way to Vermont to see him, she'd be horribly humili-
ted. Although humiliation was the least of her worries.

I'm going to trust him, she thought, gripping the edge of
he table so hard her knuckles were white. He said he had
eelings for me. Strong feelings. And he hated it when I
ompared him to Gustave, who was always changing
vomen.

So I'm not going to.

Cal may not love me. But I matter to him. Somehow.

Holding tight to these thoughts, as though they were talismans, Joanna spent the rest of the evening packing. However, she didn't get to sleep until well past one o'clock because every nerve in her body was twanging like stretched elastic. In consequence, she overslept the next morning; it was nearly noon before she pulled away from her cottage and drove up the lane in Sally's car.

Tomorrow she'd see Cal again.

She had to trust he'd be glad to see her.

She had to tell him that she loved him.

At five the next evening, Joanna was within one hundred and fifty miles of the little town in Vermont where Cal and Lenny lived. She could have kept going quite easily; but she was tired and hungry, and not at all sure she was up to meeting Cal at nine o'clock at night. So she pulled over at a pleasant country inn that was probably more than she could afford. She needed cosseting, she decided. She could use her credit card; by the time the bill came she'd have her advance from the publishers.

She went for a walk after supper, then to bed. She slept soundly until 5:00 a.m., after which she lay awake listing all the negative outcomes of her unexpected arrival at Cal's house. He was finished with her, child or no child. He'd never love her but would insist on marrying her and then taking off the very next day to Patagonia. He'd be so angry with her that he'd show her the door.

Or else the gorgeous blonde would open the door.

None of these dire thoughts was remotely comforting. At quarter to seven Joanna got up, showered, went downstairs for a breakfast that deserved more than the attention she gave it, then took a short walk around the lake that bordered the inn's formal garden. The sun on the blue water, the pure white water lilies and the quacking of an unseen duck were somewhat comforting. At eight twenty-five she set off.

It was eleven-twenty when she stopped for directions on the outskirts of the town of Madson; at eleven-thirty she turned into Cal's driveway. It was flanked by stone pillars, with a wrought-iron sign that said Riversedge, and proceeded to wind for nearly a quarter of a mile through tall elms and maples, their leaves a cool green roof. Her heart was beating very fast; when she finally drove into the open again, she gave a gasp of mingled pleasure and dismay.

A gracious double-winged Colonial house built of stone, with dazzling white trim and a slate roof set with several charming dormers; expansive stables to one side, garages to the other, boxwood hedges and mature trees shading the front walk. "I have a lot of money," Cal had said to her once. "An astonishing amount of money."

She had the proof right in front of her. How could he possibly believe she wasn't after him for his fortune? A six-figure advance might seem like a great deal of money to her; to him it would be peanuts.

She parked near the garage, and got out. There was no sign of life. Maybe he'd gone away since her phone call; she should have told him she was coming. But how could she? Wasn't she subconsciously hoping that by taking him by surprise, she'd learn his true feelings?

Her heart pounding, she walked steadily toward the handsome door with its mullioned-glass insets. The doorbell was set in highly polished brass; she pushed it firmly.

A breeze wafted the scent of the river to her nostrils; overhead the leaves rustled, as though exchanging secrets. Then the door opened. A manservant swathed in a canvas apron said formally, "May I help you, madam?"

He was neither blond nor gorgeous. In fact, he was as bald as a coot. "I'm looking for Mr. Freeman," Joanna stammered.

"He's out back. Just follow the path 'round the house through the rose garden and go past the paddock. Don' mind the dogs, they won't harm you."

"Is he alone?" Joanna blurted.

The manservant didn't even blink. "To the best of my knowledge, madam."

"Thank you," Joanna gasped, wondering if her mingled relief and terror was as obvious to the man as to her. Cal wasn't in Patagonia. He was here, in Vermont. Alone Which meant, of course, that in a couple of minutes she'd be face-to-face with him.

Knowing her whole life hung in the balance, Joanna walked around the side of the house. The rose garden was filled with late blooms nodding on their stems, delicately fragrant. On impulse she picked one, a pale cream tea rose whose petals were edged with pink. She'd give it to Cal One more way of saying she loved him.

Was she really going to tell him that?

A herb garden with an antique sundial supplanted the roses; the gray leaves and purple blossoms of sage brushed her bare ankles. She was wearing her most becoming sundress to give herself courage; it was a clear violet-blue sprinkled with flowers, hugging her breasts and baring her shoulders, its skirt coming to mid-calf. Now that she was actually here, she wished she'd chosen dungarees and a long-sleeved shirt as baggy as Dieter's pajama jacket. She was quite sure the thumping of her heart must show where the dress lay against her left breast. Cal would probably hear it, she thought desperately, and took a couple of deep breaths.

As she rounded the west wing of the house, she stopped in her tracks. A lazy curve of the river glinted in the sun caressed by the drooping fingers of willows. Sloping meadows lay between the house and the river, along with a vegetable garden and an orchard of ripening apples and pears.

o her right was a white-fenced paddock. A robin was lust-ly singing on top of a stone wall espaliered with peach trees.

All this Joanna saw in one quick instant. Because there was more. Near the stone wall was a woodpile. His back to her, shirtless, Cal was splitting logs, the thunk of the ax echoing against the wall.

He was working with a concentrated ferocity that made her heart sink. He did not, to put it mildly, look in the mood for company. Very slowly she walked toward him, her mind totally blank, her feet automatically searching out the uneven flagstone pathway.

Two dogs were curled near the woodpile, sleeping in the sun. One of them raised its head, saw her and gave a short bark; the other woke up and both got to their feet, stretched and headed up the path toward her, their tails wagging.

Mongrels, both of them. Two of Lenny's rescued animals?

As the dogs trotted past him, Cal looked around. He saw her immediately. A shudder ran through his body, his face a mask of shock. The ax continued its downward swing; to her horror Joanna saw it ricochet off the log and strike his hand. Drops of blood sprayed the sinews of the wood.

For a moment the tableau was frozen; she wasn't even sure Cal realized he'd cut himself. Then he looked down, dropped the ax and tried to stem the flow of blood with his other hand. The rose she had picked fell to the ground. Then she was running toward him, her heart racing with a new terror. "Let me see," she said urgently.

"It's nothing."

It was far from nothing: a gash in the ball of his hand at least an inch long. She grabbed his shirt from the woodpile, pressing its clean folds to the wound. "Come on," she said, "we'll have to find a doctor."

"What are you doing here?"

She said frantically, "Later—you've got to have stitches in this, it's too deep just to leave. Hurry up, Cal! My car's around the front, I'll drive you."

She took hold of his elbow and shoved him ahead of her, wondering if she'd ever forget the stark contrast of scarlet and white in the folds of his shirt. Cal, rather to her surprise, obeyed her, striding the length of the pathway past the herbs and the velvet-petaled roses. Joanna ran ahead, opened the passenger door and slammed it shut once he was in. Then she got in the driver's seat, turned on the engine and surged along the green-shadowed driveway.

At the highway, Cal said tersely, "Go left. Joanna, I have to know why you're here."

She pressed her foot to the accelerator, terrified anew by the sodden red cloth wrapped around his hand. "I can't tell you now, truly I can't—I've got to concentrate on my driving. But I promise I'll talk to you later. How far do we have to go?"

"The hospital's the other side of town."

She gave an unconscious groan of despair: the narrow streets of Madson weren't built for speed. Then, as though the word speed had conjured it up, she saw a police cruiser parked in the side road that she had just flashed past. In her rearview mirror, with a strange sense of fatality, she watched it pull out behind her, lights flashing. "Oh, no," she muttered, "I'll have to stop."

She pulled over by the side of the road. The officer got out and sauntered up to the car. "Are you aware of the limit—" he began; then he saw her passenger and the blood-soaked bandage. "Cal!" he exclaimed. "What's up?"

"Ax jumped out and bit me," Cal said with a grin; although he was, Joanna noticed with a distant part of her brain, white about the mouth.

"Okay, let's get you through town quick as we can. You follow me, ma'am."

So the little cavalcade drove very fast through the town of Madson, the siren blaring. Joanna said with a thread of laughter in her voice, "I've always wanted to go through a red light. And with a police escort, no less."

Three minutes later they drew up outside the emergency entrance of a small red brick hospital. The police officer opened Cal's door, saying to Joanna, "Park over there, ma'am, I'll go in with him. And we'll forget about a ticket this time."

Heartened by his wink, Joanna did as she was told. By the time she entered the emergency department, Cal had already disappeared. She sat down hard in the nearest chair and tried very hard to compose herself.

She shouldn't have come. Not once since he'd seen her had Cal smiled at her or indicated in any way that he was pleased to see her. Admittedly, he'd been bleeding rather a lot; but surely that wouldn't deflect a seasoned mountaineer?

The police officer strolled back in and came over to her. "They're stitching him up right now. Shouldn't take too long. You want to go and hold his hand?"

"No, thanks," she said quickly, "I'll wait right here."

"No need to speed on the way home."

"I promise I won't," she said solemnly, and watched a grin split his florid face.

"See you 'round," he said, and left as unhurriedly as he'd arrived.

She rather doubted that he would; she was almost sure she'd be driving back to Nova Scotia in short order. For a moment she had the wild idea that she should simply leave now. Flee and never come back. Why put herself through the pain of rejection?

Cal could always find his own way home.

She pushed herself partway up in the chair. Then she heard Cal's voice down the hall, and the sound of his footsteps. She sank back. Too late. Anyway, hadn't she come here to fight for him? Was she forgetting that already?

She'd never be able to face Sally and Dianne if she simply turned tail and ran.

When Cal reentered the room, his eyes flew to her. His hand was cocooned in an immaculate white bandage. He said harshly, "I wasn't sure you'd still be here."

She stood up, wishing he weren't quite so tall, so formidably self-contained. "I'll drive you home. Do you need to get a prescription or anything?"

"No, they gave me enough painkillers to stun a horse...let's get out of here. I'll never live this down, what with the police escort through town and my own stupidity."

Stupid to react to her presence? Is that what he meant? Joanna turned her back, marched outside and got in Sally's car. By the time Cal was seated, she'd started the engine and was ready to back up. Cal said flatly, "Hold on a minute. I still want to know what you're doing here."

"I'll tell you when we get back to your place and not before. I've been on the road the last two days and I need a cup of strong tea and a comfortable chair."

Briefly he gripped her wrist. "Have you lost the baby? Is that what's wrong?"

Her jaw dropped. "No! Of course not."

"There's no *of course* about it—you miscarried last October."

"I'm taking very good care of myself. Truly, Cal." Joanna shook her arm free, sick at heart that his sole concern should be the baby. "Where's Lenny?"

"Gone for the day."

Fond as she was of Lenny, Joanna was relieved; she didn't need any further complications to a day that already seemed interminable. She'd be long gone from here by the

ime Lenny got home, she thought miserably, and drove
back to Riversedge in a strained silence. Once there, she
parked by the garage again and followed Cal through the
front door.

Her overwrought nerves took in a brass chandelier, a
beautifully proportioned entrance hall and the elegant curve
of a spiral staircase. She followed Cal up these stairs, her
purse banging against her hip. A bowl of roses against the
panes of an oval window, and then the entrance to what
must be the east wing of the house. He said briefly, ush-
ering her in, "My living quarters—we'll have privacy
here."

She both needed and dreaded such privacy. Not saying
a word, Joanna followed him down a long hall decorated
with stunning photographs of various mountain peaks, into
a living room with a stone fireplace and a bay window that
overlooked the river and the faraway, blue-tinted hills.

He said with the same intimidatingly distant courtesy,
"I'll make you some tea—I'll be back in a minute."

"I can get it, shouldn't you—"

But he'd already left the room. She wandered over to the
window, gazing at a scene whose serenity was utterly alien
to her own inner turmoil. She'd say what she had to say
and she'd get out.

And this time she'd stay away from Cal. Forever.

CHAPTER FIFTEEN

WITHIN a few minutes Cal was back. "You'll have to carry the tray," he said stiffly.

Joanna went into the well-appointed kitchen, picked up the tray and carried it back into the living room. She poured two cups, passed Cal his, put hers down on a small cherrywood table and said, "I came to tell you the truth."

"And what version of the truth might that be?"

She raised her chin. "You don't have to make this more difficult than it already is."

"I've had the worst few weeks of my entire life," Cal said. "I don't feel conciliatory."

"Then I'm wasting my time."

"For the fourth time, Joanna, tell me why you're here."

She took a deep breath. It was now or never. Her voice high-pitched with nervousness, she said, "I came to tell you I'll marry you. If you still want me to."

"And what brought about this change of heart?"

Go for broke, Joanna. By the looks of it, you've got nothing more to lose. You've lost it already. She lifted her chin still higher. "I love you," she said with a complete absence of emotion.

His eyes narrowed. "You *what?* Since when?"

"I don't know—does it matter? Look, I know I'm doing this all wrong. But I had to come and see if—"

Cal reached out, resting a hand on her wrist, an inner tension in his face gradually relaxing. He said evenly, "For the last thirty-six hours I've been trying to reach you by phone. No answer. Your department at the university would only tell me you were on vacation, and you never told me the names of your friends there. Dead end.''

"Why were you doing that?" Joanna said in a staccato voice.

"My bags are packed and I have a reservation to fly to Halifax at six this evening. To see if I could track you down.''

"What for? You aren't even glad to see me."

"Glad in no way describes how I'm feeling right now."

"Answer the question, Cal. Why were you coming to see me? Because of the baby?''

"No," he said, "not just because of the baby. Because what I've discovered the last few weeks is that I can't live without you. Weeks that felt like a year, by the way.''

"You can't live without me," Joanna repeated slowly. It wasn't quite *I love you*. But it certainly wasn't *Here's the door*. She said, "I can't live without you, either. That's why I'm here.''

Although she longed for the reassurance of his embrace, Cal was still keeping a careful distance between them. "So you drove all this way to tell me you love me?" he said in an unreadable voice. "You're brave as a lion, you know that?''

"Not so brave. The next time you go mountain climbing, I won't...but I'm assuming when I say that, that I'll be with you," she babbled. "I'm jumping to conclusions. You haven't said anything about—"

"Finish what you were going to say."

She twisted her fingers in her lap. "The next time you go mountain climbing, I'll be a wreck until you get back. But I can't turn my back on loving you because you might be killed on the mountains, that's what I've come to understand the last few days. The risk of loss is part of love—its dark side.''

"You *are* brave as a lion. One of the many reasons I

was heading to Nova Scotia was to tell you I'm quitting
the mountains."

"You *are?*"

Briefly Cal described his conversation with Ludo, and
then what Lenny had said to him about her own fears. "I've
always known about luck. That one day, no matter how
skilled you are, your luck can just plain run out and that's
that. I've had a great innings. But now it's time to move
on. It took me a few days to figure all this out...but I finally
did."

"You're sure? You won't resent me and Lenny for that
decision?"

"I'm sure." As Cal got up and took a couple of steps
toward her, she, too, got to her feet. He rested his hand
on her bare shoulders, the bandage soft on her skin, and
said with a crooked smile, "Seems to me I've proposed to
you several times. Isn't this your turn?"

"You really were coming to look for me?"

"My ticket's on my bureau."

"Oh." Joanna bit her lip, her heart fluttering like a
trapped bird. "I guess it is my turn—to propose, I mean."

His smile widened; and surely that was tenderness softening the slate-gray of his eyes? "I'm waiting," he said.

Her own smile was both sudden and radiant, withholding
nothing. "Cal," she said, "will you marry me?"

"I will, Joanna. As soon as possible, and that's got nothing to do with the baby and everything to do with you."
Very gently he pushed a shiny strand of hair back from her
face. "Don't you see, you make quitting the mountains so
easy. Marrying you, living with you, will be the greatest
adventure of my life. I know you'll take me places I've
never been—you already have."

Tears filmed her eyes. "You say such beautiful things to
me."

"It's the truth."

"You don't know what a relief that is, that I won't have to wave goodbye to you not knowing if I'll ever see you again. I would've done it. But I'm so glad I won't have to."

"But you would have married me anyway."

"Yes," she said simply.

"You really do love me."

Her happiness was pierced by a sudden pang of loss: Cal didn't—couldn't—love her back. Wasn't pretending to. She said quickly, not wanting to dwell on this, "My friends Sally and Dianne arrived a couple of nights ago, told me they were sick of seeing me so unhappy and that I'd better take myself down here and ask you to marry me." She batted her lashes at him. "On bended knee, was more or less the message. But you can do without that, can't you?"

"I have difficulty imagining it," he grinned. "By the way, you haven't asked me the other reasons I was coming to see you."

"To abduct me on your prancing white stallion?"

"That, too." He traced the soft line of her lower lip with one finger, his face full of what was unquestionably tenderness. "I missed you unrelentingly, day and night. I regretted every word I'd spoken to you in anger, every time I'd pushed you away. I ached to make love with you. But I wasn't in love with you, oh, no. Not me. I'd been in love with Suzanne and it hadn't lasted, you weren't going to catch me doing that again."

"We were both running scared. Me as much as you."

"But it took me longer to stop," Cal said wryly. Putting his arms around her, as though he couldn't wait for the contact, he went on. "Yesterday I was carrying a load of logs into the house—I split a lot of wood the past couple of weeks—and thinking about the heat that birch logs throw, when it hit me that because I'd turned my back on love, my heart was as cold as the granite on the Matterhorn.

And that only you could warm it. I stacked the logs on the pile, and I looked around the basement, and for the first time I allowed myself to say that I love you. That I'll love you until the day I die. That somehow you'd found your way to the very center of my being and you weren't going to leave.''

"You love me?" Joanna repeated dazedly.

"I tried to phone you. All day I kept phoning and no answer. I was terrified that you'd moved and that I'd never find you. Or that you'd met someone else. Someone who goes lawn bowling on Sundays. Someone safe.''

"After I first met you, I dated the registrar a couple of times. He was safe and he bored me to tears.'' Joanna stood a little taller in Cal's embrace, wondering if she could trust the evidence of her own ears. "Say it again, Cal.''

"Giving me orders already?"

"You bet."

He laughed. "I could show you instead.''

"I hope you will. Soon," she said, color washing her cheeks. "But first I want to hear you say it. You know how it is when you've wanted something so badly and then you get it, and yet you don't quite believe that it's real?''

"I'm yours," Cal said hoarsely. "Joanna, I love you. I've probably loved you since the first moment I saw your face in the middle of a prairie blizzard. But it took me this long to admit it, and for that I'm sorry.''

Her voice shaking a little, she said, "You were worth waiting for.''

He undid the clasp at her nape, loosing her hair to flow free on her shoulders. "What are we standing here for when there's a bedroom down the hall?''

"I can't imagine," said Joanna, and started unbuttoning his shirt, her palms seeking the hair-roughened skin of his chest as a flower turns to the sun.

"We've got the rest of the day," he said huskily. "Just

the two of us. Oh, Joanna, I can't believe you're really here. Come to bed with me, then maybe I'll realize this is all true."

"I'm here," she said, "and this time I'm not going to go away. Ever again."

He took her by the hand, leading her down the hall into his bedroom, where they undressed each other, the leaves of the maple outside the window casting dappled shadows on their naked bodies. With slow sensuality, not noticeably impeded by his sore hand, Cal unleashed a storm of desire in Joanna, a desire he more than matched; and inevitably it mounted to its fiery release. Afterward, wrapping her arms around him, her hair coiled in his shoulder, Joanna said, "I feel so close to you, Cal—so unbelievably intimate."

"I love you. So much I don't know how to say it."

"Your body said it for you," she answered softly.

"Darling Joanna. Your hair smells like flowers, yet it's smooth and cool as the river…and I'm the luckiest of men." He hesitated. "There's something I need to say—I want you to know I'm marrying you for yourself. Yes, you're carrying our child, and that's immeasurably precious to me. But it's you I want. You."

"I know that, Cal." She guided his hand to her belly. "I realized I was in real trouble when I found out I was pregnant and I wasn't happy, even though I've wanted a baby for so long. But I wanted you more—I hope you believe me."

"Right after I talked to you on the phone and was so royally turned down, I was sore enough to convince myself that you'd used me for your own ends. That a baby was what you wanted, not me. But it wouldn't wash…I know you too well for that."

"I had you shacked up with a gorgeous blonde," Joanna replied, smiling at him through her lashes. "But then I decided to trust you. And that's when I got in Sally's car and drove here.''

He tweaked her hair. ''Blondes don't interest me in the slightest.'' Then a look of comical dismay crossed his face. ''Do we tell Lenny that you're pregnant?''

''She's a smart kid—she's quite capable of figuring out how long nine months is. In other words, yes.''

''And you're happy to have her as a stepdaughter?''

''Oh, yes. I liked her right from the start. And we share so many interests.''

''She was furious with me when I told her I didn't want her to write to you anymore. Right before she left this morning, knowing I was flying to Nova Scotia, she loaned me her rabbit's foot for good luck.''

''So that's why this has all worked out so beautifully,'' Joanna chuckled. ''I knew there had to be a reason. Do you realize if I'd left a day later, we'd have passed en route?''

''It doesn't bear thinking about,'' Cal said. He kissed her parted lips, his tongue flicking them with lazy sensuality. ''Perhaps I'll ask for the rabbit's foot on permanent loan...and now I think we should get something to eat— you haven't had any lunch. Then we could go back to bed. If you want to?''

She touched him very suggestively. ''Oh, I could be persuaded.''

''Stop that,'' he growled, ''or you'll never get lunch.''

''But I'm eating for two,'' she teased.

For a moment Cal buried his face in her shoulder, holding her so tightly she almost couldn't breathe. ''I'm the happiest man on earth right now.''

Her nostrils were filled with the heat of his skin, her hands were curved around his back, and within her his child was growing. What more could she ask?

Only that Lenny be as happy as they.

* * *

By five that afternoon, Cal and Joanna were up and dressed, and had wandered outdoors, hand in hand, to wait for Lenny. "It's so beautiful here, Cal," Joanna murmured. "I already feel at home."

"I bought the property after Suzanne died. She never wanted to live in the country. But Lenny loves it here, and so do I." He added, "You won't have to stay here all the time—we can always go to New York or London or Appenzell."

Instinctively she knew she could write here. "I can't think of anywhere I'd rather be than here with you and Lenny."

"Talking of Lenny, here she is," Cal said, his fingers tightening around Joanna's.

Lenny had just emerged through the trees, riding a bay Thoroughbred. When she saw her father and Joanna in the garden, she dismounted, looped the reins over the cedar fence and hurried toward them. Then, suddenly shy, she stopped a few feet away. Her jodhpurs had seen better days; her gray eyes were uncertain. "Hi, Joanna," she said. "How did you get here? Dad was going to Nova Scotia to look for you."

"A friend loaned me her car. Your Dad and I were on the same wavelength—we both needed to see each other."

"What happened to your hand, Dad?"

"I saw Joanna standing in the orchard and the ax slipped," Cal said ruefully. "It's nothing, half a dozen stitches. But other than that, your rabbit's foot worked like a charm."

Lenny looked from one to the other; she was obviously bursting with questions that she wasn't sure she should ask. Cal added, putting his arm around Joanna, "Joanna and I are going to get married. We hope you'll be happy for us."

"Oh, yes," said Lenny fervently. "Where will we live?"

Lenny had some of her father's directness, Joanna thought, amused. "How about here?"

"You mean I wouldn't have to go back to school in Switzerland, Dad?"

"We'll all live here, Lenny."

The dawning smile on Lenny's face emboldened Joanna. "I would very much like to be your stepmother, Lenny. I realize that'll take time, big changes can't be made overnight—but I hope you like the idea, too."

With the same fervency, Lenny said, "I've wanted that all along." She gave her father a swift hug, then hugged Joanna, too. "I was afraid you weren't ever going to see each other again. Can I be a bridesmaid?"

"You can," her father teased, "although not in those clothes." Then, with uncharacteristic awkwardness, he added, "There's something else you should know..."

"You already told me you were giving up mountain climbing," Lenny said cheerfully. "Although I haven't figured out what you'll do instead. You're too big to be a jockey."

"Para gliding?" Joanna suggested, giving Cal a sly glance from under her lashes.

"Helicopter skiing," Lenny added.

"I've always wanted to try that," Joanna said thoughtfully.

"Just as long as it's not lawn bowling," Cal said. "But, Lenny, I'm trying to tell you something. About Joanna and me. Something I'm sure you're old enough to understand. Or at least I hope you are. Sometimes when adults—"

"You mean you're pregnant?" Lenny interrupted, looking from one to the other.

Cal looked visibly taken aback that she'd guessed so quickly. "Yes. Yes, we are. That'll be another big change, Lenny. But I hope—"

''I really love you, Dad. But three's better than two and four's totally awesome.''

Cal wiped his forehead with a relief that wasn't altogether faked. ''Awesome's not a bad word for the way I'm feeling right now.''

Joanna put her arm around his waist and smiled at his daughter. ''I couldn't agree more.''

''Me, too,'' said Lenny. ''What's for dinner?''

THE ROYAL HOUSE OF NIROLI

...International affairs, seduction and passion guaranteed

Volume 5 – November 2007
Expecting His Royal Baby by Susan Stephens

Volume 6 – December 2007
The Prince's Forbidden Virgin by Robyn Donald

Volume 7 – January 2008
Bride by Royal Appointment by Raye Morgan

Volume 8 – February 2008
A Royal Bride at the Sheikh's Command by Penny Jordan

8 volumes in all to collect!

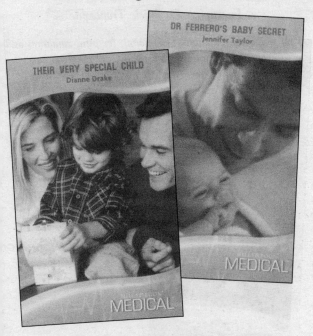

MILLS & BOON
MEDICAL™
Proudly presents

Brides of Penhally Bay

Featuring Dr Nick Tremayne

A pulse-raising collection of emotional, tempting romances and heart-warming stories – devoted doctors, single fathers, Mediterranean heroes, a Sheikh and his guarded heart, royal scandals and miracle babies…

Book One

CHRISTMAS EVE BABY

by Caroline Anderson

Starting 7th December 2007

MILLS & BOON

MEDICAL

Proudly presents

Brides of Penhally Bay

A pulse-raising collection of emotional,
tempting romances and heart-warming stories by
bestselling Mills & Boon Medical™ authors.

January 2008
The Italian's New-Year Marriage Wish
by Sarah Morgan

Enjoy some much-needed winter warmth with
gorgeous Italian doctor Marcus Avanti.

February 2008
The Doctor's Bride By Sunrise
by Josie Metcalfe

Then join Adam and Maggie on a 24-hour rescue mission
where romance begins to blossom as the sun starts to set.

March 2008
The Surgeon's Fatherhood Surprise
by Jennifer Taylor

Single dad Jack Tremayne finds a mother for his
little boy – and a bride for himself.

*Let us whisk you away to an idyllic Cornish town –
a place where hearts are made whole*

COLLECT ALL 12 BOOKS!